THE OFFICER'S PREY

Armand Cabasson

Armand Cabasson was born in 1970. He is a psychiatrist working in the North of France. *The Officer's Prey* is the first in the Quentin Margont series of thrillers set in the Napoleonic Wars, published in France in 2002 as *Les Proies de l'officier*, which received the 2003 Gendarmerie Nationale Thriller Prize. The second in the series, *Chasse au loup*, was awarded the 2005 Fiction Prize by the Napoleonic Foundation. Armand Cabasson is a member of the Souvenir Napoléonien and has used his extensive research to create a vivid portrait of the Napoleonic campaigns.

Michael Glencross

Michael Glencross lives and works in France as a translator. His most recent translations include *The Dream* by Émile Zola, *Around the World in Eighty Days* by Jules Verne and *The Châtelet Apprentice* by Jean-François Parot.

THE
OFFICER'S PREY

ARMAND CABASSON

Translated from the French by Michael Glencross

GALLIC BOOKS
London

First published in France as *Les Proies de l'officier* by NiL editions

Copyright © NiL éditions, Paris, 2002
English translation copyright © Michael Glencross 2007

First published in Great Britain in 2007 by Gallic Books,
134 Lots Road, London SW10 0RJ
This edition published in 2011 by Gallic Books

A CIP record for this book is available from the British Library

ISBN 978-1-906040-82-6

Typeset in Fournier MT by SX Composing DTP, Rayleigh, Essex
Printed and bound by CPI Bookmarque, Croydon CR0 4TD

2 4 6 8 10 9 7 5 3 1

For Emmanuelle
with whom I have the joy of sharing my life
and for Françoise

CHAPTER 1

STRANGELY, his hands were not trembling. The man was gazing at the body of the servant to whom he had been talking just a few moments earlier. His victim, now a pitifully bloodied and mutilated corpse, was real enough. But he was staring at her with as little feeling as if she were a broken doll. What made him uneasy was not that he had killed her, but that he felt no guilt. In sharp contrast to his inner turmoil as he'd stabbed the woman again and again, he now felt calm.

He stood up so suddenly that his chair almost toppled over. Time was against him. The innkeeper or one of his employees was bound to knock on the door sooner or later to ask for help serving the customers. The man knew he had to shake off his lethargy. His shoes, trousers, shirt and hair were all covered in blood. He had managed only partially to clean it from his hands and face. Impossible to run the risk of encountering a customer in the corridor. And how could he walk through the main room downstairs without being accosted by one of the infantrymen that were eating, getting drunk, smoking, chatting and leering at the serving girls? When he had entered the bedroom he had not known he was going to kill the woman. Now he realised he was trapped and his only route of escape was through the window.

The bedroom was on the third floor, under the eaves. It had rained the whole evening and heavy cloud still hid the moon.

The pitch-dark gave him a reasonable chance of being unnoticed by the many soldiers passing in the street. He opened the window and cautiously looked down. Three infantrymen were staggering along, laughing and bumping into each other. Groups of Italians and Frenchmen were arguing, neither understanding what the other was saying. The French army IV Corps was camped nearby, so the small town and all the neighbouring villages were thronged with soldiers.

Like a hussar committed to the charge, the man decided to go for it. With his bloodstained shirt concealed by an ordinary soldier's grey greatcoat, he climbed on to the windowsill and hauled himself up on to the overhang of the tiles. From there he reached the top of the roof without difficulty, crawled carefully along to the large stone chimney and hid behind it. Now what? There was nothing he could hold on to in order to climb down. In any case, that was out of the question for the time being. For the moment he stayed hidden in the darkness.

The street seemed to belong to another world; it was bathed in light and full of activity. The inns and private houses with rooms to let to soldiers had put lamps and candles in their windows. A constant stream of soldiers was arriving from outlying areas, lighting their way with torches, which made the countryside look as if it were swarming with fireflies. Most did not have the required passes, but the soldiers that were supposed to escort them back to their dreary camps were instead joining in the revelry.

The man looked at the next roof. There was a narrow street between but he should be able to leap across it. He stood up, negotiated his way round the chimney and flung himself into space. Stumbling against the other chimney, he fell forward, but managed to cling on to the ridge of the roof. A few tiles, dislodged around him, slid halfway down. He recovered himself and began moving again. He was in a hurry, trying not to think about the abyss that had opened up inside him in that bedroom, the chasm he was only just discovering. The roof of the adjoining house was rather less steeply pitched. The minutes were ticking by and he had still managed to advance only a few yards. Taking a risk, he stood up and moved forward, arms spread out, treading hesitantly like a tightrope walker. Fortunately, the ridge of the roof was a tile wide and, quickly learning dexterity, he speeded up. In this way he went past two houses, scrambled on to a raised roof and leapt across a second narrow street to land three feet below on the chimney of an inn.

By now he was almost running. Then an old tile suddenly gave way beneath him. He whirled his arms about, twisting this way and that, his body swaying as if unsure which way to fall, but eventually he regained his balance. The tile, meanwhile, continued its descent and shattered at the feet of a soldier in a grey greatcoat. The man immediately levelled his musket at the rooftops.

'Stop! Who goes there?'

'Private Mirambeau, what are you playing at?' roared a sergeant.

'A tile nearly hit me on the head, Sergeant. Someone's walking on the rooftops.'

The sergeant looked up. 'There's nobody up there, Mirambeau, just crumbling tiles that—'

The sound of firing cut short the NCO's words. The

soldier's eyes had adjusted to the darkness and he had just made out the outline of a rapidly disappearing figure.

'To arms! There's someone on the rooftops.'

Immediately a crowd gathered around the two men. A corporal, completely drunk, pointed his musket skywards.

'It's a Russian spy! Fire away like at Eylau, lads.'

He fired and two infantrymen did likewise. A hot-headed young lieutenant rushed up, sabre in hand.

'Who's attacking us?'

'Private Mirambeau's seen a Russian spy leaping about on the rooftops, sir.'

'There are three of them at least,' someone claimed authoritatively.

Further along the street other soldiers were firing or calling on their comrades to do so.

'A great big devil of a fellow!' declared one unsuccessful marksman.

His companion took aim.

'Devils don't scare me – take that!' But his shot failed to halt the moving figure.

'Surround the buildings!' the lieutenant shouted excitedly.

The gang of soldiers split into two groups which charged off in opposite directions. Some were laughing their heads off, finding, in their drunken high spirits, this manhunt even better entertainment than a game of cards.

The fugitive kept running and with each step might have fallen to his death. A bullet struck a chimney near him, showering him with fragments of stone. He could hear shouts and cries, and the sound of firing. Someone yelled: 'The Russians are taking pot shots at us from the rooftops!' and the street was soon alive with the rumour. One bullet shattered a tile at the fleeing man's feet, another whistled past his ears while a third broke a windowpane and produced a burst of drunken laughter.

Suddenly he noticed a tree growing against the back of the building. Without hesitating, he ran down the steep slope and flung himself as far forward as possible, arms outstretched. The leap seemed to last an eternity. Then foliage grazed his face. He grabbed a branch but immediately it bent beneath his weight and snapped. His ribs were struck a painful blow by another considerably thicker branch, but he clung on to it, now only a few feet above the ground. He dropped down and landed in a puddle.

He was about to rush off into the shelter of the nearby forest when a voice rang out behind him.

'Hold it. So where do you think you're going, old son? You wouldn't be the cause of all these fireworks, would you?'

The man turned round. A sergeant was pointing his musket at him, the bayonet fixed.

'Come closer to the light.'

The shouting was getting nearer. The man obeyed.

The sergeant blinked several times, straightened his musket and stood to attention. 'Beg your pardon, Colonel. I've only just recognised you.'

The man lunged forward and stabbed him with his knife, right in the heart.

'More's the pity for you . . .'

*

5

That 29 June 1812, Captain Margont watched the crossing of the Niemen in fascination. The river marked the border between the Grand Duchy of Warsaw, an ally of France, and Russia. Getting across this obstacle was therefore the first test in this campaign. A few days earlier, Napoleon and the bulk of his troops had crossed the broad stretch of water further to the north via the three bridges built by General Éblé in record time. Margont was serving in IV Corps, made up of forty thousand men under the command of Prince Eugène de Beauharnais, Napoleon's stepson and Viceroy of Italy. Now it was the turn of this force to enter Russian territory.

The regiments were impatiently crowding one another, bunching up the ranks of those in front, who were going too slowly. The infantrymen were calling the cavalry mounts 'lame hacks', 'worn-out nags' and 'meat barely good enough for the butcher's knife', to which the mounted chasseurs retorted that the battalions were just 'brainless centipedes' and the infantrymen 'big mouths on short legs'.

Perched on a hilltop, Margont could make out nothing but a seething mass of humanity. This dark, tightly packed column of men, their muskets glinting in the brilliant sunshine, cut a swathe through the green expanse of fields and the blue strip of river. The 84th Infantry Regiment of the Line, in which Margont served, had still not crossed and the men were wilting in the heat. Since it would not be their turn for some time yet, they had been allowed to make themselves more comfortable. They had fallen out of line, stacked their muskets and taken off their knapsacks before spreading out. There had been a brief scramble for the few shady spots under the trees, but now the pragmatists were dozing while the idealists hotly debated the merits of the campaign.

Margont wiped his brow with the back of his hand. The sun was giving him a headache and he regretted not being able to remove his shako, the cylindrical headgear that was so heavy. This campaign meant a lot to him. He was not the staunchest supporter of the Emperor's decisions, considering that Napoleon had let himself get carried away by his countless successes. Worse than that, the wars, which had formerly been intended to defend the state, safeguard the ideals of the Revolution and free nations from the yoke of ancient monarchies, were now turning into imperial conquests. But he admired the genius of the man, a strategist who had won so many unlikely, even impossible, victories. By defeating Austria, Prussia and many other countries, Napoleon had preserved the achievements of the Revolution: the abolition of feudal privileges, the establishment of the Constitution and the Declaration of the Rights of Man and the Citizen, including the passage that appealed so much to both heart and mind: 'Liberty consists in the freedom to do everything that injures no one else . . .'

The war between France and Russia had broken out because of the Tsar's decision to stop enforcing the blockade imposed by Napoleon with the aim of ruining England financially until she was forced to sue for peace. But Margont was not naïve. He knew that another reason for this conflict was that Europe was too small for two such powerful emperors. He himself was preparing to take part in this war for other reasons (though he would have been forced to fight anyway). Committed to the values of republicanism, citizenship and liberalism, he dreamt of the day when all monarchies would collapse and be replaced by republics that would blossom like flowers in a wasteland. Although he was now thirty-two, his ideas were the clear-cut, strongly held convictions of youth. Nevertheless, he was aware of the irony of a situation whereby, in the interests of the republican cause, he was serving a republican emperor who was becoming ever more imperialistic. Reality has an unpleasant habit of overriding one's ideals with its contradictions, disillusions and ironies. But Margont thought that it was Napoleon who was really the plaything of the Revolution and not the reverse. French soldiers carried with them the ideas of liberty and equality and these ideals took root in people's minds.

An aide-de-camp galloped down a hillside, knocking over a stack of muskets, and brought his horse to a halt in front of a group of men. Three infantrymen turned round and pointed towards Margont, and the horseman set off again in his direction. On reaching Margont, he reined in his horse, wheeling it round under control. His uniform was soaked with sweat. His chubby cheeks and round face made him look like a peach oozing its juice. Locks of fair hair were plastered to his forehead. He must have wished he was back in Alsace or Normandy.

He hurriedly returned Margont's salute and asked hopefully: 'Are you Captain Margont of the 84th?'

'That is correct.'

'In that case, I request that you follow me without further ado.'

'May I know why?'

'No. They are orders.'

This type of answer annoyed Margont. And he hated even more what he was going to reply.

'I'll follow you.'

The two men set off at a gallop. Margont turned round for a last look at the Niemen. But he would be seeing it again before long. He would even have the pleasure of hearing it flowing beneath him.

Margont took the same route as the day before, but in the opposite direction. Soon he reached the 15th Division, the Pino Division, consisting of Italians, who made up the rearguard of IV Corps. The Italians were easily recognisable from their green or white and green coats, whereas the dominant colour in the French infantry was dark blue.

After what seemed an excessively long ride, as is always the case when you don't know where you are going or why, the aide-de-camp stopped his horse not far from a blue and white striped tent. It had a four-sided roof and was big enough to sleep a dozen men. Six soldiers in green coats were guarding it: grenadiers from the Royal Italian Guard, wearing enormous black bearskins, each topped with a red plume; and guards of honour whose gilded helmets had black crests and white plumes. A very eminent person was here.

A moment later, a grenadier called out Margont's name and the captain entered the tent.

CHAPTER 2

Margont found himself face to face with Prince Eugène and immediately stood stiffly to attention. With a wave of the hand the prince invited him to sit. Two chairs, probably commandeered from a nearby farm, had been placed in the centre of the tent. As it was out of the question for a prince to sit on a seat identical to that of one of his subordinates, the guards of honour had used all their inventiveness. One of the chairs, bedecked with an elaborately embroidered cushion, had been arranged on a dais covered with a sumptuous Turkish rug decorated with red, gold and brown arabesques. It was an unconvincing imitation of a throne. The rest of the furniture was simple: a sofa used as a bed, a trunk and a trestle table with a large map of Europe spread out on it. The Empire and its allies covered the entire map with the exception of three countries: Portugal, England, and Russia in all its immensity.

Prince Eugène was thirty-one. His puffy oval face was elongated by his high forehead. His slightly untidy auburn hair detracted somewhat from the formality of his coat, with its collar heavily embroidered in gold, voluminous epaulettes and colourful medals. His uniform could not, however, disguise his youthfulness, and many thought him a man promoted too soon and too far. He was said to be constantly cheerful. That was not true. He scrutinised Margont closely, noting his attractive face, his slightly prominent cheekbones and the scar on his left cheek.

This gave him a martial appearance that held a particular appeal for Prussian ladies, as such marks were much appreciated in Berlin. His blue eyes and fair hair gave him a slightly Nordic look, whereas in fact he came from the south-east of France. The prince kicked back the dais with the tip of his boot, grabbed his chair and placed it opposite Margont's.

'Hang all this absurd protocol. We're at war. I shall come straight to the point.'

Splendid, thought Margont.

However, Eugène still hesitated. He tried to sound firm but his face betrayed his anxiety.

'I need someone for a secret mission of the highest importance. But I know nobody who can carry it out with the necessary speed, panache and discretion. You were recommended to me, hence your presence here. Secrecy is one of the key aspects of this business! If you take on this heavy responsibility and anything leaks out, you will be shot even before a court martial can be convened to sentence you.'

Margont wondered who the person was to whom he owed the pleasure of this summons.

'If you are successful, you will be promoted to major. You will immediately receive ten years' pay.'

Margont had visions of himself in a small mansion in Nîmes or Montpellier . . .

The prince continued, 'The necessary official explanations will be given but the mission must never be mentioned. Do you accept?'

'The fact is, Your Highness has not—'

'Thank you for this resounding and unqualified "yes". I

knew the Empire could count on you. Here is a quick summary of this whole wretched business. Last night in Tresno, a small Polish town near the River Niemen, a woman was murdered in her bedroom. She was called Maria Dorlovna – Polish but of German extraction. Her murder was a terrible butchery. If that were the whole story I wouldn't even have been informed of it and the military police would now be investigating. The problem is, it is possible that the culprit may be an officer serving in the army corps that I have the honour of commanding.'

Margont responded to the news with an aplomb that both pleased and amazed the prince.

'Such calmness, Captain. You barely seem surprised. It couldn't be you, by any chance, could it? That would simplify my life considerably.'

'Unfortunately, I regret to say that I must disappoint Your Highness.'

'What impertinence! Well, the person who recommended you did warn me of that displeasing trait of yours. I must confess that it made me hesitate before choosing you.'

Not enough, unfortunately, thought Margont.

'But I said to myself that a good many of our finest officers were the personification of impertinence. Look at Murat. He charges at the head of his squadrons and sometimes considers himself a one-man vanguard. Then there's Ney, the great Ney. On the battlefield he's everywhere at once, always rushing to where the action is fiercest, like a moth drawn to the light. Lasalle, too. He dubbed any hussar who hadn't died by the age of thirty a wastrel. What's more, he followed his own precept at Wagram, only a few years late. And don't all these heroes, and the Empire itself, spring from the greatest and most daring example of impertinence of all: the people of France decreeing a republic? In France, insolence is not a defect, but a badge of honour! That said, it's like alcohol: it quickly goes to your head and causes blunders, so do not overindulge.'

The prince folded his arms and stared Margont straight in the eye.

'I suppose your quip was a clever manoeuvre designed to make me choose someone else. It was crafty but it hasn't worked. Far from discouraging me, you have confirmed me in my decision. So, as I was saying, it would appear that the murderer is one of my officers.'

The prince gave Margont an account of the race across the rooftops and the confrontation between the sentry and the fugitive.

'The sentry stood to attention? Are you sure of that?' said Margont with a surprised look.

Eugène stiffened and his brow furrowed. It was clear that he would dearly have liked to say the opposite of what he must.

'I'm quite certain, thanks to the testimony of another sentry, who was too far away to intervene but who saw the whole scene. The soldier who was stabbed had the rank of sergeant. A sergeant would not suddenly have stood to attention in front of an immediate superior who had just jumped down from a roof, was not wearing regulation uniform and was not on duty. No, given the way he reacted and the speed with which he did so, he must undoubtedly have recognised an officer. At least a captain, or perhaps someone of even higher rank . . . Now then, Captain Margont, take that look off your face. Anyone would swear that you were no longer listening to me and that you were desperately searching for a way of shirking this task.'

Margont was absent-mindedly tapping the hilt of his sword.

'For it to be a captain is just about acceptable, Your Highness. But if it is someone of higher rank . . .'

'No arrests. Whether it's a captain or a major — I dare not imagine anyone above that — you will take no initiative. Nothing foolish or it's the firing squad!'

'I take Your Highness at his word.'

'You will draw up a report for me in the greatest secrecy and I will take the necessary steps.'

The prince breathed in slowly, which Margont took to be a ploy intended to give emphasis to what he was about to say.

'Captain, have you given a moment's thought to what would happen if the rumour spread that one of our French officers is a maniac who tortures and butchers Polish women? All the regiments would denounce their own captains, majors, colonels . . . Whole companies would refuse to obey the orders of the man they took to be the murderer. But, even worse, the victim was Polish and of German extraction. You can well imagine the reaction of the tens of thousands of Poles, of Germans from the Confederation of the Rhine, and of Prussians and Austrians taking part in this campaign. Already there's little love lost between the Prussians, the Austrians and ourselves. It would not take much to inflame people's passions. There would be disagreements, desertions . . . If this matter were taken up by agitators, spies and enemies of France, it could shake to the foundations the carefully constructed diplomatic edifice built up by the Emperor.'

The prince stood up and began to walk around the two chairs.

'You were at the battle of Auerstädt.'

'That is correct, Your—'

The Viceroy interrupted him abruptly with a wave of the hand. 'Of course it is correct. I know all about you. At Jena and Auerstädt we blew these wretched Prussians and their Saxon allies to smithereens. And today they are at our side, fighting with us against the Russians!'

The prince spread his arms in a gesture of powerlessness. 'Ah, the miracles of diplomacy! I shall never get used to it, even though I observe its rituals. In short, a rumour such as "A French officer is murdering and mutilating Polish women" – and "officer" would soon become all officers, and the Polish woman would become in turn German for the Germans, Prussian for the Prussians, Austrian, Saxon, et cetera – is quite enough to rekindle ill feeling in the hearts of those who lost a brother, a cousin, a friend or an arm at Jena, in Italy, at Wagram . . .'

The prince continued to walk around in a circle as if this circle embodied the problem he was unable to solve.

'When the Emperor was told about this business, he lost his temper. He began to rant at my messenger in Corsican!'

The Viceroy stopped dead. He was lost in thought and was staring at the elaborate arabesques on the rug.

'Just think about the Russian civilian population!' he exclaimed all of a sudden, raising his head. 'How could we rally them to our cause, or at least prevent them from doing too much harm to our rear? "Here come the women-killers!" Pillagers!

Yes, they'll think we are pillagers. And what about the Emperor? He'll fly into a rage again, that's for sure. Then there are the Germans . . .'

His words were becoming more and more disjointed as troubled thoughts swirled around in his head. Margont had the impression that the prince was hiding something from him. It was a vague feeling prompted by various small details: an evasive look; a hurried delivery as if Eugène wanted to convince him quickly; a puzzled expression; lips that opened as if about to say something then closed again immediately . . . It lasted a few moments, then the prince's attitude became perfectly assured again.

'Captain, you are going to unmask this man for me!'

Eugène spoke these words with incisive firmness. If he had been hesitating about whether to reveal an extra piece of information, he had in the end decided to keep it to himself.

'For the moment there are no such rumours. It should be added that I have taken every possible precaution. The person who discovered the body was the innkeeper with whom the victim lodged, a certain Maroveski. I had him arrested and he's being held in an isolated farmhouse. Officially, he robbed an officer. His gaolers speak only Italian, so he can't tell them anything. On seeing the body, this Maroveski informed a picket of soldiers on duty, who immediately alerted a captain on guard. The officer was completely out of his depth and informed my general staff. I had these witnesses interrogated by one of the captains from my Royal Guard. They told him nothing. The sentry was a long way from the murderer, it was dark and the scene lasted only a few seconds. All he noticed was that the man was between five foot six and six foot in height. A remarkably precise piece of evidence indeed!'

That leaves a mere five hundred suspects, thought Margont.

'The soldiers who kept watch at the spot until the arrival of my grenadiers, the captain on guard and this sentry were all transferred to Spain at daybreak.'

Margont managed to restrain his anger. 'But it's essential for me to question these men personally, Your Highness!'

'Well, you'll just have to do without what they would have been able to tell you. I had to nip the rumour in the bud. They are on their way to Vieja Lamarsota, Vieja Lamarora. In a word, you could say they're off to "Vieja Go-to-Hell"!'

'I regret to inform Your Highness that I decline to carry out this investigation.'

The prince gave him a taunting look, as if daring Margont to stick to this position.

'Because you think there's still time for you to set off for Vieja Something-or-Other, do you? If you refuse to help me, it won't be the road to Spain for you but the nearest wall!'

The Viceroy of Italy broke off. Margont's silence confirmed that he could continue.

'When one of my aides-de-camp, General Triaire, gave the order to go to fetch you, he led the messenger to believe that he wanted to inform you personally of the death of your brother.'

'I don't have a brother.'

'Well, you do now. Major Henri Margont, killed in an ambush on the road to Madrid a few days ago. That band of guerrillas led by the famous Mina again. Your brother was a close friend of General Triaire. That's why you were sent for. You have my deepest sympathy.'

'My friends know I don't have a brother, so if they hear that—'

'Do as Triaire does: make it up!'

The prince eventually sat down. He seemed eager to see the back of this captain who was going to lighten his burden considerably.

'To summarise, my grenadiers are guarding the innkeeper and that poor woman's bedroom. The body has been buried . . .'

The captain looked up to the heavens.

'The body has been buried!' the prince repeated unequivocally. 'All that a few soldiers and the inhabitants of Tresno know is that a woman has been murdered. They do not know that an officer is the suspect and that the victim was found in a grisly state. Now you may ask any questions.'

'Why not put the military police in charge of this case?'

'Impossible! There would inevitably be leaks. This investigation must not be carried out by a whole host of people. I need a single sleuth answerable only to me. Leaks would produce rumour, which I fear almost as much as I do the Russians. Besides, the leaks might come to the attention of the murderer, who would then discover that we knew he was an officer. We would lose our only trump card.'

Margont guessed a third reason. He was under Prince Eugène's orders; there was no one else he could talk to about this business, so to antagonise the prince could cost him dearly. Conversely, an investigator from the military police would be accountable to his own superiors. By choosing Margont, the prince ensured total control of the investigation. He would have complete freedom in deciding the fate of the culprit if he were unmasked. But if he proved to be a high-ranking officer, would he be fairly tried and sentenced, or would he be discreetly transferred to 'Vieja Go-to-Hell'?

'Why choose me, Your Highness?'

The Viceroy stood up and grabbed a document case lying on the sofa. He swiftly opened it and took out fifteen or so sheets of paper.

'You have been chosen for a number of criteria. I know everything about you, Captain. Your childhood, your short and enforced career in the Church, your military record, your opinions, the books you read, the names of your friends . . .'

'May I know how Your Highness obtained all this information? You could not have found out my life story overnight.'

The prince had the triumphant look of someone who sees his predictions coming true, giving him the misleading but exhilarating feeling of being in total control.

'A few years ago I got Triaire to draw up a secret list of individuals with various skills. My idea was to create my own network of spies. But in the end the ones the Emperor uses proved so efficient – Schulmeister is the prime example – that I abandoned my plan. However, Triaire continued to keep this register, striking out the names of those killed in combat and adding others. One day, your name cropped up.'

'Is there really only one way of being struck off the list?'

The prince ignored the question. He casually pulled the reports from his file as if pulling the petals off a daisy. The reports were in such small, compact handwriting that they looked like pages from a bible. Triaire had conducted his investigation meticulously. With every page that the prince skimmed through, Margont felt a little more exposed. At last the Viceroy looked up.

'I don't have time to go into the details of your life, even if it does seem to have been of keen interest to the good Triaire. Let's talk about the battle of Eylau, which you took part in, or rather, the aftermath of Eylau. It was at this point that you became a little more critical of the Emperor.'

Margont stared in disbelief. Only his best friends, Saber, Lefine and Piquebois, had such a clear idea of his opinions. Which one had given the information to Triaire's men? Lefine, without a doubt. In any case, he had to respond.

'Your Highness, I have always been faithful to the Emperor and to the ideals of the Revolution and I—'

'I know. Otherwise you wouldn't be on my list! Let's just say that you are not one of those who think that everything – absolutely everything – that the Emperor does is faultless and admirable. And, cautious as you are, you keep your criticisms for your closest friends.'

'Not close enough, it would appear.'

'The only close friends who keep secrets are dead ones.'

'I wouldn't go so far as that with the one who betrayed me.'

There was a change of attitude in the prince. His features softened. The Viceroy temporarily gave way to the man.

'Why this change of heart in 1807? It was the battle of Eylau, wasn't it? I have to admit that I myself . . . One may admire the tactical genius of generals, the heroism of certain soldiers and epic feats of arms, but one cannot ignore the slaughter that goes with all this. The human spirit is like blotting paper: it can absorb blood up to a point but in the end it will become saturated and overflow.'

This was not what Margont was fighting for. But Eylau had shown him what reality could sometimes do to noble feelings and good intentions. Ten thousand dead and forty thousand wounded was not just a slaughter; it was the end of the world. As a result, the Emperor had forbidden the wearing of white uniforms. Officially, it was because they were reminders of the old regime, but also it was because they made the bloodstains too obvious.

The prince had fallen silent. Was he back at Eylau or on the shore of another sea of blood? Maybe all this was a carefully staged attempt to make him more likeable in Margont's eyes. It was difficult to fathom this illustrious figure: sometimes calculating and manipulative, haughty and disdainful; sometimes sympathetic and humane. Margont was unable to say which of these facets was more genuine or to tell which would win out in the end.

'Eylau justifies the criticisms you occasionally make of some of the Emperor's decisions,' the prince concluded.

He turned over a sheaf of pages.

Margont got his comment in first. 'As does Spain.'

'Indeed. I know that you ventured the opinion that the occupation of Spain was a mistake.'

The hypocrisy of politicians! thought Margont. It was no longer the prince or the general talking but the diplomat concerned for the image of the Empire. Spain was ablaze, every peasant a part-time guerrilla: tens of thousands of Frenchmen had died in ambushes; young women were taking up arms as the need arose; the inhabitants of cities under siege were hanging those of their number who wished to capitulate; even priests in their cassocks were firing from their church towers . . . But the official version was that the conquest of Spain had not been a mistake and, no, fanatical nationalism heightened by the mystical fervour of the Spanish was not a problem.

'Well, Captain, let me tell you that I chose you for three reasons and one of them involves Spain.'

More bad news brought by a Spanish ill wind. Would they never be rid of it, even here, at the other end of Europe?

'First, according to Triaire, you are good at investigating. Secondly, you are not indispensable for the good running of your regiment. And thirdly, you are a hero of the Peninsular War, during which you were promoted to the rank of Officer of the Légion d'Honneur. This last point will ease your task and if, at the end of your enquiries, I decide to reveal the name of the murderer, no one will question your conclusions.'

The prince's naïvety was disarming. For him it was obvious that the culprit would be unmasked. How could it be otherwise, since he had given the order?

'And what excuses shall I give to leave my regiment and move about as I please, Your Highness?'

The Viceroy handed him two documents. 'Here are two passes. The first is signed by Triaire and is more than enough to open most doors for you. If you did happen to come up against any higher authority, you would use the second one, which bears my own signature. It goes without saying that this document should be used only as a very last resort.'

Margont glanced at the handwritten lines, their gracefully shaped, outsized capitals in no way attenuating the terseness of the instructions. Captain Margont had been entrusted with a mission of the utmost importance. He should be asked no questions about it. He was entitled to go anywhere – the word was underlined. His every request, whatever its nature, should be granted immediately. In the event of any disagreement concerning the said requests, the person should obey but would be entitled to make a complaint to the signatory of this order. Margont was dumbfounded. These two sheets of paper made him superior – in the context of this investigation – to a major-general.

'Power can be intoxicating . . .' the prince commented soberly. 'But you will answer with your life for the use you make of these papers. Were I to learn that you waved them under the nose of some Russian aristocrat to requisition his stately home with a view to leading a life of luxury, or that you showed them off in an attempt to seduce some beauty by playing the dashing secret agent, then it would mean the firing squad!'

'What am I going to tell my colonel? And anyone I have to show these orders to? Because I'm still bound to be asked questions.'

'Do as Triaire does. Make something up! I think I've told you everything. Any questions? Yes, you're bound to have some. Well, keep them to yourself. I'm handing responsibility for this problem over to you. You will give me regular progress reports on your investigation. And, above all, be discreet! You may leave.'

Margont was still gazing at the passes. 'They're fakes, aren't they?'

The prince was stung to the quick. 'I beg your pardon?'

'Secrecy is so dear to your heart that I take it these documents are fakes. If my investigation implicates someone powerful, and if the affair becomes common knowledge, then you will be able to disavow me. I will be called a spy or a crank, and people will claim that I wrote the safe-conducts myself.'

Prince Eugène was caught off guard. 'Well, you . . . They are a good enough likeness to serve their purpose. In any case, you now have a further reason to act with the utmost discretion. Did I not tell you that you may leave?'

Margont stood up, saluted and went towards the exit. The half-light inside the tent was oppressing him; he wanted to see daylight again, the morning light that drives away the fears of the night.

But the prince called out to him: 'Captain! The messenger I sent to inform the Emperor put forward the names of five investigators to His Majesty. You are the one the Emperor chose. He affords you his full confidence and is convinced that you will prove worthy of this honour.'

CHAPTER 3

MARGONT wanted first of all to question the innkeeper before he too was sent off to Vieja Go-to-Hell, a village that was certainly filling up quickly these days. The gaolers had been informed of the visit and took Margont to see the prisoner, though not before carefully divesting him of his weapons.

'Poor man.' These were the two words that immediately came to mind on looking at Maroveski. His whole world had collapsed. He was over forty. His ginger hair was tangled and his bulging stomach and flabby cheeks contrasted sharply with his deep-set, dark-ringed eyes. Glazed with tears, they seemed to look without seeing, and it took him a few seconds to realise that someone had entered his cell.

'Captain, I've done nothing wrong!' he exclaimed, sobbing.

'I know,' said Margont. 'How do you come to speak French?'

'I took part in the Polish campaign. God bless the French for having freed us. I was a canteen-keeper. I followed your troops and sold them good bread and vodka. Mulled wine too, and well-cooked bacon.'

'I'll see that you get all that here.'

'And eggs as well?'

'Until your stomach's full to bursting! Listen to me carefully: nobody will harm you. You're going to stay here . . .'

Maroveski let out a cry that would have melted the hardest of hearts.

'You're not a prisoner,' Margont added. 'Not exactly . . . but you knew the murdered woman. I'm in charge of the investigation and when the culprit has been arrested you can go free, provided that you never breathe a word about this business.'

'I swear it! I swear it by the Holy Virgin! Get me out of here, Captain! I won't say a thing!'

'You're staying here for the time being!'

Even though he had no choice, Margont disliked being so hard. The grenadiers of the Royal Guard were holding their prisoner in the cellar of a commandeered farm. The place was cold and the stone walls and vaults were oozing damp. Daylight entered only through a basement window blocked by a grenadier's boots. There was nothing to do here except engrave your sufferings on the walls. Margont found the place oppressive. It reminded him of his childhood years spent in a monastic cell: the sound of the bolt locking the door, the fading footsteps of the key-holder, the silence, the deadly boredom, the despair. If Margont had been locked away here he would have attempted every means of escape. Every single one.

'Do you read?'

'I never learnt.'

'What a pity. You will have good meals here, the guards will take you for walks regularly and, as soon as possible, I'll have you set free.'

Maroveski dared not speak. He was broken. His yellowing teeth bit nervously into his lower lip.

'Tell me about the dead woman,' continued Margont.

The man blanched. He could see again her bloodied body,

the expression of pain on her face. That was perhaps worse than the physical mutilations she had suffered.

'I'm not the one . . .' he stuttered.

'I know that. Calm down.'

From having been desperate, Maroveski suddenly became wary.

'Why is a captain investigating Maria's death? She was just a decent, simple girl.'

Margont was taken by surprise. The prince's political explanation would have satisfied him had it not been for those few moments of hesitation.

'They're orders,' he replied.

The stock answer of soldiers when they do not want to give one. Maroveski was used to dealing with the army, so did not pursue the matter. He dropped his suspicious air and looked sorrowful again.

'Do you know who could have behaved like this?' Margont went on.

'It's . . . Prince Charming.'

Margont stood motionless as if the slightest movement might make this first hint of a clue disappear into thin air.

'That's what she called him, Captain.'

'Have you seen him?'

'Never. All this is so strange . . . I must tell you about Maria first. She came from a good family but her parents have been dead a long time. Maria was thirty-six. Her husband was a sergeant, killed at Wagram. Since then Maria led a respectable life!'

This last sentence was spoken with deliberation. Maroveski was searching for the right words and speaking slowly.

'Maria didn't have much money. She had no family left, so two years ago she came to see me. We struck a deal. She lived in my inn for free, and did the housework and cooking and made herself generally useful. She worked hard and was polite. In three years she never had anyone, you understand. Yet with all these soldiers around here there was no shortage of men, and she was pretty, was Maria. She could have got married again or . . . entertained men. But no. I used to say to her: "Get yourself a husband before it's too late." But Maria wanted the perfect man: kind, well-mannered, knowledgeable . . . And then just the day before she died, she came back really happy – singing, even. I teased her and said: "Well, Maria, you're in good spirits today." I was teasing her but she blushed and told me she might have met her "Prince Charming". I didn't say anything. What sort of man could have seduced Maria in a day? I've had plenty of sweet-talkers on my premises: wealthy merchants, educated landowners . . .'

'Did she talk to you about him again? Did she say where she had met him?'

'No.'

'What had she gone out to do?'

'Errands for me, seeing people . . .'

'Can you give me some names?'

Maroveski shrugged. 'Maria was friends with everyone around here.'

Margont sighed inwardly. With the start of the military campaign he would never have time to reconstruct Maria's movements on that day and question the people she might have met.

'Why do you think it was this "Prince Charming" who killed her?'

'On the evening she died there were a lot of people about: soldiers and officers, all over the place. The serving girls and I were scurrying around carrying food and wine. But Maria wasn't there. I went up to her room to tell her to come and help. When she opened the door she was wearing her pretty dress, the one she wore to church. You can't imagine how lovely she looked. She blushed and told me her friend was coming to visit her. She begged me to let her off work until midnight. I said yes.'

Maroveski was more pitiful than ever. He was a prisoner twice over, of this cellar and of an unrequited love now stifled for ever by death. Margont moved automatically towards the door. He felt he had already spent too long in a locked room.

'You must surely have tried to spot her guest?'

'Yes, but there were too many people! All out to have a good time before possibly going to their deaths.'

'Didn't you see him climbing the stairs?'

'People were sitting on the steps as there was no room anywhere else. And loads were also going up to the bedrooms for drinks with friends.'

'A Prince Charming might suggest an officer,' Margont ventured.

The innkeeper did not react. 'There were officers everywhere: lieutenants, captains . . .'

'And higher ranks than those?'

'I don't know. Some customers were in civilian clothes. In any case, it was raining, so many of them were wearing greatcoats or cloaks.'

Margont wondered whether the murderer had premeditated his crime. If so, how bold of him to risk being recognised by walking through this crowd, even wrapped in a greatcoat with his collar turned up. If not, what could have led him to commit such an act?

'And what makes you think that this man really is the one we're looking for?'

Maroveski seemed to be pulling himself together. He straightened up in his chair. For the first time he looked Margont in the eye. The captain had the impression he was using him as a crutch. The Poles were a strange people. History had been unkind to Poland, a country constantly subject to invasion. Dordenski, a Polish friend of Margont's, summed it up with a quip: 'In Poland we don't erect memorials for every war or for every massacre as other countries do. That's because there aren't enough stones in our country.' And despite everything, the Poles were stubbornly refusing to give in.

'Captain, tell me first of all, what will you do with him if you arrest him?'

'He'll be handed over to the appropriate authorities, tried and sentenced.'

'But it won't be just your decision?'

Margont smiled. 'That's for sure. I'm only a captain. But the person who appointed me to this task is just as eager as I am for—'

'First he wants to know who it is. And if it's someone wealthy and powerful or important to your army? If you discover it's someone who's beyond the reach of justice, what will you do?'

'No one is beyond the reach of justice.'

'If you really think that then I understand why you were picked for the investigation. It makes it easier for them to manipulate you.'

Margont was disconcerted. There was too much truth in this assertion.

Maroveski hesitated, then decided to continue. When he recalled the panic caused by the firing and the fear of a Russian attack, he shook his head.

'I was sure it wasn't the Russians. I was afraid for Maria. I tried to get to the staircase but people were pushing me towards the exit. When I did manage to get to her bedroom door, I banged on it and called out to her but she didn't reply. Captain, the door hadn't been forced and it was locked from the inside. She'd opened the door to the man who did it. So it must have been him . . .' His fists were now clenched. 'So I forced the door open with my shoulder. It was stupid of me because he might have still been there and killed me as well. I saw Maria stretched out on the bed, and she . . . she had . . .'

Margont gave him a few moments to recover before putting his question.

'I know that my enquiries are painful but they are vital for my investigation. Do you remember anything in particular, was there some detail that struck you?'

'There was blood all over her. Her face was disfigured. I looked at her only for a moment. I couldn't stand it.'

Maroveski's expression was blank. Once more he was in a state of complete mental disarray.

'Oh, yes,' he added eventually. 'Everything was very neat and tidy. She'd made her bedroom nice to welcome him.'

CHAPTER 4

HAVING instructed the grenadiers to treat the prisoner well – instructions that he had to sketch out – Margont went to Tresno.

The village was completely unaware of the drama that had taken place. The villagers seemed obsessed with the presence of the French army and excitement was at fever pitch. A regiment was marching down the main street in orderly fashion, the soldiers trudging in step through mud that had been tramped a thousand times over. Fascinated children were crowding around, watching them, shouting: 'Drummers! Drummers!' and imitating an interminable drum roll with their fists. The colonel smiled and, waving his sabre imperiously like Jupiter brandishing his thunderbolt, pointed to the drummers, who immediately began to play. The children shouted joyfully and their faces lit up as if they were witnessing the most amazing of spectacles.

At the windows of the wooden houses, onlookers were jostling for position with such determination that it looked as if they might bring all the houses tumbling down. Polish women – equally concerned, whether they were wearing patched and faded clothes, or elegant dresses and spring bonnets – were calling out to the soldiers in halting French: 'Tell Corporal Djaczek, from the 3rd Polish Regiment, that Natasha sends him kisses.' 'Tell Private Blachas, from the 12th Polish Artillery, that all his family send their love and are thinking of him.' 'Do you know whether Ivan Naskelitch, from the 14th Polish Chasseurs, is all right?'

Everywhere soldiers were buying things, to the delight of the villagers, who all seemed to have turned into pedlars. There was a delicious aroma of sausages, which made empty stomachs rumble; elsewhere were warm clothes, knitted jackets, fur-lined – if threadbare – cloaks and fur hats. Infantrymen, collapsing under the weight of parcels, were skewering loaves of bread on their bayonets. Sergeants in charge of keeping order were checking passes and other papers. Four times out of five they frowned and began to shout, but they invariably received the same reply: 'I lost me way, Sergeant. D'you know where my regiment is?'

The only stone buildings were the inns and the church. Because Tresno was located along a busy highway, there were many places to stay and Maroveski's was the biggest. The window on the top floor was still open. Margont prayed that the scene of the crime had not been ransacked by those who had taken the body away. As he went inside the establishment, the wind shook the wrought-iron carafe-shaped sign hanging above the entrance, making its metal fastenings creak.

Five grenadiers were seated around a table, playing cards. Their captain, astride a chair, was watching his men as he stuffed his pipe. As soon as he saw the Frenchman, he got up and approached him. There was a brief shuffling of chairs and then all the grenadiers lined up and stood to attention. The Italian officer saluted stiffly. He was puzzled by Margont's two epaulettes, indicating his junior rank. Since they, the prestigious grenadiers of the Italian Royal Guard, were being forced to wait for someone, that someone had to be an important person. But Margont did not look like someone important. The Italian checked his safe-conduct, then asked a question in Italian. Margont did not understand much of it. Did they want permission to leave the scene after his investigation? He settled on this explanation, reckoning that, like Guard soldiers everywhere, they were spoiling for a fight.

'You are to remain here until further notice,' he stated slowly, pointing his finger at the Italians before indicating the ground.

His gesture was greeted by looks of disappointment. No more glorious military campaigns. Their only battles would be at cards.

'And no one is to go upstairs,' he added at the foot of the staircase, waving his hands about to halt an imaginary crowd of onlookers.

He climbed a few stairs and turned round to say with barely disguised anger in his voice: 'And I would be pleased if someone would fetch Sergeant Lefine, from the 84th.'

'Sergeant Lefine, here,' repeated one of the grenadiers, to make sure he had understood properly.

The hotel had been emptied of its occupants and the silence pervading the whole building was in sharp contrast to the hubbub in the streets. The door to the victim's bedroom was wide open. A latch on the inside had given way when the innkeeper forced the door with his shoulder. Although small, the accommodation had been carefully thought out. The steeply sloping roof made it possible to stand up straight only in the left-hand part of the room. On the right-hand side it was only possible to sit or to lie down, so that was where the bed had been set up. Alongside it, a trunk served as a bedside table. A small bookcase, an unexpected item, was tucked away in a corner. So Maria had had the advantage of being taught to read by her parents. The pages of the few books on the shelves were well thumbed. Judging by the pink or pastel-coloured covers and the engravings depicting couples walking together, they were probably romantic works, novels and collections of poetry. On a table stood a candlestick, two glasses and a pitcher of wine. A jug, a tub of water and some provisions – pots of jam, vegetables and a string of garlic – were crammed on to some shelves.

The rumpled sheets were soaked with blood. Dark red spots on the floor made it possible to discern two sets of footprints. One led from the bed to the door and was probably the result of the victim's body being moved by the grenadiers. The other went from the bed to the tub. The water inside it was red, as was the water in the jug. So it was impossible to decide whether the murderer had got rid of the bloodstains after his crime or whether the soldiers who had helped to lift the body up had simply washed their hands there. And now these precious witnesses were on their way to Spain.

'How can an investigation be carried out in such circumstances?' Margont asked himself angrily.

He spent an hour inspecting the bedroom but discovered nothing except a trace of blood on the bolt of the trunk. It was scarcely visible because it had been wiped. That seemed strange. The chest was spattered with blood as it had been next to the bed. Why then had this trace been wiped away? Was it something unconnected with the murder, the result of the victim having injured herself? Or had the murderer still been covered in blood when he opened the trunk, despite having had a quick wash?

Margont emptied it, carefully examining each dress, the spring jacket and the two nightdresses. The garments, which were folded, had nothing special about them.

He was peering at the window when a flurry of footsteps was heard on the staircase. A few moments later Sergeant Lefine stood stiffly to attention in the doorway and, with a smile on his face, bellowed: 'At your disposal, Captain.'

Fernand Lefine, who hailed from Arles, was such a quick-witted fellow that the parish priest had done his utmost to teach him to read and write. His parents, humble farmers, had got it into their heads that he would become a schoolmaster or a mayor. That showed how little they knew Fernand. He was the laziest, craftiest man in the entire region. Instead of using his talents wisely, he exploited illiterates, getting them to pay him to write their letters. He had an easy-going attitude to life and considered it really stupid to see things otherwise. One day a policeman had caught him stealing from a neighbour's vegetable garden. This representative of the law, a former soldier, had warned him that he would come back for him in three days and haul him off to prison. Lefine was then given three options: he could go to prison; he could pack his bags and prepare to spend his life as a fugitive roaming the countryside; or he could join the army, in which case the police would never dream of depriving the motherland of such a stalwart defender in these troubled times. So it was that in 1801, aged only seventeen, Lefine entered the French army. There he met Margont and the two men had become inseparable. That said, friendship, like everything else on this poor earth, has its limits.

Margont grabbed a flabbergasted Lefine by the collar and flung him to the ground.

'You miserable wretch!'

Lefine remained sitting, clutching his throat, waiting for the storm to pass.

'How could you have told my life story to the agents of that cursed Triaire? For what price did you betray our friendship? A high one, I'm sure.'

'Oh, that . . .'

'So there's something else as well, is there?' thundered Margont.

Lefine straightened his shako. His brown hair was always well cut and carefully combed. His self-assurance, knowledge and resourcefulness – a euphemism – made him a very popular figure in the 84th.

'You notice that I confess to my crime, Captain. And a crime confessed to is half—'

'That sort of stupid talk only works in the confessional.'

Margont squatted down to force Lefine to look him straight in the eye.

'Of course you confess. You're the only possible suspect! Who knew about my criticisms of the Emperor's policy after Eylau? Only Saber and you! And Saber has too much of a sense of honour.'

'But I also have—'

'Don't use words you don't know the meaning of.'

Lefine stood up again, followed by Margont, whose nervous, jerky gestures were still menacing.

'I was forced into it, Captain. It was last year. A sergeant-major sent for me. He told me he had orders from very high up. He wanted to know everything about you! Supposedly it was to do with promotion. He threatened me. He told me that if I didn't obey I'd be sent to the colonies, on the other side of the world. And on top of that I'd be downgraded to—'

Margont shook his head. 'No, no, no. You're as cunning as a monkey and in the fairground they don't train monkeys by waving a stick at them, but by throwing them peanuts.'

'They also paid me a bit,' Lefine admitted.

'You didn't have to tell them all that you knew, traitor. That'll teach me to talk too much. And save that pathetic look for the grenadiers of the Royal Guard. The Italians love *commedia dell'arte*. I should have you transferred to the navy.'

Lefine went pale. The sea filled him with panic and fear, which he had always refused to explain as if he really believed in those writhing sea monsters that adorned the oceans on maps and on public fountains.

'Yes, I wouldn't put it past you,' he muttered.

'Just because you saved my life doesn't mean that you've got the right to sell it. Now repeat to me exactly what you said to this sergeant-major.'

'Well, more or less all I knew . . .'

Margont's anger subsided somewhat at the thought that such a reply was inevitable.

'He was stupid, that sergeant-major, Captain. The more I told him, the more he paid me. So of course I told him everything.'

'Of course.'

'And after I'd told him everything I knew, I went on, making things up. Well, my imagination's boundless. Not like the sergeant-major's purse, which ran out in the end. Two or three things I made up completely: you love horses, you dream of one day breeding your own; you're in love with the pretty daughter of a Montpellier notary who doesn't want you as his son-in-law until you're a colonel; you have a distant uncle who lives in Louisiana and you've toyed with the idea of starting a new life in the New World.'

Margont smiled to himself. The file put together by Triaire was so stuffed with nonsense that it should prove impossible to separate the wheat from the chaff. He felt less cheated.

'One thing intrigues me, Fernand. You said so much that you must have known that one day I would find you out, but that didn't bother you. Why not?'

Lefine had recovered his self-assurance.

'It's true that I had underestimated your anger a bit. But above all I know how to make myself indispensable. And when someone's indispensable, what can happen to them?'

The answer was as impudent as it was true. It brought Margont back to his investigation. What if the murderer were an indispensable officer? He had asked himself that question dozens of times. He put his arm on Lefine's shoulder.

'Since you sold my secrets, I'm going to give you a taste of your own medicine. And more than you bargained for. Prince Eugène has put me in a particularly difficult position. Well, I'm going to tell you the whole story, and then you'll help me with my investigation and I'll feel less lonely in hell.'

CHAPTER 5

Lefine guessed that any mention of this business would get him into terrible trouble so, having a talent for weighing up the pros and cons, and being blessed with a pragmatic disposition, his first words after Margont had explained were: 'So what do we do now?'

Margont selected a collection of poems and slipped it into one of his pockets.

'Don't worry, I'm not just helping myself to a book for some late-night reading. The man we're looking for managed to seduce this woman in just a day. However, we know that the victim was not the sort to fall for the first man to come her way, so what could he have said to charm her so much?'

Margont brandished a second collection, like an impassioned preacher holding up the Bible.

'Look how well thumbed these pages are. She read these works over and over again. She must have thought that he matched her ideal. The description of our murderer's personality is in here.'

Lefine was sceptical. 'For a respectable woman she was a bit quick to invite a stranger into her bedroom.'

'That's easy to explain. If the murderer really was an officer, he would only have had a few hours to spend in Tresno before starting out on a campaign that might last several months. Hundreds of soldiers had come here to enjoy themselves, so the only quiet place would have been her room. She was trusting; she didn't seem to think he would take advantage of the situation.'

'Or she wanted him to do so . . .'

'That makes no difference to the argument.'

Margont leaned out of the window. He was not afraid of heights. It looked easy to him to step over the frame and get on to the roof.

'Go down and tell the grenadiers and passers-by not to panic. Tell them I'm after a deserter and, as he used to be a chimney sweep, I suspect him of having hidden away somewhere up there. Then keep an eye on me from the street.'

'Do you really expect to find something worth risking your neck for?'

But Margont was already resting his weight on the tiles. A few moments later he was doing a balancing act along the roof, the villagers and soldiers watching from below, half worried and half amused. Lefine did not let his friend out of his sight, even if it meant constantly bumping into onlookers.

'Careful with the tile to your right. It's come loose,' he shouted.

'Thanks.'

'You know it's just as easy to see from down here.'

Margont was peering at every inch of roofing, hoping to spot something the murderer might have left behind. He found nothing and every leap from one roof to the next was greeted by applause from some idiot down below. He stopped at the top of the third inn and gazed down at the street. A sea of faces was staring up at him. The people were smaller than he would have thought. He looked away, afraid that he might lose his balance. He imagined the scene. It was night-time, it had been raining, making the tiles slippery, and people were shooting at the fugitive. The man was running. Running? The mere thought of moving quickly so high above the ground made Margont tense. He deduced from this that the murderer was in excellent physical shape. He continued his progress, wondering how the man had managed to descend from his acrobatic perch. He reached the final inn. This one was separated from the next house by a gap of nine feet. Not only that, but the dwelling, made of wood, had only a ground floor and he was two storeys higher up. He thought it impossible to continue, but he wanted a second opinion.

'I'm going to take a run and a jump,' he called out to Lefine.

The sergeant began to gesticulate frantically. 'You're mad, Captain! It's suicidal! You'll get squashed as flat as a pancake! The murd— the deserter must have got down before. We just need to ask the people living in that shack whether they heard anyone fall on to their roof that night. A racket like that would certainly have woken them.'

Margont retraced his steps.

An artillery corporal, disfigured by severe burns to his neck and the lower part of his face, leaned towards Lefine. 'Ain't he a bit soft in the head, that captain of yours?'

'When he's set on something, that's all he thinks about and he doesn't take account of the risks.'

'Carelessness can prove very expensive,' retorted the corporal, slowly running his forefinger along a cheek that was as crumpled as a wet sheet.

Margont went back and stood stock-still in front of an enormous oak with some of its branches broken. There were numerous footmarks around it. A few yards away was a rough impression made by a body and in the hollow was a mixture of mud and blood. A moment later the two men were examining the scene.

'This is his route: he jumps down from this roof, breaks his fall by grasping the branches that give way, lands in this puddle, walks towards the wood . . . But from here on it's impossible to work anything out because of all the other footprints left by the men in pursuit, those who took the sentry's body away, onlookers, people out walking . . .'

'These bloody idiots have trampled over our only clue, the footprints!'

Margont's face suddenly lit up. 'They haven't destroyed everything. The puddle! Nobody would deliberately paddle in it for the pleasure of ruining their shoes.' He stared at the pool of muddy water surrounding the trunk and the roots of the tree. 'Go and fetch the grenadiers to bale it out, but make sure they don't step in it!'

Lefine, who could not stand being looked down on – unless it was to his financial or other benefit – hated the soldiers of the Italian Guard and their haughty attitude. His face broke into a sadistic smile.

'As they don't speak a word of French, with a bit of luck they may think you're ordering them to lick it up.'

'If you play that sort of game, believe me, you'll be drinking it with them.'

'I'd almost be pleased to do so.'

'Find a cobbler and get him to make a sole and a cast of this footprint. And find out which regiment the sentry who was murdered belonged to. Meet me at six o'clock at the inn at the entrance to the village. We've moved forward,' Margont concluded, rubbing his hands.

'By one step,' added Lefine.

Margont questioned Maroveski's servant girls but Maria had not confided in them about her 'Prince Charming'. After queuing up outside an eating-house to buy a sausage and a piece of black bread that cost him a king's ransom, he left Tresno.

He rode through the countryside, travelling through woods of conifer trees and across plains. He passed an endless procession of carts and wagons carrying supplies, which had already fallen behind schedule even before hostilities had begun. After asking the way, he eventually reached a village with an unpronounceable name consisting of a handful of small wooden houses scattered on either side of an almost dried-up river. There was not a single Pole to be seen in the fields or orchards. Here, too, a crowd of soldiers and locals were doing deals in the streets. Margont stopped a *voltigeur*, one of those skilful marksmen who go ahead of the troops and delight in picking off enemy officers at long range. The man was carrying two cages so full of chickens that their heads, wings and feet were poking through the bars on all sides. The poor creatures were clucking in distress but only attracted hungry looks from the passers-by.

'Do you know where Medical Officer Brémond is?'

'Building that hospital, that big shack over there, Captain.'

Margont noticed scores of soldiers busy fitting out a barn.

'It's kind of 'em to do that for us but if we shoot it out with the Russians we'll all end up inside there and more cooped up than my chickens.'

Margont entrusted his horse to some bare-chested soldiers who were chopping down trees, and approached the building. The ground and first floors had been covered with straw. It would serve as mattresses for the wounded and soak up the blood. Hammering and sawing of wood could be heard all around. Margont had the feeling that they were preparing the set for some horrible drama portraying the struggle between Life and Death. The performances would last for months and would play to a full house every day.

The humanist ideas of the Revolution, plus the experience of countless battles fought by France during the Revolution and then the Empire, had led to greatly improved medical services in the army. Credit was also due to the genius of a number of men, including Larrey with his 'flying ambulances', well-equipped vehicles specially designed to reduce the impact of travelling over rough roads; Parmentier, whose research had shown that the right diet could prevent many illnesses; and Desgenette and Percy, who had combated infections and epidemics by improving hygiene. Lastly, surgical techniques had been developed, the better to carry out emergency operations without proper equipment in the wake of the army, if not on the battlefield itself. The quality of care had therefore improved considerably, despite administrative delays and the stupid decisions sometimes taken by the imperial government. For example, in 1810, in the belief that peace had been achieved, the authorities had laid off a considerable number of medical officers, to make savings. This mistake had not been properly rectified because scant regard was paid to the quality of the training of new medical officers. As a result, some individuals were now acting as assistant surgeons after studying medicine for only a few months. Percy nicknamed them 'bogus surgeons'.

Margont was fascinated by medicine. He never tired of questioning all the physicians he came across. One day Brémond had explained to him the different types of hospital needed by an army in wartime. Next to the battlefield were mobile hospitals, which often consisted of requisitioned buildings with makeshift facilities where the most seriously wounded were given emergency treatment. The less badly wounded, who could often wait for several hours without their condition deteriorating, were transported to temporary hospitals. Mobile hospitals had several ambulances, which either collected the wounded from the battlefield or took them from the mobile hospital to a temporary hospital. The temporary hospitals were situated in the second line. They were therefore beyond the reach of cannon fire and less at risk of being encircled by the enemy in the event of a setback. Then there were the hospitals in the rear, which took in those recovering from their wounds and needing medical attention. These were usually proper hospitals situated in the nearest towns.

Margont finally caught sight of Brémond speaking to a small gathering of assistant surgeons. The medical officer had light auburn, almost ginger, hair, and whiskers that went down to his chin. His eyebrows, which were long, delicate and well arched, gave his blue eyes an even more piercing gaze. He made a point of always being impeccably dressed and had often criticised Margont for having unpolished shoes or a badly done-up collar. In fact, the medical officer's jacket did not fully meet the regulations but only a very observant person would have noticed that the last button in the bottom row was different from the other two. It had been in general use only from 1796 to 1798 and bore the inscription 'Military Hospitals' as well as a Phrygian bonnet above the word 'Humanity'.

Margont joined the gathering without being noticed by Brémond, who was engrossed in what he was saying.

'In hospitals, remember that the wound is more important than the rank. We do not treat in descending order of rank – that philosophy does not apply here – but in descending order of the seriousness of the injury. I must now speak to you about that most difficult and painful of subjects, the art of triage. Let's imagine that three wounded soldiers are brought in at the same time. The first has had his leg almost blown off by round shot. The second has been riddled with grapeshot and has suffered a dozen or so multiple fractures. The third has received a bullet in the thigh – the bone and the femoral artery have not been hit – and is screaming out for immediate treatment. If I operate straight away on the third patient I will save him. But by the time I've finished, the others will be dead. If I start by seeing to the second one he will die anyway because he is too badly wounded. By the time I've finished, the first one is dead and the third still waiting for help. If I begin with the first I will save him. Then I will treat the third one and save him too. Only the second one will die. The conclusion is that according to the order in which I treat my three patients, either I will save only one or I will save two. My purpose, then, is to teach you to sort the wounded, not to rush to treat the most spectacular-looking injury – the one riddled with grapeshot for whom unfortunately nothing can be done – and not to allow yourselves to be bullied by the one who is not seriously injured and who still has the strength to call you all the names under the sun. Of course, triage does not do away with the obligation to give emergency treatment to everyone. In the case I have just mentioned, while I began to operate on the first patient, you would have bandaged the wounds of the other two in order to reduce the bleeding. You would also have lessened their suffering with words of comfort – but not lies of the "we are going to save you and you'll suffer no aftereffects" sort – painkillers, if you are lucky enough to have any left, and hefty doses of spirits because there's nothing like it to dull the senses. Any questions before I begin my class?'

A hesitant voice was heard. 'Sir, may we go and eat first?'

'What nonsense is this? It's not eleven o'clock yet . . .' said Brémond in surprise.

But his watch showed him it was already past two o'clock. With a startled look he put it to his ear before disdainfully letting it fall back into his pocket.

'Well, it's pointless me wasting my breath if all you're listening to is the rumbling of your stomachs.'

The gathering broke up, to reveal a smiling Margont.

'Quentin!' exclaimed Brémond, putting his hands on his shoulders.

The two men had known each other since childhood and had frequently had occasion to see each other on the battlefield.

'What regiment are you serving in?'

'The 84th, with Lefine, Saber and Piquebois.'

'So you're in good company. I bet you're bored and are dreaming of a tutorial on how to fit out a hospital.'

'You've lost your bet, I'm afraid, Jean-Quenin. I've a big favour to ask you.'

'Granted. I'm listening.'

'I'm investigating a murder but it must be hushed up at all costs. I would like you to examine the victim.'

CHAPTER 6

A n hour later, after arriving back in Tresno, Margont was in a requisitioned house, shouting at a lethargic captain.

'With your grindingly slow bureaucracy I'll have to wait ten months for the authorisation to dig up the body. I might as well just pick up a handful of dust!'

'I'm very sorry. I don't have the slightest idea of how to process such a request. So I'll need to inform my superiors. Because as you will understand—'

'That's precisely it. I do not understand, Captain Ladoyère.'

'If the correct procedure is not followed, I'll be the one who gets the blame.'

'But I have an order from—'

'General Triaire, yes, I know,' mumbled the captain, looking puzzled and reading the document once more.

'So I command you to authorise me to dig up this body.'

'But is General Triaire entitled to have the body of a civilian dug up? Because I, you understand, am the person responsible for law and order in Tresno. It's my job to sort out deserters and troublemakers.'

Margont couldn't bear to look any longer at the ugly face with its flabby jowls reminiscent of a dozy bulldog. Brémond, for his part, seemed engrossed in gazing out of the window at the Polish countryside.

'Stick to the point!' exclaimed Margont.

The captain spread his arms in a gesture of helplessness. 'I've told you already. I'm responsible for law and order in Tresno. Digging up the body of a local inhabitant could arouse the hostility of the population, leading to unrest, rioting and the use of military force.'

'So what do you suggest?'

'I suggest going through the official channels. Your request will be passed on today to the appropriate person, that is to say the person above me who . . .'

'. . . will pass it on to someone else and so on and so forth. I'm going to hold you to account to General Triaire.'

'Oh, I'm not the one to be held to account. It will be the person above me because I will have submitted your request to him.' The officer was pleased to have resolved this problem and concluded: 'So we shall both have the satisfaction of having followed the proper procedure.'

Brémond turned round and, with his hands behind his back, declared quite out of the blue: 'Very well, gentlemen, we understand your position. You have your procedures and we have ours. Captain Ladoyère, I am having you and your men put into quarantine immediately.'

Ladoyère's jowls drooped a little more. At the same time the lieutenant, who was his right-hand man, and the two other soldiers present in the room turned as pale as sheets.

'I beg your pardon, sir?'

'It is possible that this woman was suffering from typhus.'

Typhus! Fourteen thousand deaths in 1796 in the hospitals of Nice alone. And even more during the military campaigns, but that was a taboo subject. Ladoyère remained petrified.

'As I am unable to examine her to prove or to disprove this diagnosis,' Brémond continued, 'I have no choice other than to assume the worst and to impose the strictest possible measures. I shall therefore have you all placed in a hospital reserved for people suspected of being infected.'

Ladoyère fidgeted on his chair. 'But if this woman had not contracted typhus, I'm at risk of infection from being in your hospital when I have no reason to be there.'

Margont nodded. 'That is correct. But we shall both have the satisfaction of having followed the proper procedure.'

Ladoyère's face dropped as if he was already contemplating the inevitability of death.

'Surely she didn't have typhus . . . it's just not possible.'

But Brémond had adopted his absent-minded look again. To the captain's dismay, he moved calmly towards the door. Ladoyère got up and walked around his desk, ready to run after the doctor if necessary.

'All right, all right. Exhume the body. I'm only a lowly captain. I obey orders from General Triaire and from the army medical service. If you'd be so kind as to put in writing all that you have just said . . .'

Brémond and Margont signed their lie and went off to the graveyard, requisitioning on their way three soldiers and some spades.

Tresno's graveyard was on top of a hill at the edge of the village. A spinney concealed its gloomy presence from the villagers. The tombs were well kept and decked with flowers.

'I don't much like disturbing the peace of the dead,' murmured Brémond.

'Neither do I, but we have to exhume this body if we want to lay this business to rest.'

One of the soldiers requisitioned in the street was Polish. He threw aside his spade the moment he realised what was expected of him. Margont didn't make an issue of it but ordered the man to stay. While the Frenchmen were throwing large spadefuls of earth over their shoulders, a woodcutter with a bushy beard, accompanied by two adolescents, suddenly emerged from the spinney. The three of them had axes in their hands. Instinctively, the Polish soldier pulled his musket, which was lying on the ground, nearer to him with his foot. The intruder began to speak. His aggressive tone made his sons blink.

'What does he have to say for himself?' asked Margont.

By now the infantryman had grabbed his musket. 'He's saying that the French are pagans who have killed their priests, that the Revolution has destroyed the churches, that Napoleon is the Antichrist and that each of his armies is one of the heads of the dragon of the Apocalypse.'

'What else does he have to say?'

'Begging your pardon, Captain, he thinks that you're digging up this poor woman to have your way with her.'

'Charming.'

Eventually, the cutting edge of the spades struck the lid of the coffin. Margont wiped the sweat off his face and nodded towards a nearby building.

'We're going to transport the coffin over to that barn. Only the medical officer and I will examine the body. You will wait for us close by. And keep that lunatic away. I don't want him trying to find out whether a Frenchman is as hard to split in two as the trunk of a fir tree.'

The place was empty. Margont was glad of the smell of straw, not for any nostalgic reason but because it would partially cover up the odours emanating from the body.

Brémond seemed equally hesitant but declared: 'Better to get on with it straight away. The waiting is sometimes worse than the deed itself.'

The boards of the coffin, made of pine, had been carefully fitted together, and for some strange reason the lid had been sealed by knocking in a large number of nails.

'Were they afraid she might get out or something?' said Brémond in surprise.

'It's the lips of the villagers that they most wanted to seal.'

Using the point of his sword as a lever, Margont prised open the lid. The two men immediately looked away. Prince Eugène had been in such a hurry to have the victim buried that she had not even been washed. She was still wearing the dress she'd had on at the time of the murder. The garment was torn and spattered with congealed bloodstains. Brémond pulled himself together by concentrating on the scientific aspects of his task.

'The body has bled heavily, so a number of the wounds were inflicted before death . . .'

Margont was staring straight at his friend and looking down as little as possible.

'What? She was mutilated while still alive?'

'A wound inflicted post mortem produces little loss of blood because the heart is no longer beating.'

'But people would have heard her screaming. The inn was heaving with customers that particular evening.'

Brémond bent forward until his face lightly touched the victim's. It was like a lover's final kiss to his beloved. Margont was sweating; he could see spots in front of his eyes and, fighting for breath, he felt as if he would choke.

'A disorder of the nervous system . . .' mumbled Brémond.

'What do you mean?'

'Not her, you. You're as white as a sheet. Sit down on the ground or you'll collapse.'

Margont obeyed meekly.

'And yet I've seen plenty of mangled bodies . . .'

'Yes, but in wartime. Here we are on the threshold of another realm: madness. War is also a form of madness but we understand its objectives and its mechanics.'

Brémond rummaged in one of his pockets, took out some tweezers and thrust them into the corpse's mouth. He immediately showed his findings to Margont.

'Feathers and a tiny piece of material. The murderer pressed a pillow against her face to smother the screams.'

'There was no pillow in the bedroom.'

'It's in the coffin. Under her head.'

Margont had collected himself. He rose to his feet but held on to the edge of the coffin for support.

'I'm not the right person for this investigation. I can't even bear the sight of the victim, so how could I face the person who committed this abominable crime?'

'I'm going to let you into a secret. When I'm confronted with a wounded soldier, I feel incompetent. I say to myself there are too many things I don't know and that medicine doesn't know very much either. I feel as if I have only the smatterings of a science that is itself incomplete. However that may be, remember that if this woman had been my wife, you are the one I would have asked to find her killer.'

Margont forced himself to look at Maria Dorlovna. The thorax, abdomen, arms and legs were covered in bruises. Brémond pointed to the forearms.

'The wounds are especially numerous in this area. She was trying to protect herself by putting her arms in front of her.'

The doctor took the victim's hands and carefully examined each fingernail.

'While defending herself she must have scratched her attacker. Sadly, she kept her fingernails very short. If they had been longer we might have found beneath them some of the murderer's hair or a piece of skin, evidence that he had suffered a gash to his face, torso or arms. I've examined very many wounded bodies in the course of my career but I have to admit that this is the first time I've seen such an atrocity. I've counted more than thirty wounds but none was immediately fatal. The murderer avoided the heart, the carotid arteries and the larynx. He left the vital organs intact in order to keep his victim alive as long as possible while he was cutting her up. She died in fact from loss of blood after several minutes of agony. He did not wish merely to kill her; he also wanted to torture her.'

'From what you've said, it may well be that the culprit had medical knowledge.'

'Yes, but he may not have been a doctor. Any butcher or farmer knows how to kill an animal swiftly, and without causing unnecessary suffering, by severing its carotid artery. Besides, plenty of soldiers have experience of hand-to-hand combat and know where some of the vital organs are. An average French hussar knows as much about this as many physicians. Our friend Piquebois will confirm that for you, believe me.'

'What weapon was used?'

'A knife fitted with a blade of approximately . . .' Brémond thrust his tweezers into several of the wounds '. . . four and a half inches. Considering the violence of the attack and this bruising around the points of impact I think he plunged the blade in up to the hilt. So it was a small knife with a straight blade. The murderer is right-handed. Have you seen her face?'

Margont took a close look at the Polish woman's features and had to prevent himself from retching. The eyebrows had been scorched or perhaps cut off. Maria Dorlovna seemed to be staring up at him, wide-eyed. The eye sockets had been damaged by the flame from a candle, and her unseeing eyes, streaked with black stains, seemed to be crying tears of wax. Her mouth was twisted with pain. Margont was mesmerised as Brémond methodically continued his analysis, examining the limbs, touching them, feeling their weight, measuring the size of the injuries. However, at times the medical officer's hands trembled slightly, affecting the accuracy of his actions.

'The burns as well as several other wounds were inflicted after death. He used a candle to singe the eyes, the breasts and the skin in some areas. I think he was significantly calmer at that point compared to when he struck the first blows because the damage is more deliberate: the marks are symmetrical, inflicted with less violence . . .'

'And yet he must have realised that she was dead!'

'Certainly, but that didn't stop him. So, in addition to making his victim suffer, he also took pleasure in mutilating her.'

'Perhaps he was also thinking about the shock the person discovering the body in such a state would feel. If that was the case, he certainly achieved his goal with me.'

'Don't do yourself down, Quentin. I know you well. "The reed bends but does not break." '

Finally, the medical officer examined the crotch.

'Sexual intercourse did not take place. That's all I can tell you. We could carry out an autopsy but I'm not sure it would tell us any more. In any case, I don't have time to do it. As you know, I have my work cut out improving our temporary hospitals, training assistants on the job . . .'

'Of course.'

'There's just one aspect that intrigues me.' The doctor took the right hand. The tips of the middle finger, thumb and index finger were spattered with black marks. 'It's ink.'

'She must have written a letter recently,' Margont suggested. He changed his mind at once. 'Not one letter in isolation but a whole series. And yet she had no family.'

'She was working at an inn, you told me. Perhaps she kept an account book . . .'

'The person who employed her told me she helped out with the serving and did the housework. There was no mention of account books.'

The two men replaced the lid of the coffin.

'Good luck, Quentin. Don't take unnecessary risks.'

Margont nodded assent. It was Jean-Quenin's stock remark, the advice he gave to his friends before every campaign. And in peacetime it was, 'Eat less, and less quickly', 'Take more exercise' and 'Don't read at night in poor candlelight.'

'The same to you, Jean-Quenin, and thanks once again.'

Margont helped to reinter the coffin, then walked down the hill from the graveyard on his own, trying to think of other things. But every time he set foot on a bump or bulge in the ground he thought he was treading on and desecrating a tomb.

CHAPTER 7

DURING the return journey Margont thought back over his life. He often did so at the start of a campaign. His past reminded him of a baker's dough that had been kneaded by too many hands, each with their own idea of what shape to give the future loaf. Eventually, he had been brave enough to choose his own way, despite the opposition of those around him. Arrogance had saved him from doing what others wanted.

He was born in Nîmes in 1780 into a family of winegrowers and his father, Georges Margont, had died of a fit of apoplexy in 1786. As his mother could not provide for her son and two daughters, she decided to move to Montpellier to live with her brother, Ferdinand Lassère, a hardened and religiously inclined bachelor whose ambition was to turn the young boy into a priest or a monk. 'What an absurd idea!' Margont frequently exclaimed, remembering the time when he was forced to read the Bible and to pray every day.

His uncle sent him to study at the Benedictine abbey of Saint-Guilhem-le-Désert. This monastery, founded more than a thousand years earlier and situated in the gorge of the River Verdus, was a resting place on the pilgrimage route to Santiago de Compostela. Its architecture was a mixture of Romanesque and Southern French styles. Built on to the magnificent, astonishingly high nave were a cloister and a few buildings that marked the boundaries of a verdant quadrangle. For four years this place had been Margont's whole world. He had practically never been allowed to leave it. When he had complained about the lack of freedom, the monks had tirelessly repeated to him that solitude would open up his mind to God.

At that time the community of Saint-Guilhem-le-Désert was a far cry from what it had been in centuries past. Although only six monks remained, life inside those walls still continued in the time-honoured tradition: long hours of prayer, meditation, contemplation and services. Fortunately for Margont, study also played an important part in the activities of the monastery. He was taught reading, writing, Latin, Greek, mathematics, history, geography and theology. His marks were good or outstanding except in theology, where his results were nonexistent because the simplest of questions ('Who died for us on the Cross, Quentin?') elicited a deliberately wrong answer ('Joan of Arc, Brother').

In a monastery almost everything is forbidden, particularly anything you might want to do. So Margont spent hours reading in the cloister garden. This space represented the last bastion of freedom, even if it was surrounded by monks and walls. Words gave him access to other horizons, other thoughts and other lives. No one around him seemed to understand that without books he would have ended up not a monk but insane. Nobody, that is, except Brother Medrelli, a well-respected monk who taught history and mathematics. It was he who took this rebellious pupil under his wing. He became his mentor and gave him private lessons, in addition to the already extensive regular curriculum. He hoped to see him become a cardinal. According to the monk, when this young 'believer' claimed he was without faith, he was being insincere. Brother Medrelli was open-minded, understanding, tolerant and warm-hearted. He provided Margont with a constant supply of books and allowed the boy to accompany him on the rare occasions when he went for a walk (even if it meant running to catch up with him at the Devil's Bridge, as happened on one famous occasion when he attempted to escape). Margont gave him the affectionate nickname 'my friend the citizen-monk'. Even today the two men still often wrote to each other.

In 1790 the Republic, as represented by the National Assembly, abolished all religious communities. Margont cried as he emerged from the main door of the abbey. He was free.

He returned to his uncle's in Montpellier. Lassère still wanted to make a priest of him. Father Medrelli, knowing him better, wrote suggesting he should take up medicine. His mother, for her part, wanted him to buy back the family vineyards in order to follow in his father's footsteps.

'To satisfy you and to please my uncle as well, perhaps I could make communion wine,' her son would sometimes say bitterly. It was no longer the walls of Saint-Guilhem-le-Désert that closed in around him but everyone else's wishes.

Thankfully, at Brother Medrelli's insistence, Margont continued to study. He still read voraciously and loved to go for long walks through the streets of Montpellier. During his adolescence he became an ardent supporter of the republican cause and decided to get involved in politics. The world was changing and he wanted a hand in making it change even more and faster. His plan met with a frosty reception as at the time a number of politicians had lost their heads in more ways than one.

In 1798 he enlisted in the army and followed Bonaparte on his Egyptian expedition. On his return he had time to indulge his love of haphazard study. But from 1805 onwards there was one war after another. He had taken part in numerous battles, including Austerlitz, Auerstädt, Eylau and Wagram, and had had the opportunity to live in Berlin, Vienna, Madrid and many other places, making up for the time wasted within the four square walls of Saint-Guilhem-le-Désert.

Since then, like many others, he had been waiting for peace. A genuine peace, not a new peace *para bellum*, like that of Amiens in 1802 or Tilsit in 1807, during which all the countries concerned were actually levying troops and putting the finishing touches to their future battle plans. He wanted this forthcoming peace to be based on republican and humanistic ideals and for that he was prepared to fight, for the rest of his life if necessary.

Margont met up with Lefine as arranged. The inn had a low ceiling and was poorly lit by tallow candles that emitted foul-smelling smoke. There were tables of all shapes and sizes: round tables, workbenches, chests, casks. Business was business. For the owner of the place a military invasion meant first and fore-most an invasion of customers. Despite the sticks of furniture, many soldiers were forced to remain standing, drinking beer straight from jugs or gnawing on chicken bones. Margont had to push his way through to Lefine, who was sitting at a barrel, dunking pieces of bread in a bowl of lentils.

'Let's go outside,' shouted Margont, struggling to make himself heard above the din.

Lefine wiped his plate clean and followed Margont, his mouth full and a satisfied look on his face. In the streets the commotion was still at its height. French soldiers were jostling one another to get into a packed tavern. Italian dragoons from the Regina Regiment were roaring with laughter at the sight of one of their number, dead drunk, trying his best to climb on to a horse. His green coat was covered with mud and he'd lost his helmet. When he finally scrambled up on to his mount he was warmly applauded. He raised his hand in triumph, slid to one side and, feeling himself gathering momentum but unable to rescue the situation, crashed to the ground again. This was greeted with even more cheering. Margont turned a blind eye towards this sort of disorderly behaviour so long as it did not degenerate into looting and fighting. Knowing that thousands of people were going to die, it was natural to want to live every minute to the full rather than obeying orders and doing nothing for hours, just waiting for the signal to be given to move on.

'So, what have you found out?' asked Margont.

'Not much. The murdered sentry belonged to the 2nd Battalion of the 18th Light Infantry. There's no way of knowing where he was buried.'

'What do you mean, no way of knowing?'

Lefine was furious at not being congratulated for the quality of his work.

'Have you seen the crowd milling about here, Captain? It took me more than an hour to find someone who knew him. I went to find the battalion: nobody knows where Sergeant Biandot was buried. His friends believe he was assassinated by a Russian partisan. I did the rounds of the local graveyards. No grave has been dug recently except for the Polish woman's. I came back here and questioned the grenadiers of the Royal Guard as best I could, but they weren't in the know.'

'What about the footprint?'

Lefine took a wooden sole out of his pocket.

'The cast didn't prove anything. It belonged to an ordinary, large-sized shoe. But here's what the cobbler I found managed to make.'

Margont examined the object. He lifted up his foot and held the sole firmly against his own. It was about an inch longer than his.

'It's not you,' concluded Lefine.

'So, to sum up, our fellow belongs to IV Army Corps – since the other corps are too far away from Tresno – he's athletic and has experience of hand-to-hand combat. He's an officer, between five foot six and six foot tall and we know his shoe size. He's right-handed. Finally, he's a "Prince Charming". How many suspects are we left with?'

Lefine looked up. 'Let's say . . . four hundred?'

'There's no way of discreetly enquiring about the movements of four hundred people on the night of the murder, especially when these four hundred blend in with forty thousand others.' Margont stared at the wooden sole. 'This is the only clue the "Prince Charming" has left us, like a Cinderella of crime. But I doubt whether it's enough to find him.'

The sun had almost disappeared below the horizon and shadows were spreading over the plains and forests. The areas still bathed in sunlight were shifting and shrinking inexorably. The man was gazing in fascination at the sight. Recently he had felt that his mind was affected by similar phenomena. Dark thoughts were slowly clouding his certainties and his plans for the future.

The people he had killed – whether enemies in combat or others, such as the Polish woman or the sentry who had almost trapped him – had revealed something to him. Or, rather, someone: himself.

The whole of that day he had relived the evening he had spent with Maria, tirelessly adding an excess of detail to his memory of the scene: the words they exchanged, the decoration of the room, the dancing shadows cast by the guttering flames of the candles, the joyful expression on Maria's face as they clinked glasses. One detail in particular had amused him: each time Maria blushed, she immediately rearranged her hair with the palm of her hand. He had liked that particular gesture because he had interpreted it as fake shyness. When she had invited him into her bedroom, he was convinced that she was going to give herself to him. But all Maria wanted was to hear him declare his love for her once more. She had refused to give in to him and suddenly he had wanted to make her suffer. That had given him more pleasure than words could express.

And today, as he looked at his soldiers – ranks he was once so proud of, the tightly packed bodies whose impact was irresistible, the dense mass, dark and bristling with muskets – all he could think of was the blood running through their veins. In his imagination he had stripped them of their bones and their flesh, reducing them to nothing more than an intricate network of blood vessels branching out in all directions. As if all that mattered to him from now on was blood. Had he become a monster? The question haunted him. There must be others like him. How many of them had enlisted in this army for the sole pleasure of seeing blood flow? If he happened to meet up with one of these predators, would he recognise him? And would such a being unmask him?

He looked down at his horse pistols with their ornate butts. One pull of the trigger and his life would end here and now.

He felt like a drifting skiff. Gradually, land was coming into sight. But where exactly would he come ashore?

CHAPTER 8

LEFINE was fast asleep when suddenly he felt himself being tossed about. A light dazzled him. It was the flame from a candle. Someone was shaking him. He opened his eyes and recognised Margont's face.

'Wake up, Fernand. I've had an idea.'

Margont was speaking in a muffled voice, scarcely able to contain his impatience. Several noncommissioned officers were stretched out on the floor of the tent. A shape lying rolled up in a blanket switched from its right side to its left, grunting as it did so.

'All right? Are you awake? Get dressed. I'll wait for you outside.'

Lefine pulled on his trousers, gritting his teeth. Captain or not, he was going to hit this unwanted visitor with the butt of his musket and then go back to bed. Bedraggled and furious, he joined Margont. The captain was already on horseback, holding a second mount by the bridle.

'Everyone's asleep!' Lefine protested in a low voice, pointing towards the field with a sweep of his arm.

The area was covered with tents and bodies resting out in the open. Margont did not even hear him. He was engrossed in his thoughts.

'Do you remember the ink marks on the victim's fingers? Of course you do, I told you about them.'

'Yes, so what?'

'A private diary! I'm sure she was keeping a private diary. Everything makes sense. She enjoyed collections of romantic poetry, she called the man she had feelings for a "Prince Charming": just the sort of person who—'

He suddenly broke off. He had just remembered the trace of blood that had not been properly wiped off the bolt of the trunk. Perhaps Maria had mentioned the diary to her killer. Once his murderous rage had passed, he had become worried about it. His victim might have written down his name, his rank, his regiment . . . So he had searched the room thoroughly. There was no mark on the clothes. He must have unbolted the trunk and then, realising that he was going to leave fingermarks, had gone to wash his hands so that no one would know he was looking for something. Then he had continued his search. But if these assumptions were correct, despite his crime, the man had remained cool-headed enough to unfold and refold every item of clothing. Such self-control seemed unbelievable to Margont. Or rather, he did not want to believe it.

'The question is: did he find this diary?' he murmured to himself.

Lefine was combing his hair with his fingers.

'So you want us to go and look for this notebook, do you? It'll still be where it is now tomorrow morning,' he grumbled.

'Get into the saddle! Don't call me ungrateful: I'm giving you this horse to thank you for your help. A Pole sold it to me for a fortune.'

Lefine stroked the animal's neck and lifted one of its legs to examine its shoe.

'Into the saddle, Fernand. Do you know the proverb "Never look a gift horse in the mouth"?'

Lefine obeyed, waiting until later to assess the value of his new acquisition.

'If this diary did exist, you or the murderer would have found it. Why would this Polish woman have hidden it when no one came to see her?'

'That was part of the game. If you are going to write a private diary, you don't leave it lying around on a table; you hide it carefully. It's obvious you don't know much about women.'

'The women I associate with have nothing private, neither diaries nor . . . well, that's how it is.'

Margont woke the grenadiers of the Royal Guard by clapping his hands and talking fast and furiously. The Italians looked at him with a mixture of fear and anger. For them there was no doubt that this hothead who had turned up in the middle of the night was raving mad. The two Frenchmen went up to the attic room on their own. Margont started with the bed, lifting up the mattress. Lefine unsheathed his knife and ran the blade between the joins in the floorboards.

'You never know, we may come across a hoard of gold . . .' he mumbled between yawns.

After an hour they had discovered nothing.

Lefine leant against the wall. 'You have to know how to be a good loser. Can we go back to bed now?'

'You'll have all the time in the world to sleep when you're dead. I would have thought that someone with such a well-developed practical sense as you would have guessed where the best hiding-places were.'

'No idea,' sighed Lefine.

'Use your imagination. Ask the advice of my uncle in Louisiana.'

'Yes, that was a good one! You should have seen that sergeant-major scribbling away furiously. His quill was scratching the paper joyfully and the idiot, so happy to please his master, was smiling like a dog wagging its tail.'

Margont folded his arms. 'If this were your bedroom, where would you hide your private diary, the one in which you noted down the sums received for selling the secrets I confided in you as a friend?'

'Where no one would think of looking for them. So, outside the room.'

Margont shot out of the room. At the end of the corridor was a locked door.

'That must be a loft used as a storeroom or larder.'

'Too risky, the innkeeper and his employees must go there regularly,' Lefine remarked. 'But up there . . .'

Margont looked up. Enormous beams were holding up the roof.

'She could reach up there by standing on a chair . . .'

Lefine went back into the bedroom to get one but Margont jumped up and grabbed a piece of timber supporting several beams, hauled himself up and sat astride it. Nothing. He dropped back down to the floor with a loud thud.

'I was wrong.'

'At last he admits it!'

'Or else . . . I've had another idea. I'm leaving. Stay here and keep looking! Try to get the Italians to help you. I'll be back in less than an hour.'

Lefine was ready to fall asleep on his feet. 'Well, go wherever you want! And when you come back empty-handed we'll each get a spade and go digging all around the inn just in case Maria buried it! Then we'll dismantle Tresno, a plank at a time!'

Margont went to see Maroveski again. The innkeeper was not asleep. He was pacing around the cellar. He didn't say a word when he saw Margont enter, escorted by three of his gaolers. He'd given up expecting anything of them. The rings around his eyes had become puffy and were darker. Margont glared at him.

'I believe you took a document from Maria's bedroom just after she died, a notebook or something similar.'

'I haven't stolen anything. I don't even know whether Maria had—'

Margont interrupted him curtly. 'You must have heard of this diary from one of your servant girls or from Maria herself. And you took it away because you thought you'd find a clue in it leading you to the murderer. You wanted to settle the score with him personally, didn't you?'

'I can't read.'

'Either you can read or you'll get someone to read it to you. If you wanted to make out you were a half-wit, you should have done so from our first meeting. Now it's too late for that. I'm going to have your cell searched from top to bottom. But I warn you that in any case you will not be released until the end of this campaign or until the culprit has been arrested. So you're going to remain a prisoner for some time. If you hide any evidence from me, we'll both be losers. The only winner is the murderer.'

Margont turned towards the Italians. But he said to himself that if Maroveski didn't speak up now, they would find nothing because the diary would be only a figment of his imagination.

'Wait,' interrupted Maroveski in a resigned tone of voice.

He scratched at the ground in a corner of the room and unearthed something. It was a notebook with a bunch of roses painted on its cover. Margont wanted to take it but Maroveski held on to it for a moment.

'Swear to me you will burn it when all this is over. I don't want soldiers reading it for entertainment or for it to lie around for years with loads of other papers.'

'I swear.'

Margont briefly flicked through the pages of delicate handwriting. He then went to look for Lefine, whom he found arguing with the grenadiers of the Royal Guard, which was predictable.

He flourished his find in front of his flabbergasted friend and exclaimed: 'We need an interpreter, straight away!'

The two men spoke to every civilian they came across in the street. And when they did eventually find someone who knew both French and Polish, they had a devil of a job persuading him to translate their document. The old man was holding by the bridle three scrawny mules that must have been around when his grandparents were born. So they wanted him to do them a favour, did they? Very well, with pleasure. But in exchange, they had to buy his mules.

'For that price, can they translate Polish too?' enquired Margont.

He threatened to call in the imperial police until the Pole agreed to sell him only two of the mules but for three-quarters of the price of the three because there was, of course, a discount for buying the three, which you lost if you only took two. In the end Margont handed him a few coins and managed to convince him that if he refused he would have these wretched beasts hanged just to put an end to the discussion. Both arguments were effective, especially the first, and the three men moved away from the crowd.

'Begin at the end.'

Gnarled fingers turned the pages over.

'It's a woman recounting her day.'

The Pole spoke in a quavering voice. Margont nodded several times to encourage him to speed up.

'June 27. An incredible, wonderful thing has happened to me. I was going to the market and I still had a few things left to buy. There were a lot of soldiers in the streets. It was unpleasant to feel all those men staring at me and to hear them laughing. I didn't understand their jokes but it was easy to guess. Almost everything I wanted to buy had been sold and what was left cost four times more than usual. A tall soldier—'

The old man broke off. 'I don't know the French word for this. It's the colour of hair that's like red.'

' "Ginger", yes, "ginger". Carry on.'

'A tall, ginger-haired soldier appeared. He'd been drinking and was talking very loudly. He grabbed my dress and said something before bursting out laughing. I think he was saying he wanted to buy it. He began to lift it up. You could see my calves. I was very frightened; I screamed. I think some soldiers were telling him to stop but they were afraid of him. I started to cry and to . . .

'What do you say when you move your body about?' asked the Pole, shaking his fists.

' "Struggle" or "defend yourself". Don't stop at every word you have difficulty with: carry on reading.'

'Then a man arrived. He said something and the soldier let me go. The one who'd attacked me was shouting but my saviour remained calm. He was tall and well dressed. The soldier wanted to punch him but my saviour hit him with his cane and the other man fell over. Then he gave me his arm to accompany me back home. He did not speak Polish but knew a little German and we were able to talk. He is called Pierre Acosavan. He's kind, polite and told jokes that made me laugh. He also loves poetry. He seemed to like me. He told me that he had to follow the army but promised that after the campaign he would come back to Tresno to see me. I don't know who came up with the idea first, but we've arranged to meet again at my place tomorrow evening. I still blush at having agreed. But there's nowhere else to go: everywhere there are soldiers who've had too much to drink. I made it clear to him that it was just to talk. My God, how could I have invited a stranger back to my room? There'll be lots of people at the inn. If he behaves badly, all I have to do is scream. But I always worry about everything and I'm sure all will be well. On the way home, something incredible happened. A trooper came trotting up. He looked all around him. Suddenly he rushed up to Monsieur Acosavan, saluted him and called him "colonel". I couldn't make out the rest but I'm sure I heard "colonel". Monsieur Acosavan interrupted him, smiled, said goodbye to me, promising to come back the following day, and went off with the trooper. My saviour's a colonel! I can hardly believe it. I hope he'll come back tomorrow.'

The Pole looked up and smiled, pleased with himself.

'Is that all?' Margont asked him.

'Yes. There's no continuation.'

Margont thanked him and left, accompanied by Lefine.

'To the best of my knowledge there's no Colonel Acosavan in IV Corps. It's definitely a false name but I want you to check it out all the same.'

Lefine had turned pale.

'We're looking for a colonel, are we? You must tell Prince Eugène that he needs to replace you.'

Margont spun round to face his friend. 'Certainly not. The prince would have had a captain arrested for such a crime, but a colonel . . .'

'It could be a colonel without much of a reputation so he'll go to prison. In fact, he'll be advised to commit suicide before the trial to avoid a scandal that would damage the army. Or it could be a famous and respected colonel and . . . he'll get a rap on the knuckles and be let off.'

'I sincerely hope you're mistaken. Perhaps someone very important may be asked to sort out the problem he presents. But I have my doubts and I don't want to take risks. So we won't inform the prince; we'll just carry on.'

Lefine had by no means reached the same conclusion.

'It's a colonel! A colonel! Rabbits never attack bulls.'

Margont walked away without answering him.

CHAPTER 9

MARCHING on and on – there was no end to the marching. For days the Russians had been falling back, abandoning large tracts of territory. A stray *voltigeur*, his musket slung over his shoulder and munching an apple, could inadvertently capture a whole village, or rather what was left of it, because the enemy was employing a scorched-earth policy. The Russian soldiers and peasants were setting fire to everything: fields, dwellings, stables, barns . . . and all this with the blessing of the Orthodox priests, who were setting their own churches alight. The population would then take refuge in the forests or follow the retreating troops.

The consequences for the Grande Armée were catastrophic. Until then the French had been able to live off the villagers during their campaigns. Italian, Austrian, Prussian or Polish peasants had welcomed them with varying degrees of enthusiasm, according to the country. In Russia, the French could rely only on military supplies but these supplies were too far behind. Napoleon led one forced march after another in his attempt to catch up with the Russians, and the heavy wagons laden with food and forage were lagging far behind, bogged down and jammed together. Thousands of men and horses were stricken with hunger, exhaustion and disease. Deserters, marauders, wanderers and stragglers hovered around the army in their tens of thousands, more on the look-out for chickens than for Russians, even though they came across the latter more often and were massacred in ambushes. A quarter of the army had been lost in this way but, despite the suffering, the morale of the troops remained high because they did not question the Emperor's genius. They grumbled but kept advancing.

Everyone in the Grande Armée wondered why the Russians kept falling back. The Russians were wondering too. Alexander's forces were impatient to engage in combat and were bemused by the retreat, but the massive exodus continued. The combatants found it demoralising to abandon large portions of their country without a struggle, knowing that their villages were being burnt to cinders and their families exiled to some as yet unknown destination.

There were two possible explanations for this pull-back. Some supported this strategy, which weakened the French and was easy to implement, thanks to the sheer size of the country and the paucity of its resources. It was a procedure that had proved effective in the past. The Scythians, semi-nomadic tribes who lived in the area between the Danube and the Don, had used it centuries earlier against the Romans. Peter the Great had done the same to weaken the Swedish army of Charles XII before crushing him at Poltava in 1709. Napoleon had procured documents about this war. The most distinguished supporters of this point of view were General Barclay de Tolly, the commander-in-chief of the Russian forces, and Tsar Alexander I himself. But the pressure of those in favour of a direct encounter was becoming such that they would have won the argument had it not been for another factor: the state of the Russian army.

Against Napoleon's four hundred thousand men, including sixty thousand cavalry and twelve hundred guns, the Russians could line up six hundred thousand men . . . on paper. In reality, after deducting the auxiliaries, and the phantom soldiers, who existed only for the purpose of embezzling their pay, there were just over four hundred thousand men. And these were very scattered: facing the invading army in Finland, in Moldavia, on the Turkish border, on the Dvina and the Dnieper, in the garrisons, in the interior of the country . . . The immediately available forces amounted to two hundred thousand men but the crowning misfortune for the Russians was that they were divided in two: the western army, commanded by General Prince Barclay de Tolly, consisting of fifty thousand men, and the southern army, under the orders of General Prince Bagration. Napoleon had attacked with bewildering speed and since then he had been urging his troops on in order to defeat these two armies separately, a tactic he had employed brilliantly in the past. So the Russians were pulling back hurriedly in order to link up before deciding on a possible confrontation on favourable ground.

The monotony and inaction of the interminable days of marching preyed on Margont's mind. What was worse was that his investigation was advancing as laboriously as this campaign. He had been obliged to go back to the 84th to avoid arousing suspicion with his repeated absences. He had given Lefine the task of using any pretext to recruit a handful of reliable soldiers to gather information discreetly about all the colonels in IV Corps. There were about forty of them. None, of course, was called Acosavan. No witnesses could be found to a brawl involving a tall, ginger-haired soldier and a civilian, or to the sighting of a colonel in civilian clothes in Tresno. The investigation had quickly eliminated any who were too small, too tall, left-handed, invalids (of which there were plenty, since a colonel was duty-bound to lead his regiment into battle, which inevitably brought down a hail of bullets on him) and those who were known to have spent the night of 28 June in the company of such and such a person.

By 15 July, Lefine had been able to draw up a preliminary list of a dozen or so names. It included two that Margont would have preferred not to see: Colonel Pégot, who was in charge of the 84th of the Line, and Colonel Delarse, one of General Huard's aides-de-camp. Delarse commanded the 1st Brigade of the Delzons Division, which included the 84th, together with the 8th Regiment of Light Infantry and the 1st Croat Regiment.

Lefine and his men had then begun to reconstruct the movements of the suspects on the night of the murder. The fact that Margont had always been exasperated by the question of shoes in the French army had given him an idea. One of a French soldier's best weapons was indeed his shoes. The imperial troops were second to none in their ability to cover long distances in record time. Napoleon had brilliantly incorporated this advantage of speed into his strategic calculations when launching his infantrymen on frenzied, crazed, hellish marches. As a result, in 1805, on the way to Austerlitz, Margont had seen soldiers literally die of exhaustion. Others fell into such a deep sleep that the officers could not wake them, even by prodding them with the points of their sabres. They had nevertheless continued to advance with the result that, thanks to some skilful manoeuvres, Napoleon had succeeded in preventing the Austrian army of General Mack from linking up with the bulk of his forces. The Austrian army had finally been encircled in the city of Ulm. The Austrians had lost twenty-five thousand men, whom they sorely missed a few days later during the battle of Austerlitz . . .

Yet, despite the obvious importance of mobility for the regiments, the shoes used by the Grande Armée were very badly designed. There was no difference between right or left: the soldiers' feet shaped the shoes during the march. There were only three sizes: small, medium and large, so it was hard for feet of other lengths. The shoes were supposed to last for five hundred miles, but many of the suppliers swindled the army and often, if you set off from Paris with new shoes, you ended up in Brussels barefoot.

Margont had decided to take advantage of this paradox. He had suggested that Jean-Quenin should write a letter asking the regimental cobblers to answer a list of questions. The medical officer claimed he wanted to do some research into the shoes in order to rethink their design. Lefine met the cobblers, read them the letter and immediately drowned them in a sea of words. He talked on and on. Sometimes his slick talk endeared him to them and he obtained all the information he wanted; other times he infuriated them and people said all they knew just to get rid of this wretched sergeant. Casually slipped in among the questions was one about the shoe sizes of the senior officers . . .

But this painstaking task proved to be unbearably slow.

The complete translation of the private diary had taught Margont nothing new. Maria Dorlovna suffered from loneliness. Being of a sensitive and dreamy disposition, she fed her hopes by reading romantic literature. Her writing was steeped in poetic melancholy, a feature that was all the more remarkable given that few women of her class had the opportunity to learn to read and write. She had believed that a miracle was possible. What had her murderer done to seduce her so quickly? What, then, could a Prince Charming possibly be like?

July 21 started badly for Margont as that morning bore an annoying resemblance to the preceding ones. How ironic to be constantly singing the praises of freedom and yet to be himself a prisoner! Where was the freedom to go where you liked? He had to continue advancing in this cloud of dust that the road to Moscow had turned into. Where was freedom of speech? Tiredness often made it impossible to talk. The laborious progress of the Grande Armée reminded Margont of his years spent in the abbey of Saint-Guilhem-le-Désert. The old stone walls had been replaced by vast plains. Certain moments from his life there came back to him as if linked to the present by a common thread of hopelessness. He pictured himself again scraping away night after night at a stone hidden under the bed of his monastic cell. He had never succeeded in dislodging it. He remembered the obdurate expression of certain monks when he pleaded with them to let him accompany them on visits outside the monastery.

As a child his mind had been an empty vessel in an empty, locked room. Then he had discovered books and had feasted on words, dreams and the promise of travel. But even today he still retained this searing memory of emptiness. He still needed to fill himself up: with food, with any kind of learning, with reading . . . So he had devised all sorts of strategies for warding off boredom, this nothingness that threatened to swallow him up. He had learnt the rudiments of Russian; recited to himself entire monologues from plays, throwing himself into the roles; written articles for the newspaper he wanted to launch; scribbled notes and sketches in a notebook in the hope of having his memoirs published . . . And, to that end, he said to himself, in order to give an accurate idea of this long march in a work about the Russian campaign, he would have to leave dozens of pages blank. He had read all the books he had been able to bring with him: *Candide*, *Hamlet*, *Macbeth*, a treatise on ants – creatures whose ingenuity and tenacity fascinated him – and accounts of travels in Russia. He had been compelled to lighten his load by leaving these works by the wayside, hoping that they would be picked up by someone else. No soldier in his company had wanted them. Many of them could not read, and in any case with a kitbag containing three shirts, three pairs of socks, three pairs of gaiters, two pairs of trousers, dress uniform and the regulation ten kilos of rations . . . He frequently listened to the soldiers recounting their life stories, whilst being careful not to tell his own. Lastly, like the other captains, he spent a ridiculous amount of time trying to maintain order.

The columns of soldiers were becoming more and more ragged, the ranks slacker and slacker. Exhausted stragglers, left behind by their regiments, attracted the attention of sergeants, who gesticulated at them, but to no avail. Some collapsed, overcome by sleep as if hit by a thunderbolt. Others lengthened their stride to regain their position before falling behind once more. Sometimes the officers turned a blind eye, but those in command could also prove ruthless. A flurry of punishments would then be meted out and surreal scenes would ensue: here three infantrymen being forced to wear their uniforms back to front as a mark of dishonour; there a straggler running back and forth between two columns of soldiers ten times without stopping; yet another miscreant being put on guard duty every night. There seemed no limit to the inventiveness of the punishments.

Fortunately, the men were united by a feeling of camaraderie. When a young recruit threatened to fall by the wayside, one veteran carried his musket and another his kit. When some of the men could no longer keep up, the regiment imperceptibly slowed its pace, or lieutenants would be furious to witness a sudden general outbreak of blisters and corns. Resupply problems had become so severe that officers sent detachments out looting to bring back what they could, which in most cases meant little or nothing. Everyone always volunteered for this sort of mission, despite the considerable risks posed by the Cossacks.

Originally, the Cossacks were free peasants and soldiers who fought the Russians, the Poles or the Tartars but now they were subjugated by Russia. Enamoured of nature and freedom, always on horseback, armed with lances and fanatically devoted to the Tsar, these marvellous horsemen were key elements in the Russian army. Highly mobile, swift and unobtrusive, they attacked isolated groups and concealed Alexander's troop movements by disrupting reconnaissance expeditions and making it impossible to estimate their number by their constant comings and goings. At the head of the Cossacks of the Don was Hetman Platov, who had sworn to bring Napoleon back to St Petersburg in chains.

On that day, the 84th had just been given permission to make a halt. The soldiers lay down so quickly that the regiment looked like a house of cards blown over by the wind. Two corporals dragged the sick horses to one side. Because of the shortage of fodder, the animals grazed on wet grass, unripe rye and even straw from the roofs of the *isba*s, which gave them serious bouts of dysentery, which weakened them even more.

Margont lit a fire and boiled some water, into which he dropped a handful of rice. Saber and Piquebois did likewise. As he waited for the rice to cook, Margont stretched out on the grass and began to munch a biscuit, his only pleasure of the day. Lieutenants Saber and Piquebois were Margont's other two close friends. Irénée Saber was a very self-assured man and too full of himself. His handsome face could look surprisingly arrogant when it broke into a sardonic smile. Though generous by nature, he was consumed with overwhelming ambition. In his youth, Julius Caesar had wept before the statue of Alexander the Great who, in his youth, had already conquered an empire. Saber, at thirty, inwardly broke down in tears before both Caesar and Alexander. He was only a lieutenant! Not even a major! When would he have a colonel's epaulettes? Why had he not been decorated on the evening of the battle of Wagram? Had no one noticed that, without him, all would have been lost? Saber was jealous of Margont because of his higher rank but he also looked down on him because there was no doubt that by the age of thirty-two he, Saber, would be at least a colonel, perhaps higher . . . much higher.

Poor Saber. Rather than his military career, it was his lack of sincerity and narrow-mindedness that had become legendary (and then only in the small world of the 84th). So, when a soldier was too obstinate, it had become customary in the regiment to call him 'as pig-headed as Saber'. Yet Irénée Saber had a brilliant mind. He had a real tactical sense and was able to grasp the deployment of troops and to work out the movements generals expected of them. He had an eye for all this on the battlefield, where all that most people could see was smoke, blood and indistinct masses of troops. In short, he could read pattern in chaos. But as he refused to question his own judgement, he was equally capable of displaying the clear-sightedness of a marshal and of raving like a madman claiming to be Napoleon. A little more flexibility would have turned his intelligence into genius. Margont was convinced that his friend would go very far. But what was very far for Margont was only halfway for Saber.

Lieutenant Piquebois had been very similar, before becoming very different. Aged thirty-three, he behaved as if he were fifty, with the result that he was often taken for a young-looking fifty-year-old. He had fallen madly in love with the daughter of a rich cloth merchant from Uzès. Étienne Marcelin, the young woman's father, had not approved of this match. Piquebois had been studying medicine in Montpellier but for some strange reason he was to be seen every day in the taverns of Uzès. He had sailed the seas during his 'I shall be a ship's captain' period and he had lived in Africa for two years during his 'I shall make a fortune out of cocoa' period. On his return, he declared that he was going to emigrate to South America. His journey to Peru never got any further than the Peyrou Gardens in the heart of Montpellier . . . Marcelin had therefore said no, categorically. His daughter, Anne-Lise, had become distraught, with the result that the veto was qualified: 'No, unless you acquire a respectable social position.' 'But I'm studying to become a Protestant minister,' Piquebois had explained, though no one seemed aware of this new calling. ' "Minister" is not a social position, it's a theological position,' Marcelin had retorted. Piquebois guessed that this subtle distinction had something to do with income. He therefore gave up his religious studies before they had started, together with his interminable medical studies, naval studies and chocolate studies in order to enlist in the army. Nothing can compare with the army in wartime as a way of climbing the social ladder. For a long time Uzès had mocked 'Piquebois the chocolate soldier'. In the cafés bordering the superb main square, all the inhabitants of Uzès had drunk to his health: 'Heaven forbid that anything should happen to him! But let's not worry too much. The sound of cannon fire isn't often to be heard in Montpellier.' Everyone had assumed that Piquebois was still there, dead drunk, snoring under the table like his fellow medical students, a young Rabelais without the inspiration.

To general surprise, Piquebois reappeared in full hussar's uniform, his hair braided into elegant little plaits, sporting a bushy moustache and a smile on his face. In every house people exclaimed: 'Has our chocolate soldier changed into a hussar? Let's drink some of this magic cocoa straight away.' Marcelin, thoughtful father that he was, had found plenty of better matches (better in his eyes, at least, and weren't they the only ones that counted?). However, Anne-Lise, who was as stubborn as her father, had turned them all down. He eventually accepted the marriage, which was celebrated in the cathedral of the former duchy of Uzès.

Piquebois had not chosen the hussars by accident. Turbulent, fun-loving young men who lived their lives at a frantic pace were attracted to the hussars because everything they did was fast and furious. Instead of talking, they yelled; instead of drinking they got slewed; and they picked quarrels with anyone who wasn't a hussar (while also getting into arguments with hussars from other regiments). Piquebois performed heroically on the battlefield but took even more risks away from it. He had nearly broken his neck by jumping out of the window of an inn in which he had thrashed a cuirassier. He was frequently picked up by the police 'more dead than drunk'. He had also wounded two men in duels: one because of the accidental clash between two sabre scabbards – he let his own drag along the ground because he enjoyed the sound of it scraping over the cobbles – and the other because of a look he judged 'full of innuendoes', though what the innuendoes were, no one ever knew, not even the man on the receiving end.

Despite this tendency to play with fire (or perhaps because of it) Piquebois had been promoted to the rank of lieutenant. Everything changed on the day of the battle of Austerlitz. On 2 December 1805, Napoleon broke through the centre of the Austro-Russian army. In a final attempt to avoid catastrophe, the Russian Imperial Horse Guard launched a furious counterattack. Napoleon himself considered the charge admirable. Piquebois mingled with the cavalry of the French Imperial Guard (he already considered himself one of their number) who were racing towards the Russians. He did not see the triumphant conclusion to the battle because a bullet struck him full in the chest. He swore it was fired by Grand Duke Constantine himself, and when a man had undergone such suffering, he was allowed one final boast.

It took him a whole year to recover. But his fellow medical students and hussars were in the habit of saying that he never fully recovered. He did indeed change completely. No more heavy drinking sessions, duels, bragging or student pranks. Piquebois began to enjoy the quiet pleasures of an afternoon spent listening to his wife playing the piano, or chatting with friends while smoking a pipe. Considered unfit to serve in the hussars, he was transferred to the infantry and was very happy there. From then on Piquebois determined to become a serious-minded officer. 'Serious-minded' — a word that had never before existed in his vocabulary. His wife, delighted by this change, said to him one day: 'It took a bullet to kill the eternal student in you. Now I have a man for my husband.' Those who had formerly accompanied him on his escapades ruefully came to the same conclusion, and his squadron organised a funeral for 'Hussar Piquebois'. They solemnly buried his saddle and cavalry sabre before going to get drunk to celebrate his resurrection in the vast world of spoilsports.

The aftereffects, his world-weary look, his air of moderation and the wrinkles etched into his forehead by the months of suffering, had prematurely aged him. But despite his settled existence and his old man's ways – such as when he complained about the weather while mentioning his rheumatism – his former squadron swore that the old Piquebois wasn't completely dead and that his ghost would rise up again from the charnel house of Austerlitz and fly back to his earthly frame to take possession of it once more. Then they would go and dig up his saddle and sabre – which they had buried in a field near Uzès in the hope that that would have a healing effect on the patient – and they would drink themselves senseless to celebrate the event. Because when a hussar fell on the battlefield he didn't finish up like Piquebois. Certainly not. The Valkyries appeared from the heavens and carried him back to Valhalla singing of his exploits, a Valhalla that inevitably resembled an enormous tavern in which you got drunk with pretty girls on your knee before galloping off into the plains to mow down the enemy hordes.

Saber was polishing his shoes but they never shone enough for his liking. He was thoroughly annoyed. The Russians kept falling back but he couldn't run after them indefinitely. How could he finish this campaign with the rank of colonel if the enemy didn't play its part? Glory was awaiting him; he had a schedule to keep to. Piquebois stuffed his pipe calmly. Smoking eased his hunger. Lucky man. Saber was now furiously rubbing his shoes as if the whole Russian army had launched an attack on his feet.

'Let's smash their faces in again like at Austerlitz and then all go back home in triumph. An army that retreats without fighting!' he exclaimed like a judge speaking to a person who has committed the most heinous of crimes.

He did not even notice the nervous twitch affecting Piquebois's face at the mention of Austerlitz.

'I think the Russians will fight like fanatics,' said Margont.

'Have you been reading that sort of nonsense in books?' replied Saber immediately. 'When we catch up with them they'll be sorry not to have kept us on the go even longer.'

The atmosphere was gloomy as they ate their meagre meal. Margont kept seeing Maria's martyred body. These images haunted him frequently and he tried to keep busy at all costs, to combat not only the boredom but also the memories that filled the void in his mind when he was insufficiently active. The atrocities had shaken his conception of humanity.

Margont smiled, thinking that he was conducting the investigation so tenaciously not so much to obey Prince Eugène as to fight for his principles. He thought back to Maroveski's question that had made him so uneasy: why should a captain be interested in the murder of 'a girl of no importance'? For Margont everyone had their value. However, the prince was likely to think of Maria as the equivalent of a speck of dust. An officer guilty of a crime, political stakes . . . yes, but why had Prince Eugène seemed so hesitant at the end of the meeting? Margont felt there was an element missing; the prince had concealed something from him. A link between the victim and him? It seemed absurd – even if absurd things did occur constantly on this earth. Doubts about the murderer's identity? A hidden clue? But which and why?

Margont decided to write a letter to request a new meeting with the prince on the pretext of evaluating the situation. Never mind if it did not result in anything. Since the beginning of this campaign Margont had invented a new motto for himself: 'Better to do something futile than nothing at all.'

Just when the order was given to march on, Margont spotted Lefine catching up with the regiment. He was on foot and so tired and covered in dust that he looked like a ghost. Margont's heart began to race. Was there something new? Was there at last something else going on other than an endless march?

CHAPTER 10

M ARGONT took Lefine to one side, into the remains of an *isba*, its blackened walls still smoking. Lefine patted his uniform half-heartedly to remove the dust.

'I wonder why the Russians build their houses out of ash. Whatever . . . My horse is dead.'

'Come off it. Who did you sell it to? A trooper? A canteen-keeper?'

'It shivered night and day. It was going to die anyway so selling it didn't make any difference except that I made a bit of profit as well.'

'I gave it to you to make you faster, not richer. But never mind that, what do you have to report?'

'Four suspects.'

Four. It was few but still too many.

'Are we definitely right to eliminate the rest?'

Lefine took several sheets of paper out of his pocket and carefully unfolded them.

'Here's the list . . .'

Margont took the document from the sergeant's hands.

'. . . of all the colonels in IV Corps. The names struck off are in the clear and written next to them is the reason and the name of the person who gave it.'

'Excellent work. So who do we have left?'

'Colonel Étienne Delarse. We know him by sight . . .'

Margont's face clouded over. 'What bad luck! Still, as he's part of our brigade it will be easier to keep an eye on him.'

'Colonel Maximilien Barguelot, commanding the 9th of the Line, 1st Brigade, 14th Division.'

'I don't know him.'

'Colonel Robert Pirgnon, 35th of the Line, 2nd Brigade, 14th Division.'

'Never heard of him.'

'And Colonel Alessandro Fidassio, 3rd Italian of the Line, 3rd Brigade, 15th Division.'

Margont looked up from the list. 'General Pino's Italian Division? An Italian?'

'Precisely. The men who got this information cost me a fortune. The rascals were holding out their grubby paws every day, keeping on about all the harm this investigation was doing them, and I often had to—'

Margont interrupted him by giving him a purse. 'That's for the rascals holding out their grubby paws.'

Lefine spread out the coins in the palm of his hand. 'That'll barely cover the costs. And that's being optimistic.'

'Are you sure a name hasn't been struck off by mistake?'

'We know when the victim died. It took some time to do but we managed to reconstruct the movements of quite a few of the suspects at around midnight. Only the remaining four were away from their regiment that night without us knowing where.'

'So it's very likely that the murderer is one of these men. Perfect. I want to know everything about them: their lives, their careers, their friends, their interests, their plans, their temperaments . . .'

Lefine shook his head to indicate he was throwing in the towel.

'No, Fernand. You're going to continue helping me. I still haven't forgiven you for betraying me and, in any case, it's an order.'

'It's an abuse of power.'

'Prince Eugène promised me a handsome reward, remember. I'm offering you half. Yes, I know, that'll barely cover your expenses. Count yourself lucky that I'll share the money in the event of success but not the punishment in the event of failure. You're going to find me eight men as resourceful as you – two per suspect – but less grasping, otherwise your expenses really will be out of control.'

Lefine had the worried look of a card player watching the stakes increase too quickly for his liking.

'It's too much work! Anyway, I don't know any of the sort of men you want.'

Margont nodded in encouragement. 'No, but you do know darned well how to spot them and convince them to do what you expect of them. And find me men who are discreet and reliable! Otherwise, instead of gold, all you'll have is the lead pumped into me by the firing squad, and then you'd need to invent the philosopher's stone to turn it into gold.'

Lefine was furious. He often took advantage of his friends' generosity but was of course outraged when he was repaid in kind. He puckered his lips and sweat left dirty streaks on his dusty face.

'It's an abuse of power!'

'Go and complain to Colonel Delarse. There's only a one-in-four chance that he'll slit your throat.'

Margont mounted his horse. At last he was going to break free of the tedium oppressing his mind.

'I want the people you choose to keep watch over the suspects day and night. Meanwhile, I'll try to put faces to the names.'

With that he galloped away. Lefine aimed a big kick at one of the walls of the *isba*, which almost collapsed on top of him.

Margont decided to begin with Colonel Barguelot of the 9th of the Line. He galloped up to the columns of regiments and squadrons, and the convoys of guns, caissons and wagons. The numbers were still not complete. Many troopers were on foot, carrying their saddles on their shoulders. All around lay the corpses of horses that had been pushed to the side of the road. Margont wondered how his horse could bear such a sight.

He would need two hours to obtain a good cover. He rode up to Chief Physician Gras, who directed the physicians of IV Corps and handed him a letter written by Jean-Quenin Brémond. The medical officer claimed he was carrying out a study into the risks of the spread of typhus in the army and requested that the bearer of his message be allowed to question physicians and senior officers about this matter. Chief Physician Gras gave his consent on condition that the general staff of IV Corps were also in agreement. Margont decided to use the document signed by Triaire to avoid this procedure but he still had to explain the reasons for his visit to one of the aides-de-camp of General Broussier, commanding the 14th Division. The request was passed on to the general, who in turn gave his consent . . . providing that every brigadier-general was informed of the information gathered.

Unfortunately, General Bertrand de Sivray, commanding the 1st Brigade of the 14th Division, was a great friend of Colonel Pégot's, from the 84th, and he bombarded Margont with questions. Yes, Colonel Pégot was well. Yes, he too was very worried about the shortage of supplies and the number of deserters. Yes, he had authorised the formation of detachments to go foraging for food. No, he did not think that a clash with the Russian army was imminent. Yes, the general's best wishes would be passed on to him. When Margont was eventually able to leave, he still had to question Colonel Gaussard from the 18th Light Infantry as well as the physician for that regiment before going on to the 9th of the Line.

Colonel Barguelot was riding at the head of his regiment, surrounded by three captains and three majors to whom he was talking merrily. He had light, somewhat curly auburn hair, a large, almost massive, face and a nose that was long but flattened at the end as if permanently pressed up against an invisible window. Carefully trimmed whiskers accentuated his sticking-out ears. When he stopped speaking, his lips automatically reverted to a complacent smile. Margont stopped his horse, saluted, introduced himself and handed over the letter from Medical Officer Brémond. Colonel Barguelot glanced through it perfunctorily.

'Typhus? Well, yes, of course.'

His uniform had very little dust on it because he brushed it off with his hand frequently and carefully. In the same way he stroked his gold epaulettes and his Officer of the Légion d'Honneur cross. When he gave the document back he had a sardonic look on his face.

'So what is Medical Officer Brémond planning to do?'

'He wants to get a clearer idea of the situation, Colonel. He also thinks there are ways of improving prevention—'

The colonel interrupted him with a weary gesture. 'Well, get on with it: improve it, improve it.'

'Could you tell me how many—'

'Consult the regimental physician about that.'

The discussion was evidently about to come to an end.

'Colonel, you must be wondering why I've been given the task of gathering this information when I don't belong to the army medical service.'

'No, I haven't asked myself that question.'

Margont's explanation that he had survived typhus thanks to Medical Officer Brémond remained buried at the bottom of the pile of lies he had built up since the beginning of this investigation. The colonel had turned towards one of the majors. Margont no longer existed so far as he was concerned.

Contemplating the small circle of officers that surrounded Barguelot, laughing at the slightest of his jokes, the captain declared: 'I did not realise that you too had been promoted to Officer of the Légion d'Honneur, Colonel.'

Barguelot looked at Margont again, this time piercingly.

'I was a captain in the 16th Light during the battle of Jena. It was my regiment and the 14th of the Line that in the morning restored the situation on the left flank. Then Jouardet, my major, after taking over the command of the regiment when Colonel Harispe was wounded, handed his battalion over to me. My men and I were at the head of the 16th Light and we were even in front of the 105th, which launched the assault along with us. We swept aside the Hahn and Sack Battalions and took the whole of the Glasenapp Battery – fourteen fine guns that we turned against the enemy.'

Colonel Barguelot continued his account, going into unnecessary detail, describing the devastating effects of the guns taken from the Prussians or telling how he had saved the life of Colonel Habert from the 105th. He revelled in the telling of his own tale. The officers who accompanied him seemed to be drinking in his every word, though they must have heard this story many times. Eventually, the last Prussians surrendered, Barguelot received his decoration and the tirade came to an end.

'But you said "you too" concerning my decoration. Who were you referring to?' he asked finally.

'Myself, Colonel. I was promoted to the rank of Officer of the Légion d'Honneur in Spain.'

The brevity of this announcement disconcerted Barguelot somewhat. How could anyone resist the pleasure of recounting military prowess?

Margont realised that the colonel's eau de Cologne – which he used liberally – was familiar to him. Saber spent a fortune getting hold of it because the Emperor occasionally used it.

Barguelot nodded his head like a horse-trader spotting a good animal. 'Well, I congratulate you, Captain. It's always an honour to meet a man of real worth.'

For Barguelot this sentence had the merit of being a

compliment received as much as given. The colonel held out his hand to Margont who, rather taken by surprise, belatedly held out his own.

'Captain Margont, I've invited some officers from my regiment to dine with me tomorrow. Please join us.'

CHAPTER 11

THE afternoon was drawing to a close. In order to spare Nocturne, his horse, Margont had wanted to take a short cut through the woods to rejoin his regiment. Once again he had overestimated his sense of direction and had lost his way. After cursing the Russian forests he reassured himself that even the most inept of people was bound to be able to find an army of several thousand men. The smell of soil and rotting leaves filled the air, and for company he had only the soft sound of hoofs on a carpet of fir needles and moss, and the sharp snap of branches.

After a short time Margont reached a clearing. It was quite wide, forming a triangle with sides measuring more than a hundred yards. He had emerged close to three sentries, who immediately levelled their muskets at him. Realising their mistake, the soldiers lowered their weapons before saluting him with an obvious lack of military discipline. The open space dipped in the middle and along the bottom of this hollow ran a river that in the summer drought was now no more than a stream. Five grenadiers were filling their gourds and leather water bottles. A little further upstream five chasseurs were watering their horses. One sergeant did not take kindly to drinking water flavoured with horse spittle and straightened up to hurl abuse at the chasseurs. Noticing that one of the horse-men was a lieutenant, he had to content himself with ordering his men to stop what they were doing until the 'animals had finished splashing around'. Nocturne pulled up sharp when it caught sight of the stream and began to trot down the slope. Margont gave it a friendly pat on the neck.

'Yes, it's all right, we're going to have a drink. And, luckily, it's the 19th Chasseurs. We're back with our corps.'

The silence was shattered by confused shouting. Margont saw one of the three sentries go charging down the slope without his weapon. A galloping horseman caught up with him and sliced his head off with a swipe of his sword. Two shots rang out. The grenadiers let go of their gourds and swiftly levelled their muskets. Margont unsheathed his sword and turned round. Fifteen or so Cossacks had sprung out of the forest. Their blue trousers, jackets and caps showed they were regular troops. They yelled as they charged, levelling their lances. The shock tactic was a total success. More shouting compounded the French soldiers' confusion: other Cossacks had appeared to catch them in a pincer movement.

The officer leading the assault bore down on Margont. The captain attacked him without mercy, convinced he was about to die. He did not attempt to run his sword through him in case it remained stuck in his opponent's body, but struck him a fearsome blow to the shoulder. The blade sliced right through to the bone. A young Cossack, armed with a lance, immediately set upon Margont. The lance – which in Western Europe was considered a weapon of the Middle Ages – was longer than the sabre and gave the charging horseman the advantage because it allowed him to strike first. Conversely, in hand-to-hand fighting it reduced the chances of success because it was unwieldy and took away the initiative. Margont faced him and suddenly landed on his back before he could even attempt to parry the blow. Fortunately, the point had only pierced his coat and the thin layer of flesh covering his ribs. Before he had fully recovered his wits, he instinctively rolled over to narrowly avoid being trampled by another Cossack. This one let out a 'Huzza!' full of burning anger, and tried to pin him to the ground. His lance grazed Margont's arm. The Frenchman picked up his sword and rushed towards his mount to grab his horse pistols, vowing to blow the brains out of the next Cossack who tried to spear him. One of the horsemen guessed his intention and galloped towards Nocturne, yelling as he did so. Seeing how reluctant the horse was to give up on its master, he flung the lance in its direction. Nocturne fled at a gallop.

Margont faced up to the Russian who was charging towards him. This time it would be sword against sabre and, as his adversary was at least ten years younger than he, Margont could reasonably bet on his own superior technique. The Cossack followed the same reasoning and turned tail.

The Cossacks now scattered in all directions, like a flock of pigeons flying off when a child rushes into their midst. The forest soaked them up immediately, like blotting paper. Three of them were strewn across the clearing. Four infantrymen and one chasseur had also perished. In the stream a grenadier on all fours was spitting blood. The sergeant was supporting another who had the point of a lance still embedded in his thigh. The lieutenant from the chasseurs was pressing a hand to his forehead to stanch the blood that was running into his eyes.

Margont was surprised by the tactics of the Cossacks, who

had no sooner come than gone. They had the advantage in numbers, the speed of their horses and their wretched lances. Why did they not continue? Why did they break off a fight that would probably have ended with the death of all the Frenchmen? It was obvious that their aim was to harry. The element of surprise had reduced their losses: if they had persisted they would have paid heavily. They preferred sudden raids to drawn-out action. Margont attempted to lift his spirits with the thought that in a Cossack raid, time was on the side of those under attack.

The lieutenant came galloping up to him. The poor fellow held his sleeve to his forehead and his face was spattered with blood, making him look like an écorché.

'Captain, would you care to join us in pursuing these bastards?'

'There were fifteen or so on my side. How many were there altogether?'

'Two groups of about fifteen sons of bitches.'

'Do you expect just the five of us to chase after them?'

'They've spread out. I'm hoping to surprise a small isolated group who—'

Margont shook his head. 'If you set off on their trail and they decide to face up to us, they will regroup immediately. If they prefer to flee, they will scatter in all directions.'

The lieutenant took his sleeve away from his wound but had to put it back again immediately.

'With your permission, Captain, I shall leave you.'

Margont gave an impatient wave. 'Off you go. Go and charge at them if you haven't had your face smashed in enough.'

The chasseur went back to his men and led them off towards the woods, sabres drawn.

Margont was still cursing as he rejoined his regiment. His life might have come to an abrupt end in some godforsaken clearing in the middle of nowhere in the vast empty spaces of Russia.

Despite his fright, his mind was racing. Four suspects! Why had night fallen already? Why should he have to waste time sleeping when there was so much to be done? The 84th had set up camp on a muddy plain. Some soldiers were already asleep, wrapped in poor-quality blankets and huddled against one another out in the open. Here and there men were pitching tents or collecting deadwood to make fires for warmth and to cook up a miserably meagre broth.

Margont tied Nocturne to a stake. The animal's ribs were sticking out from under its skin and its scrawny look was in sharp contrast to its stomach, which was bloated with gas. He stroked its neck a long while. Then he took it by the bridle and led it to a wood where he set it free. Margont wanted to give it a last chance of survival, or at least allow it to die peacefully. Nocturne gazed at him for a long time without moving before disappearing into the darkness.

By the time Margont caught up with Lefine, Saber and Piquebois, his comrades were roasting a chicken and it took all their combined authority and rank to keep the famished spectres clustering around them at bay.

'A good catch! Who do we have to thank for this?' Margont exclaimed gleefully.

Lefine bowed his head. Margont tore a leg off the bird.

'Just now a soldier asked me how many days we were from Moscow. "Four? Five? More? Are you sure?" he said to me. If the infantrymen had maps there'd be three times as many deserters and you'd need to fire a shot to protect this meal. I can't stay because I've still got things to do.'

He motioned to Lefine to step aside for a quiet word.

'I've had a brief talk with Colonel Barguelot. I'll tell you the whole story later. One thing struck me: this pseudonym "Acosavan" is odd. It doesn't sound French or Italian. Why not choose a simpler or more believable name?'

'Yes, it surprised me a bit as well. I'd hoped the murderer would have chosen a pseudonym resembling his real name, one with the same initial or a shared syllable. But this idea didn't get me anywhere. There's an Alméras, but he's a brigadier-general. There's also a Colonel Serrant, who's in command of the 8th Light, and a Bertrand in the 106th of the Line but both of them have alibis. I really thought I'd got it with Colonel Banco! "Banco" and "Acosavan": one syllable and four letters in common. But this fellow Banco is in command of the 2nd Italian Mounted Chasseurs and spent a good part of the night of 28 June looking after the animals in his regiment. Another of those who get on better with the horses than with their riders. I can quite understand it, though. When you're at war you end up preferring animals to men.'

'What name would you make up if you wanted to mislead someone? Knowing you as I do, I assume you're well versed in such matters.'

Lefine blushed. 'I'd keep the same initials.'

'Why?'

Lefine pointed to the hunting knife in his belt. His initials were engraved on an impressive-looking blade. He had spent a fortune purchasing it in Spain, but the quality of the materials and the skill of the craftsmanship justified the cost. What a shame the Spanish had given up the game they traditionally hunted to go after French soldiers instead.

'So that my belongings don't give me away. Added to that, it's very difficult to make up a new signature and manage to reproduce it. With the same initials that's a good start and you just scribble something after. Not to mention that my initials are part of me and I want to keep them.'

'What a lecture! I suppose you've cheated like this before.'

'A bit. But it didn't involve you.'

'Don't go on about it or I'll lose my temper again.'

'So I would choose "François Lechu" or "Francis Lacet", a name that's easy to remember – it would be idiotic to make a mistake – but not too unusual or too ordinary, like "Dupont".'

Margont nodded. 'We're in agreement. But the point is that "Acosavan" meets none of these criteria.'

'If all he wanted was a pseudonym for a couple of days, he must have said whatever came into his head without thinking any more about it. In any case, now that we are down to only four suspects it's clear that no name bears any relation to "Acosavan". All this is pointless. It was something to chew on when there were no other clues, but that's no longer the case.'

'Think about it all the same. We'll talk about it again some time.'

'How stubborn can you get!'

'Good. Now I'm going to try to meet Colonel Delarse.'

As Margont was walking away, Piquebois strode after him and caught him up.

'Is everything all right, Quentin?'

'Of course it is. Why do you ask?'

'It's the expression on your face. You look excited and worried at the same time. My comrades in the hussars and I were like that just before a charge.'

'I got lost in the woods and was attacked by some Cossacks. The devils well and truly sent me to the ground. But all's well.'

'If that's all it was . . .' concluded Piquebois, looking unconvinced.

In spite of its losses, the Grande Armée – which IV Corps had met up with at Glubokoe – was still very impressive. There were troops stretching as far as the eye could see. From one end of the plain to the other you could see campfires and tents. The woods overlooking the nearby hills also seemed alive with fires, and the same was true of the crests of the hills further away. This immense expanse of lights seemed to reflect a distorted image of the starry sky. Margont felt reassured. In the face of adversity, the feeling of being part of a group was a source of comfort. He gnawed at his bone, snapped it to suck out the marrow and could only bring himself to throw it away when he reached Colonel Delarse's tent. The sentry pointed his bayonet at the intruder.

'Halt. Who goes there?'

'Captain Margont, 84th of the Line, 2nd Battalion. I wish to meet Colonel Delarse.'

The sentry disappeared into the tent and reappeared a

moment later accompanied by Colonel Delarse himself.

'Captain Margont. I've heard so much about you. Do me the honour of coming inside.'

Taken rather by surprise, Margont obeyed without a word. Tall but frail-looking, Colonel Delarse was approaching fifty. His energetic, determined movements seemed ill suited to his slight frame. His bony, emaciated face gave an unpleasant preview of what his head would look like once he had been reduced to a skeleton. Delarse looked sickly, weakened and debilitated. He inevitably made one think of his doctor and the medicines he must have been taking. One wanted to express one's sympathy before suggesting to him that he should lie down to conserve his strength. In fact, the feeling most of all engendered was the desire to get away from him as soon as possible, because he reminded one of death, and one's own last moments were time enough to be thinking of that. But there was a life force struggling against this generally deathly appearance. His light blue eyes stared out with interest and liveliness. Margont wondered whether such an individual was physically capable of leaping from roof to roof and killing a sentry with a single knife stab. His conclusion was no, and he held back a sudden feeling of anger. What sort of work was this? Shouldn't this suspect have been ruled out?

Colonel Delarse sat down on a chair and invited Margont to do likewise. The tent had been carefully laid out. The bed was heaped with numerous blankets and an eiderdown. There were no fewer than three chests. A small desk, placed just next to a brazier, was barely visible beneath a pile of papers: notebooks, reports, drafts and letters. The washroom was hidden by a screen. It was decorated with a classical fresco depicting athletes whose magnificent bodies were in sad contrast to the colonel's.

'I have been given to understand that you are an Officer of the Légion d'Honneur. I offer you my congratulations,' Delarse declared warmly.

Prince Eugène was right. This distinction immediately earned Margont the esteem of numerous soldiers, which opened many a door.

'I'm pleased to meet you,' the colonel went on. 'I have almost twelve thousand men under my command – since I assist General Huard,' he added somewhat reluctantly. 'But I am anxious to get to know personally all the promising officers serving in my brigade. It's a crime not to exploit everyone's potential.'

These last words were uttered with an energy bordering on anger.

'My friend Colonel Pégot says that you are tenacious and resourceful but that you think too much.'

'Is it possible, Colonel, to think too much?'

'Let's say that when a superior accuses you of thinking too much it's because he resents the fact that you think differently from him.'

'What about you, Colonel? Do you never happen to think too much?'

'Every day.'

Delarse took a bottle and filled two glasses.

'I come from the Charentes. This cognac is a bit of my native land that follows me in my campaigns. I've got another bottle for Moscow. I'm longing to open that one.'

The colonel cupped his glass in both hands to warm the alcohol.

'What is the reason for your visit?'

'Typhus.' Margont handed over Brémond's letter.

The colonel read it carefully and responded immediately: 'Typhus is only in an endemic state in the brigade. As soon as there is a suspected case, the soldier is isolated and put in a special field hospital. His kit and his tent – if he has one – are burnt. Those who have been sleeping alongside him are put into quarantine but are given double rations because malnutrition is a breeding ground for typhus.'

'That seems ideal to me.'

'To discover the exact number of people put into quarantine, you'll need to speak to the physicians attached to each regiment. May I enquire why you have decided to concern yourself with typhus?'

'I find inactivity a burden.'

'Personally, I find it deadly. But before long the Russians are bound to stop falling back. They'll fight to save Smolensk. It'll be a slaughter. We'll suffer too but their army will be blown to bits.'

The colonel was becoming more and more excited.

'The Tsar will be on his knees but the Emperor will be able to spare his dignity by throwing him a few crumbs. He'll agree not to deprive Russia of the provinces she stole from the Poles; he won't restore Greater Poland; he will be magnanimous. In exchange, he'll force Alexander to implement the continental system. And where will the English ships go if Europe welcomes them with round shot? Without ports you lose control of the seas and oceans, and without control of the water, an island is lost. So – at last! – the English will also sign the peace treaty, one laden with punitive clauses that will weaken them. Thus we shall be able to expand our colonies and acquire new ones, and people in India, Africa, Asia or America will henceforth say "*Bonjour, monsieur*" instead of "Good morning, sir".'

The colonel raised his glass as if he were already celebrating the capture of Bombay. Margont did not like this vision of the campaign; it was too militaristic and political for his taste. There was no mention of freedom for the muzhiks, the peasant serfs; nothing about reforming Tsarist society, the dashing of the hopes of their Polish allies . . . Still, the two visions were not totally incompatible. He took a swig of cognac and tried to make the pleasant burning sensation last as long as possible.

'I can see that you're a great reader, Colonel.'

'I'm finishing a book about Joan of Arc. What a fascinating destiny! And to think that she was even frailer than me. Colonel Pégot tells me that you also are a great reader.'

Margont pointed at one of the books lying on the desk. 'Yes, but not *The Gallic War*. You read Julius Caesar whereas I read Cicero.'

'What's wrong with that? Isn't a general worth as much as a philosopher?'

'The only problem is that Caesar had Cicero executed.'

'You have a sharp tongue, Captain. Too sharp. But that's often the case with serving soldiers.'

The colonel took a chessboard out of one of the chests. The wooden pieces were delicately carved: infantrymen armed with halberds for the pawns; caparisoned chargers for the knights;

elaborate mitres for the bishops; and crenellated towers for the castles. As for the kings and queens, they looked truly regal. Delarse was delighted to have an opponent.

How odd, thought Margont, that no sooner has he begun to respect someone, than he's in a hurry to challenge them.

'Let's see if you'd make a good general. The guest has the first move.'

After a courageous last stand, the white king capitulated on an almost deserted chessboard. Margont had been unsettled by Delarse's game plan. The colonel had played a particularly aggressive game, never hesitating to exchange pawns, knights, etc. Margont had not even had time to bring his defensive game into play.

'If only the Russians could attack instead of running away from one chessboard to the next,' Delarse declared pensively.

'Please allow me a return game, Colonel. I hate losing.'

'I do understand.'

Delarse was already enthusiastically setting up the board again. He was the type of officer who, in answer to the standard question, 'Which regiment do you command?' dreamt of one day being able to reply in all modesty, 'All of them.'

The sentry came bursting in.

'Colonel, sir, the head of bread supplies and the head of meat supplies wish to speak to you.'

The colonel stood up. 'I'd forgotten about their visit. The return game will have to wait for another time.'

Margont saluted him and, just as he was leaving, declared: 'I'm very sorry I was not a more worthy opponent, Colonel.'

At chess, only at chess, he added to himself.

The man was not worrying about the investigation into Maria's murder. He felt perfectly safe, hidden among the unending column of soldiers. In any case, crimes were so seldom solved . . . No, what bothered him was what was happening to him. As he walked on amongst the infantrymen and the dust, one thing became obvious to him: his fascination with death was not something recent.

As a lieutenant he had often gone into hospitals to view the dying. He attempted to capture that fleeting moment between life and death, the moment when the body becomes immobilised, when breathing itself ceases. He tried to commit to memory the change of expression on those faces at that fateful instant. But even a few years before that, death and suffering had attracted him. He attended autopsies, giving as an excuse his intention to study medicine. At the time he had put it down to a morbid curiosity. He had even read up on different types of coma. He wondered if there was one deep enough to present all the outward signs of death. During the dissections he enjoyed imagining that the man whose muscles had been separated and whose gaping abdomen was being prodded by the doctor's instrument was still alive and that, although his coma prevented him from moving, his conscious mind enabled him to have a clear idea of what was happening.

In fact his fascination with death seemed to go even further back than that. As a child he had loved graveyards. He'd spent whole days in them. He knew where each tomb was, the names and dates of the dead . . . He was curious to know what corpses looked like after a day, a week, two weeks . . . He enjoyed watching apples on which he had drawn features rot away. They were his skulls whose skin withered as the flesh became damp and soft. He watched them shrivel and gradually disintegrate.

Even as a child . . . he had revelled in the death throes of ducks wounded by his father when out hunting: their fruitless attempts to get off the ground and fly again; their long silky necks twisting in a dance of death; the sharp crack of their vertebrae when he broke their necks to put them out of their misery.

The fact was that he had always been attracted by death, pain and blood, and he wondered why it had taken him so long to realise this obvious fact. It was yet one more question demanding an answer. His life seemed to have become a series of riddles.

CHAPTER 12

THE day of 22 July was particularly gruelling. IV Corps had covered fifteen miles and it was the third successive day that they had kept up such a pace. Margont spent the afternoon attempting to get hold of a horse. In vain. Even the mounted chasseurs had been ordered to give up their mounts to the gunners to enable them to make up full teams. So that evening he went to Colonel Barguelot's on foot.

Twenty or so officers – captains and majors as well as a lieutenant-colonel – were sitting on the grass around a long white tablecloth that had been placed on the ground and laid with extraordinarily luxurious tableware: plates of Dutch china, crystal wine glasses, decanters, silver cutlery . . . Servants in powdered wigs were bustling about filling glasses and carving a roasted pig coated with a creamy sauce.

Margont put his shako and sword down on a table cluttered with headgear and bladed weapons of all shapes and sizes. He noticed a silver scabbard on which had been engraved in elaborate lettering, 'Colonel Barguelot. *Semper heroicus*'. 'Ever the hero.'

The colonel spotted him and, pointing at a place not far from his right, exclaimed: 'Here's Captain Margont! I'm always pleased to welcome a man of merit. Let's put an Officer of the Légion d'Honneur between a major and a lieutenant-colonel.'

The higher one's rank, the closer one was placed to the head of the table. As Margont was taking his place, he could sense he was being stared at by all the majors who had had to move down one place. Barguelot introduced his officers to him.

'Captain Margont received his decoration in Spain,' he explained. 'Ah, Spain, what an ill-fated country. Believe it or not, I almost got torn to shreds in Madrid during the revolt of 2 May 1808, their wretched "*dos de mayo*". The whole city went mad that day. I was calmly walking the streets with my friend Lieutenant Carré . . . Carrier . . . Damn, what was his name? Anyway, in a word, we were meeting up with two Madrid girls in a park when we noticed a sorry-looking dragoon. The poor chap had lost his helmet and his horse, and was breathless from running, sabre in hand. By the time I'd realised it was not a hallucination, a crowd had gathered at the end of the street and had started rushing towards us. Men and women, old people and children, some dressed in rags, others well dressed . . . One of the ringleaders was brandishing a rope with a noose at the end of it. My friend and I started to run. We fled down one narrow street after another until we emerged in a square, to be confronted by a horrific scene: the naked and emasculated bodies of two Mamelukes who had been hanged upside down on the façade of a house that some lunatics were setting fire to. The rabble was still on our tail. They caught up with the dragoon, who was out of breath, and tore him to pieces. When we reached the park where we had our rendezvous, we hid behind a hedge. But, believe it or not, the two traitors with whom we should have been billing and cooing pointed us out with their fans. '*Por aquí! Por aquí!*' The bitches! Determined to die fighting, we turned to face our attackers. I ran my sword through three of the insurgents and my friend . . . Carsier, Carrier . . . did the same but, alas, he was pitchforked. I held out against this horde of fanatics for a few more minutes. Then, thank God, the cavalry of the Guard suddenly arrived in the park and cleared the area.'

The conversation about Spain became heated. Why did the Spanish resist the French presence so fanatically? Why did they reject the fruits of the Revolution? Why did they rise up *en masse* to defend a society that oppressed them? Margont felt particularly unsettled by these questions. Another debate also occupied their minds: would it not have been better to have got out of the Spanish quagmire before launching the Russian campaign? The Spanish campaign was mobilising a considerable number of French and allied troops to face up to the Spanish, the Portuguese and the English. In addition, there was concern about the Emperor being such a long way from the battlefield, especially since the English were involved.

Margont was watching Barguelot. It is said that all roads lead to Rome. Here, all comments led to Barguelot. So what if a captain had been at the battle of Roliça? He, Barguelot, had been at the battle of Gamonal. So what if someone admired Goya's paintings but expressed doubts about their feelings for France? Colonel Barguelot announced that he knew the great painter well and, moreover, that the latter had started work on the colonel's portrait. In a word, whenever someone had taken a hundred prisoners in one battle, Barguelot had captured three hundred in the next one, and it was as if each well-known person had said to himself, 'Now that I'm famous, it's time I met Colonel Barguelot.'

A servant placed a thin slice of pork on each plate. The finest tableware could not make up for the lack of food . . . Margont was very surprised to note that Barguelot ate nothing. He was not even served any food and did not touch his wine even though the claret was excellent, despite leaving the slightly bitter aftertaste of homesickness. Margont discovered that Barguelot had distinguished himself in numerous battles, owned a château near Nancy and had married a wealthy baroness, Marie-Isabelle de Montecy. Barguelot also mentioned his ancestors. He was from a long line of Dutch soldiers, the Van Hessens. His grandfather, the youngest son, had inherited nothing and, out of spite, had settled in France. He had had only one child, a daughter, so the Dutch name had died out. A procedure was under way to add the name Van Hessen to that of Barguelot.

At the end of the meal, Barguelot motioned discreetly to one of his servants. The man took his glass, poured a little more wine into it and placed it directly in the colonel's hand. Barguelot rose to his feet and everyone did likewise, holding their glasses.

'What a shame I haven't had time to give you an account of the liberation of Copenhagen in 1638 by the Dutch fleet. One of my ancestors was involved as a ship's captain. His ship was at the head of the squadron and distinguished itself by running the Swedish blockade. But it will have to wait for another time. Gentlemen!'

He brandished his glass and twenty others did likewise.

'To Moscow, soon to be Paris's little sister!'

'To Moscow!' all the officers replied in unison.

These fine words revitalised them as much as the good claret and they went their separate ways cheerfully enough, while all around them the horizon was studded with fires gleaming in the night sky. The next day the French would as usual be tramping through ashes.

The days that followed proved particularly frustrating for Margont. Despite all his efforts, he was unable to meet the other two suspects.

Colonel Fidassio was never available. Captain Nedroni, who assisted him, stood in the way. He played the role of compulsory go-between, the one who each time was sorry to say that the colonel was too busy for the time being but who would be delighted to pass on a message.

Nedroni took pride in his appearance without being ostentatious. His dark hair made his complexion look even paler, a feature that distinguished him from the other Italians.

Colonel Fidassio, whom Margont had managed to glimpse from a distance, seemed preoccupied. He rode alone, some way off from his regiment. The colonel was approaching thirty-five. His hair was brown, his huge face rendered even more thickset by his broad cheekbones. This brief portrait, sketched hurriedly and from afar, was all that Margont could obtain.

As for Colonel Pirgnon, he seemed very elusive. He was only rarely to be found with his regiment. Sometimes he would accompany a detachment out foraging for food; sometimes he would engage in conversation with the chief physician or with the person in charge of fodder; sometimes he would go off on a reconnaissance mission or gallop around on a horse taken from a Cossack to try to break it in. Margont had not managed to catch sight of him even once.

Lefine had recruited some men he could trust and the four suspects – four because Lefine, unlike Margont, considered that Delarse should not be ruled out – were watched discreetly day and night. Except for Pirgnon, who was followed whenever possible.

Time went by agonisingly slowly. Until 26 July.

On the morning of 26 July, IV Corps was in a state of feverish excitement. The Russians were there! Was it true? Or was it just a false rumour? No! The previous day the 1st Light Division of the 1st Reserve Cavalry Corps had engaged with the enemy in a serious skirmish. As was his custom, Marshal Murat, who was in command of this corps, had led a charge and wrought havoc. But the Russians were still there.

Prince Eugène was deploying his troops. An assault seemed imminent. Margont was waiting patiently at his position, in the Huard Brigade. This brigade belonged to the Delzons Division and, since this division was the spearhead of IV Corps, it would be in the front line of the attack. Like most of the officers and soldiers, Margont was completely unaware of the situation. He did not know if he was going to charge ten thousand Russians, fifty thousand, a hundred thousand . . . or three hundred thousand. Many of the combatants had come to terms with their ignorance of what was really at stake in the fighting, but not Margont. No, not knowing anything was exasperating for someone like him, who was so eager for knowledge of even the most useless kind (although for him it was impossible for any knowledge to be useless). So he did his best to make judgements from what he could observe.

Prince Eugène was prancing about from one end of his army to the other, followed by his flamboyant retinue of aides-de-camp, orderlies and generals. Everywhere troops were taking up position. The 8th Hussars, in their green pelisses, red breeches and shakos, had massed further ahead in the plain, in two lines. The Delzons Division was on the move – a long and broad column, dark blue and white in colour, topped by a forest of bayonets that glinted in the sunlight. Several regiments followed, wondering which of them would enter the combat and which would be held in reserve. The artillerymen were busy positioning their guns, crowding together to push a cannon or unloading munitions from the wagons. Elsewhere, squadrons of chasseurs were lining up, and regiments in column formation were hurrying forward. In the front line, skirmishers standing a few paces apart were taking shots at the Russians. The battlefield consisted of slopes, some of which were wooded, which meant that the Russians could not be seen. Only plumes of white smoke were visible from where their guns were firing.

'Begging your pardon, Captain, but do you think this is the battle we've all been waiting for?'

'How should I know?' Margont replied curtly, without turning his head.

'There wouldn't be all this commotion just for a few Cossacks, would there?'

Margont had no appetite for talk, least of all for small talk. He was inspecting the lie of the land. In what direction would they be made to charge? Probably straight ahead. What could be seen from that forest of birch trees opposite him? Was there an easily defendable position that he could fall back to with his men if the attack went badly?

'What's that road over there, Captain?'

Margont sighed heavily and turned towards the chatterbox. The soldier could hardly have been fifteen years old. His face was covered in red or suppurating spots.

'How old are you, boy?'

'Twenty!' the other replied, thrusting his chin out defiantly.

'Say eighteen and you'll be scarcely more credible.'

'Twenty, Captain! And I've already caught the pox!'

Margont smiled. He'd wanted to make him think acne was the pox.

'You're a canny one, but stop talking so much. Make the most of the silence. There'll be enough of a din when everyone starts firing.'

The young man puffed out his chest. A captain had just paid him a compliment! If it had been up to this adolescent, he would already have charged at the enemy with a thousand others like him, before even waiting for the artillery to prepare the ground.

'Begging your pardon again, Captain, but why don't you wear your Légion d'Honneur?'

Margont should really have been expecting this one.

'So that I don't lose it, and so as not to annoy the Russians even more. Wearing your Légion d'Honneur is like sewing on to your chest the inscription "Shoot at me".'

The reply disappointed the soldier and he made no attempt to disguise it. Margont was not surprised. His reply had two advantages: it was sincere and it shut the other person up.

'Captain Varebeaux and Sergeant Parin wear theirs.'

At this, the boy stood stock-still and did not utter another word.

Margont went back to examining the area. He was scrutinising the road to Vitebsk when a series of thunderclaps rang out. Tongues of flame and coils of thick white smoke were spewing from the French guns. Immediately, the gunners scurried about like excited ants. They were putting the guns back in place to compensate for the recoil, stuffing the water-soaked sponges of the rammer into the muzzles of the monsters, filling their long, hungry mouths with gunpowder, wadding and round shot, cramming it all down, then training it to adjust the aim . . . Finally, the firer, linstock in hand, looked straight at the chief gunner, waiting for the order to fire. A heavy, dense smoke built up around the batteries. The sound of mighty, ear-splitting explosions could be heard. A hail of round shot rained down on the woods opposite the Delzons Division. The foliage of the birch trees rustled and clusters of torn branches fell to the ground. A shell exploded in a bush and two mangled bodies were tossed into the air for all to see. A roar of triumph greeted this horrific spectacle.

'So, Captain, is it the Russians or not, today?' asked Lefine as he reached Margont. 'Whatever the case, company morale is good. For the time being . . .'

'Fernand, I've been thinking a lot about this name "Acosavan".'

Lefine blinked. 'Well, this is hardly the moment, that's for sure!'

'After a lot of thought I realised that "Acosavan" is an anagram of "Casanova". Perhaps it's only a coincidence. But if it's not, we can say that this man possessed a particularly ironic sense of humour. He was swearing to be faithful to Maria and love her for ever while his pseudonym was spitting in her face.'

'Very interesting. Perhaps we could talk about this again after the battle, because I don't know whether you've noticed, but there is indeed going to be a battle. I suggest that first we deal with the Tsar's armies. Then we can resume this conversation somewhere quieter. A mass grave, for example. Who knows?'

At that, Lefine went back to his position, muttering, 'Between Saber, who wants to change all the battle plans and give Prince Eugène a piece of his mind, and this one with his head in the clouds, we've got a right pair! It seems to me that in this army the dafter you are the higher up you get. Apologies to the Emperor. If only they'd let sergeants take command of the army, everything would be fine, I can tell you.'

Eventually the order came through to move forward. The Huard Brigade, consisting of the 8th Light, the 84th of the Line and the 1st Croat, was at the front, to the left. Margont still did not know if he was heading towards practically empty woods or a teeming mass of enemy soldiers. In fact, near the village of Ostrovno, Murat's cavalry and IV Corps had just engaged in a skirmish with the left flank of the Russian army. The latter was made up of the 4th Corps, commanded by General Count Ostermann-Tolstoy, reinforced by dragoons, hussars of the

Guard, Soussy's hussars and the artillery. He was also going to receive the support of General Konovnitsin, who had been put in command of the 3rd Division of the 3rd Corps. It was not yet the general assault the French so yearned for, but it might well turn into it.

CHAPTER 13

Part of the French infantry had deployed in line and was resolutely moving forward. At the head, lieutenants and captains were flourishing their swords or using them to point towards the enemy and exhort their men. They advanced with colours flying and drums beating. It was impossible not to think about death. Some were praying quietly; others humming martial tunes. They touched their amulets: a fiancée's lock of hair, a wedding ring, a letter, a bonesetter's charm. The loud-mouths were boasting, 'They still ain't going to get me, just like at Eylau!' 'Here I am!' 'Stick around, green coats! I want my Légion d'Honneur, I do!'

Margont, at the head of his company, was for his part struck by the beauty of the world around him: the soft green of the plain, the darker green of the woods, the blue sky. What a shame about the heavy roar of gunfire. His blue eyes took in the greenery opposite. He remembered a childhood friend, Catherine: an adolescent love affair they had shared one summer in the countryside and broken off the following one. In between had been ten months of painful waiting and an exchange of letters riddled with spelling mistakes. What could have become of her? She was probably bringing up children while he was perhaps going to die like a dog in some foreign place.

He suddenly felt a violent shove in the back and fell flat on the ground. Ten or twelve soldiers slumped down behind him.

Margont, staggered, still had no idea of what had just happened. A soldier rushed towards him. People were shouting. A black cannonball rolled swiftly along the grass, not far away. Another bounced off the butt of a musket lying on the ground, making it explode. Saber, wearing white gloves, lifted his friend up, grabbing him under the arms.

'Are you all right, Quentin? Are you hurt at all?'

Margont managed to get up unaided. He was covered in dirt. Next to him a sergeant was dusting down his uniform.

'Those Russian bastards! They think we're already dead and buried, but we'll show 'em.'

The line of infantrymen was filing past them. The woods were flecked with puffs of white smoke, large and small. Many Frenchmen were already strewn over the plain. Some were groaning as they tried to get up. Others were waving their arms pitifully or seemed to be asleep.

'This time we won't be tilting at windmills, eh, Quentin?'

Saber's face wore a triumphant smile but Margont could read the fear in his friend's eyes. Saber was putting on a self-assured air that would have charmed many a Parisienne. He was inventing his own stereotype, that of Lieutenant Saber the intrepid officer of the Imperial Army. He felt intuitively that over the years stereotypes sometimes became truths accepted by everyone.

Margont picked up his sword and the two officers resumed marching. The round shot and shells had made breaches in the line. Colonel Delarse, on horseback, was already twenty paces ahead of the brigade. A shell sprayed the infantrymen following him with splinters.

'The devils can fire all right,' muttered Saber, putting on a brave face.

The drummers beat the charge. The soldiers knew that music well enough! The line rushed forward, shouting. A corporal near Margont doubled up, clutching his abdomen. He did not fall but remained bent in this position, motionless.

A fusilier let out a squeal and began to limp, repeating, 'They got me, the bastards!'

Saber pushed him forward with a violent kick up the backside. 'Actors belong in the theatre. Real soldiers are in the front line.'

A lieutenant carrying the eagle standard was hit in the torso. Staggering, he handed over the precious banner to one of the supply sergeants of the flag escort, just before falling to his knees gazing at his wound. Two soldiers turned round to flee. The one faking an injury immediately did likewise.

Margont pointed his sword straight ahead. 'Gentlemen, you're wrong. The enemy is in this direction.'

Saber struck one of them on the thigh with the flat of his sword. 'Get back into the ranks!'

The three men obeyed. Saber was often very forceful in driving away fear in others, probably because he also thought it effective for himself. The line was now followed by a large straggling group of soldiers, out of breath or slightly wounded. At last they reached the wood. Then, for the first time since the start of the campaign, Margont sighted the Russian infantrymen. They were dressed in white trousers, green coats and black shakos. The officers had cocked hats with white plumes, worn in the Napoleonic style, or caps. The Russians were squaring up to the French, supported against tree trunks as they took aim or reloaded, or massed in the line waiting for contact, bayonets pointing straight in front. Others were gathered around the gunners, who were hurriedly reloading.

The impact of the wave of French soldiers breaking against the wall of Russians was fearsome. A Russian colonel on horseback lowered his sabre and shouted something out when the French were a few paces away from his infantrymen. The enemy line opened fire, disappearing amidst coils of white smoke to the accompaniment of thunderous noise.

The French fell to the ground on all sides. Delarse's horse was killed outright. The beast crashed to the ground before rolling on to its side, crushing the colonel's thigh so that he clenched his teeth to stifle his cries of pain. Soldiers hurried to his rescue. The animal was quickly turned over and, as soon as Delarse was on his feet again, he limped back to his men. Butts were coming down on jaws, bayonets and sabres being thrust into flesh relentlessly, muskets being· fired at close range. Margont, Saber and a few ordinary soldiers set upon the defenders of an artillery gun. Margont deflected a bayonet and ran his sword through the infantryman holding it. Saber slashed an artilleryman armed with a musket before pointing his sabre towards the officer commanding the gun.

'I challenge you.'

'Delighted, Lieutenant,' the Russian replied in French, while saluting him with his sabre.

The fools, thought Margont. Saber positioned himself side on and lunged forward, aiming for the head. The Russian parried and counterattacked. Saber leapt nimbly to the side and sliced his opponent's wrist three-quarters through. The officer turned pale, dropped his weapon and reeled. Saber put the point of his blade to the man's throat.

'Sir, you are my prisoner.'

The Russian gave a vague sign of acknowledgement, blinked and fell unconscious. Saber set about bandaging the officer's wound. There were only two gunners left, encircled by a dozen Frenchmen. The first was sitting astride a soldier lying on the ground and hammering away at the man's face with his fist. A blow from a musket butt rendered him unconscious. The second had only a fuse in his hand. The infantrymen keeping him at bay turned their heads in the direction of a nearby explosion and immediately the Russian rushed towards his gun. Margont had been suspecting such a ploy and leapt towards him. But he saw to his horror that the Russian was not attempting to fire the cannon and thus send Saber and those around him up in smoke. No, what he intended was to thrust the fuse into the bunghole of a powder keg. Margont brought down his blade on the Russian's hand, slicing through the tendons and putting a quick end to his action. The gunner stood still as he was surrounded by men with bayonets. He clasped his wound with his left hand. Margont and he looked at each other bemused, the captain astonished by this suicidal gesture and the Russian rather embarrassed, like a child caught with his finger in the honey pot. Margont struck him a brutal blow in the face with the hilt of his sword. The Russian hunched up, screaming.

'Pull yourself together, Captain, I beg you,' a sergeant intervened.

Margont did not hear him. He was hurling insults, taut and wild with anger.

'Poor fool! Madman! Fanatic!'

The prisoner was hastily led away in tears. Margont, motionless, arms dangling by his sides, watched the gunner leave.

The attack had been short-lived. Clusters of soldiers were still fighting but most of the Russians had fallen back. In the distance lieutenants could be seen waving their sabres to rally their men while the colonel who had given the order to fire, recognisable by his portliness, was breaking his horse into a trot to spur his troops on. The Russian musketeers were hastily reloading; the wounded bandaging a hand, an arm, a calf, a thigh or a forehead . . .

Colonel Delarse was shouting furiously: 'Charge! Charge! Don't let them recover! Come with me, Huard Brigade! Forward all!'

But the French were hesitating. He noticed Margont and rushed towards him.

'Captain Margont, set an example! Charge!'

'Colonel, the Russians far outnumber—'

'So what? They're only Russians! There were far more of them at Austerlitz.'

A roar of triumph interrupted the conversation.

'The Russians are scarpering!'

The enemy front was retreating in good order. The French infantry, galvanised by the spectacle, rushed forward with a great roar. Then the Russian line changed shape. Its mass gradually thinned out as the numbers fleeing increased. It began to move faster and faster. The potbellied colonel seized hold of a flag and brandished the Russian double-headed eagle. The emblem stood out majestically against an orange disc rimmed with gilded laurel leaves and crested with a crown. The light green background bore a white diagonal cross decorated with laurel leaves and gilded crowns. Suddenly, without any warning, the Russians took to their heels. It was like a long dyke that had just given way under pressure. The French, giddy with success, were running around, leaping over the corpses and the tree roots. They felt capable of pressing on as far as Moscow in one go.

Margont stopped to take stock of the situation. He could hear the sound of fierce shooting on his right, way behind. He looked about anxiously for a senior officer. In vain. He grabbed a corporal by the arm, bringing him to a halt.

'Where are Colonel Pégot and Colonel Delarse? And General Huard?'

'I don't know, Captain.'

Margont let him go and the NCO rushed straight ahead. Margont noticed Saber, who was examining the pelisse of a hussar lying at his feet.

'Irénée, we've gone too far forward. We risk being surrounded.'

Saber noted the irresistible momentum of the French, who were carrying with them Russian musketeers, foot chasseurs and hussars, like a river sweeping twigs and branches along with it.

'That's clear, but we still have to pursue them to prevent them regrouping.'

'But what about us? Shouldn't we regroup, perhaps?'

'I quite agree. Let's catch up with Pégot or Delarse.'

'But where on earth are they?'

'Where? In front. Where do you think?'

The two men began running once more. Saber had the quirk of occasionally putting his hand on a tree trunk. He wanted to 'touch wood' whenever he was fighting. But he'd rather have been cut to shreds than admit it.

Twenty or thirty yards further on they reached the edge of the wood. Colonel Delarse was trotting back and forth to muster his troops. He was riding a magnificent Russian stallion. Victory could disorganise regiments as much as defeat. Delarse was signalling to the stragglers to hurry up, and to the over-eager to slow down. Soldiers of the light infantry were herding the prisoners together. A lieutenant from the 8th Light was brandishing a sabre of the Russian hussars.

'Victory! Victory!'

The French were bewitched by this magic word. The roar spread faster than a powder trail, and muskets and sabres were brandished aloft. Margont could not resist a smile. He was alive and they had won! By the time they had regrouped they would be ready to follow hot on the heels of the Russians, and capturing them would be as easy as picking flowers.

'Moscow, here we come!' shouted Saber.

'Moscow, here we come!' replied the whole line in unison.

'Long live the Emperor! Long live Prince Eugène!'

There was a proverbial saying that a soldier or junior officer could see no further than the end of his company. Nothing could be truer. The Huard Brigade, although it had broken through the Russian lines, had indeed advanced too fast and too far. It now found itself in the middle of the Russian army, cut off from all support. The risk of being encircled was the price it paid for its daring. Margont noticed a stirring in the wood opposite, which was separated from them by a clearing two hundred paces wide. Something was moving; something huge. Margont attempted to convince himself that it was merely an illusion produced by the wind making the bushes and the foliage sway. But it was not that. A sort of Leviathan of the forests was crawling towards them, camouflaged by the vegetation.

Margont was about to speak when someone yelled out: 'They're coming back!'

CHAPTER 14

Silhouetted figures appeared. They were everywhere, crowded against one another.

'They pulled themselves together quickly,' murmured Saber admiringly.

Margont knew that his friend was mistaken. The Russians were too numerous for them to be the remnants of the regiments that the French had just broken through. So what now? Were they going to fight again? And then? It wouldn't be the first time. Margont realised that the shakos of these particular Russians were topped with long black plumes. Only certain regiments of grenadiers and carabineers wore this distinctive item of uniform. It meant that he was dealing with crack troops. Eventually, the enemy poured out into the clearing, wave upon wave of Russians in serried ranks. The wood and the forests seemed to be spewing them forth.

Russian reserve troops had rallied their fleeing comrades and were now launching a counterattack. The French opened fire and Margont saw the green coats turn red with blood, and dozens of Russians collapse in a single movement. The moment of contact produced a roar of explosions and shouting. Margont was running, his sword in one hand and his pistol in the other. He was aware only of what was happening immediately around him. A grenadier took aim at him. He hurled himself at the man, deflected the weapon by a sword stroke and thrust the blade into his torso. Another grenadier charged at him to run him through but Margont shot him in the chest with his pistol. Two grenadiers simultaneously impaled Margont's neighbour to the right, while the one to his left was hit full in the face by a musket butt. Margont recoiled but tripped over a corpse and found himself on the ground. Just as he was getting up, he had to ward off another bayonet attack. His assailant brandished his musket aloft with the intention of shattering his skull. Swiftly, Margont struck him a violent blow to the heel with his sword. The grenadier collapsed, howling. A Russian sergeant, thinking that Margont was wounded, merely hit him on the shoulder with his musket butt without even stopping running. Margont let out a cry of pain. A grenadier ran over his body at the double and two other Russians leapt over what they assumed to be a dying man.

Margont jumped to his feet. There were still a few Frenchmen frantically jabbing away with their bayonets or whirling their muskets so as to knock out two Russians at a time. But most were fleeing, swept away by the tidal wave of Russians. Arms were raised, begging for mercy; men on the ground were being run through with bayonets . . . Margont broke into a run to get back to his own men. He went past a captain trying to get up at the same time as training a pistol. This officer shot a grenadier and, in reprisal, four Russians fired at him at point-blank range. The chaos was indescribable. A Russian was running in front of Margont but the captain refused to strike an enemy in the back, as much out of pity as out of a sense of honour, but also because he was himself terrified of feeling a searing pain, of falling and turning round to see a grenadier above him, wielding a bloodstained bayonet.

Margont pushed the Russian forward with all the strength he could muster and the man fell sprawling to the ground.

Margont turned round. A horde of Russians were at their heels. He saw to his horror that a Croatian infantryman was rushing at him and getting ready to fire. It was indeed he, Margont, who was being aimed at and, what is more, by someone from his own side! He thought, Already . . . The weapon went off and Margont could no longer hear the yelling and the crackle of gunfire. The Croat overtook him at top speed, brushing past him without taking any more notice of him than if he had been a fallen tree. Margont could feel no pain. The bullet had missed him. He could still see the expression of terror on the soldier's face. He said to himself that the man would have trampled over his own mother without noticing her if she had had the misfortune to be in his way.

The French were hurriedly withdrawing to the wood they had gone through in triumph a few moments earlier. Three Russian foot chasseurs suddenly emerged from a tangle of bushes. They levelled their muskets, calmly took aim at the routed Frenchmen and killed one apiece. Two more appeared further on and claimed two more victims. Then another, but he missed his target. They had been hiding during the Russian defeat and were now taking advantage of the reversal of the situation. Each time a chasseur showed himself, a terrible lottery began. The fleeing soldiers continued to run, repeating inwardly: 'Not me, not me.' The shot was fired, a man collapsed and the others breathed a sigh of relief.

In this odious little game, Margont's officer's epaulettes increased tenfold his chance of being picked. Margont trusted himself to his lucky star but, by the look of it, that star was not shining as much as his golden epaulettes because a chasseur hidden behind a tree stump suddenly stood up and took aim at him. Margont risked his all and rushed towards the soldier, yelling as he did so. The Russian was taken aback. He took longer than planned to aim and this delay annoyed him. Just at the moment when he was at last going to fire, Margont leapt to one side, then unexpectedly changed direction once more, while continuing to run towards the Russian, shouting and brandishing his sword. Margont was near, very near; the chasseur had him in his line of sight. Margont made as if to jump to the side once more. The Russian anticipated this change of direction, which never happened, and fired too much to the left. Suddenly, he threw his weapon to the ground and fled.

Margont stopped to get his breath back. He turned round towards his pursuers. The Russians were progressing, pointing their bayonets in front of them. He noticed a Russian captain intrepidly leading his company on. The officer had lost his shako. He was running, brandishing his sabre in his outstretched arm. Margont did not want him to be killed. Here was someone of the same rank, the same age and the same enthusiasm that had driven him in his early battles, before Eylau and Spain. It was like seeing his own image reflected in a Russian mirror. The grenadier must have been hit by a bullet since he crumpled on to his side. Margont felt a tug on his sleeve.

'Got to get out of here, Captain. Things are going badly,' someone declared in a tense voice.

'Leave him. He's already dead,' another called out.

The soldier let go of his sleeve. The Russian officer straightened up by leaning on his elbows. Margont started to retreat again. He noticed Colonel Delarse at the edge of the wood and hurried towards him. Delarse was furious.

'Those wretched Russians. They're like swings: the further you push them away the faster they come back at you. Get your breath back, Captain Margont. You're more asthmatic than I am.'

'Colonel, where's General Delzons? Where's the Roussel Brigade? And the Sivray and Alméras Brigades?'

'The whole handsome lot are on their way, Captain Margont.'

The reply was only for form's sake because it was quite obvious that the colonel had no idea of what was happening.

Margont turned round and gazed at the French artillery at the other end of the plain. He peered at the groups of troopers and the comings and goings of the messengers. Somewhere over there was Prince Eugène and his general staff. Margont knew that his chances of survival depended on decisions being made there. Prince Eugène seemed as remote a figure as God and, at this moment, more powerful than the Almighty Himself. The Russians were still following on the heels of the Huard Brigade. Margont told himself that he had to keep on running, running to the other end of the plain, to the French artillery. That was where his own side was: batteries, fresh troops eager to fight it out, Eugène, Murat . . . Then he noticed Russian hussars galloping across the plain. The French were caught between a rock and a hard place.

Colonel Delarse urged his horse into a trot. He looped back

and met up with Margont again after a brief but unsuccessful attempt to rally the fleeing band of soldiers.

'Let's go straight through them,' he exclaimed, pointing at the troopers with his sabre.

It was at that moment that the hussars charged. The French infantrymen were too disorganised to form square, a formation that would have provided effective protection against cavalry. They immediately paid the price: the cavalrymen wove in and out of the scattered groups, encircled some and began slashing and hacking on all sides. Some hussars went at it furiously, as if intent on massacring the brigade single-handedly. Others were content merely to gallop towards a handful of men and fire pistol shots before tugging the reins and pulling away. This tactic bore fruit: groups harried in this way were slowed down considerably. The Russian infantry eventually caught up with them and slaughtered them. Margont heard the sound of a horse galloping behind him. His neighbour to the left collapsed whilst a hussar rode past with a blood-soaked sabre in his hand. Another hussar suddenly appeared from behind him. He stood up in his stirrups until he was almost fully erect, holding his sabre aloft. Margont brandished his sword above his head and managed to deflect the blow. The horse continued running and curtailed the engagement, and the two men escaped with only sore wrists. Another cavalryman, coming in from the right, pointed his sabre towards Margont and spurred his horse into a gallop. Margont faced up to him and stared at the blade he was to ward off. The hussar veered away at the last moment and gave up on him.

Margont turned round and saw the frightening spectacle of

the green infantry arriving at the double, bristling with bayonets and now close to him. He raced once more towards his own lines. In turn a hussar spurred his horse on towards Margont. If Margont did not stop to face up to him, the cavalryman would kill him. And if he did stop, his opponent would ride off, like the previous one, leaving him in the hands of the infantry. Margont threw his sword to the ground like a panic-stricken deserter. This gesture convinced the hussar that he was being handed an easy victory and he did not turn his horse away. But at the last minute, Margont spun round. The Russian was standing up in his stirrups, flourishing his sabre. Margont leapt at him and clung on to his pelisse. As he leant to the side to deliver his blow, the hussar lost his balance and the two men fell. Margont immediately picked himself up and ran towards the horse as the hussar recovered from his concussion but not from his surprise. Margont mounted the animal and spurred it into a gallop, roaring with laughter.

He caught sight of Delarse grappling with three hussars, attracted like wasps to his honey-coloured braiding. Margont would have attempted to help him if he'd been armed. He had to make do with trying to find where the Russian hussars stowed their horse pistols. The colonel was amazing. Staying perfectly straight on his mount, he thrust his sabre into the side of the adversary to his right. He immediately withdrew the blade and swung round sharply to slash the face of the cavalry-man attacking him on the left. The last Russian, who was further behind, trained his pistol at the colonel's back. Darval, Delarse's adjutant, who had himself just finished dealing with another hussar, brought his sabre down on the pelisse slung over the Russian's left shoulder. This popular mode of dress protected the arm undefended by the sabre. The blade sliced through the garment, which softened the blow enough to prevent a serious wound. The hussar turned tail and fled.

Margont was stunned. He, who was always criticising his friends for judging people by appearances and having preconceptions, was now quite by accident being taught a lesson on the subject by Delarse! Margont had thought the colonel was at death's door but he now had to admit that there was far more life in him than in those two hussars who had set upon him. He immediately restored Delarse to the status of possible suspect.

The situation remained critical: the Huard Brigade was pouring back to the French position in disarray. A captain galloped up to Margont and bombarded him with questions. Where was General Huard? What were the enemy forces? Margont did not reply. He was merely an empty shell, staring at a man who was gesticulating and raising his voice. The officer trotted away, shaking his head.

Russian and French soldiers were engaging in bayonet duels, shattering bodies with their musket butts, relentlessly shooting one another . . . The artillerymen, in their blue coats and trousers, were regrouping around their precious guns. A chaotic mêlée was taking place amidst swirling dust. The hussars had changed tactics. They were no longer harrying but charging and slashing at anything blue. Their dexterity was impressive. Margont noticed one galloping his way through. A horizontal sword-stroke to the right sent a gunner crashing to the ground, then a sideways stroke to the left made a soldier fall to his knees clutching his face, and a vertical stroke to the right sent a lieutenant toppling backwards . . . His horse shuddered and collapsed on to its hindquarters, like a dog sitting! Margont had never seen anything like it. The animal was bleeding profusely from its right flank.

Someone grabbed him by the arms and shook him frantically.

'Captain, do something! Save us!'

It was the young soldier who had criticised him for not displaying his Légion d'Honneur. Tears were streaming down his face. He was talking incoherently. He ended by saying that they had to run away but, confused and distraught, he made straight for the Russians. A musketeer whirled his weapon about and brought it down on the nape of the boy's neck, sending him to the ground. The Russian brandished his bayonet but Margont rushed at him and smashed straight into him, this time knocking him down. He picked up the musket and hammered his opponent with the butt.

'Enough! Enough! Enough!' he yelled as if he were the one being hit.

But he continued to strike him. When the Russian raised his arms to his face he gave him a blow to the stomach and when the Russian put his hands on his stomach he smashed his jaw or his ribs.

A hussar arrived at a gentle trot as his horse had been slowed down by the hand-to-hand fighting. Margont left the musketeer in order to hit the cavalryman in the stomach with the musket butt. The horse decided to take its master back towards his lines, bent double. The pounding of horses' hoofs could be heard. Its intensity was increasing rapidly until it became deafening. Murat's lancers were charging, flying to the rescue of the artillerymen and the Huard Brigade. The Russian infantry were well and truly run through. By flinging themselves flat on their stomachs they were beyond reach of the cavalry's sabres but not of the lances, which struck them in the back. The 92nd of the Line arrived in a column and enthusiastically joined in the fray. Then it was the turn of the 8th Hussars to charge. The Russians were at last pushed back after suffering considerable losses.

CHAPTER 15

THERE were dead and wounded everywhere, as far as the eye could see. Margont, still suffering from concussion, was leaning against a weeping willow – a bittersweet irony. In some places, bodies were lying still locked in a deadly embrace. A magnificent grey horse was lying on its side, scraping the ground with its hoofs, trying to get back on its feet. All that was left of its forelegs was stumps. Everywhere men were groaning, crying, calling for help, pleading with the survivors or insulting them for their indifference. Many of the wounded were clamouring for a drink. Margont began to wander among them, tossing aside an empty gourd here and picking up a full one there from a dead body where it was no longer needed. He wondered about this question of thirst. Was this how the body tried to make up for the loss of blood? Or was it a psychological reaction? People often said, 'If you're wounded, drink some wine.' Did they think the body short-sighted enough to mistake one sort of red liquid for another?

'Thank yer, officer, sir. Will yer 'ave some wine as well?' asked a French grenadier, handing his gourd to Margont.

His thick blond moustache glistened with drops of water. He was clenching his stomach to stanch the flow of blood.

'Sorry, too much wine is bad for the health,' Margont answered him.

The soldier began to laugh but pain contorted his smile. 'That's a good one, Captain!'

Margont only had to stretch out his arm to open the knapsack of a Russian musketeer lying flat on his stomach. He took out a flask, opened it, tasted the contents and handed it to the grenadier.

'Vodka?'

The man's moustache twitched with pleasure. 'Is it Russian wine?'

'Stronger stuff than that.'

The grenadier downed what was left in the flask in one gulp.

'I feel like searching all the kitbags on this bloody plain!'

Margont patted him on the shoulder and moved on, motioning to some exhausted stretcher-bearers.

He stopped in front of a young hussar. He had been slashed across the chest with a sabre. Something was poking out of his slit coat. Intrigued, Margont took hold of the object. It was a small Russian icon of a slender Virgin Mary holding the new-born Christ in her arms. Strangely, the look on the mother's face was uncertain: her joy seemed tinged with sadness, as if she had an intuition that her happiness would end in suffering. Margont replaced the icon on the corpse's heart. A little further on he came across the body of the musketeer he had struck. The Russian was breathing oddly, breathing in and out in short gasps, as if wanting to taste life a little longer, on the tip of his tongue, before dying. Margont again motioned to the stretcher-bearers and moved on. He was lucky enough to find his sword, then spent the night going from one wounded soldier to the next, giving them a drink, promising to have a letter delivered to a wife or relative . . .

Just before dawn, he was so exhausted that he could hardly keep his eyes open, so he slowly made his way back to his regiment. Despite all his efforts and those of the numerous volunteers, there seemed to be just as many calls for help. He passed a dozen or so infantrymen of the 92nd attempting to put out a fire by urinating on it in one concerted effort. But the men were so drunk that the spurts of urine merely soaked their trousers, giving rise to screams of laughter or scuffles. This scene encouraged Margont to indulge in his favourite game: watching people.

Many others had also decided to give some meaning to their lives by helping the wounded. Some acted out of high-mindedness; others out of superstition, to thank Heaven or fate for having spared them; others out of a sense of guilt, to justify having survived. Margont called them the 'saviours'. But a considerable number of soldiers preferred to avoid this harsh reality by drinking themselves into a stupor or deserting. Some even ended up committing suicide. These were the 'runaways'. There were other categories: the profiteers, who stole from the dead and the wounded who were too weak to defend themselves.

Margont sat down against a birch tree, utterly spent. A few feet away a strange spectacle was unfolding: in front of other lancers and laughing French hussars, a Polish lancer was embracing a Russian hussar. The two men were not fighting but dancing, albeit clumsily. A waltz. The Russian appeared to be dead drunk. Another Pole also wanted to dance with the hussar but he accidentally let go of him and he collapsed. He was not so much dead drunk as dead. The second Pole got him back on his feet, grabbed him around the waist and in turn began to dance, egged on by the audience. These belonged to the category of the 'exorcists'. They indulged in morbid games and their imagination was boundless. But the rule was always the same: to poke fun at death, to demystify it, to debunk it. By acting like this they were less afraid. However, they sacrificed some of their humanity in the process. Were they really winners in the end? Then there were the 'dumbstruck', who wandered about aimlessly, silent, cut off from the world, unable to take the slightest initiative; the 'desperate', who wept endlessly and who needed to be watched in case they blew their brains out; the 'believers', who prayed, hoping to find a mystical meaning in this chaos . . . Then, to bring this incomplete catalogue to a temporary conclusion, there was the vast group of those who thanked one another for having provided mutual support, who celebrated the baptism of fire of the younger ones, who boasted of their exploits . . . These Margont dubbed the 'reckless but harmless' or the 'humane', because one way or another everyone belonged in part to this group.

Margont slid slowly down the tree trunk and stretched himself out on the ground. The grass stroked his face. Sleep felled him more effectively than the gunfire from a whole Russian battery.

The Russians withdrew the following day. It was not the titanic confrontation between the two armies that the Emperor so greatly longed for. It was 'only' the fighting at Ostrovno.

*

Margont felt himself being unceremoniously lifted up. He mumbled something, was dropped and went crashing to the ground. He leapt back up, his hand on the pommel of his sword. Two infantrymen in bloodstained uniforms were staring at him in consternation, open-mouthed and pale-faced with huge purple rings around their eyes.

'We had no idea, Captain . . .'

'Yes, we had no idea . . .'

'But we would have realised, Captain . . .'

'You had no idea what?' yelled Margont.

His anger paralysed the two men. Then he noticed a cart on which French corpses were being piled up. There was another for the Russians.

'You wanted to throw me into that cart, didn't you?' he shouted.

'But the thing is . . . you were lying there like that . . .'

'But we would have realised that you weren't . . . that you weren't you know what,' the second gravedigger assured him.

Margont looked at his uniform. It was spattered with blood, the blood of those he had wounded or killed, the bodily remains of men blown to pieces by round shot.

'Check that all those you've put in that wretched cart really are dead,' he ordered, more by way of punishment than in the vain hope of saving anyone.

The soldiers carried out the order, still terrified by what they had superstitiously thought was someone rising from the dead.

Margont ascertained the whereabouts of his regiment. On his way there he looked at his watch, an extravagance that had cost him a fortune but whose mathematical precision was in keeping with his own methodical mind. It was four o'clock. He did not grasp immediately what the two hands were stubbornly telling him. He called out to a cavalryman from the 9th Chasseurs who was wandering about in search of a comrade. The fellow confirmed that it was already late afternoon. Margont also learnt that more fighting had taken place that very morning, near Vitebsk, though it had not lasted long.

Margont bought a handsome horse with a brown coat and a black mane from a crafty mounted chasseur, who swore that he had set off on the campaign with a spare mount. The beast was surprisingly robust and well fed.

'He's called Wagram,' the seller explained.

'For the price you're charging me, you could have included its Russian saddle.'

'Not at all, Captain! It's my horse! He's called Wagram!'

'That horse is more likely to be called Ostrovno than Wagram.'

At that moment Lefine arrived.

'So you've just joined the hussars of the Russian Guard, have you, Captain?'

'He's called Wagram!' the chasseur stubbornly maintained.

Margont shrugged his shoulders. 'Wagram or Jena, as long as it's not called Eylau or Spain.'

The chasseur walked away grumbling about his poor old father who'd bled himself dry, struggling to plough a barren field in order to be able to buy Wagram for his son from the meagre proceeds of his hard toil. His poor father must now be turning in his grave, hearing today the insults of 'certain people'.

Lefine felt the horse's flanks. 'I've never seen such a fat horse.'

'But all our horses were like that before the start of the campaign.'

Lefine continued to stroke the animal's belly. He was envious of this stomach, which was so much fuller than his own.

'He's so impressive that next to him our cavalry look as if they're mounted on dogs. What's he to be called, then?'

'Macbeth.'

'Macbeth. What gibberish is that? I prefer Wagram. I can show you a good shop for a saddle,' he added, indicating the battlefield with a broad sweep of his arm.

'Let's go back to the regiment for news of our friends.'

'On that very subject I'm pleased to find you still in one piece. Antoine, Irénée and I have been looking for you everywhere.'

'I was knocked out by a musket butt,' Margont lied.

'Before returning to the regiment, I'm going to take you somewhere. But first I want to tell you what Colonel Delarse has been up to. The farce began as soon as the fighting had ended. The colonel wanted an interpreter. While everyone was scurrying around trying to find one for him, he was moving from one prisoner to another trying to make himself understood, because patience isn't his strong point. Dozens of people were staring at him goggle-eyed, not understanding a word. He was shouting: "Where is Lieutenant Nakalin? Lieutenant Nakalin, you ignorant peasants!" In the end they found a Russian trumpeter who spoke French.'

'Why didn't they get a Polish lancer to act as an interpreter?'

Lefine looked up to the heavens. 'They'd brought the colonel at least fifteen of them but he sent them all packing. He's no longer on speaking terms with the Poles. He thinks they waited too long before charging to extricate us from the green coats.'

Margont gritted his teeth.

'Well, yes. It is pretty stupid, of course,' Lefine concluded.

'As he can't blame it on bad luck, he's blaming it on the Poles. It's a typical reaction. The Russians, Prussians and Austrians have been doing the same thing for centuries. So then what happened?'

'In a nutshell, the Russian translated but they were still no better off. Would the colonel give up? No chance. He then did the rounds of the hospitals. He didn't find out anything about the mysterious Nakalin, so off he went to walk around the battlefield with his musician, questioning the wounded who hadn't yet been picked up.'

'Does your story have an ending? I should remind you that you're not being paid for wasting your breath.'

'The colonel eventually found his Nakalin. His horse had been disembowelled by a cannonball and had fallen over, trapping his rider's leg. I'm taking you to them. They're playing chess.'

The scene was unreal, absurd. Whilst all around them men were limping about or supporting their bleeding companions, Colonel Delarse and his Russian lieutenant were playing chess. Each seated on a box, they were moving their pieces whilst the grass about them was strewn with remains: sabres, shakos, bayonets, cannonballs, knapsacks, muskets.

'No sooner has he emerged from one slaughter than he's rushing into the next,' muttered Margont.

French officers were watching the game, which cannot have helped the concentration of the Russian, a solitary red pawn surrounded by fifteen or so dark blue pawns. Nakalin was barely twenty. His dark curly hair was dishevelled and his uniform speckled with blades of grass. He had a disconcerting way of playing. He almost never looked at the chessboard and when it was his turn, his startled look gave the impression that he was seeing the position of the pieces for the first time. He would immediately seize one of them and move it somewhere else. You could have sworn that his decisions were totally random. He would look away before he had even finished placing his bishop or his knight and would once more immediately lose himself in contemplation of the flood of wounded. Colonel Delarse seemed puzzled. He would think long and hard but when he placed his fingers on a piece, it was to play it. 'A piece touched is a piece played': he adhered strictly to the rules. When attacked by the queen, the Russian responded by moving his knight, without even a cursory glance at the chessboard. Margont was fascinated by the fact that this man was capable of memorising the game so well that he could play in his head. Delarse took the knight and smiled. Not for long. The Russian had conceded the centre of the board but, when he unleashed his attack to the side, his moves considerably restricted Delarse's room for manoeuvre.

'Mate within six moves,' Nakalin announced.

Delarse was shocked. He lost within four.

'Checkmate. There was a better combination,' the Russian declared soberly.

'Let's have another game!' exclaimed Delarse, who was already lining up his troops again.

'I'm tired. I've been wounded.'

'Are you conceding the return match?'

'"Concede" and "surrender" are words that have no equivalent in the Russian language when the motherland is at war.'

Delarse began a new game but the lieutenant did not move a single piece. After a few minutes Delarse stood up in annoyance.

'Very well. You've won the game with the little wooden soldiers. But I'm the one who won the game out there on the plain! The battlefield is strewn with green pawns and red knights.'

At last the Russian came to life. His cheeks reddened and his expression became more animated.

'Yes, but that particular game is not over yet . . .'

Delarse turned towards one of his captains. 'I want him to be well treated! See that he has a tent, blankets and proper food. Because when I defeat him I don't want him to be able to say he was in a weakened state. Let him have a chess set as well! I don't want him claiming that he was prevented from practising.'

The colonel then strode quickly towards Margont.

'So, Captain! You are dishevelled and badly shaven. Why do you look like a beaten man?'

'I apologise, Colonel. But thanks to us the Russian army had a close shave.'

'When one has wit, one should put it to better use than trying to be clever.'

'By playing chess, for example?'

Delarse turned round to watch Nakalin, who was being led away by two soldiers. The Russian was walking with his arms folded, as if out for a stroll.

'What an odd character! I might as well have been playing on my own.'

'True indeed. It seemed as if everything around him was more interesting than the game: the singing of the birds, the cloud formations, the weather . . .'

'He'll escape.'

'Worse than that, it's as if we haven't even captured him. Colonel, may I enquire how you met him?'

'He's a well-known chess player. He was born into the Ukrainian nobility and leads a dilettante life. He does nothing, has no interests, forgets to attend dinners he's been invited to . . . He lives only for chess. But what a player he is! He has beaten Tsar Alexander himself, the Emperor of Austria, General Bagration, General Kutuzov . . . Here's an amusing anecdote about the latter. That crafty old fox Kutuzov was being given a hard time when he 'accidentally' knocked the chessboard on to the floor. He apologised, explaining that the loss of an eye in the war had affected his sense of distance. But to Kutuzov's chagrin, Nakalin declared that it didn't matter, picked up all the pieces and put them back exactly as they were. Kutuzov was then beaten soundly by his opponent. How I would have liked to see his face that day! I know all this because I'm a member of several chess clubs. Nakalin has acquired such a reputation that he spends his whole life being invited to various European courts and by keen chess players. His travels are paid for and he goes from palace to stately home – a very nice life. He's the only person in the world to have defeated as many generals as the Emperor. But in his own field. Unfortunately, his successes are more of a curse than a blessing because it is increasingly difficult to rouse him from the apathy he's helplessly sinking into. One match is not enough to stimulate him. He needs to play against ten opponents at a time and be literally surrounded by chessboards. Or else play blindfolded, with a friend whispering the other player's moves in his ear. He cannot do anything except play chess. Not even be a real soldier because he was accepted into the Guard and given a commission only because he beat Grand Duke Constantine Pavlovitch.'

Colonel Delarse's face clouded over with regret. If only he had managed to beat Nakalin! Then, indirectly, he would have demonstrated his superiority over all the others: the Tsar, Kutuzov, Bagration, Emperor Francis I . . .

The man was wandering amongst the bodies, the air pungent with gunpowder, burning and blood. Everywhere there were bodies lying on the grass. And yet he felt at ease. It was as if this charnel house had become his true home. He told himself that he was going mad but it was a madness he revelled in.

He thought again about all those years it had taken him to discover his liking for death. One part of him had had to fight night and day against these desires before finally giving in, utterly exhausted. Or perhaps it was because of the war. He had witnessed so much killing . . . Differences and limits seemed more and more blurred. He felt nothing but confusion.

CHAPTER 16

THE following day Margont was summoned again by Prince Eugène. He had to wait a long time until the comings and goings of generals, aides-de-camp and dispatch riders had ceased. It was like some kind of ball. A constant stream of cavalrymen dressed all in blue and gold came prancing along before merging into the excited throng surrounding the prince. The latter had sought out a shady grove. With his general staff around him, he seemed to be listening to four conversations at once. He had to commit everything to memory, make decisions about it all and ensure that his orders were faithfully carried out. The discussion concerned troop deployments, the enemy's presumed routes of retreat, tactical possibilities, early estimates of losses, the names of officers who had distinguished themselves or not lived up to expectation . . . The Emperor, exasperated at seeing the Russians escape his grasp once more, had unleashed his fury on all and sundry and, when the Emperor was angry, his rage made the whole army tremble. The tension on these faces was in sharp contrast to the calm that prevailed on the plains and in the surrounding woods.

Eventually, the prince was able to extricate himself and motioned to Margont to join him. Margont saluted him respectfully, noting that Eugène was under so much pressure that he frequently gave people murderous looks.

'Captain Margont, I'm glad to know you've survived,

because your brigade got into serious difficulty.' But the prince spoke mechanically, as if commenting on the fine weather. 'Let's go for a short walk. Be brief and give me good news!'

Having decided not to talk about the four colonels he suspected, Margont was glad not to have to discover how Prince Eugène would have reacted to such bad news.

'I've scarcely made any progress, Your High—'

'Oh, no! Oh, no!'

The prince did not shout, he yelled. He sat down on a tree stump and motioned to his escort to move away. The grenadiers of the Italian Royal Guard deployed around them. Margont was enjoying the refreshing shade and the tranquil surroundings. Now that the guns had fallen silent, the birds were singing once more. The grove looked like a corner of paradise that had accidentally fallen to earth. The blood rushed to Eugène's face.

'A supply system that supplies no one, the desertions, the Cossacks, the Russians whom we constantly lose track of, this gruelling pursuit of the enemy that's about to resume, and now you! Tell me everything.'

The 'everything' in question took less than a minute. The prince folded his arms.

'Carry on talking. And if you've nothing to say, just move your lips. Otherwise that lot will pounce on me.'

Margont followed Eugène's gaze and noticed a new gathering of messengers and officers waiting patiently or impatiently in the company of General Triaire.

'Don't worry about your investigation remaining confidential,' the prince said at once. 'Your brigade suffered a humiliating reverse in the Russian counterattack. All those watching our conversation will think that you're reporting back to me on the conduct of your superiors.'

Now it was Margont's turn to become annoyed. He was likely to be taken for one of the prince's spies or an informer. If this rumour spread, he would lose most of his friends and be treated like an outcast by his own regiment. Nevertheless, he took advantage of the opportunity to ask the question that had been troubling him since the start of the investigation.

'Well, Your Highness, if we have to speak, it might as well be about something interesting. May I know why finding this murderer means so much to you? I know the official reason but I wondered whether there was another.'

Surprisingly, instead of snapping at him, Eugène remained calm.

'Captain Margont, either you are exasperating or you are very perceptive. In fact, you are both at once. When one is perceptive, one is often exasperating.'

That's normal, given that we live in a world that operates on lies, Margont added to himself.

Eugène was reticent. He glanced again at the messengers waiting patiently. With a wave of the arm he could summon them to his side and Margont would be swallowed up in the excited throng. Margont decided to press home his advantage.

'The reasons you have put forward to explain my investigation are valid, that's certain. However, I have been wondering about your personal interest in this. General Triaire would easily have sufficed. But you and the Emperor himself! Could there be a more personal reason, Your Highness?'

'You are wrong about the Emperor. He takes the political

aspect of the problem very seriously. As far as I'm concerned, the answer is yes and no. Perhaps. In fact, probably not . . . There was another murder, just before the start of the campaign. I found this coincidence disturbing.'

Margont almost flew into a rage, something he did rarely. His meetings with the prince were really not good for him.

'Another murder? And you didn't tell me about it?'

'No, because the culprit has been arrested.'

This new lead had scarcely come to light and it was already being snatched away. However, Margont noted that the prince did not seem convinced.

'I should be grateful if Your Highness would tell me the story so that I can form my own opinion. Above all, do not hesitate to give me all the details. Paradoxically, the more details I have, the clearer things will become to me.'

'Very well. This business occurred about a week before the murder of the Polish woman. Our corps was still in Poland and we were putting the finishing touches to the preparations. The Emperor wanted to be kept informed of everything. Every subject held his attention: the numbers and quality of the troops, the calibre of the officers, the supplies, the reserves of ammunition, the artillery, the clothing, respecting the privileges granted to my Royal Guard, the pay, maintaining discipline, relations with the Polish population . . . And His Majesty would not tolerate any delays or approximations or disappointing answers! In a word, my general staff and I were constantly in demand. So I was careful to organise regular entertainments. A mind that enjoys itself from time to time works better than one that is subject to permanent pressure.'

The prince cast another annoyed glance in the direction of poor General Triaire, who was attempting to stem the flow of missives.

'One evening, a grand reception was given by Countess Nergiss, a Polish sympathiser. I should point out that I was not the instigator of this event. It was entirely conceived and organised by the countess. There were four hundred guests at the very least. Perhaps you were there?'

'Unfortunately not. I am not of high enough rank to be invited.'

'Lay your hands on our murderer and that sort of disappointment will be a thing of the past.'

'I knew about the celebration but I didn't hear anything about a crime . . .'

'Let me continue. Countess Nergiss is as rich as Croesus and she had set her sights on an ambitious promotion for her husband, who is a general. She hoped that, if General Prince Poniatowski happened to be wounded or killed, her husband would replace him in command of V Corps, the Polish Corps. Can you believe it? So she had been preparing this reception for weeks, even before the Grande Armée reached Poland. To her chagrin, the Emperor informed her at the last minute that he would not be able to come as he was with the bulk of the army much too far north of the castle. Only IV Corps was camped nearby. The countess therefore fell back on me in her calculations, hoping that I would plead her cause with His Majesty. To make her tactic less obvious, she had decided to dazzle me. I must admit she succeeded very well. What splendour!'

The prince must, though, have been used to this type of

event. Margont told himself that the countess must have beaten all records for extravagance.

'She had invited the full complement – the full complement! – of my senior officers.'

Margont attempted to disguise his dismay. His suspects had therefore all been invited to this reception.

'Each guest was allowed to bring up to three people. When I arrived – late because I was being informed about last-minute problems practically all the time – it was only to discover a crowd of officers, Polish nobles, notables, wives, children, soldiers on guard duty . . . all of them being pampered by an armada of servants. Try to imagine an immense castle. As it was a clear night, the countess had set up outside an endless array of buffets: Polish, French, Italian, Danish, Indian, Creole . . . Valets provided the lighting by standing still with lanterns in their hands. Any sensible person would have planted stakes in the ground to hang the lanterns on, but no! Why make savings when you can throw money out of the window? Orchestras, dotted around the grounds, were giving concerts while fireworks crackled in the sky. To mark my arrival, the entire surroundings were briefly illuminated by sparkling showers of light and thousands of fireworks. It was like being back in the extravagant era of the Sun King. But it was even better than that because this time I was the Sun King.'

Margont blinked. How could anyone be so rich? And how could they waste so much money?

'It was so luxurious it was grotesque,' concluded Eugène. 'But it was ideal for taking your mind off things. I whispered to Triaire that one or two more evenings like that and though I wasn't sure whether the count would be given command of V Corps, I'd be pleased to offer him that of IV. The countess seemed to me quite a pleasant person, in the sense that she knew how to avoid overstepping the boundaries. That's a very rare quality among courtiers. So she vaunted her husband's merits – he's serving in the Polish Corps – but she interrupted herself before my irritation surfaced. She had one strange quirk: she would disappear every hour and come back showing off a new dress and different jewels, in a crescendo of extravagance. That's exactly it! With her sapphire necklace and her champagne-coloured diamond . . .'

The prince had raised his voice. There was a tense sadness about him. He seemed caught in a moment of futile protest against a past that could not be altered.

'If Countess Nergiss had not been so obsessed with luxury, everything would have turned out differently, and a young lady I thought highly of would still be alive. In short, the evening continued its pleasant course, interspersed with the extravagant follies of our hostess, including cut-crystal glasses that she cheerfully invited her guests to toss into the air as soon as they were empty, a hunting party—'

'But it was night-time.'

'Do you think that was a problem for the countess? She had illuminated one of her woods with lanterns and had it surrounded by beaters before getting the gamekeepers to set the deer loose. I admit that we killed far more lanterns than deer. When the wood started to catch fire because of the oil from the lamps that had been hit by the bullets, the countess declared that it did not matter. However, this silly game came to an end and the fire was brought under control at an early stage. The countess's next stunt was to parade past me the one hundred and twenty horses of her stud farm before presenting me with one of her handsomest stallions. That evening was a folly, I tell you! On the stroke of eleven, the master of ceremonies – a man always stiff and mannered – announced that a play was to be performed. Immediately, swarms of servants busied themselves in setting up an open-air stage and laying out hundreds of chairs. When the actors appeared, I was astonished. Because I knew them.'

The prince's voice had changed, becoming less cold and more human. His account sounded less like an official report and had become more personal. Eugène even seemed on the verge of tears. But the exercise of power had taught him to hold his emotions in check, in the same way you would train a dog. No tears flowed.

'Yes, I knew them. It was a Parisian company I had often seen perform. Oh, they're not very well known but . . . you're bound to know . . . As the whole of Paris knows about it, I suppose you do too.'

Margont noted that for the prince Paris was synonymous with the whole of France, that is to say, a hundred and thirty départements, including Amsterdam, Brussels and Rome.

'I know Your Highness is having an affair with an actress.'

Eugène seemed about to fly into a rage.

'Not an actress, an opera dancer! And an affair, an affair! One does not say to a prince that he's having an affair or has a mistress. One says he greatly admires such and such a young lady. So, as you know, I greatly admire an opera dancer.

Getting to know her has brought me into contact with other people from the world of entertainment. This friend of mine was very close to a person of real talent, Élisa Lasquenet. It was this young lady who performed for us that evening before being murdered. No one could fail to find her utterly charming. She was only nineteen and yet she already acted divinely well. I never tired of going to applaud her in her all too rare appearances. Oh, if she had lived, I swear to you that she would soon have had Paris at her feet.'

Margont said to himself that in addition to his opera dancer, the prince must also have 'greatly admired' this Élisa Lasquenet.

'This woman had a wonderful talent, Captain, wonderful. What a waste. And all because the countess wanted to please me! After finding out well in advance – doubtless via her husband – that IV Corps would be passing quite close to her castle, she did some research into my tastes. She then offered this troupe of actors a princely sum to get them to come to Poland, thinking that I would be easier to influence than the Emperor. As in billiards, she wanted to hit the Emperor indirectly and I was the cushion. There's calculation and determination for you! Heaven forbid that I should ever make an enemy of a woman like that!'

The prince paused. When he resumed, he spoke more quickly.

'The performance lasted a good hour and a half, then the actors mingled with the guests. Élisa was stabbed a moment later, in one of the castle bedrooms that she was using as a dressing room. She had gone there to remove her stage costume.'

The account had speeded up considerably. Detailing the festivities, yes; detailing the murder was altogether another matter.

'The countess noticed that the young actress whom she had engaged at great expense was slow to return. She sent her housekeeper "to ensure that Mademoiselle Lasquenet had everything she needed". The servant came back saying that there was no answer to her calls. She had not dared to open the door. The countess went to the room herself and discovered the body. What self-control! She did not scream but ordered the master of ceremonies to keep guard at the door and came to inform me of the tragedy. At most she looked a little pale. She begged me not to let news of this incident get out, in order to preserve her reputation. I agreed with some relief, as I already had enough problems with the campaign without having my officers being suspicious of one another. The countess continued to supervise the party, though she did bring it to an end early. When people asked for Mademoiselle Lasquenet she said that she was unwell and resting. None of the guests were aware of anything at all!'

It's she rather than her husband who deserves to be the possible replacement for General Poniatowski in command of V Corps, thought Margont.

'She had paid the actors to speak their lines but she paid them double for keeping quiet. For my part, I informed the Polish authorities, demanding of them the utmost discretion. Fortunately, the culprit was arrested the following day.'

'Really?' said Margont in surprise.

'He admitted to the crime. He's an unstable Polish layabout, a lunatic who has already been put away several times. He passed himself off as a servant and melted into the crowd of domestics, which enabled him to have access to Mademoiselle Lasquenet.'

That's why he kept on so much about the servants: he wanted to convince not just me but himself as well, thought Margont.

'Why did he murder this actress, Your Highness?'

Prince Eugène seemed taken by surprise. 'Why? How can you tell what's going on inside the head of a madman?'

Obviously. It was so simple. This disturbed individual might well be the culprit. But he could just as easily be the ideal scapegoat for investigators eager to please the prince.

'I am listening, Your Highness.'

'But my account is at an end. Your task and this crime are probably not related.'

Eugène rose to his feet. This way of seeing things suited him best.

Margont interjected once more, 'I would very much like to ask Your—'

'Did you say something, soldier?' the prince interrupted.

Margont was indeed a soldier. However, the words could also mean that if he persisted he risked losing his epaulettes and having his pay divided by twenty. He felt he was approaching a defining moment. It was impossible for him to carry out a thorough investigation under such conditions. Either he did what the prince wanted and scuppered his investigation or he stood up to him. Eugène's behaviour was completely contradictory. On the one hand, he wanted the murders of this actress, the Polish woman and the sentry to be solved. On the other, he was afraid of facing up to the possibility that one of his officers was a criminal. Saber was always talking about plans and tactics – Margont thought that his friend would have been proud of him at this moment: he had just worked out a strategy for making the prince talk.

'How could an intruder have made his way into the castle when there were so many people present?'

The prince frowned. 'Do you listen to me when I speak? I've told you more than once that there was a host of domestics. He passed himself off as a valet.'

'Your Highness, servants wear servants' clothes. Here's a man who arrives dressed like a beggar – because you said yourself he was a layabout, so I imagine—'

'You imagine far too much. He's said to have stolen a servant's outfit. The Polish authorities have investigated the matter, I'll have you know.'

'Their investigation lasted less than twenty-four hours as—'

'If a case is solved in twelve hours that does not automatically make it a miscarriage of justice.'

'Did people notice this madman in the course of the evening?'

'The question was put to a few trustworthy servants – and only them in order to prevent the spread of rumour – and admittedly the reply was no. But the countess had taken on a large number of staff solely for the duration of that evening's entertainment. None of her usual valets would have had any reason to pick out one new face among the employees because they were all new.'

The prince was getting annoyed. He was going to break off the conversation. Margont nodded his agreement.

'Perfect, Your Highness. I'm quite prepared to believe in the efficiency of the Polish investigators. Would you be so kind as to explain to me how this man proceeded?'

'The day before the reception he entered the house of one of the countess's servants and stole his outfit. The servant thought it was an ordinary theft. The theft was confirmed by the domestic in question after he had been traced.'

This story was so full of improbabilities and extraordinary coincidences that Margont did not even bother to make a list of them. On the other hand, his strategy was working. Eugène was not fully convinced of the guilt of this deranged man but he wanted to believe it. Margont was toying with this element of doubt like someone pulling at a loose thread, and gradually Eugène's confidence was fraying. Margont had reversed the roles of prince and captain and this was exactly how he planned to conduct the conversation.

'There's one thing I don't understand, Your Highness. This man killed without a motive . . .'

'Not without a motive, but because he is mentally disturbed.'

'But how can he be mentally disturbed when he kills if he is perfectly sane when he is planning the crime? We know that he did some research, drew up a plan, stole a servant's outfit . . .'

'How should I know? I'm not a specialist in these disorders.'

'If I may be so bold, neither are the Polish investigators. I assume that one of them has been questioned.'

'Of course not, because the culprit has confessed.'

'How was this man tracked down?'

'He had already committed a public order offence in the past. So the investigators questioned him, as they do all the usual suspects.'

Margont was furious. So much for the ideals of the Revolution and the rights of man! Were all men equal then, except the insane?

'I see. "Insane and therefore suspect." Or even better: "Insane and therefore guilty."'

'He confessed! And no force was used to make him confess. I'd sent one of my aides-de-camp to make certain of that.'

'May I talk to this aide-de-camp?'

'Yes, but after the campaign is over because he stayed behind in Poland to follow the trial.'

They were going round in circles but Margont remained unruffled.

'How did the suspect confess, Your Highness? Did he give his own version of events or did he accept the one presented to him?'

The prince seemed exasperated by this conversation but was unable to bring it to an end.

'Well, the facts were put to him and he admitted to them. It was quicker that way because he seemed incoherent. According to the report I was given of his interrogation, his explanations were hopelessly confused. For example, he would break off in the middle of a sentence and remain silent for several minutes, for no apparent reason, before continuing to talk but about something completely different in the same rambling manner. And he didn't even seem to be aware of these inconsistencies.'

'What are we to think of a confused mind that carries out a consistent plan in masterly fashion? Did he even understand what he had been made to confess to? I don't doubt that he admitted to doing it. What's surprising is that he didn't also admit to being responsible for the double murder on the Lyons mail-coach, Marat's assassination, the booby trap that almost blew up the Emperor in Rue Nicaise, and to being the man in the iron mask.'

'Don't overdo it. I don't need you for that. At least I asked that, in view of his mental disorder, he should not be sentenced to death. That's something.'

So they even wanted to execute him, did they? Margont felt nauseated.

'I'm going to order a new inquiry,' continued the prince. 'I admit that your argument does trouble me. However, I've often had positive reports about the efficiency of the Polish authorities.'

Margont did not doubt that. He sensed a presence behind those who had conducted this mockery of an investigation. Countess Nergiss. The prince was so eager for this case to be solved . . . Bribing one of her servants and one or two Polish notables was neither here nor there in terms of expense as far as she was concerned. Margont had mixed feelings about this woman. Either she had been seduced by power or else she had acted out of love, to fulfil her husband's dream. If that was the case, her ambition was rather moving and Margont could not bring himself to dislike her.

'Nevertheless, it has to be him,' muttered Eugène.

'How did events that evening unfold?'

'The murderer mingled with the guests. That must have been the case because there were sentries all around the castle and such a large number of people present . . .'

Of course he mingled with the guests because he was one of them! Margont exclaimed to himself. Still, at least the prince was co-operating now.

'He went into the dressing room . . .'

'How did he find it?'

'Just after the performance a crowd of spectators hurried into the dressing rooms to congratulate the actors as they were removing their make-up. I went in myself. It was easy therefore to locate the place. The actors then went back out into the grounds. Mademoiselle Lasquenet returned to her dressing room later so her murderer then took an enormous risk in following her there because an admirer might have tried his luck with her, or a servant might have encountered him or heard him. He acted very swiftly, otherwise someone would certainly have caught him in the act. He entered the room. Mademoiselle Lasquenet was not worried. All she needed to do was to shout and a servant would hear her. Besides, either the murderer was disguised as a valet and she thought he had been sent by the countess, or he introduced himself as one of the guests. If that were the case, actresses are used to this sort of situation and know how to deal with people tactfully. The man took her by surprise and stabbed her twice. She died before she even had time to scream. So, as you can see, this crime is different from the one involving the Polish woman.'

'But it's very similar to the one involving the sentry – killing someone outright by stabbing them only twice. Besides, we can't say whether the murderer would have mutilated his victim or not if he'd had time.'

'On that subject, there is one detail. The murderer cut out her tongue.'

Margont shuddered. He could never get used to horror. 'The tongue . . .' Now it was his turn to feel unsettled. Fortunately, he had shaken the prince sufficiently to persuade him to provide all the details.

'I've thought about it long and hard. An anecdote can perhaps explain such a cruel act. By the end of the performance, the audience was completely enthralled. Seeing this, Countess Nergiss suggested that the actors should give a repeat performance of certain scenes according to public request. Everyone joined in the spirit. They were even asked to recite speeches from other plays and were then applauded enthusiastically. From time to time someone asked a question. How could such and such an actor play such an odious character? Did they themselves feel anger when their character was angry? Opinions differed. Some of the actors maintained that you had to use your sensitivity and your emotions to "become" your character in order to perform the role properly. Hence a considerable limitation of roles because any given person could not "become" just anyone. Others thought that the actor remained an actor pretending to be the character. Therefore he had to use first and foremost his intelligence. Hence the possibility for a gifted actor to take on any role. In a word it was the insoluble debate begun by Monsieur Diderot.

'Mademoiselle Lasquenet favoured the second point of view and proclaimed that she could play absolutely any role. Another actress, whose only fault was to be less beautiful and less talented than her stage partner, jealous of being eclipsed, challenged her to play a whore. How childish it was! They were no longer two young women but two adolescent girls ready to pull each other's hair out. Mademoiselle Lasquenet gave a very convincing demonstration and even went as far as to caress her breasts. At that moment, the real spectacle was not what was happening on stage but on Countess Nergiss's face. Mademoiselle Lasquenet continued in her role, this time using her tongue. She ran it over her lips quite indecently . . . The countess suddenly rose to her feet to applaud and the audience did likewise whilst Mademoiselle Lasquenet, whose cheeks were bright red, bowed politely, still surprised by her own boldness. That was what must have infuriated the murderer and driven him to take such risks. That's why he cut out her tongue. Such cruelty unleashed by the shamelessness of a susceptible adolescent girl!'

The silence that ensued made the two men ill at ease.

'Your Highness, General Triaire must provide me with an exact list of guests.'

'Exact, exact . . . He'll note down the names of those he saw.'

'Can he try to establish who was absent at the time of the murder?'

'That's impossible. More than an hour elapsed between the moment Mademoiselle Lasquenet went to change and when the housekeeper knocked on the door. We do not know at what precise time the murderer stabbed her and it took only a few moments. His absence was probably not even noticed and, even if it had been, so many people were coming and going to the buffets, flitting from group to group or goodness knows what. In any case, who would care about someone's absence in such a crush?'

'Could General Triaire also do a sketch of the state of the bedroom: the position of the body, the—'

The prince gave a nervous laugh. 'Are you mad? In any case, nobody entered the bedroom except the countess and the investigators.'

'Do we know how the murderer got rid of any bloodstains that might have—'

'I don't know if any attention was given to those details. There was only one thing that struck the investigators. At one point they thought that the murderer had stolen the tongue because it was nowhere to be found but it had in fact been hidden in one of the pockets of the victim's cloak.'

The prince's furrowed brow and his tightly folded arms betrayed his tension. If he had hoped that Margont would dispel his doubts, he really did have cause for annoyance.

'I think I've told you everything about this sad event,' he concluded. His sentence had the ring of a funeral oration.

'I am indebted to you, Your Highness. May I leave?'

'Keep me regularly informed by sealed letter addressed to General Triaire. Ask to see me only if you have something new to tell me.'

Eugène then dived into the mass of messengers whilst Margont lingered in the grove. His thoughts were jumbled and incoherent. Could this affair be linked to his investigation or not? He was not at all convinced of the deranged man's guilt but nor was he convinced of his innocence. On what basis could he assume that the person he was tracking had also killed the actress? What was the significance – if any – of cutting out her tongue? Unable to make up his mind and torn between various suppositions, Margont was struggling to find a connection between these disparate elements.

That same evening, as he was recounting his conversation with the prince to Lefine, he received the list of guests. Almost two hundred officers from IV Corps. And Triaire pointed out that this list was almost certainly incomplete. Predictably, the names of the four suspects were among them.

CHAPTER 17

THE march resumed its tedious course. The road to Moscow, attractively lined with birch trees, was so dusty that every breath was agony for the lungs. Sometimes they advanced laboriously in the unbearable heat, making a rush for any stagnant water hole, even if it meant suffering diarrhoea. Sometimes they were soaked to the skin by rain or bombarded by hailstones. At night they shivered with cold and got very little sleep. Everything in this country seemed to be on an excessive, inhuman scale. There was also the constant smell of putrefaction coming from the thousands of dead horses, a smell that was all the more abominable as it presaged the slaughter to come. More than a third of the army was sick or off foraging for food and three-quarters of the eighty thousand horses that had set off on the campaign had perished. But the French continued to move forward in the sweltering heat through a countryside that consisted of plains, hills, marshes, forests and charred remains.

Jérôme Bonaparte, the Emperor's brother, King of Westphalia and a poor tactician who was well out of his depth as commander of VIII Corps, manoeuvred particularly badly. He let slip the opportunity of attacking Bagration's army. Napoleon, furious that this mistake had allowed the Russian army to escape destruction, relieved him of his command. Out of pique, Jérôme left the army and returned home, taking with him his Royal Guard. The consequences of this error were very serious: the two Russian armies had almost linked up with each other and Barclay de Tolly and Bagration were able to meet up at Smolensk, one of the most important and beautiful cities in Russia. The Russians were determined to defend it, at whatever cost. 'At last I've got them!' exclaimed Napoleon. On 16 and 17 August the battle raged. The French had already seized a large part of the town when, during the night of 17 to 18 August, Barclay de Tolly once more ordered a retreat.

Bagration was appalled. The two generals were proving to be exact opposites. Barclay de Tolly had a cold disposition. A man of unfailing composure, he was polite, patient and methodical. He never got tired and frequently went without a meal. He was a very competent general and continued to implement a scorched-earth policy even though his general staff, his soldiers and the Russian people were unanimously against it. His unpopularity was growing as the French army progressed. Bagration seemed to have an aura of heroism about him and was fêted all the way from St Petersburg to Siberia. He was combative, courageous to the point of foolhardiness, and each step backwards by the Russian army mortified him. But Barclay de Tolly's main objective was to protect his troops, and to continue fighting in Smolensk would have prejudiced any attempted retreat. The Russians would have been hindered by the congested streets and would probably have ended their withdrawal at the very bottom of the Dnieper, the river that ran through the city. So the Russian army abandoned its positions under cover of darkness, taking with it the icon of Our Lady of Smolensk and setting fire to the city.

IV Corps did not reach Smolensk until 19 August, too late to take part in the confrontation but early enough to witness the consequences.

Working separately, Lefine and Margont had each been gathering information about their suspects. Three days earlier they had decided they would pool the results of their investigations the moment they arrived in Smolensk. Since then Lefine had disappeared. Margont had organised a search for him but to no avail and he was becoming increasingly worried.

Three-quarters of Smolensk had been burnt but it was still a superb and fascinating city. It stretched out along the sides of a valley at the bottom of which flowed a river, the Borysthen. On the left bank stood the old town, surrounded by a red-brick wall with whitewashed battlements. These fortifications were twenty-four feet high, eighteen feet wide and included twenty-nine towers. On the other bank the dwellings were more recent and unfortified.

When the 84th entered the city, a deathly silence hung over it. Whole areas had been reduced to ashes. The column progressed through the smoking rubble among which lay bodies that were charred, shrunken and twisted like vines. In the streets strewn with wreckage and corpses, blood was mingled with mud. Here, a shell had torn a dozen or so Russian grenadiers to shreds. Death had taken them by surprise: they still had their muskets slung across their chests. There, a large shack had been the scene of fighting before collapsing in flames, killing the combatants on each side indiscriminately. No sooner had a fire been put out than fighting flared up again amongst the rubble. The fires had been so extensive that they had covered everything with a fine layer of dust, a sort of grey, warm shroud that disintegrated when touched.

Most of the inhabitants had fled with the Russian troops, but some had remained or were coming back. They were looking for relatives, begging for help in removing huge piles of wreckage, recovering anything that had escaped destruction. Although the dead were being tossed into carts and mass graves were being dug everywhere, some of the bodies had begun to decay and the air was contaminated by a vile, clinging odour. You had to press your sleeve against your nostrils to block out the smell of death. Hunger and confusion had unhinged the minds of most of the soldiers who were indulging in a frenzy of looting. They were storming grocers' and butchers' shops – or at least what was left of them – and smashing in the doors of houses that had withstood the flames with the aid of charred timbers.

The 84th reached the area allotted to it and was given permission to seek out supplies. Colonel Pégot reminded everyone that ill treatment of civilians or prisoners, theft, rape or the refusal to obey gendarmes would result in severe punishment, which often meant death. No sooner had he finished speaking than his regiment vanished about their business.

Margont was marching in the company of Saber and Piquebois.

'Why did our corps arrive after the battle?' asked an outraged Saber. 'We are incredibly badly led! What can Prince Eugène have been thinking of? There's more of the Eugène than the Prince about that one!'

Neither Margont nor Piquebois replied. It was quite impossible to discuss this subject with Saber. Saber detested Prince Eugène, who, in his opinion, was the Viceroy not of Italy but of upstarts. The son of Alexandre and Joséphine de Beauharnais, he found his life transformed when his mother had taken as her second husband a certain up-and-coming Bonaparte who quickly became known simply as Napoleon. Thus, in 1805, at the age of twenty-four he had been promoted Viceroy of Italy by his stepfather. Saber had already taken his revenge mentally many times on what he considered to be the ultimate betrayal. He frequently imagined himself – albeit in a few years' time – receiving his marshal's baton from the Emperor's own hands and declaring loudly enough for Prince Eugène to hear: 'I thank Your Majesty with all my heart. My mother will be overjoyed to learn of this appointment to which she has contributed so much . . . by educating me and helping to make me the man I am.'

The prince was not totally devoid of qualities as a military leader. Everyone acknowledged his courage at least. Or rather, almost everyone, because Saber could not be made to accept this indisputable fact. 'Of course it's disputable, because I dispute it! He's just the stepson of the right person!' he would say angrily. And he would draw an unfortunate parallel with the prince's opera dancer, asserting that it was natural that someone who was so good at mimicking a real general should have fallen in love with a 'stage Cleopatra'.

Two dogs suddenly leapt out of a narrow street and barked at the three officers.

'Look – even the curs hate us now!' fumed Piquebois.

Saber reached for his sword. 'They're as hungry as we are. It can't be nice to be seriously wounded and have to contend with the likes of them.'

A little further on he picked up a Russian shako decorated with a brass grenade with three flames shooting up from it, symbolising an explosion. He prised the metal plaque off with the point of his knife and stuffed it into his pocket.

'A souvenir. I have an infantryman's grenade with one flame, a grenadier's grenade with three flames, and the double-headed eagle of the soldiers of the Guard. A complete set.'

Piquebois merely shook his head, whereas a few years earlier he would have rolled up his sleeves for fisticuffs over this trophy.

'You're missing the cross of the national guards, which has the engraved inscription, "For Faith and the Tsar".'

'I don't take account of the militiamen,' Saber retorted contemptuously.

'Well, you'll see when you come across them whether they take account of you.'

Margont's horse whinnied frequently. Swarms of insects were swirling around the carrion-choked city and clusters of flies were massing on the animal's eyes as if they were lumps of caviar. The three Frenchmen went past an Orthodox church. The walls had been blackened by smoke but the gilded cupolas of the bell towers sparkled in the sun. It looked like a palace out of the Arabian nights. Families in tears crowded around the altars. A few heaps of rubble further on, they joined a handful of inhabitants in clearing away wreckage as they'd been told it was an inn famous for its larder. When they eventually cleared the trapdoor to the cellar it opened to reveal not smoked hams but a pale-eyed, terror-stricken young girl and her mother. The woman was clutching the child in her arms and could not be persuaded to let go of her. The man who had spoken of the larder explained in halting French that he had 'lied a bit' to save his wife and daughter.

'But why lie like that?' exploded Saber. 'We are French officers. Had you told us the truth we would have worked twice as fast.'

All the Russian understood of course was the word 'lie' and he quickly handed over a bag to Saber. It contained slices of meat. The French were reluctant to deprive this family but the man rubbed his stomach and smiled. Piquebois, whey-faced, looked closely at the food.

'It's not beef.'

'They wouldn't poison us, would they?' said Margont with a worried look.

'It's not horsemeat, is it? You wouldn't have dared . . .' asked Piquebois.

The Russian nodded several times. 'Good horse, yes. Killed yesterday.'

Piquebois was a sorry sight. His slavering mouth gave him away but he declared: 'Not for me.'

'You won't last long if you don't eat as much as you can when you have the chance,' Margont pointed out to him.

'By chewing horsemeat I'd feel as if I were eating one of you because you and the horses are my best friends.'

He walked off, a pitiful sight, while Saber was already skewering the slices with the bayonet of a musket found lying on the ground and was holding them over the still-glowing embers of a beam.

As soon as Margont had eaten his fill, he abandoned Saber and went off in search of Lefine. He decided to do the rounds of the hospitals. He reached what had been a fine-looking square. Sappers were chopping down blackened trees to prevent them from crashing on to the buildings. The park was turning into a wasteland. Four blocks of houses gave the rectangle an elegant symmetry. But their façades were riddled with bullet holes and one of them had lost its roof. A phenomenal number of cannonballs were scattered on the ground. Württemberg gunners, easily recognisable by their black-crested helmets, were placing the ones that could still be used in a cart. They roared with laughter when someone held up a cannonball that had been flattened like a pancake or taken on a bizarre shape. This must be what Württemberg gunners found amusing.

Carts were piling up at the foot of the three buildings left intact and more were constantly arriving. They were carrying all the world's woes: the wounded. The forest of arms raised in pleas for help, the chorus of groans, the trails of blood, the mangled bodies . . . Margont had the greatest admiration for those who tended to these men: medical orderlies, helpers, surgeons, physicians, pharmacists . . . He wondered whether Lefine was somewhere among these unfortunates. One of them escaped by hopping from a wagon as if leaving this place meant escaping death itself. Two soldiers tried to reason with him but he yelled: 'They're going to cut my leg off! Without my leg who's going to look after my farm?' How far away the fine ideas about humanism and freedom now seemed . . .

Margont noticed Jean-Quenin Brémond. The physician was going from cart to cart, a dazed look on his face. His dark blue uniform was spattered with bloodstains. Brémond pointed with his finger at those who were to be treated within the hour, specifying the exact order. The wounded were pleading with him, threatening him, insulting him, promising him a fortune . . . In exchange for an operation they were offering him a horse, a house, a daughter in marriage, a wife's virtue . . . Who could blame them? When Brémond turned his gaze on a cart, the dying attempted to smile and joke in order to appear less as if they were dying, while the less seriously wounded pretended to be worse by swearing they had been bleeding for hours. It was unbearable, unbearable. Helpers took charge of those selected amidst insults, spitting and tears. 'There's room for all of you. We'll settle you all in. It just needs time' was their constant reply.

Margont called out to Brémond but the medical officer took a while to recognise him. In hell it always takes time to realise there can still be good news.

'You're not wounded, are you, Quentin?'

'No. Have you seen Fernand? He's disappeared.'

'Yes, he was wounded on 17 August in the assault on Smolensk. What was he doing there, so far from IV Corps?'

'It's my fault. He's been helping me with my investigation. I'll never forgive myself, damn it!'

Brémond was exhausted. His intonation was dull and flat, out of keeping with what he was talking about.

'It's just cannon-shock syndrome. As of this morning he's cured and he's helping to settle in the wounded.'

Margont was not reassured by these words. 'But what's cannon-shock syndrome?'

'When a cannonball passes very close, really very close, to a soldier, it sometimes happens that the blast of air can knock him over. It's not serious from a physical point of view but feeling death come so close often affects the mind. Fernand could not speak a single word. Either he screamed or he remained silent. As he was covered in the blood of the person blown up by the cannonball he ended up here.'

'Will he suffer any aftereffects?'

'Possibly. But he's cheerful and confident by nature, so we can hope he won't. Otherwise, he may lose his zest for life and start going on about the misery he has witnessed, thinking himself damaged by life and the army.'

'I'll let you get on with your work.'

Brémond was so shattered that he had to struggle to keep his eyes open.

'There are so many wounded that we're short of everything. We're using tow instead of lint, paper instead of linen. Even the medical orderlies are performing operations . . . and soldiers are being brought in who haven't been wounded but are suffering from depression. They've lost their appetites, can't sleep, don't talk any more, cry all the time and have lost the will to live. Lost the will to live! And what about me? What am I supposed to do for them? I can't operate on wounded minds, that's for sure.'

At last Margont found Lefine. He was going to and fro among the carts but there was no sense of purpose about his movements. He waved his arms around as he spoke and then walked off in the middle of a sentence, picked up a shako and handed it to its owner, who couldn't have cared less. When he spotted Margont he rushed over to him, as happy as could be.

'My favourite captain! Come here. I've got some news for you!'

'Are you sure you're going to—'

'I've spoken to some friends of Colonel Pirgnon and our Italian colonel. I was in the process of talking to one of them when—' Lefine stopped suddenly. His high spirits had evaporated. 'I hadn't realised we were exposed . . . The Russian cannonballs suddenly began to rain down. He was talking to me . . .'

Margont put a hand on his shoulder. 'Fernand, you should get some rest. We'll talk about it tomorrow or another day.'

His friend was puzzled. 'No. It's better to be active rather than sit alone in a corner thinking. Otherwise I keep imagining myself back there, talking to that lieutenant from the cuirassiers.'

'Come on then!' exclaimed Margont, taking his friend away from the place that had such a bad effect on him.

'Are we still a long way from Moscow, Captain?'

'Just over two hundred and forty miles.'

'Two hundred and forty? What a swine of a country! What about going back for a swim in the Gardon?'

Margont started speaking in conspiratorial tones, glancing around as he did so. 'Talk more quietly. Some officers are having deserters shot by the dozen.'

'If Jean-Quenin brought back a few broken skulls with their

foreheads slashed by sabres and blasted by cannonballs or with all their bones broken by grapeshot, and exhibited them in the anatomy museum of the medical school in Montpellier, perhaps people would think twice before going off to tickle one another with bayonets . . .'

'You must be joking. People would be only too eager to continue adding to the collection.'

Margont was looking for a way of helping his friend to get over the emotional shock that seemed to have transformed him. It was as if the blast from the cannonball had made him lapse into a second childhood. Lefine found the slightest thing amusing, almost getting himself bitten by a stray dog when he tried to stroke it, and his naïve comments were in sharp contrast to the usual pragmatism of this wily old monkey.

They settled themselves down in a house fortunate enough to have escaped the fire. Its good luck had not, however, extended as far as to protect it from looting. They picked up some chairs and sat down in the middle of a chaos of clothes and broken crockery. Someone had discovered a sack of flour. A quarrel had ensued and the sack had been torn open. The flour scattered on the floor was witness to human folly. There had been a fight and there were traces of blood amidst the confused pattern of footprints. The winners had then tried to gather up this precious powder. Judging by all that remained on the floor, both parties would have been better off sharing out the contents of the sack while it was still intact.

'In Russia traces of flour are like bloodstains: it means someone is going to die,' Lefine declared.

'No! We aren't going to die of hunger any more. We're

going to find enough food supplies here,' Margont lied. 'On the subject of our investigation, I've thought hard about Élisa Lasquenet's murder. All the same, it's very odd, a tongue cut out and slipped into the pocket of a cloak.'

'So?'

'Do you remember the anagram "Acosavan", "Casanova"? Well, the mutilation of this actress seems to be saying: "She would have done better to have held her tongue instead of provoking me by running it over her lips." '

Margont stopped talking to allow Lefine to express an opinion but the sergeant failed to respond.

'If I'm right, then there really is a connection between these two crimes. It's difficult to define: it's a sort of signature in the form of a cruel and coded play on words, which must greatly amuse the murderer. A biting and humiliating form of mockery that looks as if it's intended to add insult to injury. I admit that this is quite a bold piece of speculation but it seems to me far more credible than the "confessions" of that poor madman. There's also another element in common: the mixture of love and death. In both cases, what would have aroused desire in normal people provoked extreme violence in the murderer.'

Margont stretched out his legs and made himself more comfortable, trying to relax. If his hypothesis was right, his investigation was taking an even more sinister turn. On the one hand, there was the possibility of earlier crimes and on the other . . .

' "Bad luck comes in threes", as the saying goes,' Lefine added, following the same train of thought.

'Let's put that to one side. What have you got to tell me?'

Lefine admired his friend's pugnacity. However, Margont did not know his own limits or how to avoid going too far and risking his own neck.

'I had one sighting of the indefatigable Pirgnon.'

'So he really does exist. I'd almost begun to doubt it.'

'He was exhausted. He was leaning so far forward that his head was resting on the neck of his horse. I was able to talk to one of his lieutenants. His overwhelming vitality has made him very popular. He gets up at the crack of dawn and is the last to go to bed. He converses with the regimental doctor, inspects the wagons, interrogates the prisoners, goes off on reconnaissance, checks the stocks of ammunition . . . Apparently, his theory is that, in the face of such a shambles, one must react decisively. He frequently reviews his troops with the result that the 35th are a very handsome sight with their shining muskets and their trousers and gaiters as white as the Alps. Robert Pirgnon is forty-one and comes from a bourgeois Lyons family. He attended a military academy and came out placed near the bottom of the ranking. He was in the Prussian campaign and then served for a long period in Spain. It seems that he made a lot of money there by looting the palaces of captured Spanish generals . . .'

Lefine's eyes lit up, as if reflecting heaps of imaginary gold. Margont was pleased to see his friend's normal look return.

'Well, you see, if you'd been less lazy and if you'd worked hard at school you might have got into a military academy and would be a captain or a major by now and I'm sure you'd have helped yourself to booty like he did over there.'

'Ah!' sighed Lefine ruefully.

He consoled himself with the thought that it was never too late to do the right thing.

'He was living it up in Madrid . . .'

'A seducer, was he, our Prince Charming?'

'Not quite. He didn't chase after the local beauties. He was more interested in high society, doing the rounds of dinners and balls, military parades and bowing and scraping at court.'

Margont had difficulty disguising his disappointment.

'For example, they say that one day Pirgnon invited the King, Joseph Bonaparte, to dinner. There were about thirty guests, including some bigwigs from the general staff. Pirgnon served a wonderful wine, a first-rate burgundy from before the Revolution! He uncorked it himself and served the King. Joseph emptied his glass and was fulsome with praise. Pirgnon served him again. Joseph again emptied his glass. Pirgnon was about to pour him a third but he refused because he had already had a few aperitifs and, as you know . . .'

'Yes, the Spanish think he's an alcoholic and nickname him "Pepe Botella", "Joe the Bottle". He must have wanted to avoid feeding the rumour. So then what?'

'Then Pirgnon grabbed the neck of the bottle and tipped it upside down over a vase, declaring: "The King has finished drinking." Everyone looked shocked while the roses soaked up the wine. Apparently the King found it very amusing. I would have had him shot.'

'How can people waste their time at such social gatherings?'

'It's even worse than you think. Captain Suenteria, from the Joseph Napoleon Regiment, told me that one day Marshal Marmont decided to give a grand reception while he was passing through Madrid. Marshal Soult, who had quarrelled with Marmont and was also in the capital at that time, immediately arranged a ball on the same evening. All the cream of Madrid society was invited to both places so was forced to choose its camp. When evening came, Pirgnon went to Marmont's, saluted the marshal, helped himself to a glass of punch, danced three waltzes, disappeared, reappeared at the other end of town, saluted Marshal Soult, drank a glass of port, joked with Soult's general staff, left again, turned up once more at Marmont's for a toast before downing champagne at Soult's ... and so on, for the whole night. Neither marshal suspected a thing and subsequently they never failed to invite the colonel on a regular basis.'

'It's absurd! I can't understand the logic of it.'

'But you're going to like this Pirgnon, Captain. He has a passion for art and literature. He transformed his residence in Madrid into a veritable museum and loved showing people around. He also set up a literary salon, the Cervantes Club.'

'Excellent! That's how I'm going to meet him! I'm going to talk to him about literary salons! What more do you know about this?'

'His club was quite open ... to men. Women were excluded, with one or two exceptions. The members were French or Spanish, military personnel or civilians. They met regularly to talk about books, recite poetry, argue about the translation of such and such a line of Shakespeare ... Just like your club.'

'Except that in mine women are welcome. Does he have any brothers or sisters? Did he distinguish himself in any battle in particular?'

'He's an only son. From a military point of view, he's not like Barguelot and Saber, who won every battle single-handed. Pirgnon has never displayed exceptional courage or tactical sense. But he's an excellent organiser. He juggles with figures, manages the supplies, talks very little to his soldiers and officers. He treats people rather "mechanically", so I've been told. For him, if a soldier is well dressed, well fed and well equipped, then he's a machine that's going to function properly.'

'I see. He's the "military metronome" sort. Then after that, for some unknown reason, he'll babble away in his literary salon about humanism and the beauty of literature.'

Lefine folded his arms, pleased with himself and waiting to be congratulated.

'Yes, bravo. Good work, Fernand.'

'So much for Pirgnon. On to our Italian. This one counts as two because Captain Nedroni sticks to him like a leech. Fidassio and his shadow Nedroni. Fidassio is an only son. He's thirty-five. His mother's a countess – a grand lady from the aristocracy of Rome, extremely wealthy, very beautiful and prematurely widowed. What do you expect if you marry a man three times your age?'

'So Fidassio had a very elderly father.'

'You said it! Because the countess is such a charming woman – she's reputed to have a fiery temper – Colonel Alessandro Fidassio was brought up by his "father", who hated his wife for making him look ridiculous by having so many lovers. The count retired to his country estate, taking his son with him, and sent his wife money in exchange for promises of reasonable behaviour and discretion. He can't have been paying enough. On the day of Alessandro's fifteenth birthday, his mother made a sudden reappearance in his life. Finding him very presentable, she took him away with her like a pretty plaything to exhibit in Roman high society, which was beginning to tire of the countess's love affairs.'

'She redeemed herself by using her son to restore her image as a mother. Bravo.'

'Yes, but according to the people I questioned she became deeply attached to Alessandro. From then on she had only one idea in her head: that he should become someone important. He was a very average student, so goodbye to being a scholar. He was clumsy, so goodbye to being a surgeon. He wasn't a good public speaker, so goodbye to being a politician. So she decided to make a soldier of him and that seemed to please Alessandro. He did well in a prestigious Italian military academy and was promoted to the rank of lieutenant. Then I was given to understand that his mother used and abused her connections and her wealth and more besides . . .'

'I get the picture.'

'And so within a few years the lieutenant turned into a colonel. She was the one who forced him to volunteer for this campaign. Her son had never taken part in a battle or even been outside Italy, so his career was stagnating in a provincial garrison. She thought that the Russian campaign would be a jolly jaunt beneath triumphal arches and an ideal springboard for Alessandro to be promoted to general.'

'Quite an ambitious programme.'

'Fidassio is taciturn and prefers being alone. Nobody really seems to know him in his regiment, apart from Nedroni.'

Margont tried to remember the captain's features and that look of his, both polite and firm.

'What do you know about this fellow?'

'Countess Fidassio was rather worried about sending her son to Russia. After all, war can, sometimes, kill. She'd already thought about this problem. Whilst buying her son the rank of colonel, she asked for a small bonus, like any good customer about to make a large purchase.'

'The rank of captain for Nedroni.'

'Exactly. Silvio Nedroni was born into a poor family from the lower nobility. He's thirty-two and is said to be the son of one of the countess's lovers. In any case, she considers him as her second son. An indiscreet person implied to me that this maternal feeling was born of the countess's sense of guilt. It's true that it was her relationship with Silvio's father that caused the child's mother to leave home. Anyway, the countess enabled him to enrol in the same military academy as Alessandro and she always saw to it that they kept an eye on each other. But Nedroni is far from stupid and he owes his social advancement as much to his own ability as to the countess's money and connections.'

'So if Fidassio is the murderer, and if Nedroni knows about it, he might be tempted to cover up for him. Let's add Nedroni to our list as a possible accomplice.'

'Fidassio has a weak spot: gambling. He bets a lot and owes money to several officers. He's deliberately slow to settle his debts, so sometimes they diminish because the creditor dies. I've found out that he owed a large amount to a certain Captain von Stils – I don't know what regiment he belongs to – and to Lieutenant Sampre, from the 108th. But in the fighting at Mohilev, Sampre was trampled by one or two Russian battalions. Eventually his body was fished out of the river, at the foot of the dyke he'd been trying to storm.'

'Have you discovered how much Fidassio owed Sampre?'

'Five hundred francs.'

'Oh, as much as that! I want you to find this von Stils for me.'

Lefine went purple with anger. 'How about finding him yourself?'

'Colonel Pégot is infuriated by my comings and goings. He's ordered me to limit my movements.'

'But how am I going to find this von Stils fellow in the middle of hundreds of thousands of men?'

'Don't be so defeatist. The name von Stils could be Prussian, Austrian, Bavarian, Saxon or from Baden or Württemberg. The Austrians and Prussians are too far away, so start with the Confederation of the Rhine.'

Lefine's face was a picture of woe. Margont pretended not to notice and explained his plan.

'Find this von Stils and send him to me. I'm going to put it about that Sampre had asked me to recover the debt for him in the event of his being killed so that I could send the amount involved to his family. Von Stils and I will then both go and find Colonel Fidassio.'

'Poor Fidassio. He's going to find himself once more saddled with a debt of five hundred francs that he thought was dead and buried.'

'What else have you discovered?' asked Margont calmly.

Margont knew that a tensing of the muscles was the first sign of annoyance in his friend but he had rarely seen him clench his fists and hold his arms to his body so tightly. It was like a leather strap shrivelling up in the sun.

'Captain, our corps arrived here after all the others. If we don't look for somewhere to stay now, we'll end up sleeping in the open.'

'We're investigating a murder and you're talking to me about a comfortable lodging?'

Lefine suddenly went for him, like a cat leaping at a bird.

'I almost got myself cut in two by a cannonball because of this investigation! Have you ever seen someone getting sliced up a yard away from you like a log being chopped?'

Lefine stopped shouting. He was surprised to find himself still standing, leaning so far forward that he was holding on to his friend's chair with both hands.

'Forgive me, Fernand. Come on, we'll go and find ourselves some decent quarters for the night. And something to eat, as well.'

Lefine slowly straightened up.

'Like a log, I tell you.'

CHAPTER 18

IV Corps had been ordered to find quarters in the suburbs of Smolensk. Now everyone was fighting for the best places. Lefine and Margont's accommodation was beyond their expectations. Piquebois, Saber and a certain Captain Fanselin had taken over nothing less than a palace. Lefine stood awe-struck in front of its yellow façade decorated with white stucco. The pediments of the windows were overladen with elegant arabesques. Broad columns with acanthus leaves framed the door, and smaller classical columns rose up from the balcony to support the overhang of the roof, which was crowned by a cupola. Despite its originality, the palace had adhered to the traditional rules of houses of the Russian nobility. The main building was linked to two wings by semi-circular galleries, thus creating an elegant space at the foot of the edifice. Unfortunately, the right wing had burnt down.

Saber, overjoyed at having found accommodation worthy of him, was in full flow.

'It's the residence of a family of Russian aristocrats of Polish extraction, the Valiuskis. They've stayed on. I'll introduce you. They love the French! The count has only one aim, for the Emperor to deprive Russia of the area from the Niemen to Smolensk and recreate Greater Poland. He even said to me: "Remember, there'll always be enough room in Poland to bury all the Russians found there, either dead or alive." He's having a banquet prepared for us.'

'A banquet?' repeated Margont, sceptical at the prospect of such delights.

'You should see their daughter! Such noble beauty . . .'

Saber could already see himself as a general, Count of Greater Poland, spending the summers in 'his' palace in Smolensk and wintering in Paris.

'But it took some doing, I can tell you. The building was swarming with cuirassiers when we arrived. So I went to find their lieutenant to explain to him politely that these quarters had been allotted to the 84th Regiment and he sent me packing. Me, Lieutenant Saber!'

'That's unthinkable!' Margont exclaimed, pretending to look shocked.

'I swear to you it's true! I returned with Piquebois, and a Red Lancer, who also wanted to settle in here. You should have seen how Piquebois sorted them out. There were ten cuirassiers in the drawing room, so Piquebois planted himself in the middle and exclaimed: "Good God! My lodging's crawling with silver-shelled beetles!" Then he grabbed the lieutenant by the sleeve, just as if he were picking up a real beetle by the leg! He dragged him outside with such confidence that the other fellow acquiesced without complaining. It almost led to a duel when Piquebois added, "A big mouth but a small sabre."'

'Oh dear! I hate it when he starts acting the hussar again.'

'A cuirassier began to protest but our Red Lancer yelled: "What the hell are you doing here in your fancy get-up? Out! Obey orders!" when he had no damned right to be there either.'

At that very moment the lancer came up to them. He bowed politely. He had a strange bearing, bow-legged as if he were permanently in the saddle, with or without a horse. Ever the cavalryman. His auburn hair hung down in small plaits and his moustache curled up at both ends.

'Allow me to introduce myself: Captain Edgar Fanselin, 2nd Regiment of the Chevau-Légers Lancers of the Guard commanded by General Baron Édouard de Colbert-Chabanais. Ten years of loyal service and morale always excellent. Long live the Emperor!'

'Long live the Emperor!' exclaimed Saber and Margont a few moments later.

Fanselin was a handsome man and seemed amiable enough, but there was something intense about him. It was the look in his eye. It was impossible to define this something, or to give it a name, but its presence was undeniable.

'To whom do I have the honour of speaking?'

'Captain Margont, 84th . . .'

But Fanselin had already embraced him before immediately releasing him.

'He has the Légion d'Honneur and the rank of Officer, what's more. He's a man of courage! Lieutenant Piquebois told me about you just now.'

The three men walked as far as the entrance to the palace, followed diffidently by Lefine, who didn't know if he could accompany the officers into the central building or whether he had to make do with the left wing that the soldiers and NCOs had taken over. Margont motioned to him to join them and the sergeant's face broke into a smile once more. Captain Fanselin explained how, as he was walking through the city, he had decided to settle himself here – and nowhere else. His tone gave the impression that it would be more difficult to dislodge him than ten cuirassiers. Saber could not take his eyes off the flamboyant uniform. The short jacket – the kurtka – was crimson and decorated with a blue breastplate. A blue stripe ran down the sides of the trousers, which were also crimson. The headgear was a chapka of red linen with a white plume.

Is a general of the Red Lancers more or less prestigious than a Polish general and count? wondered Saber.

The majestic-looking entrance hall was of white marble. Statues of muses or goddesses stood next to armchairs with embroidered upholstery. A red and gold stucco frieze, close to the ceiling, matched a colossal gilded chandelier containing fifty or so candles. Paintings depicting the inevitable classical ruins decorated the walls. Saber flung his sabre and shako on to an armchair and, pointing at a tall double door, invited his friends to follow him. He already considered himself at home. Captain Fanselin seemed to want to examine each canvas.

'Look at the effect of calm produced by this colonnade in the middle of this park. The place doesn't exist and yet how I would like to be there.'

'If you like the painting so much, Captain, take it,' said Lefine.

'You have a sense of humour, Sergeant,' Fanselin guffawed.

Lefine couldn't see what a sense of humour had to do with his suggestion. Fanselin turned round and spoke to Margont enthusiastically.

'The world is full of misery, but when I see these artistic

masterpieces I say to myself that all is not yet lost. Like you, I have suffered from this gruelling march. However, I have no regrets and I shall often think of all these peasants whose world will never extend further than the patch of land they cultivate.'

In the next room they were confronted by a double flight of steps. At the sides were two doors framed by still lifes. An elderly man suddenly appeared from the right-hand door. The bald crown of his head was encircled by an abundance of grey hair. He looked like a Caesar with a garland of grey laurels. On his huge nose was a pince-nez behind which sparkled small brown eyes. He was dressed in black trousers and a pearl-grey shirt over which he wore a mauve waistcoat.

'Count, allow me to introduce my—'

Saber broke off when he saw the joyful expression on the other man's face. Even his wrinkles seemed to smile.

'A Polish officer!' he exclaimed, embracing Fanselin.

'You are mistaken, Count. I am French. It's my Polish-style uniform that has confused you. I am a lancer of the Guard.'

'If you are a lancer then you are at least half Polish. The lance is our national weapon,' replied the count.

It was obvious from the warmth of the introductions how pleased the count was to welcome the Frenchmen. The burnt-out villages seemed a distant memory. No matter how friendly Count Valiuski tried to be, he still radiated an aristocratic authority. It was evident in his discreetly refined and assured gestures, in the modulations of his voice, which was husky with age, in his confident air. Such manners had been fashioned day after day by a sophisticated education, the result of generations of careful thought. Margont felt there was something familiar about the count but he was unable to say what.

'Please forgive me for not arranging for my major-domo to welcome you but he has left. Half of my servants fled the city when your army's arrival was announced. The rest are in the kitchens or preparing your bedrooms. Dinner will be served at eight o'clock, if that is convenient to you.'

That was convenient to everyone. Here everything was convenient to everyone.

'Please excuse me but I must go and settle some important matters and talk to my wife and daughter, whom you will meet this evening.'

'Your French is remarkable,' Saber complimented him.

'All the French are remarkable!' retorted the count.

He quickly walked away, exclaiming: 'Long live a free Poland!'

A servant accompanied the Frenchmen to their bedrooms. His eyes were red from crying. He did not utter a word. Fear tightened its grip on his throat, like a foretaste of the noose. Margont thought that Russian propaganda must have spread the rumour that French officers enjoyed testing the sharpness of their sabres by decapitating prisoners and that they loved to hang the servants after breakfast, which of course consisted of a roasted new-born baby. He handed the Russian a coin, which he took, trembling and utterly confused. So he wasn't going to be killed? He was being given a tip? Where was the trap?

Margont examined the marquetry furniture closely. The four-poster bed looked so comfortable that it might have been an evil spell. Sleeping Beauty must have lain down on a similar mattress, which would explain her story. In the tapestries, handsome gentlemen were depicted bowing to ladies, who were pretending to be flattered or whispering to one another behind their fans. The statue of a centaur decorated the mantelpiece. It symbolised Russia's untamed spirit.

Margont stood stock-still in front of a mirror. He thought he looked thin and tired. But he had that determined expression that came with critical times, a look that was too harsh, too severe and surly. Even a slightly forced smile scarcely softened its sternness. What if this campaign stops at Smolensk? he wondered.

He went across the corridor to Lefine's room. Through the windows he could see the soldiers from his regiment. In the area at the foot of the palace a bear keeper was making his animal perform tricks, and dozens of infantrymen had formed a circle around the spectacle. Thunderous applause greeted the bear as it got back up after a forward roll. They were as happy as sandboys.

Lying on his bed, Lefine was gazing at a painting he was holding. But what he was really examining was the gilt frame.

'You'll lose one stripe for each painting that goes missing,' Margont warned.

Lefine casually put the picture down on his bedside table.

'Not interested. I thought you were Irénée. He's furious I'm here. When he took his shako off just now I thought he was expecting me to put it on a hat stand for him. It wouldn't surprise me if he told me to clear off.'

'Well, if that does happen, send him to me and we'll soon see which of you will be the first to leave. You've got your palace, so now you can finish off your report.'

But Lefine remained motionless, studying the cherubs chasing one another in the clouds in the stuccoed world of the ceiling.

'What for?'

'What for?'

'Why are we searching so hard for this colonel? Because he's killed someone? So what? How many deaths have there been since the start of this campaign? Ten thousand? Twenty thousand? No, far more. And that's nothing compared with what will happen when we encounter the whole Russian army.'

Lefine was sincere. A part of him really had been cut in two by that cannonball.

'You're going to tell me that the soldiers are fighting for "valid" reasons,' he went on. 'Their country, their ideas, glory, for social advancement . . . Well, that's exactly it. It's because of your fine ideas that you've been so keen on this wretched investigation from the start, but if we take on a colonel, we risk having our lives buggered up.'

'Fernand . . .'

'Buggered up! With a snap of his fingers a colonel can have us transferred to a nice little French outpost miles from anywhere in the middle of the Spanish countryside. We'll take over from the sentries who had their throats slit by the guerrillas the preceding week, before our own corpses are replaced the week after . . . But a colonel doesn't even need Spain to get rid of us. He needs only to send us both on a foraging expedition and the Cossacks will enjoy nailing our remains to the fir trees for the crows to feed on.'

'Prince Eugène is supporting us.'

'Politicians and princes only ever support themselves! If you were so sure of the opposite, you'd have told our dear prince that we suspected a colonel.'

Lefine was beginning to turn red as if the words he was saying were going back down his throat, blocking and obstructing his breathing.

'If the Russians don't get us, this investigation will! And you know that perfectly well. That's the worst thing about it! But dear Captain Margont is on the side of justice – he can't stand the idea of heinous crimes going unpunished. You're the plaything of your ideals.'

'Well, we're all the playthings of something or someone. Better to be the plaything of my ideals than of greed.'

Margont stood still after giving this stinging reply. Being attacked for what he believed in body and soul put him on the defensive. For the moment he could handle it but if he were provoked further he might become dangerous. Lefine sensed this.

'Nothing will make you give up this investigation except a bullet between the eyes. That's the radical way of dealing with fanatics. Despite all those years you spent with them, those Holy Joes forgot to tell you that the good Samaritans always end up being tortured and hacked to bits by the crowds they wanted to save. And afterwards they become martyrs and people light candles to ask favours of them.'

A few moments of silence elapsed before Margont spoke.

'I don't think I have the right to ask you to do more than

you've already done. You're free to let this business drop.'

Fernand smiled a sad smile, more depressing than tears.

'I can get out of this business whenever I like and I won't lose any sleep over it. It's you I want to extricate from it before it's too late.'

'That's a waste of time.'

'What a fanatic! It's absurd! Why should we risk our lives for a few crimes when there's butchery right, left and centre? Find me one sensible reason to continue.'

'If we don't arrest this man, he may do it again.'

'So what? One more death just means three more spadefuls of earth in a common grave. What difference will it make?'

'It will make a difference to the women we save.'

Lefine sat on the edge of the bed. 'Yes, that does mean something.'

Then, suddenly, he resumed his report, speaking quickly to prevent dark thoughts from interrupting the course of his life again.

'Colonel Maximilien Barguelot is thirty-nine. His father died when he was a child. His mother and two sisters live in Amsterdam but he has settled in Paris and leads a life of luxury. He attended the military academy at Pont-à-Mousson, then took part in a large number of campaigns. He distinguished himself at the battle of Austerlitz where he was said to have been wounded but he never mentions this episode. He served in Prussia, Spain, Austria . . . He enjoys an excellent reputation among officers . . . who don't serve under him. He's not liked by his men because he openly despises them. He takes his sycophants with him everywhere and they move up a rank once they've flattered him sufficiently. He claims to be descended from a long line of Dutch and French military men: some are said to have liberated Copenhagen, others America. There's no way of knowing if it's true. He does speak Dutch. That's been confirmed. He married a beautiful and rich heiress and owns a château near Nancy. He was promoted Officer of the Légion d'Honneur . . . but in December 1808. Surprising, don't you think?'

'In 1808? Two years after Jena? It took a long time to reward him.'

Lefine was beaming. He loved work that was well done and few things gave him as much satisfaction as a well-built house or a carefully crafted piece of furniture, especially when it belonged to him.

'I found a former lieutenant in the 16th Light who was with him at Jena — Lucien Fardès, who's now a captain in the 13th Light. Would you believe it, Barguelot really was at Jena and that whole story about the capture of the Glasenapp Battery is true. But this exploit occurred without Barguelot, who'd been wounded as soon as the first shots were fired.'

'Seriously wounded?'

'A sprained ankle while charging. Barguelot came limping along after they'd seized the guns and were already turning them against the enemy. Barguelot kept on shouting, "Let's avenge our men!" as if he'd almost been killed ten times over. Fardès even claims to have seen him thrust his sword into a dead body to add colour to his blade and to his version of events.'

'But didn't Fardès denounce this felony?'

Lefine shook his head. 'Fardès knew nothing about Barguelot's version. Barguelot had to wait until he'd left the

16th Light before changing his story. How could he dare to lie about this matter when the reasons for awarding this decoration could be checked in official publications? No, that would have been suicidal for his career. The only explanation is that officially he really was rewarded for his "action" at Jena. He may have bribed officers to submit false reports about his heroic conduct to the Emperor.'

Margont could scarcely contain his anger. For him, the Légion d'Honneur represented something sacred. Just as an atheist should not spit on the Bible or the Koran, you did not wear a Légion d'Honneur to which you were not entitled.

'Perhaps he did deserve his distinction but not because of Jena,' ventured Lefine.

'Well, of course. He seized three Austrian guns at some fashionable gathering. What else do you know?'

'He has some strange habits. He never eats in public. He takes his food where no one can see him, always in his tent, alone or in the company of Coubert, one of his servants.'

'That's odd. Have you spoken to this fellow Coubert?'

'No. I was afraid he'd warn his master that he was being investigated.'

'You did the right thing. Any other strange habits?'

'I was told that he was a superb fencer. He often boasts about it but he's never been seen practising. One day, during an official dinner, Marshal Davout suggested a friendly duel because he'd heard about Barguelot's technique from a former cadet at Pont-à-Mousson. Well, Barguelot refused! At first the guests thought it was out of modesty . . .'

'That's absurd!' exclaimed Margont, laughing.

'But despite all the marshal's polite requests, Barguelot refused to cross swords. The marshal was so surprised that he should decline such an honour that he didn't even get angry. And, to cap it all, Barguelot as usual didn't touch a thing on his plate.'

Margont was distractedly stroking the edge of a desk.

'It's incomprehensible.'

'That's it,' declared Lefine with a look of satisfaction. 'What about you? What have you found out about Delarse?'

'Étienne Delarse is forty-five. He comes from the Charentes nobility. His father was called Louis de Larse but he was one of the few aristocrats who sincerely believed in the Republican cause. Louis de Larse had his name changed to 'Delarse' and died at the battle of Fleurus – on the right side, ours, not on the side of the English and the Royalist émigrés. Colonel Étienne Delarse suffers from severe asthma, which has dominated his life. He was a sickly child and his attacks nearly resulted in his death on several occasions. They thought he was done for and would not live beyond the spring because of his allergies to pollen, rather like the last autumn leaf falling very late. His mother spared no expense in getting him the care of famous doctors. She spent entire nights listening to him fighting for breath, holding his hand, convinced that he was breathing his last.'

Lefine, who feared disease as much as the open sea, shuddered at the description of these moments of agony.

'Yes, I've already heard about his asthma. Soldiers he'd punished made up a little song that enjoyed a certain success. The chorus ran like this: "Delarse in winter beats the lot! Delarse in spring ain't half so hot . . ." '

'I learnt all this from Chief Physician Gras, who's treating him at present,' Margont continued.

'Does he still have attacks?'

'Regularly. And Gras is very worried about it. He thought I was a friend of the colonel's and he told me what he knew in confidence so that I could back up his advice to Delarse to spare himself. But Delarse won't hear a word of it. All you have to do is ask him to rest and he'll get on a horse and start jumping over obstacles. To everyone's surprise, Delarse reached adolescence and beyond. He entered a military academy and came out amongst the top few but his career has been constrained by his illness. On several occasions he has been forced to hand over to his second in command. They say that he has the talent and intelligence of a general and that all he's short of is breath. Believe it or not, several times he had to insist on taking part in this campaign. The general staff thought that Russia would be bad for his lungs. Those on high are convinced he won't last out the war, which is why he hasn't been given a regiment. They preferred to place him beside General Huard but the general already has an aide-de-camp. Delarse's exact position in the hierarchy is unclear. Let's say he acts as a secondary aide-de-camp, even though one is enough for Huard. Delarse is disgusted because he's convinced that if it weren't for his asthma he'd be at least a brigadier-general and on equal terms with Huard. And the worst thing is that he's undoubtedly right.'

Lefine unbuttoned his gaiters and took them off, then removed his shoes and the remains of his socks. His feet were covered in blisters and sores.

'At one time,' Margont went on, 'he even consulted

clairvoyants and the like to try to convince himself that there was an afterlife.'

Lefine began to laugh but Margont interrupted him.

'Don't make fun of him. Who knows what you would have done in his place? I also discovered that for three years Delarse had a mistress who was fifteen years older than he. She must have looked like his mama . . .'

'Don't make fun of him. Who knows what you would have done in his place? There's just one question left.'

'Exactly. Which of the four most resembles a Prince Charming?'

'Not Delarse.'

'Not Delarse,' repeated Margont.

'I'd put my money on Pirgnon, with his artistic and worldly tastes.'

Margont ran his fingers through his hair. It was a habit of his when he was lost in thought. In Madrid a pretty girl had once said she found this attractive. Oh, the girls of Madrid . . . But it was such a woman who had pointed at Barguelot with the tip of her fan . . .

'I would rather vote for Barguelot, with his luxurious lifestyle and gift of the gab.'

'Yes, Barguelot or Pirgnon. And there's still our Italian.'

Margont screwed up his eyes. 'That one really is beginning to annoy me! I simply have to find a way of meeting him at last.'

There were still two hours left before dinner. Margont decided to try to find Colonel Pirgnon.

The bodies had been cleared from the streets and the pools of blood were being washed away with large pails of water. The Emperor had issued orders to prevent looting, and soldiers and gendarmes were ensuring that these instructions were obeyed.

The neighbourhood allocated to the 35th of the Line was in a pitiful state. Men were settling in beneath portions of ceiling that had not collapsed, attempting to fill in the gaps in the roofs with planks blown off by cannonballs. In some cases, those in possession of houses that were still intact were persuaded to sell their places for a fortune. Margont saw a grenadier hand over three paintings, a silk dressing gown and a sable fur hat to a *voltigeur* in exchange for a position near a fireplace.

Colonel Pirgnon had ensured he was well provided for. His quarters were in a baroque-style mansion. Along the pastel-coloured façade, high windows alternated with fake white columns set into the wall. Above the door was an oval window. On the top floor other rounded windows relieved the geometrical rigour of the whole. A flight of steps led up to the front entrance. At ground level soldiers could be heard joking through the basement windows. The entrance hall was enormous. To the right a wide semi-circular staircase broke up the symmetry that had once been the golden rule for façades.

Margont was surprised to find a queue of soldiers from various regiments waiting patiently on the steps. They were carrying a motley collection of objects: a candlestick, vases of various shapes, crockery, porcelain or ivory statuettes. Margont quickly climbed this spiral of greed. His face was expressionless. As he went past, some clasped their treasures to them for fear the captain might take possession of them. A sergeant-major was acting as the doorman. He saluted Margont and, interpreting the captain's attitude as a sign of impatience in selling an item of great value, immediately let him in.

Colonel Pirgnon was examining an icon being shown to him by a Westphalian infantryman. It was of the Virgin Mary holding the Christ Child in her arms. The gilded background was damaged but the two faces remained strangely intact. It was not a miracle, however.

'You filthy dog! You've scraped away all the gilding!' exclaimed Pirgnon, making the Westphalian step backwards. 'You have defaced a work of art!'

The German fled. Pirgnon showed the painting to Margont.

'A painting of the "tenderness" type by the Stroganoff school! And he scraped it with a knife . . .'

The colonel had tears in his eyes. He was tall and well built. His slightly curly, brown hair and his rounded face gave him a placid look. Margont saluted him.

'Captain Margont, 84th Regiment, Huard Brigade, Delzons Division . . .'

'Yes, yes, but if everyone begins like that I'll be spending the whole week in Smolensk. What have you got to sell me?'

Seeing Margont's reproachful look, Pirgnon scowled.

'Oh, I see. You're judging me. May I know the reason for your visit, Captain?'

'Well, Colonel, I've heard that you were the driving force behind the Cervantes Club in Madrid and I myself belong to a literary salon.'

Pirgnon's expression brightened but his pleasure was mixed with wariness. 'Oh, really? And where is that?'

'In Nîmes.'

'And what did you do in your literary salon? Because there are salons and salons.'

'Oh, it's not one of those society salons where people go just to be seen. If that's what people want they can go to Madame Cabarrus's or Madame de Montesson's. I've never been invited, but in any case an evening of deadly boredom is too high a price for me.'

Pirgnon folded his arms. 'How I do sympathise. And what's the name of your salon? Who are its members? What do you do there?'

'The Roast Duck Club.'

Pirgnon seemed put out. Obviously it was far less elegant than the Cervantes Club. His large pink cheeks and huge head made him look a bit like a baby still.

'I have to admit I don't get it, Captain.'

'The members argued about what to call our club. The Cicero Club, the Voltaire Club, the Molière Club . . . But there must be dozens of Voltaire Clubs and Rousseau Clubs in every town.'

'Two Voltaire Clubs were indeed created in Madrid. They had a violent argument about who came up with it first.'

'I trust they both had their comeuppance, so to speak. Well, in a word, we were wondering whether our debates were in the spirit of Rousseau; Molière had his devotees and Voltaire was beating Virgil hands down, which led the poet's supporters to claim that once more the moderns were shafting the ancients. At this juncture I remarked that the only point we were all agreed on was the desire to sit down to a good meal together. My suggestion had in its favour the fact that even if it didn't please many, it didn't offend anyone. And as we had before us at the table six splendid roast ducks . . .'

Pirgnon invited Margont to sit down.

'For Cervantes it was easier. As the instigator of the project and the highest-ranking officer, I chose the name. As literary salons are all the rage, everyone wants their own and all too often society gatherings pompously call themselves "Madame So-and-So's literary salon". People read out poems stolen from those more inspired than themselves, after carefully tinkering with the lines in the naïve belief that they will not be found out. Each member is eager to laugh at the others' offerings in the hope that they will reciprocate. So everyone leaves full of unearned praise. Some even convince themselves that they can "improve" Ducis's rhyming couplets.'

'Our salon is open to all; no account is taken of social background or income or connections, to the chagrin of the prefect who is still not a member. To join our club all you have to do is read out a text you've written that appeals to the members, and be capable of making appropriate comments on political, literary and philosophical topics. During our meetings we submit our writings to critical scrutiny, we discuss works we have read, we argue . . . A sense of humour and a love of rhetorical debate are highly appreciated. Perhaps it's the influence of the Roman amphitheatre that we can see from the windows of our salon. Our most lethal weapon is wit and we finish off those we have wounded with the cutting edge of irony before being reconciled around the inevitable roast ducks.'

Pirgnon grasped Margont's hand and shook it warmly.

'I admit you without further ado to membership of my next salon: the Moscow Club. I hope we will also number some Russian members. Ah! Moscow . . . We all dream of it, don't we?'

Pirgnon began to display his acquisitions. A silver samovar that he liked so much that he had taken to drinking tea for the sole pleasure of using it. An iconostasis, a wooden screen decorated with icons, used for separating the nave from the sanctuary in Orthodox churches. Pirgnon explained that at the centre of the iconostasis saints were depicted interceding with Christ on behalf of the faithful.

'What about you, Colonel? What do you ask of the saints?'

Pirgnon looked at Margont in surprise. He pointed at the paintings he had bought from some Italian soldiers who had been preparing to make a fire out of them so they could cook their meat.

'I was – indirectly – one of the instigators of the decree of 14 Fructidor in the year IX, by order of which the Consulate created fifteen museums. The very idea of a museum fascinates me: bringing art within everyone's reach. Show a Leonardo da Vinci to a tramp or a road sweeper and you open windows in their minds. In antiquity the Greeks reserved seats in their amphitheatres for the poor so that they could see Sophocles being performed. I shall give some of these treasures to museums. Man is nothing, only art matters.'

Margont remained silent, even if this statement shocked his sense of values.

'But,' added Pirgnon, 'as I'm not a saint worthy of an icon, I shall keep the iconostasis and the samovar.'

He strode over to an impossibly cluttered corner of the room and rummaged among a jumble of paintings and elaborately framed mirrors before straightening up triumphantly, holding a canvas in his hands.

'Do you know what this is?'

Margont had no idea. The portrait of a young woman in a pale green dress made him feel uneasy. Strands of her long, wet hair stuck to her face. Strangely, she was standing in a riverbed, indifferent to the icy water swirling around her delicate waist. Stranger still, her pallid complexion contrasted with the beauty of her features. Her skin seemed to be fashioned from the same snow that lay on the ground round about.

'She looks rather poorly,' Margont ventured.

'That's not surprising. She's dead. She's a rusalka. In Eastern European folklore, when a young girl commits suicide by drowning herself, she becomes a rusalka, a creature of the waters who uses her female form to seduce passers-by before drowning them. Some claim that it's in order to devour them, others that it is simply the reflex action of her suffering soul, condemned to wander because it may not enter paradise.'

'I wonder whether they co-operate with the Cossacks because one of them almost skewered me next to a river.'

Pirgnon was studying the rusalka's expression. The seductive look she was displaying had a hint of coldness about it.

'What realism! But let's not be morbid. Do you enjoy classical mythology, Captain?'

'Absolutely.'

'The Russians do too!' Pirgnon exclaimed, delighted that the whole world shared his passion.

In fact, Margont was not madly keen on this topic but he was glad to get away from the rusalka. The colonel stepped over rolled-up carpets, inviting Margont to follow him. He was so devoted to Greek and Roman culture that anything remotely connected with it was carefully exhibited, contrasting with the surrounding mess and waiting only to be seen by the visitors Pirgnon would bring along. It seemed highly unlikely that French museums would ever get a glimpse of these marvels . . .

'Here is Minerva, my favourite goddess.'

Margont went closer to examine in detail a buxom-looking woman girded with a coat of mail. She was combing her tumbling mass of golden hair whilst watching over an array of vases and sculptures.

'You see, Captain, Minerva is the Roman goddess of wisdom and the arts. But the Romans – unlike the Greeks, for whom she was Athena – also gave her a martial dimension. To such an extent that the Roman legions dedicated their war treasures to her. So it's natural that I should give her pride of place in this collection, don't you think?'

Margont agreed, not knowing what else to do. He did not know how to react to this remark. Was it humour? Or irony? A show of contempt towards him because he had been shocked by the systematic looting of Russia's artistic heritage? Pirgnon's personality seemed indistinct to him, elusive.

The colonel, carried away by his guided tour, was now pointing at another subject. It was a gigantic fresco occupying an entire wall. A mass of combatants were slaughtering one another at the foot of walls lined with defenders. The figures, some naked and some wearing helmets and breastplates or sheltering behind broad, decorated shields, were attacking each other with a ferocity that was convincing in its realism. The complexity of the setting was in contrast to the sobriety of the colours, which were limited to either black or ochre. Margont recognised the Trojan War. The Trojans had made a sortie to attempt to recover the body of Hector, one of their heroes, whom Achilles had just struck down.

'The centuries pass, men remain the same,' Margont remarked.

'Men? You mean the gods! Well, demigods. Achilles was the son of Thetis, a sea nymph, and of an ordinary mortal, hence his extraordinary destiny.'

Of all the warriors swarming across the canvas, Pirgnon had eyes only for Achilles, his arm brandishing a forbidding-looking spear and his foot resting on the face of the dead Hector. The Trojans would not recover his mortal remains and for twelve days Achilles would drag them behind his chariot around the tomb of his friend Patroclus, himself slain in combat by Hector.

Pirgnon spoke of Hercules and his mythical labours, Ulysses and the adventures he had on his travels . . . His knowledge of ancient mythology seemed as inexhaustible as the horn of plenty. He was passionate about it and his enthusiasm was infectious. Antiquity made him radiant.

As time was getting on, the sergeant-major came to make sure that all was well. In fact, it was on his side that everything was going badly: on the staircase the soldiers thought that Margont was exhausting Pirgnon's purse and there was almost a riot. So Pirgnon ordered the next salesman to be sent in and turned towards Margont.

'Captain, I must ask you to leave me but I am counting on you for my Moscow Club.'

Margont saluted and went out. He had at last managed to meet the elusive Pirgnon but he didn't feel any the wiser. Delarse, Barguelot and Pirgnon: he hadn't really been able to eliminate any of the three. And he was fuming at still not having had the opportunity to talk to Fidassio. He chased away these thoughts as he wandered along the streets, feasting his eyes on Russian architecture, gilded domes and the orchards that carpeted the steep slopes surrounding the city.

CHAPTER 19

A T precisely eight o'clock in the evening, Margont made his way to the Valiuskis' drawing room, wearing his full-dress uniform. He cut a fine figure in his brilliant white trousers, immaculate dark blue coat, gilded buttons, epaulettes and with his self-assured air. He was disappointed to notice that exactly the same could be said of his friends. Worse than this, Fanselin's scarlet red was particularly striking because of its unusually bright colour. A servant in fir-green livery and white silk stockings begged them to forgive the count and the two countesses, who would be arriving shortly.

The walls of the room were covered in brown wooden panelling. Lefine found this oppressive, as if he were in the cabin of a ship, so he stayed near the window and, having pulled back the heavy yellow, silver-fringed curtains, observed the comings and goings in the street. Piquebois was examining a collection of pipes closely, lost in admiration for the boundless imagination shown by their makers in varying the shapes and sizes. He wondered if it was possible to do the same with life, to make each day in some way unique. Saber, who was comfortably installed in an armchair, was running his fingers along a harpsichord, content to run up and down the scale, while Fanselin seemed fascinated by a globe, which he turned incessantly.

'There's so much to see in the world. Have you travelled widely?' he asked.

'No. There's too much blue on the maps,' Lefine asserted coldly, without turning his head.

'Apparently between the United States and Canada there are lakes as big as seas. It's hard to believe. I absolutely must go there to see them with my own eyes.'

Margont settled himself down between a large harp and a fireguard. Then he immediately got up again to make his way towards a small bookcase placed in a poorly lit corner of the room.

'It took him less than a minute to find it,' Saber joked.

French literature figured prominently: Voltaire, Rousseau, La Bruyère . . . What was more, these works were in French. Russian society was francophile, except when it came to political ideas, whether revolutionary or imperial.

The servant reappeared and made an announcement:

'Their Excellencies Count Valiuski, Countess Valiuska and Countess Natalia Valiuska.'

The count was still wearing the same clothes. He was not the sort of man to change half a dozen times a day. His wife was wearing an elegant violet outfit. An ivory locket with an effigy of the Virgin Mary proclaimed her faith in the face of 'republican heathens'. She looked worn and tired, but dignified – dignified above all and at all times. Her grey hair was drawn back, emphasising the severity of her features, a severity further reinforced by her stiff bearing and disdainful expression. However, age had commenced its slow and cruel work. It was like being in front of a deposed empress.

Natalia had just celebrated her twenty-fifth birthday. She had long suffered from being overshadowed by two such powerful personalities. But she had eventually progressed from the difficult position of obedient, inhibited child to that of a young woman capable of defending tenaciously that indefinable, unique quality that every individual possesses. She was wearing a white dress with a moderately low neckline that would only have shocked the most hypocritical religious bigot. Her gilded belt was tied very high, just beneath her breasts, so that her dress billowed out, disguising her waist and emphasising her height. Her delicate features were framed by her long auburn hair but this impression of fragility was now quite out of keeping with her character. Her narrow nose and thin lips set off her blue eyes, which observed the five Frenchmen with a curiosity tinged with reserve. She was magnificent.

The introductions were brief and the count was careful to make them informal. Clearly determined to ignore this, Saber bent himself double to kiss the hands of the countess and Natalia in a perfectly executed movement. They had only just sat down when the count launched into an interminable speech that was part glorification of Poland, part anti-Russian diatribe and part history of the Valiuski family, peppered unfortunately with a series of questions.

It transpired that the Valiuski family came from the Polish nobility. After suffering revolts, invasions and civil wars combined with wars of religion, Poland had been partitioned three times between Russia, Prussia and Austria, in 1772, 1793 and 1795. The last scramble for territory had resulted in Poland's disappearance pure and simple. When the count recalled the resurrection of the Polish state by Napoleon in 1807 under the name of the 'Grand Duchy of Warsaw', his voice quivered with emotion. If Fanselin had been struck by the distant Americas or mysterious Africa on the globe, the count had eyes for nothing on it except Poland. Smolensk had been captured by the Russians even before the first partition but the Valiuskis had always considered themselves as Polish.

'You do not allow lines on a map to tell you who you are and whom you should serve!' exclaimed the count, pointing to the world spinning around beneath the lancer's fingers.

It was just as well that there were five of them to answer his questions. Why had the Emperor not yet announced that the territories taken from the Russians had been handed back to Poland? Why had the Grand Duchy of Warsaw not been swallowed up in a larger territorial unit called Poland?

How was it possible to tell such a warm-hearted man that the Emperor had made no promises about the resurrection of Poland because he did not want to offend Austria and Prussia, his new-found allies, who could still smell the powder of the French gunfire at Austerlitz, Jena and Wagram? Besides, the Emperor wanted to negotiate with Alexander and, if his plan came to fruition, its price would be to give the area invaded back to Russia. Napoleon knew that one of the preconditions to any talks with the Tsar was to rule out categorically the restoration of a Polish state. Piquebois proved to be surprisingly diplomatic in finding the right way of putting it: the Emperor rarely set out his plans but what was certain was that he always saw through to the end whatever he had in mind. The count pretended to be taken in. But there was nothing you could teach a Valiuski about politics. He prayed every night for the situation to get worse. The more the French suffered, the more obdurate Alexander would become. Then the stakes in this war would rise spectacularly, as would the Emperor's exasperation until he crushed the Russians and imposed an unconditional peace. This was the count's point of view: a desire for the storm to break and for the wind to blow in the right direction, extending the Polish border far into Russia . . . all the way to Smolensk.

Margont noticed that the countess was proving distinctly less friendly towards them than her husband, especially in the presence of the servants, whom she addressed in Russian. He would have given a lot to understand the meaning of her words. Was she criticising the presence of the French in her house? Had she condemned their lack of piety because they had not crossed themselves in front of what Margont had later realised was an icon chest? A pro-French count and a pro-Russian countess: the Valiuski family and its property would survive the war. Did not the winners always reward those who had supported them in times of crisis? Natalia seemed to disapprove of this two-pronged approach but she remained silent. Tea was served. Seeing the simmering water come pouring out of the spout of the samovar as the chill of the evening descended was one of those small pleasures that would put anyone in a good mood.

When the count had stopped monopolising the conversation, Saber was quick to take over. He constantly sought Natalia's attention, questioning her about her activities and marvelling out loud to himself about the things they had in common. Incredibly, he too adored music, reading and going for walks.

The countess did not like the idea of Saber wooing her daughter. He had after all only one fringed epaulette whereas his fellow officers, with the exception of Piquebois, had two. She was not absolutely sure but she thought that this single fringed epaulette indicated a lower rank – and therefore poorer prospects. She decided to engage in conversation only with officers who were 'properly epauletted', so in her opinion Saber and Piquebois were beyond the pale. As for the non-commissioned officer, he simply did not exist.

The count had read his wife's thoughts. Considering Saber to be overstepping the mark, he took advantage of one of the Frenchman's mistakes. Saber had tried to show off by talking about the battle of Wagram and was about to launch into a description of one of his rescue missions when the count exclaimed: 'So you were at Wagram, were you? There were plenty of Poles at Wagram!' He then rained questions on him. Saber thus became a prisoner of Wagram, releasing Natalia.

'What do you like about Russia?' asked the young lady without directing the question at any of the Frenchmen in particular.

Saber was furious but he could scarcely abandon the Polish Chevau-Légers as they were about to charge.

'What I like most in Russia is Poland,' Piquebois calmly declared.

Fanselin was more reserved. 'So far all Russia has had to offer us is being fired on amongst the ashes, but I'm sure there are fascinating things to discover.'

'Such as?' asked Natalia.

'I've no idea, but if they're there, I'll find them.'

Fanselin then began to talk in a voice that the others did not recognise, a voice simultaneously full of wonder and laden with sorrow.

'In Sweden there are regions entirely given over to nature where there are only lakes and forests as far as the eye can see. When autumn comes the leaves display an infinite variety of shades. In Italy, ancient monuments have miraculously survived and it would come as no surprise to encounter men in togas, talking in Latin. In the south of Spain, western Christian art and the Muslim art of the Moors are fused in a harmony that is unique in the world, thus succeeding where men have failed. I lived in these three countries for several months before tiring of them. But I know that one day I will discover a landscape and a culture that will make me feel truly at home. That day I will lay down my arms and settle down. Perhaps I will at last find my paradise in Russia. Perhaps not.'

Natalia nodded distantly, meditating on these words.

'What about you, Captain Margont?'

'Each country has its own culture, and every culture is by definition fascinating. I have come here to encounter Russian culture and to bring to it republican ideals.'

The young woman seemed put out.

'To encounter Russian culture? Are you not aware that the victors always destroy the culture of the vanquished? What did the conquistadors retain of the culture of the Aztecs and of the Incas? Nothing as far as I can see, apart from slaves, land and the gold obtained from melting down their jewels.'

'Well, perhaps they missed exactly what was most precious. Like the magpies, they went straight for what glittered.'

'So what do you know about Russian or Polish culture? You'll tell me that the peasants dance on their haunches, kicking their legs in the air, that the priests have funny long beards, that people travel around by sleigh in the winter and that the bell towers of the churches have decidedly odd roofs . . . Well, if that's what Russian culture is for you . . .'

'All that is indeed part of it. But an essential element of this culture seems to me to be tenacity. During some fighting I saw a whole row of Russians fall to the ground when under fire by our company. There were only three soldiers left standing. Do you think those three surrendered? No, they fought hand to hand with determination, as if they'd been facing up to us right in the middle of their battalion, packed tight against one another. There are traces of this Russian fighting spirit to be found in you.'

The young woman blinked. She had never been spoken to like this. Her mother had noticed how troubled she looked but, having a poor command of French, she did not properly understand the reason.

Thinking that her daughter had been shocked by the virile account of some martial exploit, she was quick to declare: 'War is a terrible thing. It's better not to talk about it.'

Piquebois sat up in his chair. 'How skilful you are, Countess, at summarising the situation and solving the most difficult issues.'

The countess smiled at him politely to thank him for his compliment, its biting irony completely escaping her. She announced that it was time to go for dinner and rose to her feet. Her husband took her arm. Fanselin did likewise with Natalia, his privilege as a member of the Guard.

As they made their way to the dining room, Saber whispered to Margont: 'Trying to seduce the young countess, are we? A château and the title of count for the price of a wedding ring is a pretty good way of recovering one's costs. It's pathetic! Watching you boast about your military exploits like that . . .'

'But my dear Irénée, it's your own reflection you're looking at.'

'Pathetic!'

The immense dining room was decorated with tapestries depicting impenetrable forests or waterfalls in which water sprites were bathing. The Russians excelled in the use of coloured glass in their lighting. Thus the emerald glass in the stem of the chandelier created a play of light with the crystals, which blended well with the tones of the tapestries. The tablecloth was dark green and matched the colour of the rims of the plates and the count's coat of arms. These arms, depicting a silver-headed bear on a fir-green background, appeared on the middle of every plate, were engraved on the crystal glasses and chased on the silver cutlery. Images detailing the construction of the château, stage by stage, were painted on to large porcelain vases, which alternated with three-legged crystal vases. Margont noticed that the bright light that evening was provided by a clever arrangement of mirrors and chandeliers, but, by extinguishing only a few candles, an intimate effect could be achieved.

The count and his wife took their seats at either end of the table. The count had placed Margont on his right and his daughter on his left. The countess had Fanselin on her right and Piquebois on her left. Saber was sitting between Fanselin and Natalia, and Lefine was opposite Saber. Margont appreciated the comfort of the chairs, which were quite unlike the Empire style, with its mixture of classical, Greco-Roman influences and military grandeur. How could the Emperor like those rigid geometrical lines and annoying edges that no plane was allowed to smooth? Still, even if that aesthetic showed scant regard for the functional, at least it did so with panache.

The count said grace and the meal began with an enormous plate of zakuski, that traditional assortment of appetisers and starters, including meat vol-au-vents, black bread canapés with multicoloured garnishes, croquettes, mother-of-pearl spoons filled with caviar . . .

'I love Russian architecture,' Saber announced to Natalia.

'In that case, why are you shelling it?'

Saber was flabbergasted. He had not seriously imagined that anyone could resist his charm.

'My dear Natalia,' the count interjected in a paternalistic tone of voice, 'you are giving an opinion on a subject that is beyond you.'

'The Emperor's policies are beyond us all,' Margont remarked.

They are beyond even your Emperor, the countess thought.

Margont realised what was familiar about the count: he reminded him of Saber. It was those gestures full of 'natural superiority' that Saber strove awkwardly to imitate. Saber's attitude made no sense. He had remarkable qualities as a strategist and was wasting his time learning the rules of polite society and trying to make an impression. Nature had given him a precious gift but he complained about the quality of its wrapping.

The zakuski were followed by red soup made with peppers and sour cream in the Ukrainian style. The count once more launched into the history of the Valiuski family. Unfortunately, this time he began with the battle of Tannenberg, or battle of Grunwald, which had taken place in 1410. It was after this that Ladislas II Jagiello, King of Poland and Grand Duke of Lithuania, had rewarded the Valiuski family by ennobling it and giving it a bear as its coat of arms. The bear because those 'grizzly peasants' had carried out a massacre and had seized an enemy standard, that of Johann von Redern, the commander of Brathian and Neumarket. The banner was white and decorated with three stag horns joined at the base. The count was sorry not to be able to show it to his guests but it was hanging in one of his country houses near Moscow.

'Then we'll be seeing it soon,' decreed Fanselin.

The count gave a detailed account of how the Teutonic Knights were crushed by the army of Ladislas II Jagiello. As it happened, in 1809 Napoleon had ordered the dissolution of this religious and military order and the count drew a host of other parallels between France and Poland, their common enemies and desires. His fervent wish for the restoration of Poland clouded his judgement: he sincerely believed that the futures of France and Poland were inextricably linked, a notion that history had categorically confirmed many times, in his opinion.

While Saber was dreaming of being a Polish count, the count

was imagining himself living in a Greater Poland . . . Margont wondered, then, what he himself aspired to. Normally his immediate, idealistic response to such questions was the liberty of nations, an end to the slaughter, a stable peace in Europe, the spread of republican ideas . . . But that evening he was weary. All he wanted was to have a pleasant time. Noble aspirations are considerably diminished by hunger and tiredness.

Natalia was not listening to her father. In any case, she had heard him recount the battle of Tannenberg so often that she was beginning to wonder whether she'd actually taken part in it. Margont intrigued her. He seemed different from the men she had so far met. Her father had always given her orders. Her admirers, of whom there had been a considerable number in recent years, seemed equally authoritarian. They never bothered to listen to what she said to them and assumed she thought the same as they. And these were the best of her suitors, those who accepted the idea that women could have an opinion – although they should not express it. Things had come to a head at the beginning of the war. She had received a procession of officers in the palace: a captain from the hussars of the Guard, an elderly infantry colonel, a lieutenant from the Preobrajensky Regiment (above all, remember to congratulate him for being in the Guard, her mother had told her a hundred times), and a surprising number of aides-de-camp. In any case she thought it stupid that there should be so many of the latter. Since all the regiments hated one another and their officers sometimes went so far as refusing to speak to one another, what was the point of lining up so many messengers? In fact, she knew full well that nobles fought over the positions of aide-de-camp for the simple reason that they had less chance – relatively speaking – of being exposed to enemy fire.

All these visitors had behaved in an extraordinarily inept manner. Most of them had promised to bring her back a French flag topped with its eagle emblem. They thought this would please her but the idea horrified her. A piece of bloodstained material together with the certainty that its bearer, like its escort, had been exterminated and that the flagpole had been removed from their dead fingers: what a delightful present! Anyway, they already had the one seized at Tannenberg, so how many more did they need? A Cossack had even promised her Napoleon's head, probably confusing her with Salome. She was eternally grateful to her father for his pro-Polish views, without which she would have been married off to a Russian aristocrat long ago. But her relative freedom was nearing its end. Her mother had given her six months to make her choice from the list of names she had drawn up herself 'to help her to avoid making a mistake she would regret for the rest of her life'. The war had forced a postponement of the deadline because announcing an engagement to someone who might be killed soon afterwards would have put her in a difficult position with regard to the surviving suitors.

Oh, the war! Men waged war for a thousand different reasons but what difference did victory really make? She could find only one answer: the colour of the uniforms and the designs on the banners that would be hung up in the drawing rooms. Might Margont be different? She wanted to provoke him, to push him to the limits in order to study his reactions. Oh, she was under no illusions. He would probably maintain an indignant silence like Lieutenant Saber, or order her to be quiet, just as her father did. Or, even worse, he would behave like her suitors, greeting her comments with a kindly and unbearably patronising smile. In that case she would quickly drain her glass to prevent herself from throwing its contents in his face.

When the servants brought in the coulibiac, salmon in pastry, with mushrooms, celery, onions and dill, she said to Margont: 'Here's a little more Russian culture for you to devour.'

'Well, you devour our writers: Voltaire, La Fontaine . . .'

So he had noticed the books? An accident, no doubt.

'So you know the fables of La Fontaine, do you? They make edifying reading. "The Wolf and the Lamb" for example. "Might Is Right".'

'Dear Natalia,' the count interjected, 'having sung all summer, the cicada was caught unprepared when the north wind blew.'

Which was supposed to mean: if the cicada Natalia continued to mock, eternal winter – that is, the marriage she so much feared – would come earlier than expected.

'*Dura lex, sed lex*,' Margont summed up.

'But Natalia is always happy to please her parents, Captain,' the countess claimed. 'Do you not say in France "blood will out"?'

'Well, we usually say, "What a woman wants, God wants." Mademoiselle, I quite understand that our enforced presence is annoying. However, Russian hospitality . . .'

'What do you know about Russian hospitality?' Natalia asked.

'Well, it's said that samovars are pot-bellied because people want to be sure there's always enough boiling water to be able to serve tea to all the guests.'

The young woman was surprised. So he knew that, did he? He really was not like the others. She wanted to scratch this varnish just to check.

'What present would you offer your hosts by way of thanks?'

Her mother smiled, interpreting the question as the expression of a child's greed. In her mind there could be no other explanation.

'Poland! Poland!' whispered the count, beaming.

Natalia stared at Margont, wondering whether he too was planning to present her with standards, guns and heaps of corpses.

'The promise to give them an equally warm welcome in France. But without the caviar, I'm afraid . . .'

Natalia then asked with false naïvety: 'Would my father also have to come in uniform and accompanied by five hundred thousand soldiers?'

'We'd have enough cannonballs to feed the lot of them,' muttered Saber in his corner, without turning his head.

The count was furious. With a discreet gesture he ordered his army of servants to enter the battlefield. The salmon coulibiac was replaced by a hare *à la polonaise*. Bacon, lard, fresh cream, juniper and caramel: extravagant but delicious. It was served with potatoes and red cabbage. All the guests rejoiced at the sight. Fanselin's joy was the most intense, such was his love of discovering new flavours, in the widest possible sense of the word.

'Natalia plays the harpsichord very well,' announced the count.

The young countess gracefully placed her napkin over her mouth so as not to be seen gritting her teeth. So they also expected to make her play after the meal, did they?

'It would seem that she doesn't play enough, since it is said that music soothes the savage breast,' Margont joked.

Natalia was flabbergasted. So now she was being attacked on ironic territory, her territory! Because if they took away her irony, how else could she express herself freely? The colour of the feathers of her nightingales and the length of her shawls?

'A soldier presumes to explain to me how music soothes the savage breast,' she retorted.

'I'm a soldier only because we are living in a time of war.'

'What will you do when the peace treaty has finally been signed?' asked the countess.

In the countess's mind the question was a tactful way of finding out about the officer's wealth. Admittedly, she thought him low-ranking. But he did belong to the French army, the only one in which any soldier could climb to the very top. She had learnt that Murat was the son of an innkeeper. Yes, an innkeeper! Really, that was quite ridiculous! He had begun his career as an ordinary soldier. Today, at the age of forty-five, he was a Marshal of France, Grand Admiral of France, Grand Duke of Berg and of Cleves, a prince and, to cap it all, King of Naples. The son of an innkeeper King of Naples! Oh, the French and their Revolution. No respect for the rules and for social barriers.

Margont put down his knife and fork to reply. His dreams were even more appetising than the famous hare à *la polonaise*.

'Well, I would like to launch a newspaper.'

A newspaper. How terribly amusing! thought the countess. She invented on the spur of the moment a short proverb: 'Innkeeper, King of Naples; journalist, King of the Alps.'

'A journalist?' Natalia said in surprise.

Given the interest her daughter had shown in the captain, Countess Valiuska decided on reflection that he was not at all amusing. She was already beginning to worry that her adage might become: 'Innkeeper, King of Naples; journalist, Count Valiuski.' There was no question of letting that happen.

'I love writing and—'

But Margont was interrupted by Piquebois. 'Are you seriously considering launching a newspaper? My dear old friend, it's impossible. Censorship will close it down within weeks and the law will force you to pay the state-appointed censor out of your own pocket.'

Margont agreed, his lips puckering up with anger. 'Yes, you have to feed the hand that bites you.'

'And he's entitled to comment on every line, on the lay-out . . . In any case, there's a decree prohibiting more than one newspaper per département, so your project will just join a long waiting list that the prefect will sit on every morning.'

'I know all that. Before 1800 there were more than seventy newspapers in Paris. Today there are only half a dozen left. The commission for the freedom of the press is practically alone in showing real support for the freedom of the press because it considers itself incompetent to judge newspapers and never gets involved in anything. Such are republicans! Now it's censorship that should be censored.'

Fanselin was also interested in the subject.

'The only interesting things left to read are the bulletins of the Grande Armée.'

Piquebois looked sceptical. 'I admit I like reading the bulletins but the truth is distorted by propaganda. There are the enemy who died on the battlefield and those who died in the pages of the bulletin and often a lot more appear in the second category.'

' "The pen is mightier than the sword",' said Margont ironically.

'It's true that in the bulletins everything looks straight-forward,' Saber added. 'They announce that the Austrians took a thrashing here and the Prussians there . . . Fine, but we aren't told how difficult it was or what price was paid.'

Fanselin raised his hands to concede the point. 'I know. I know the expression "to lie like a bulletin". But I like the bulletins of the Grande Armée because I was mentioned in them in relation to the battle of Essling. It was this bulletin that later opened the doors of the Red Lancers for me. What I also like is that you really feel something when you read them: emotion, enthusiasm and even elation! It's quite something when the French army manages to break through the Austrian army! Never mind if they claim that twenty thousand Russians ended up at the bottom of a pond at Austerlitz when really it wasn't even a quarter of that number.'

'Which is a great shame,' murmured the count.

Margont, wild with joy, was pointing at Fanselin. 'Well said. If you write, it's to give the reader a thrill! Words combat the tedium of the daily routine.'

'In that case one wonders why there are any newspapers left,' Saber remarked.

'Why do you say that?' asked the count, whilst, to the chagrin of the French, who were expecting dessert, the servants brought in paprika poussins, three per person.

Margont stared at the little birds placed in front of him. He hadn't started on them yet but already felt almost sick from overeating. A captain in the French army defeated by three little birds, how sad . . .

'Censorship means that all the newspapers say the same thing in the same way, namely that everything the State does is wonderful,' he said. 'It's the daily imperial litany.'

'They should all print the same headline, "Fantastic!" every day,' Piquebois suggested.

Natalia seemed disappointed when she said to Margont: 'Things don't look very promising for your plans.'

'I've already thought about this problem. Until such time as censorship loosens its hold, I might launch a monthly periodical devoted to theatre and the arts. There would be literary criticisms, theatre reviews . . . and by slipping in references in these articles it might be possible to deal with politics indirectly.'

Saber was highly amused. 'A newspaper full of literary criticism and theatre reviews? What an idea! And why not recipes as well?'

'Why not, indeed?' retorted Margont, smiling complicitly at Natalia as she glared at a Saber still roaring with laughter.

'Don't listen to him, Quentin,' advised Piquebois. 'When the newspaper appears, Irénée will keep coming to ask you why there's nothing about him on the front page.'

'In any case, the mere fact of talking about a newspaper encourages debate and stimulates freedom of expression,' Margont concluded.

For the rest of the meal the count carried on talking, convinced that the guests were eagerly awaiting the next instalment of the history of the Valiuski family. When the dessert did arrive it was on a silver platter carried by two servants. The French looked dubiously at the golden or meringue-topped brioches and the cakes spiced with honey.

Seeing their embarrassment, Natalia declared: 'Don't forget that after the meal you still have the entire Russian army to gobble up.'

The count cast a deeply reproachful look at his wife. This, in his view, was where the education she had chosen had led her daughter. Mothers often stand quite alone in these cases. Fanselin and Margont both smiled to indicate that they were not offended.

The meal finally ended with strongly brewed smoked tea accompanied by milk, honey and caramels. The servants poured into the cups some of the contents of the chainik, the small teapot kept on top of the samovar, before adding some hot water from the samovar itself. Natalia discreetly observed Margont's hands, his rather slender fingers, the way he held his cup . . . For some unknown reason, this pleased her.

Countess Valiuska rose just as they were taking away the samovar and said that it was time she and her daughter went to bed. Margont was sorry to see Natalia leave and surprised to see her return a moment later. Her mother was following her, like a spectre ensuring that the soul in its charge does not flee the underworld to which it must be taken, namely the boredom of the bedroom. Natalia went up to Margont and handed him a book entitled in French: *Extraits de la littérature française*.

'This is for you, since you are so fond of words. You can return it to me when your army comes back via Smolensk.'

A few minutes later, settled in the red drawing room, Margont was still thinking about Natalia while the count sang the praises of the vodka produced on his estate. Margont could see the gestures of the count and his friends but could not hear what they were saying. Without thinking, he swallowed a mouthful from the glass he had been served and the sensation of burning caused by the vodka brought him back to reality, a reality now interwoven with uninteresting snippets of conversation. The evening had been wonderful because it had been outside the war, outside time.

CHAPTER 20

WAKING up was particularly unpleasant. The previous evening's reception seemed to belong to an already distant past. A servant came to wake Margont, saying that an officer, Captain Dalero, from the grenadiers of the Royal Italian Guard, was demanding to see him. Dalero was wearing a green jacket with a white leather cross-belt. He looked enormous with his huge red-plumed bearskin busby. Like Margont, he was ill-shaven and his uniform was crumpled, but it seemed to matter more to him. His swarthy face was marked by a strange semi-circular scar that ran along the top of his left cheekbone. Margont wondered whether it was self-inflicted, to give a more martial appearance. Dalero immediately took Margont outside. He was walking so quickly that the three grenadiers accompanying him had difficulty keeping up. As for Lefine, he had been alerted but was still getting dressed in his bedroom.

'I've been sent by His Highness Prince Eugène. The person you are looking for may have killed again.'

Margont turned pale. He thought of Natalia, however absurdly, since several dozen members of his company had quarters in the château. Besides, Dalero and he were moving away from the Valiuski residence. However, two images became superimposed in his mind: Natalia lying on her bed and the tortured body of Maria. The vision of Natalia became clearer and Margont had the impression of actually being in her presence. Her body had been slashed with a knife; her hands were clutching her slit throat; her hair, clotted with blood, partially covered her face; her naked body was in an obscene posture deliberately chosen by her torturer. The more Margont tried to banish this scene from his mind, the clearer and more credible it became. An extreme tension came over him. He saw himself confronting the murderer. He leapt on him, ran him through repeatedly with his sword, stopping only to gaze at a lifeless figure at his feet. He was astonished at the violence of this image and tried to rid himself of his fear and hatred. To no avail. Captain Dalero noticed nothing. He was displaying the detachment that Margont had felt until he had opened the lid of Maria's coffin.

'The prince is furious with you!' Dalero announced. 'Why do you give him so little news? Why hasn't the murderer been identified yet?'

Margont spread his arms. 'When, of course, it's so simple . . .'

'We can speak freely: my men understand only Italian and the prince has put me fully in the picture. What new information have you got?'

'Nothing,' Margont lied. 'We have thirty or so suspects but some are high-ranking. There are even some colonels on the list!'

'Colonels . . .' Dalero repeated as if he needed to hear himself say it for it to sink in.

The streets were practically deserted. They came across only a few stray inhabitants or drunken soldiers staggering about.

'Discreet as always!' exclaimed Dalero. 'That's the only

aspect of your investigation the prince is satisfied with. I've had the servants of the house questioned: the victim was . . . what's that delightful way you have of putting it in France? Oh, yes, a "man-eater".'

'No, not a man-eater!' Margont cut in.

Dalero raised his eyebrows. 'And why not a man-chaser?'

'I won't answer that. Since my discretion is the only thing that's valued I might as well keep it.'

'Very well. So be it. The woman was called Ludmila Sperzof. She had married Count Sperzof, a captain in the hussars who was killed during the war against the Turks. The servants of the house were very fond of the captain and hated their mistress: they spoke their minds about her. She was always having affairs with other men, even with hussars serving under him. I was told all sorts of stories: that she had a relationship with so-and-so, that all Smolensk knew, that she didn't even mark the anniversary of her husband's death, that sometimes she had two hussars in bed with her at the same time . . .'

'Are you sure it wasn't one of the servants who killed her?'

'You're going up in my estimation. I don't think so. I'll get to the crime soon but allow me to finish the account of the Sperzof couple. An elderly retainer, a former hussar who served under the captain, gave me to understand that the count, in despair at his wife's behaviour, blew his brains out. His hussars covered up the deed and the following day they charged with his body, leaving it behind on the battlefield before going back to collect it with full military honours.'

'So officially it's the Turks who get the blame and not the sultana . . . What sort of men did she choose as her lovers?'

'I didn't go into that amount of detail but her maidservants were vying with one another to give me the sauciest snippets. The countess was particularly fond of military men, especially those with a violent streak. Incidentally, one night one of them tried to rape a chambermaid.'

Margont was at a loss. 'Are you sure of the truth of what you were told? Perhaps one of the servants had a grudge against the countess and slandered her.'

Dalero shook his head vigorously. 'I questioned eight servants and they all said the same thing. The countess often entertained officers and plied them with drink. Sometimes she didn't even bother to go as far as the bedroom and the meal turned into an orgy. The countess also involved a pretty maidservant with morals as loose as hers and threw her out of the house when she became pregnant.'

'But surely not all her lovers were military thugs, were they?'

'Yes, they were. People who behaved normally didn't interest her. Some tried their luck – because the countess was beautiful and wealthy – but to no avail. Only brutes. The lover she kept the longest, that's to say three months, was a lieutenant in the dragoons called Garufski. One day he thrashed a manservant because his bathwater had gone cold. On another occasion he hit a female servant and broke two of her teeth.'

Dalero was gripping the pommel of his sabre with his white glove. He was smiling. He looked frightening.

'I'd like to get my hands on this Garufski.'

Margont scratched the palm of his hand by stroking his day's growth of beard.

'Let's get back to the murderer we're hunting for. It's certainly not the same man who killed our Polish woman and this countess.'

'Well, I'm convinced of the opposite. The victim was riddled with stab wounds. I was told that the Polish woman had received the same treatment. In my opinion, such cruelty is the trademark of the person we're after. But you'll see that for yourself.'

The group arrived in front of a large residence whose pastel-coloured façade was black with soot. A grenadier from the Royal Guard who was guarding the entrance stood stiffly to attention. Only Dalero and Margont went inside the house.

'How did she meet her murderer?'

'At nightfall, she went out "hunting for a lover" – that was how the servants put it. To avoid being attacked by someone not of her choosing she was escorted by Yvan, a giant muzhik.'

'Why didn't you tell me this earlier? I absolutely must meet him.'

'There he is.'

Dalero pointed to a tiny room beneath the stairs. Cubbyhole would have been a better description. A man with an unkempt beard was lying on a straw mattress that took up all the space. He was so tall that his legs hung over his pallet. His cream tunic was bloodstained. He was dead.

'Yvan was utterly devoted to the countess. He acted as her bodyguard, preventing his mistress from being harassed by men she had thrown out of her bed, and as her "emergency lover" at "slack times". He lived below the stairs so that he would be woken by anyone going up or down.'

Margont entered the boxroom. He examined the cloak lying on the floor and found a pistol and a hunting knife in one of the pockets. Dalero gazed at the body in disgust. He regarded it in the same way as he would some hideous beast killed in a hunt.

'So the countess went out last night with Yvan. She must have roamed around before meeting a man who suited her. All three came back here. The servant who saw them return said it was about one o'clock in the morning. The "lucky man" wished to remain anonymous because he was wearing a cloak with a hood that he kept on, even as he went up the stairs.'

'So he already knew he was going to kill her.'

'The servant didn't see the man's face. All he can say is that he was rather tall.'

'What about his boots, his hands, his outfit? Did he notice nothing?'

'No. The countess was talking and laughing. He was not speaking. When the countess went upstairs with someone, no servant was allowed to follow. Yvan would be sleeping in his cubbyhole and woe betide anyone who woke him!'

'Poor fellow. He was jealous.'

Dalero's brow furrowed. 'Jealous of a woman like that? Anyway . . . the countess often sent her lovers packing after an hour, an old habit dating from the time when her husband would return late after playing cards. The man would then go back downstairs, which would wake Yvan, who would open the door for him. Then the countess would order Yvan to change the dirty sheets . . .'

'Yvan was waiting for the guest to depart, since he was dressed,' Margont remarked. 'There was no sign of a struggle. Without warning, the murderer thrust the blade of his knife into Yvan's heart.'

'Just as with the sentry.'

Margont quickly climbed the steps. When he saw the victim, the face twisted with pain and the body slashed all over, it reminded him of Maria Dorlovna in her coffin. It was the same murderer. There were two new victims and part of his theory had just collapsed.

The countess's naked body was lying on the bed, in the middle of a large bloodstain. The wounds seemed even more numerous and horrible than on the first victim. Part of the muscles of the forearm had even been sliced through to the bone. To stifle his victim's screams the killer had done the same as with Maria: the pillowcase had been bitten and torn and was soaked with saliva and blood. Other details seemed to have no apparent significance. The killer had laid opened oysters upon the victim's slashed breasts. He had heaped nuts on her genitals and smeared mulberries over her face, staining it black with the crushed fruit. Lumps of fat had been left on her stomach. A book had been placed in her left hand, open at a map of Africa. The cover torn from another book with a Russian title had been placed on the left thigh while the pages lay scattered across the floor. Finally, tea leaves had been strewn around her feet.

Captain Dalero had not gone beyond the door frame. Unable to go back because of his sense of duty and unable to go in because of his revulsion, he was literally trapped between cowardice and madness.

Margont guessed what he was thinking and declared: 'Captain, could you find a servant to translate the titles of these works?'

Dalero could then beat an honourable retreat, which he hastened to do. Margont gathered the books and picked up a few torn-out pages. He studied the bloody footmarks that led from the bed to the bowl of water standing on a table. An old man arrived a few moments later.

'I translate,' he declared, with a strong foreign accent.

He examined the book covers that Margont handed to him.

'Book of maps and military book of war against Turks by Colonel Uchekin. The count liked very much.'

'Where were they kept?'

'Drawing room below.'

'What about the oysters and the fat?'

'Kitchen or larder.'

'Good. So no one must be allowed to go into those rooms until I've inspected them. No one, is that clear?'

The servant seemed relatively unperturbed at finding his mistress in such a state. Margont asked him why.

The servant shrugged. 'Me always say she finish like that. Now she burn in hell and she enjoy that.'

'Nobody deserves such a death.'

Margont stood there without moving for a considerable time, observing these details. All this had a meaning, of that he was sure. It was a new mystery but even more difficult to solve, given the almost unbearable sight of this mutilated body defiled by food.

When Lefine arrived, he found Margont in the corridor in

the act of smelling a bunch of dahlias and assorted roses displayed on a pedestal table. Lefine prepared to enter the bedroom but Margont suddenly raised his arm.

'I strongly advise you not to.'

Lefine obeyed. Margont asked the servant to leave and waited until he was far enough away before continuing, 'Are you sure that your men were keeping a careful eye on our suspects?'

'They are perfectly trustworthy. If one of our colonels had gone out during the night, they would have seen him, would have informed us immediately and would have followed him. In my opinion we've made a mistake: none of the four is the killer.'

Margont sighed. 'Unless this man realised that he was being spied on. Perhaps he eventually noticed that the same soldier was often glancing at him or perhaps one of the people we've questioned to build up a picture of him went and told him about our investigation.'

'But my men and I have been very careful when trying to worm things out of people to play it casual, as if we were just passing the time of day.'

'If the person we're after has discovered he's being watched, he must have left his quarters in secret. Have you seen the size of the palace we've been billeted in? And the colonels are even better provided for. If you know you're being spied on, nothing would be easier than to slip out of one of the many windows on the ground floor.'

Lefine was staring down at his boots like a naughty boy who'd been found out.

'It would take a whole company to watch all the possible

exits. Obviously, my men were only keeping an eye on the doors.'

'He sneaked out and went in search of his prey, laughing at how stupid we'd feel the next day.'

'I'm very sorry . . .'

Margont patted him on the arm. 'It's not your fault. The worst thing is that even though he knew he was being watched, he still managed to get out to commit another crime. It's something he can't control; he has to give himself over to this butchery. So if we don't arrest him, he'll strike again. And this time there's no comparison with the considerable risks he took in murdering Élisa Lasquenet – if he really was the culprit – and Maria Dorlovna. He's greatly improved his technique: no haste, no more escaping across the rooftops, he didn't attract attention . . .'

'Are we going to call in Jean-Quenin to examine the body?'

'What would you expect from an examination?'

'Well . . . nothing.'

'I too would like something to cling on to, to be able to say to myself: "This is what I must do and when I've done it, everything will become clear." I don't think Jean-Quenin would be able to teach us anything and I don't have the heart to ask him to devote two hours of his time to us when he's rushing around tending the wounded. Fernand, my theory of the Prince Charming doesn't stand up: this victim only liked rough soldiers.'

The killer seemed to have a very sharp mind and a talent for acting. He had quickly surmised that Maria Dorlovna wanted a man able to show tenderness and refinement . . . so he had become that man. And he had had no difficulty in becoming the military tough liking a good screw for Countess Sperzof. Margont was no longer looking for a Prince Charming but for a chameleon.

Dalero joined him again. Margont was surprised to see that he had shaved. He must have used his knife or a servant's razor. He had also had his coat pressed. He seemed restored, using his image as a crutch to lean on. Without saying a word, he went into the bedroom to examine the body. Lefine forced himself to do likewise so as not to be the only one to avoid that painful experience, but he came out again almost immediately.

On his way out, Dalero said to Margont: 'Good. I shall write a report at once about this new crime and about the progress of your investigation. The prince will have it within the hour. Take care in the fighting. Don't expose yourself to too much danger.'

'Why so much concern for me?'

'Because if you get yourself killed, I'm the one the prince will appoint to replace you.'

CHAPTER 21

THE man was slumped in an armchair, in one of the drawing rooms of his quarters in Smolensk. Nothing in this wonderful room could hold his attention, not the height of the ceiling – quite out of proportion – nor the furniture with its embroidered upholstery, nor the chest of drawers inlaid with panels of Chinese or Japanese lacquer . . . His mind was occupied by images of other things. He was recalling the feelings that had overwhelmed him while he was torturing that woman, especially when he had disfigured her face. The mutilations had rendered that body anonymous and his imagination had seen the reflection of other faces in this mirror of blood: the shy wife of one of his officers; a former lady-friend to whom he had been very close; women he had come across in the street . . . On the other hand, he had killed the servant on the spur of the moment because he had been frightened. That giant with arms and legs like the branches of an oak tree could have broken his neck with one swipe, like a bear. He regretted the hastiness of it. He would have liked to tie the beast to his straw mattress and cut him up bit by bit. But the exquisite taste of pleasure was mingled with a feeling of anxiety.

A few days earlier he had visited a field hospital. Oh, the wounded! He had looked at them writhing like the worms he used to cut in two as a child. The funniest thing was that people had thought it was compassion. Compassion! Seeing these

255

anguished faces smile at him as if he were a saint had doubled his pleasure.

The following day, as he was exploring the area, he had noticed that a man he had seen the previous day near one of the wounded was riding some way off from his escort. He had assumed he was a marauder, except that he saw him later and then understood. He suspected that someone was investigating the murder of the Polish woman but he had been amazed to realise how far the investigations had progressed without unmasking him. It must be because of Maria's private journal. What an absurd idea to write everything down in a notebook perfumed with dried rose petals! Maria had told him about it as you tell someone a secret as a mark of confidence. She had immediately added with a sway of the hips that she would never let anyone read it, not even him. As if he could be interested in such childish activities! It was only afterwards, just after killing her, that he had remembered that lieutenant who had come galloping up to them from nowhere and saluted him saying: 'Colonel, an urgent message for you!' The bloody fool! He had given clear instructions about who was replacing him that day! He had not told anyone where he was going so this lieutenant must have scoured the countryside to find him. The fathead! He must have seen that his colonel was in civilian dress and in the company of a lady. The lieutenant had paid heavily for his blunder. At Ostrovno he had sent him time and again to the front line carrying missives of little importance. In the end the young officer had been cut to pieces by grapeshot. And the message he was carrying said basically: 'Beware of the enemy artillery.'

If he had not been overwhelmed by fury as he was stabbing

Maria, he would have remembered to force her to tell him where she had hidden her notebook before finishing her off! His emotions and desires sometimes impinged dangerously on his reason.

The result was that now he was being spied on. So he had decided not to kill again until the end of the campaign. Then he would be transferred somewhere and there . . . In Smolensk, he had not been able to stop himself from striking again, but it was imperative from now on that he should lie low. Those spying on him would eventually tire of doing so. However, despite his resolutions, he was not sure he would be able to restrain himself for such a long time.

IV Corps was given the order to cross the Dnieper. Margont had to resign himself to saying his farewells to the Valiuski family while the colonel of another corps was already taking possession of the place.

As Margont was getting into the saddle he noticed Countess Sperzof's old servant. He was hurrying as fast as his advancing years allowed. His cheeks were puffing in and out as he struggled for breath.

'Captain, sir, something's missing . . .' The servant closed his eyes as if he were going to drop down dead at the hoofs of Margont's horse. After catching his breath he declared: 'Captain, something's missing. A ring. The countess had the ring yesterday evening, the count's ring with the family emblem: the two birds.'

'Someone's stolen her signet ring, have they?'

Margont thrust his hand deep into his pocket but the servant stopped him.

'No money. If you want to thank, arrest man who did it and go back to France. All.'

'I'll find this man. The rest is outside my control.'

The old man looked bewildered. 'Why all that on her, oysters, tea . . . ?'

'I haven't the slightest idea.'

The servant left, taking his fears and his queries with him.

Margont turned to Lefine. 'I know why he stole the signet ring. He wanted a souvenir like when you keep the menu from a wedding to remind yourself of a very enjoyable occasion.'

Napoleon and his entourage were weighing up the situation. There were now only one hundred and fifty thousand men left in the Grande Armée. Soldiers were shooting the looters until their arms ached from firing, but to no effect. Hunger, fatigue and despair were winning and, every day, more soldiers disappeared. The Emperor had taken advantage of the stop at Smolensk to restore some order to this chaotic army. Should they go on?

Marshal Berthier, the Emperor's close friend and confidant, wanted to leave it at that. They had already conquered enough land for 1812. The army should take up its winter quarters and continue the war in 1813. Others wanted to bring the campaign to an end. They could not see the point of it. It was a very diplomatic way of not saying what they really thought: that Napoleon was waging this war because he did not like sharing part of the throne of Europe with Alexander. Murat even went as far as to beg the Emperor on bended knee to give up on Moscow as the city would be their downfall. But Napoleon was not accustomed to half-victories. He wanted Moscow. He was convinced that the Russians would fight to save their old capital (this was how it was referred to now because a century ago the administration had been transferred to St Petersburg, the new capital) and that he would therefore at last have the chance to crush their army. Then the Tsar would definitely agree to negotiate, he thought. Furthermore, the Emperor feared the reaction of the countries he now ruled. How would Austria, Prussia and the German states of the Confederation of the Rhine react if he did not win a decisive victory over the Russians when he had four hundred thousand soldiers at his disposal? Silent curses were likely to degenerate into protest and then open revolt. In any case, was he not Napoleon? So Moscow it would be.

On 23 August, IV Corps resumed its march. The palette of feelings amongst the soldiers ranged from the dull grey of gloom to the jet black of despair. There was often the scarlet of anger too. Many had thought the campaign was over and nobody wanted to resume this hellish march.

Lefine had managed to obtain a konia, a hardy Russian breed of horse. These beasts were very small and the French who rode them became figures of fun, their huge bodies perched on what looked like ponies, their legs dangling to the ground.

The previous day Lefine and Margont had returned to Smolensk. They had inspected the houses where their suspects had been staying on the night of the murder. The buildings were enormous and it would have been easy to slip away from them. They had decided to recruit a few more men they could rely on to back up their spies. The surveillance operation would continue even though it had been unmasked.

The 84th had just set off when Margont gave a start. He went pale. Lefine, who was riding alongside him, stared at him in consternation. He'd already seen similar faces, those of comrades hit by bullets. Margont seemed to have taken the full force of a noiseless explosion.

'Are you all right, Captain?'

'I think . . . I think I've understood why the killer spread food over the body of the second victim and why he tore out the pages of a book.'

'Really? So there's an explanation for that, is there?'

'It's another of his coded plays on words. He smears mulberry jam over the face, places an atlas on the body, the remnants of a book – only the remnants because he had torn out the pages – lumps of fat, or rather grease, oysters, nuts, tea leaves. Mulberry, atlas, remnants, grease, oysters, nuts, tea: MARGONT.'

Now it was Lefine's turn to be hit by the silent bullet.

'But . . . how . . . ?'

'After discovering he was being watched, he in turn must have enlisted the services of a spy. The spy must have followed one of your men. So he traced you and then me.'

Lefine looked around him anxiously. 'What if he chops our heads off? Who's to say we won't end up one morning with mulberries smeared all over our faces?'

Margont was looking more and more composed. His coolness was a mystery to his friend. He could remain calm in a situation like this but, conversely, become panic-stricken by the inactivity that Lefine found pleasantly restful.

'He must think that killing us would be a mistake. We'd be replaced by Captain Dalero and if he disappeared someone else would take over. It's better for our suspect to know exactly who he's dealing with. In fact, there's even some good news.'

The 84th was passing through a village that the Russian army had set fire to as it fell back. It had left behind about sixty wounded who could not be transported. Almost all had died and Portuguese soldiers in brown uniforms were burying them.

Who can see any good news around here? wondered Lefine.

'If our man had wanted to murder us,' Margont went on, 'he wouldn't have let us know that he'd identified us.'

The argument did not allay Lefine's fear.

'Why, then, did he warn us that he knew who we were?'

'For the pleasure of showing that he's cleverer than us and to inform us that if we get too close, he knows who to strike.'

'Better and better.'

'We need to be on the look-out. Perhaps we'll be lucky enough to spot someone spying on us. We'd need only to catch the rascal and make him talk in order to trace our man. But I don't believe that will happen. He wouldn't take such a risk. We're probably no longer being watched.'

'Really?' replied Lefine, who'd already spotted three suspects.

'And that's not all. If the spy employed by our man has followed you, since you regularly visit our henchmen, it's possible that the killer has discovered that we have three other suspects and that he now knows their names. Still, at least I'm now convinced that the person we're after also killed Élisa Lasquenet.'

Smolensk was gradually receding into the distance, in a bluish haze that made it look unreal. The Grande Armée seemed like an immense shipwrecked vessel abandoning the island on which it had just run aground to sail off again into unknown waters.

CHAPTER 22

NOTHING, absolutely nothing was happening, and this nothing was making the French army desperate. The Russians continued to fall back. Whole regions were being invaded with hardly a shot fired, but all they found was ashes.

For many, the lack of action was an ordeal because it made the agonising wait before the fighting even longer. For Margont being inactive was like being dead. Advancing in a column was killing the days; all those regiments were grinding them to dust. He salvaged a few hours by talking to various people, but the march made those without horses short of breath. He made up short stories, plays and even changes to the Constitution. But tiredness drained his mind. These pointless, wasted days ebbed away like blood oozing from the veins of a wounded man. To combat his melancholy, he forced himself to shave every day and spent time dusting down his uniform. His theory was this: since a nice glass sometimes makes a drink taste better, why should the same not be true of uniforms and soldiers? His efforts paid off. A little. His smart appearance and the impeccable creases in his uniform – in the mornings, at the start of the day's march – helped to contain his distress. In addition, he kept volunteering for things: patrolling to obtain provisions, sending messages . . . His Russian horse was sufficiently tough to withstand the extra miles and, paradoxically, the effort alleviated his own weariness and tiredness. Fortunately, the day of 2 September was so eventful that it managed to revive him just as he was teetering on the brink of depression.

The morning had begun in the normal, tedious way. Margont was spending – or rather wasting – his time roaming around. He was bringing deserters and marauders back to the ranks, knowing full well that they would slip away again as soon as his back was turned. He also expended a great deal of energy jollying the stragglers along. He tied their knapsacks to his saddle to lighten their load, used diplomacy, threats, encouragement . . . But hunger and fatigue dogged the soldiers' steps. Margont gazed at the endless succession of columns on the plain. The ranks were slack, the uniforms filthy and a great many men were missing, a great many. The horizon, consisting of interminable stretches of plains, hills and forests, seemed to lead nowhere. Margont decided to fall back in with his battalion.

Of the many strange phenomena that occurred in armies, one of the most curious was rumour. News that was more or less true sprang up somewhere and developed like an epidemic, spreading joy, hope or fear and unfailingly nonsense. During this campaign, everything moved slowly apart from rumour. It had its own way of galloping from one mind to another, of disturbing the rearguard before, a moment later, exciting the vanguard. It was like a swarm of sparkling fireflies flitting from someone too talkative to someone else too credulous, before frightening the army corps commander himself. Today it was in one person's head and tomorrow in the heads of the whole army; now in the Russian plains and in three weeks' time in the Paris theatres. How did it perform its magic? No one knew. Margont lent an ear and reaped a good harvest.

The long-awaited great battle was going to take place because the Russian generals had become so exasperated at having to fall back that they had rebelled and hanged the Tsar in their anger. There was nothing left of the Russian army. Almost all its men had been killed at Austerlitz and its survivors had been exterminated at Eylau, Friedland and Smolensk. So they were chasing a ghost. There would at last be a confrontation in less than three days. This was bound to be the case because the Russians were ruined and desperate and could no longer retreat. But that rumour had been heard every day since the crossing of the Niemen two months earlier . . .

Another fashionable opinion was that Alexander was falling back so far that this campaign would end up in India. Margont smiled to himself as he imagined this bizarre scene. Would Napoleon meet the same fate as Alexander the Great, seeing his soldiers mutiny on the banks of the Ganges and refuse to continue their astonishing series of victories? Or, on the contrary, would he watch them scrambling aboard every imaginable vessel in their haste to add the other side of the river to the Empire? He would then be able to exclaim: 'Now I am mightier than the great Alexander!'

Apart from rumour, there were constant conversations – but only in the mornings before tiredness took its toll. The problem was that by this point every soldier had already told his neighbour his life story, including details both real and invented. A scar-faced sergeant with a drooping moustache suggested attacking the Prussian and Austrian contingents 'just to keep our hand in'. His joke produced gales of laughter in the battalion. Margont wondered if this reaction would be enough to start a rumour and, if so, whether he should note down how these strange psychological shifts of mood came about. Saber rebuked the sergeant sharply. A few minutes later, the man could be seen running along the column, red-faced and brandishing his musket in the air, tirelessly repeating as he paused for breath: 'Long live our friends the Prussians! Long live our friends the Austrians!'

Lefine caught up with Margont.

'So, Fernand? Anything new from your men?'

'Naught but the dusty road and swaying sward.'

'Very funny. And what about von Stils?'

'Two of my friends are actively searching for him.'

'Good. Where's your knapsack gone?'

Lefine displayed a pair of dice and kissed them.

'*Voltigeur* Denuse has been carrying it for me for the last fifteen days, then it'll be Sergeant Petit's turn. Unless they get themselves killed, which would be the sign of a bad loser.'

'You're always playing with words, and people and the rules. One day it'll end in disaster.'

'In any case, life always ends in disaster.'

Lefine pointed at his shoes. They were worn through. Not even a vagrant would have wanted them.

'I'd be surprised if my soles lasted out until Moscow.'

'As long as it's only your shoes that get left behind on the plain.'

'You really have the knack of restoring the morale of the troops, Captain. Have you stopped gathering up your stray sheep to set them back on the right path to Moscow?'

'The shepherd's tired,' Margont sighed.

'I understand. Apparently the Emperor wants to have all the marauders shot as an example, which is the same as telling one half of the army to execute the other.'

'The worst thing is that it's not even certain whether the right half would be doing the shooting.'

A cavalryman hurtled down a hill and spurred his horse into a gallop to catch up with the column. He looked splendid in his yellow dolman and gilded helmet with a black crest and white plume.

Saber went up to Margont. 'Just look at him! Who does he think he is?'

'What is he?'

'A show-off.'

Margont tossed his head impatiently.

'He's a trumpeter from the Württemberg Mounted Chasseurs,' a corporal decreed.

'A trumpeter!' Saber said angrily. 'A trumpeter without a trumpet wearing a captain's epaulettes?'

'There are a few yellow jackets among the Neapolitans,' said Lefine, suddenly remembering.

Saber shook his head. 'Saxony Life Guards!'

'Correct, Lieutenant!' shouted a voice from the ranks.

The officer was getting closer. Seeing Margont and Saber, he turned in their direction. His lofty bearing and disdainful air immediately earned him the regiment's hostility and Saber's hatred.

'Just because he's dressed in yellow he needn't think he's a ray of sunshine,' muttered Lefine.

The Saxon brought his horse to a halt in front of Piquebois.

His cheeks and nose were red from sunburn. This colour contrasted with the limpid blue of his eyes, which resembled two small lakes in the middle of a face on fire.

'Captain von Stils, from the Saxony Life Guards.'

Piquebois introduced himself and the Saxon carried on immediately, as if he did not really care who he was dealing with as long as they knew who he was.

'I'm looking for Captain Margont. He's serving in your regiment.'

'You've knocked on the right door, Captain. Here he comes now.'

Margont and von Stils saluted each other. Von Stils seemed put out.

'A corporal came to tell me on your behalf that Colonel Fidassio from the 3rd Italian of the Line owed you some money and has been slow to settle up.'

Margont wanted to give Lefine a hug.

'Absolutely. But whenever I try to have a talk with Colonel Fidassio, Captain Nedroni, his adjutant, stands in the way.'

'His adjutant stands in the way?' the Saxon spluttered. 'And my letters are never answered!'

'Since I'd heard that Colonel Fidassio was also in debt to you I thought that a joint approach might be more . . . profitable.'

'I'm delighted to accept. If you're available, let's solve this problem straight away.'

Margont agreed and made his horse do an about-turn.

'The Italians are to the rear.'

'Even further to the rear? For almost the last hour I've been going up and down your army corps in search of the Pino

Division and people keep telling me to go and look further to the rear. Are these Italians of yours still in Rome?'

Saber asked to accompany them. Margont agreed reluctantly. The plain, which stretched out as far as the eye could see, nevertheless seemed too narrow to him for two such large egos.

The riders were advancing at walking pace. They came across some stragglers who speeded up when they knew they were being watched, sleeping infantrymen and marauders. Von Stils looked them up and down contemptuously until they bowed their heads. A soldier from the 8th Light, his chest criss-crossed with two strings of sausages, saluted the three officers.

'Looters do not salute!' thundered the Saxon.

Margont, watching the feast move off, was practically drooling.

'You speak good French,' he declared to von Stils in an attempt to get to know him better.

'It's easy. French is a shallow and simplistic language.'

Margont refrained from retorting that it was minds not languages that were shallow and simplistic. They continued their journey in silence. Margont gazed at the plain. This unbelievable expanse of greenery was too great not only for the eye but also for the mind itself to take in. How could any country be so vast? It had swallowed up an army consisting of four hundred thousand men like a giant might have swallowed a chickpea. Saber grabbed his gourd and took a good swig of water. Margont did likewise but the tepid water hardly slaked his thirst. He noticed that von Stils was not drinking although his lips were cracked and the heat stifling. If the Saxon thought that this made him in some way superior, he had obviously not realised that the sun would always win in the end.

'Were you at Jena?' he asked out of the blue.

Margont shook his head. 'We were at Auerstädt.'

'It's the same thing, isn't it? The same day, two battles between the French and the Prussians allied with the Saxons and the same result: a complete victory for the French. Whether we were at Jena or Auerstädt in Prussia, each year we mourn the 14 October. I was at Jena, the Beviloqua Regiment, the von Dyhern Brigade, the von Zeschwitz 1st Saxon Infantry Division. You crushed us, slaughtered and decimated us . . . No, you did even worse than that.' He gave a sad smile and added: 'You said I spoke your language well but I still can't find the right word to describe what you inflicted on us.'

'Flattened,' Saber kindly suggested.

Von Stils suddenly turned towards him. Margont noted that the Saxon exercised far better control over his thirst than over his anger, whereas with him it was the opposite.

'You flattened us,' the Saxon continued, emphasising the word. 'Everything happened so fast . . . How can a war be lost so quickly? Do you play chess?'

'Not very often but one of my acquaintances does,' Margont replied.

'Well, it was exactly like fool's mate. The game has only just begun when your opponent tells you it's checkmate. We were defeated, humiliated and sickened. I remember envying my comrades who'd been killed. To forget this disaster, I had myself assigned to the cavalry. I left the woman I loved, stopped seeing my friends, gave up my law studies, changed my haircut and moved house . . . It was as if everything belonging to the past was cursed. In fact, when all's said and done, perhaps I really did die at Jena. Poor Louisa, she never understood. In a word, on this road from Paris to Moscow I feel I am moving in the wrong direction. I'm told to shout, "Long live the Emperor!" when I'd like to yell, "Fire for all you are worth!" The game of political alliances really is too sophisticated for my sense of patriotism. But I shall obey orders and fight bravely. And like my King, I pray that Napoleon will throw us a few crumbs of territory at the end of his Russian feast. However, you will excuse me if I'm not the most cheerful of companions. My legendary good humour has been . . . flattened.'

Margont forgave von Stils his haughty air. It was his way of keeping up appearances. They met a score of Polish lancers who were escorting Russian prisoners. Von Stils gave the Russians a pitying look. It was as if he were one of them.

'The Cossacks! The Cossacks!' Saber yelled suddenly, galloping forward.

Margont and von Stils unsheathed their swords with equal speed while the Poles turned in their direction. Saber was tearing across the plain, his sword drawn, not noticing that a lone lancer had followed him in his charge. Far from there, at the edge of a wood, three Cossacks were watching him. All were armed with lances – their best weapon, their standard, their trademark and, on top of all that, an extra limb. When Saber had covered three-quarters of the distance, they disappeared under cover of the trees.

'He's been flattened,' von Stils declared.

'Made a laughing stock would be nearer the mark.'

Saber resigned himself to turning back. Wild with anger, he was gesticulating, his sabre still in his hand.

'Oh, the bastards! The swine! They aren't soldiers, they're clowns!'

Margont pointed at his sheath, urging him to put his sword back in it before he hurt someone. Saber thought that he was indicating more Cossacks and made his horse do a half-turn. He turned round again, more furious still.

'They're taunting me from the woods, are they? Is that it? Curse these wretched Cossacks! Why do they keep scattering like sparrows? What's the point?'

'Ask your horse. Even he knows the answer to that,' Margont interrupted.

The poor animal had come to a halt. Mouth open, nostrils quivering, it was attempting to recover its breath. This type of repeated effort would kill it before long. It was impossible to get Saber to calm down.

'They aren't soldiers but militiamen! No, they aren't even men, they're too savage. Always yelling as they gallop, like wild animals. Centaurs . . . centaurs that have survived from the beginning of time! Why didn't you follow me? I demand an answer!'

Von Stils stroked his mount's neck. 'I belong to the heavy cavalry. Our horses are stronger but have less stamina. They're intended for charging in line, not for this type of chase.'

'Quibbles! Quibbles!' Saber exclaimed in the triumphant tones of a lawyer who has just unmasked a case of perjury.

'Irénée, pull yourself together.'

'And what about you, Captain Margont? What's your excuse for inertia?'

'I'm past the age of playing hide and seek in the woods.'

Saber bowed his head. 'Gentlemen, allow me to take my leave.'

With that, he tried to spur his horse into a gallop but in its weakened state the animal only managed a fast trot.

'Why does your friend hate the Cossacks so much?' von Stils enquired.

'Lieutenant Saber is very chivalrous and the Cossacks' sudden raids are the opposite of his idea of a heroic military confrontation. As the Cossacks also have the bad taste to actually be successful . . .'

'It's true that the French military hate being defeated by peasants in rags. It goes back to the battle of Agincourt.'

'Jena, the Cossacks, Agincourt. Could we stop talking about war, please?'

Von Stils nodded slowly. 'With pleasure.'

He then launched into a long speech about Saxony. He described his country methodically and in detail, like an art expert analysing a painting by an old master. However, his chauvinism distorted the picture. The rivers were as clear as crystal; the towns the most beautiful in the world; the Saxon people possessed all possible qualities and a few more besides; the forests inspired poets, and you hadn't really lived unless you'd visited Saxony . . .

Margont listened attentively and interrupted him to ask questions. He was preparing for the moment when he would try to find out more about Fidassio.

The two men met up with sixty or so gunners officered by the occasional Polish lancer. For the past few days there had been torrential downpours, turning the road into a vast quagmire. A gun had become bogged down in a rut and eight gunners were trying to free it. The soldiers were struggling with all their might, some leaning forward and shoving with the full weight of their bodies, others pulling on the wheels strenuously enough to tear ligaments. The team of horses was also doing all it could. But the cannon would not budge. Knees bent, the soldiers sweated, swore, and held their breath . . . to no effect. Margont said to himself that the whole army was like this cannon, bogged down and struggling against all the odds to continue its advance. Von Stils once again wore an expression that was both conceited and melancholy. He was gazing at the artillery pieces.

'The famous Gribeauval cannon. Their muzzles have blown apart more than one enemy army.'

Margont went up to a captain who was nervously dusting off his jacket.

'Where's your escort?'

'The Poles, you mean? Oh, heavens! A good third of them have deserted, another third are roaming around in search of food and the rest have gone to hunt the Cossacks over there,' replied the gunner, pointing vaguely towards a wood in the distance.

'So what are these Polish lancers doing with IV Corps?'

'What of it? You're with a Saxon Life Guard yourself! Their major was wounded in Smolensk. His men stayed with him and, now that he's recovered, they are trying to rejoin their regiment. What a bloody shambles this campaign is, don't you think?'

'You're exposing yourself to—'

Margont did not finish his sentence. A roar rose up from the plain. 'Huzza!' Three hundred Cossacks had suddenly emerged from a wood and were bearing down on them. They were dressed in black or navy-blue uniforms. The few Poles present rushed at them, considering the Cossacks their eternal enemies. As they too were wearing navy-blue uniforms, it was difficult to distinguish them from their opponents. Bodies fell to the ground and were trampled, the wounded screamed, pistol shots punctuated the air and strange entangled shapes moved about . . . The Poles were quickly overwhelmed and the Cossacks sprang up from all sides in the midst of the gunners. The gunners shot the Cossacks at point-blank range and were spiked through in return. A lieutenant close to Margont was nailed to a munitions wagon by a spear neatly thrust through his heart; the teams of horses were bolting, the Cossacks yelling at the tops of their voices: 'Huzza! Huzza! Huzza!'

Margont charged. A young trooper, hoping to cover himself in glory by capturing a French officer, rode straight at him. With disconcerting ease he turned his lance round. He was no longer brandishing the point but the end of the shaft. Margont attempted to ward off the attack with his sword, felt a violent blow to his breastbone and fell. He landed on his back and the pain took his breath away. Hoofs galloped past close to his eyes, throwing earth on to his face. The Cossack nimbly dismounted. He must have been sixteen. He could have been a little boy, really happy at the idea of giving his father a present but slightly worried because he was after all in the middle of a battle . . . His prisoner looked in a poor state and he didn't know how to set about taking him away. Margont tried to move but his back gave him terrible pain. He felt like a wretched insect crushed by a shoe, surviving only to endure agony. The Russian placed his pike on his throat.

'I won't move,' Margont said in Russian.

The adolescent looked at him wide-eyed. It was inconceivable to him that this man could speak his language because the French were agents of the devil. He carefully examined his captive's uniform. Yes, he definitely was a Frenchman.

'You are my prisoner!' he proudly exclaimed.

'I don't doubt that for a second,' replied Margont.

The Russian removed his belt and set about tying the Frenchman's wrists. Margont feared the moment when the adolescent said to himself that it would be much easier to kill him than to take him prisoner. All around them the Cossacks looked as if they were celebrating rather than fighting. They were whirling and galloping about in every direction, like leaves blowing in the wind, triumphantly yelling 'Huzza!' Their frenzy was indescribable: they ran their opponents through until their lances broke, fired their pistols, slashed around with all their might and rode their horses at the gunners to trample them. The Poles showed equal ferocity in the combat. They were fighting as if each Cossack killed freed one square yard of Poland crushed beneath their horses' hoofs.

The French were defending their guns. Gathered around their cannon, they gave as good as they got. They were taking advantage of the mêlée to put their muskets against the bellies of Russians engaged in sword duels before firing. They cut into the enemy with their bayonets, swords and even knives. The Cossacks were drooling over the artillery. An elderly sergeant was jealously guarding his Gribeauval and his gunners, like a cockerel guarding his hens.

After smashing two skulls with his musket butt he shouted: 'God Almighty! What would the Emperor say if they nabbed our fire-belchers? What a disgrace that would be!'

These words galvanised the defenders. Margont was struggling to his feet when the first sign of an adverse wind made the Cossack storm die down. A substantial party of Polish lancers had appeared from a distant wood and was galloping towards them.

'The escort's coming back!' yelled someone.

Margont rejoiced at the thought that these troopers had finally realised they had fallen into a trap, pursuing a decoy intended to lead them away from the convoy. Then he thought that perhaps the Poles had deliberately gone off on this false trail to encourage the Cossacks to attack at last. The adolescent who had captured him was looking at him with an expression of deep sorrow. There were still a few wisps of straw left in his tousled ginger hair from where he had slept. One felt like removing them with a paternal gesture and sending him back out to play. Margont had taken his expression to be one of disappointment but it was more one of guilt. He seemed to be about to apologise. He unsheathed his sabre and approached the captain intending to execute him. Margont rushed him. The Russian brandished his sword but the Frenchman barged into him and his shoulder charge sent him flying to the ground. The shock revived the pain in Margont's back, giving him the impression that his opponent had, in spite of everything, managed to thrust his sabre into his backbone.

There was a sign of hesitation in the Cossack attack, clearly perceptible by the dying away of the shouts of 'Huzza!' The Russians decided to release their prey. A horseman stopped beside the adolescent and shouted something to him as he stretched out his arm. The young man shook his head and again faced up to Margont. If he couldn't take back a captive, at least he'd have the lovely epaulettes that he'd snatched from an officer's dead body. Margont easily rid himself of the belt that was shackling his hands. There were almost no Cossacks left. One of them broke away from the group who were fleeing and came galloping back towards the convoy. Aged about fifty, bearded and with wavy ginger hair, he rode his horse between the two adversaries, made it rear up and grabbed the adolescent more by the scruff of the neck than by the collar. The boy shouted out but nimbly threw himself on to the horse's back. They fled just as the Poles reached the guns and skewered the last remaining Russians as they would chickens or turkeys at Christmas: one after another and without ever feeling sated.

Saber was also back, alerted by the firing. His exhausted mount covered the last few yards at walking pace, its weakened gait contrasting with the efforts of its rider to make it gallop off in pursuit of the enemy.

'Did you see that, Quentin? They deliberately chose to attack after I'd left.'

Saber really believed he was well known in this part of Russia and that when they talked among themselves the Cossacks would sometimes say: 'So let's attack this convoy. It's poorly guarded.' 'No, my friend, because Lieutenant Saber's with them.' 'Oh! If Saber's there, there's no point in even thinking about it.'

Margont was having difficulty walking and was trying to recover his sword, his shako, his mount and his pride. He needed a warm, comfortable bed. Yes, that was exactly it – a warm, comfortable bed.

Saber looked him up and down. 'That's the second time the Cossacks have unhorsed you, isn't it? Next time, throw yourself straight to the ground. You'll save time.'

Saber often tried to outshine his friends with this type of withering remark. For him, glory was not something to be shared. Every man has his limits, so Margont moved towards Saber to grab him by the sleeve and unhorse him, to see which of the two would be the next to end up on the ground. Saber thought it preferable to move away.

Von Stils came back, with a haughty look on his face. His heavy cavalry sabre was bloodstained. He dismounted and wiped it clean with the tunic of a dead Cossack.

'I killed two of them. I imagined I was charging at two French hussars.'

Margont eyed him coldly. 'If you hate us so much, why don't you go over to the Russians? Instead of dirtying this tunic, put it on.'

The Saxon sheathed his sword abruptly, slamming the hilt against the sheath. 'A Saxon wears a Saxon uniform and obeys the King of Saxony.'

'To be faithful to one's ideals or to one's duty . . . I would have chosen ideals. Your fringed epaulette has been cut off by a sabre.'

Von Stils looked at his left shoulder. 'Not content with trying to run me through, they want to strip me of my rank as well!'

Margont and von Stils went to the aid of the wounded. Saber was barking orders for setting up a gun in firing position. The gunners were rushing about, laboriously pushing the wheels, busily bringing round shot. They were obviously very willing but Saber was hurling abuse at them: 'Layabouts, bunglers . . .' However, there was very little likelihood of the Cossacks coming back. So much wasted effort to unhitch the gun, put it into position and load it before firing it at ant-like figures, and then hitching it up again . . . Margont realised that his friend was frightened. Saber was carefully avoiding looking at the wounded. His aim in putting this gun in a firing position was not to create more victims but to prevent him from seeing the ones already there. Saber completely blotted out this aspect of war. He wanted to fight, but like a child with tin soldiers which don't bleed when they're knocked down. So he remained on his horse, sword in hand, ready to order a gun to be fired at Cossacks who never came. When the last of the wounded had been tended and put into a cart and the bogged-down gun pulled out of its rut, an annoyed artillery captain, his arm covered in blood, came to retrieve his cannon. The convoy moved off again.

Saber, Margont and von Stils abandoned it. In the distance could be seen the front of the Pino Division.

The Pino Division was in an appalling state. It was trying to find provisions in an area that had been set on fire by the

Russians and pillaged by all the regiments that were ahead of it. The men's gaunt and haggard faces were worse than any Margont had seen so far.

As the three riders trotted up to the 3rd Italian of the Line, Margont asked: 'Do you often play with Colonel Fidassio?'

'Yes, because he loses.'

'How does he play?'

Von Stils did not seem surprised at this question, as if everyone had a gambling instinct. And perhaps that was true.

'He takes no risks, constantly undervalues his hand, is suspicious of his own partners. He continually loses money – a lot of money – but when he wins, he's as happy as a sandboy.'

'I'd like to play a few rounds with him.'

'He's stopped playing now that no one will give him credit.'

'Who does he still owe money to?'

'A few of his subordinates who don't dare to ask for it back!'

'Does he owe any to that guard dog of his, Captain Nedroni?'

'As far as I know, Nedroni doesn't gamble. He merely follows behind Colonel Fidassio to negotiate his debts by staggering the repayments, reducing the amount in exchange for a letter of recommendation . . .' Von Stils at once added with a sneer: 'Yes, that's exactly it! Captain Nedroni follows behind his colonel!'

'I'm afraid I don't really understand what you're getting at.'

'I think those two are sodomites! Now do you understand better?'

'Personally, I don't have any prejudices against such men.'

'Neither do I, in fact. Only against bad payers.'

'Are you sure of what you're suggesting about their relationship?'

'No, but it wouldn't surprise me.'

Colonel Fidassio was riding some way off from his regiment, as was his custom. He turned pale when he noticed von Stils. Nedroni, who was at his side, immediately galloped up to meet these unwelcome visitors.

He brought his horse to a halt in front of them, to block their way, saluted politely and said: 'May I enquire as to the reason for your visit?'

'I am Captain von Stils, from the Saxony Life Guards, and this is Captain Margont from the 84th,' the Saxon replied in a curt tone of voice. 'We've come to talk to Colonel Fidassio about the debts he's supposed to have paid us some time ago.'

'I'm extremely sorry but that is impossible. Commanding the regiment occupies all the colonel's attention.'

Von Stils turned even redder than from exposure to the sun. 'It's a matter of honour, sir! I insist!'

Nedroni remained courteous but firm. 'It's impossible and I'm sincerely sorry. But if you're willing to leave me a message, it will be delivered in the shortest possible time.'

'A message!'

'Yes, we do have a message,' Margont intervened. 'Tell the colonel that we are going to ask General Dembrovsky to order your colonel to receive us immediately.'

Nedroni was taken by surprise. 'You aren't going to pester a general about money problems, surely?'

'Deliver your message by all means,' said Margont sarcastically before setting off towards the brigadier-general and his aides-de-camp, who were surveying the surroundings through field glasses from the top of a hill.

'Very well,' Nedroni conceded. 'Please follow me, but be brief.'

When they reached Colonel Fidassio he was conversing with a major of the chasseurs. As this officer was French, that was the language the two men were using. The colonel's face betrayed his dismay.

'Have you deployed your squadrons to protect our flanks?'

'Yes, Colonel,' the chasseur assured him.

The major looked puzzled. It was clear that Colonel Fidassio was faced with a difficult choice. The chasseur couldn't see what the problem was and was cursing himself for his lack of perceptiveness.

'Yes, but aren't your squadrons too spread out? If they are too spread out they won't be able to stand up to a large-scale attack at one particular point. Tell your troopers to be at the ready but not too spread out. There needs to be a happy medium between being spread out and grouped together.'

'I'll transmit your orders immediately, Colonel.'

'Everything in life is a question of a happy medium. "Always a little, never too much!"'

Always a little, Colonel, never too much, thought Margont.

The chasseur went away feeling he had not properly understood his instructions. Fidassio seemed to be about to call him back to add or subtract something but he restrained himself. Nedroni's knuckles were white from holding the reins so tightly.

'Colonel, these two officers wish to speak to you. I told them how overburdened with work you were but they insisted. They quite understand that you can only give them a few seconds.'

The few seconds in question seemed longer to Fidassio than eternal damnation. His face fell when Margont informed him that he'd been entrusted by the late Lieutenant Sampre with the task of recovering the dead man's debt. Fidassio explained that he did not have the requisite amount on him but paid each of the two men a down payment of two hundred francs in exchange for a receipt. Fidassio kept looking at Nedroni for help. It's Nedroni who's the colonel and Fidassio his shadow, concluded Margont.

He and von Stils set off again. Margont turned round. Fidassio seemed more downcast than ever as Nedroni talked to him. Nedroni gave the Frenchman a look of hatred. He was angry with him for having guessed his friend's secret, for discovering that a colonel's magnificent epaulettes were too heavy for Fidassio's shoulders and that Nedroni was helping him to bear this glorious burden. 'Why did my mother want to make me a colonel?' Fidassio must have lamented to himself. Yes, of course. But also, why had Fidassio gone along with it? It was true, however, that colonels always obeyed generals.

CHAPTER 23

A T the end of August the Tsar promoted General Kutuzov to generalissimo and the latter thus found himself in command of the Russian army. Barclay de Tolly had been demoted because the public were exasperated by his successive retreats. The choice of his successor had proved difficult. The Tsar did not like Kutuzov and criticised him for 'having obeyed too well'. It was no secret that at the battle of Austerlitz, Kutuzov had advised against withdrawing troops from the plateau of Pratzen, the centre of the Austro-Russian position, and sending them to try to break through the French right flank. But despite this advice, the Tsar ordered the manoeuvre, falling into the trap set by Napoleon, who had not given ground on his right flank but had happily broken through the weakened enemy centre. But, because Kutuzov was so popular, the Tsar was forced to choose him. Kutuzov was sixty-six. He was considered an old man because he frequently dozed off – even during councils of war – because his excessive weight made it difficult for him to mount a horse, and because he was lethargic by nature. A pupil of Suvorov, one of the greatest Russian strategists, he had lost an eye during one of the many campaigns he had fought. Caution was one of his watchwords and he loved to give the impression that he was a crafty old fox who said nothing but took in everything.

Kutuzov was convinced of Napoleon's superiority and

wanted to continue the scorched-earth policy. But now Moscow itself was under threat, Moscow the cradle of the nation! The Russian people were wondering how things could have come to this. Public opinion and the Tsar's decision had combined to force a confrontation on Kutuzov. Deeply religious and fatalistic, he now considered that a clash between the two armies was a necessary evil. Napoleon would at last have his battle.

Kutuzov chose an area close to the village of Borodino as the battlefield. Whilst the Russians called the confrontation the battle of Borodino, Napoleon preferred to call it the battle of the Moskva. The Moskva was a river nearby, and although Moscow itself was still more than ninety miles away, calling it the battle of the Moskva made it sound as if they were just outside the city walls. This was in a way correct because if the Russian army were crushed, Moscow would inevitably fall into French hands.

One hundred and fifteen thousand Frenchmen and allies, and their five hundred and ninety cannon – all that was left of the Grande Armée – were preparing to attack one hundred and fifty-five thousand Russians equipped with six hundred and forty cannon, which were often of larger calibre than the French ones. The Russians had set themselves up along a convex front more than six miles long. The terrain was winding and undulating, interspersed with small woods and bushy ravines, and bordered by forests of pine and birch. The Russian right wing, commanded by Barclay de Tolly, came up to the villages of Borodino and Gorki and their environs. The River Moskva flowed along this side. In the centre was the valley of the Kolocha, a tributary of the Moskva.

To the rear on a hillock, the Russians had built an entrenchment called the Great Redoubt or the Raevsky Redoubt, named after the general commanding it. This redoubt was the cornerstone of the Russian centre and it was an impressive construction. It extended for more than one hundred and eighty yards and was protected by a wide ditch. An earthwork had been built in front of it and to the sides. To the rear, a gorge, blocked off by a double stockade, enabled the defenders to come and go. Embrasures had been made to allow nineteen cannon to be fired. In addition, General Raevsky had had 'wolf holes' dug in front of the position in order to halt a possible cavalry charge. The large number of infantrymen given the task of protecting the Great Redoubt – twenty battalions – had positioned themselves wherever they could: in the Semenovskaya Ravine, on the slope of the hill and to the left of the redoubt, and in the village of Semenovskaya.

The Russian left, commanded by Bagration, had also been reinforced with fortifications – three redoubts, which were very close to one another. They were dubbed the 'Three Flèches'. Lastly, large numbers of reserve troops were stationed behind the Russian position.

Napoleon came face to face with the Russian army on 5 September but the battle did not commence until 7 September. The two armies made good use of this respite to observe each other. The French rounded up as many laggards as possible and awaited the arrival of part of the artillery, whose progress had been impeded by the rain. The Russians were also gathering their troops and fortifying their entrenchments.

On 6 September the Russians held a spectacular religious ceremony. It consisted of a procession of icons, including the Madonna of Smolensk, which was reputed to make armies invincible. Priests in full ceremonial vestments marched at the head, followed by generals and soldiers singing hymns or saying prayers. Kutuzov, like many others, knelt as the holy images went past. The effect on the Russians was to rouse them to a frenzy. It was no longer a war but a crusade against the devil himself. And, during the night, the large doses of vodka that had replaced the holy water made the troops more euphoric still.

The Russian plan was essentially defensive: to hold their positions and to bleed the French army dry with their artillery. Decisions would then be made according to the enemy's actions and reactions. The plan was that General Tuchkov, on the left of the army, would go around the enemy's right wing to attack it on the flank and to the rear, but that proved unworkable.

In fact, since the Russian left flank had received reinforcements and was defended by the Three Flèches, Napoleon deduced that it was the weak spot of the Russian strategy. This, then, was where he decided he would try to break through. Initially, Prince Eugène would attack the Russian right as a diversion. He would be 'content' to take the village of Borodino, to contain the Russians and to surround the Great Redoubt. Ney, Junot and Murat would attack the centre and Davout and Poniatowski the left flank. When the French right wing had broken through the enemy left, it would fall back on the centre and sweep away everything in its path. These were the plans of the two camps. But nothing went according to plan.

The night before the battle, the soldiers talked or got drunk. On the French side there was the dull rumble of troops moving around to take up position. Latecomers kept arriving and then going off in search of their regiments.

The 84th had already taken up its position and was making the most of the night's respite. Margont was visiting the men of his company, sitting with them around the campfires. Despite the slaughter to come, morale remained high. At last they were going to confront the Russian army! No more marching until they were exhausted or tramping through mud or nearly going mad from hunger . . . They had faith in Napoleon's genius and no one doubted that the Russians would be annihilated. Margont was making sure that all was well, giving instructions, reassuring his men . . . They liked him and were always pleased to make room for him.

'Captain, what runs faster than a galloping horse?' asked an old corporal whose right eye was permanently watching the left one since a bullet had deformed its socket.

'No idea.'

'A Prussian after the battle of Jena!'

There were roars of laughter. Margont himself merely smiled. When soldiers told one another this sort of nonsense, they were in a really good mood.

'Begging your pardon, Captain, but what's that scar on your cheek?' enquired a soldier who had just about enough teeth left to bite open his cartridges before pouring the powder into the barrel of his musket. If it hadn't been for his three incisors and one canine, he would have been discharged from the army.

Margont absently ran his finger along the scar. He didn't like talking about it.

'Well, let's just say that like everyone else involved in the Spanish campaign, I brought back a little souvenir . . .'

A cuirassier appeared in the light of the campfire. The flicker of its flames was reflected in his breastplate and helmet.

'Do you know where the 5th Regiment of Cuirassiers is?'

'Yes.'

'Easy.'

'Are you sure it's so simple?'

At that, all the infantrymen pointed their fingers in different directions and shouted out amidst general laughter: 'It's that way!'

The cavalryman wanted to leave but Margont held his mount by the bridle.

'Where's your greatcoat? In one of your saddlebags? Roll it up and place it across your saddle in front of your private parts. Because tomorrow when you charge, the Russians will riddle you with bullets. Your breastplate and your helmet will protect your body well but not down there. Your rolled-up greatcoat will prevent you from being castrated. What would your pretty filly think if, after letting her young stud go off to war, she saw only an ugly fat gelding come back?'

The cuirassier set off without answering.

Margont got up, gave his apologies and went to the next

campfire, despite the request to 'stay a bit longer'. There, some soldiers were listening to Second Lieutenant Galouche read extracts from the Bible. Margont remembered prayers at Saint-Guilhem-le-Désert. He put his hands together and entwined his fingers, as he used to do. He silently asked Heaven for the battle to cause as little bloodshed as possible, for the Russians to be defeated and for the war to end. And if the Tsar capitulated, then England would be forced to negotiate. Probably. Then at last there would be peace.

A little further on, Saber was busily cutting the Russian army to pieces. With the aid of a stick he was drawing a plan on the ground for the benefit of his supporters – soldiers who swore by him and already imagined themselves colonels of the future marshal of France. There were arrows in all directions; the Great Redoubt had already fallen – rather too quickly in Margont's opinion – and the Russian Guard was rushing into this 'death trap'. Saber had in fact ordered the French right wing to fall back to make the Russians think that there had been a rout on that side. The Russians had been quick to send in all their reserves, including the Guard, to finish smashing through the right enemy flank. Then Saber ordered the cavalry of the Guard to charge at their flank and break up their columns. The Old Guard followed and finished them off. It was obviously very effective in the sand since Saber was energetically wiping out Russian squares and columns. But he was taking no account of the human factor. Even if the Russians actually believed they had broken through the French right, how could anyone be sure the French would not think the same? And if they did, then the left wing and the French centre, thinking the right wing had been routed, would in turn break up in disarray . . . Any movement towards the rear was dangerous because it very soon led to all sides following suit.

Piquebois was smoking his pipe some distance from the others. Lying on his back, with a treatise on astronomy resting against his knees and his head on his knapsack, he was gazing up at the sky. His eyes were full of stars.

'Why do you have such a passion for them?' Margont asked him.

'Because they're so far away.'

Margont then caught up with Lefine, who was selling phials containing a greenish liquid. It was his 'remedy for fear', an infusion of verbena and eucalyptus. Margont grabbed him by the collar and, when they saw the expression on the sergeant's face, all his potential customers immediately realised that the product was a swindle.

'Ripping people off again!' thundered Margont.

'It works. It's been scientifically proved, Captain. The truth is that you're against progress.'

'Give me your report instead of adding fuel to the flames.'

'If I had fuel I wouldn't waste it, I'd drink it, even if it were lamp oil.'

Margont let go of Lefine, who made a show of readjusting his collar.

'My men will try to keep an eye on all our suspects during the combat.'

'Excellent, I'm relying on them.'

'Captain, aren't you afraid?'

'Why? Do you want to sell me that filthy potion of yours?'

'No, seriously . . .'

'Of course I am. But my fear doesn't paralyse me and doesn't ruin my life. So I can consider myself content.'

Margont walked away. He wanted to sleep for a while. Lefine downed three of his phials in quick succession. He didn't think it would work, but just in case . . .

His heart was pounding. The Russians were here at last! He was convinced that the Emperor was going to see to them in his own way and he already felt sorry for them. While waiting for the general assault, he had just made up a new game that he found very entertaining. The aim was to imagine the worst possible death for Captain Margont. His wishes were then arranged in ascending order of preference.

For the moment these were the results: For round shot to blow his arm off and for him to lie for hours watching the blood pour out of his stump; for grapeshot to make mincemeat of him; for a blow from a sword to smash his teeth and slash his face from ear to ear; for a hail of bullets to burst open his spleen, liver and bowels; for him to be seriously wounded, unable to move and left behind in a corner of the battlefield feeling the crows pecking his eyes out; for all that to happen at once.

For him, Margont was a louse he hadn't yet managed to crush. And if he didn't disappear, this louse would end up, like any other, getting squashed.

*

At three in the morning the order of the day was read out to the troops. It was the Emperor's address:

'Soldiers, here is the battle you have yearned for! From now on victory depends on you. We need it; it will guarantee us plentiful food, good winter quarters and a swift return to the homeland! Conduct yourselves as you did at Austerlitz, at Friedland, at Vitebsk, at Smolensk and may all the generations to come proudly hail your conduct on this day. Let it be said of you: "He was at that great battle beneath the walls of Moscow!"'

Colonel Pégot went to find Margont just after the speech had been read out. The cheering and the shouts of 'Long live the Emperor!' meant that he had to take Margont to one side to make himself heard. Napoleon had decided to reinforce IV Corps for the battle so he had placed the Morand and Gérard Divisions under Prince Eugène's command. Some of their regiments had, however, lost a very large number of officers.

'Officers are therefore being temporarily assigned to other regiments. These are orders,' explained Pégot. 'At the battle of Smolensk, the 13th Light lost one-third of its strength and about thirty officers. Consequently, I'm transferring you to it.'

'That's out of the question, Colonel. I want to remain with the men from my company. I know them and I . . .'

Pégot shook his head. He was a pitiful sight with his bloodshot, dark-ringed eyes.

'It's only for the duration of the battle. One of the battalions of the 13th Light is without its major. I'm putting you in charge of it. You will take Saber, Piquebois and Galouche with you and you will give them the remnants of two companies each.'

He was being put in charge of a battalion, was he? Promotion was close. To refuse the battalion was to refuse promotion. Margont wanted to ask something but Pégot was already off, waving him away.

'No time, no time. I have to find some gunners to make up the numbers in our artillery companies, horses for our cavalry and our cannon, and I need to patch together what's left of the companies . . . What a life! And on top of all this they're taking my officers away.'

The sun rose. Napoleon exclaimed that it was the sun of Austerlitz, the one that had broken through the clouds on 2 December 1805 to hail the victory. But today the sun was dazzling the French and showing up their positions. The sky was clear. Dew moistened the grass, pleasantly cooling the atmosphere. It could have been a beautiful day.

CHAPTER 24

A T five thirty a battery of the Guard's artillery fired three shots, giving the signal for hostilities to begin. The roar of artillery fire was already deafening a few minutes later as the French attacked at several points. In both camps they were saying: 'This is it at last.'

Time was passing. The Morand Division was positioned in the front line on the left wing, in column by regiment, motionless, awaiting orders. Elsewhere there was slaughter; here there was waiting.

Margont rode along the ranks of his new battalion. He tried to reassure those who were as white-faced as a Russian winter, and to calm down those who were overwrought. The soldiers were glancing up and seeing cannonballs buzzing through the sky. One young chasseur was marvelling at the scene. He found the masses of French and Russian troops rushing at each other 'fantastic', the exploding shells 'amazing', and the thunder of the cannon 'awesome'. Exhilarated by the sight, he was gazing up at the black shapes flying over him.

'And that? What's that?'

Margont went up to him and removed the bayonet from his musket. Otherwise in a couple of minutes he would accidentally have run his neighbour through. He slid it into its sheath.

'Only when we launch the attack.'

The soldier had still not taken his eyes off the spectacle overhead.

'They look like huge insects!'

'They are in fact insects. Their precise scientific name is *Russiae rondishoti*. This subspecies of the bumblebee family is a large spherical insect with an especially hard shell. They are clumsy and awkward and not very good at flying, so they always end up on the ground. They don't sting but crush their prey beneath their weight. As they are gregarious by nature, when one of them arrives near you it's always followed by the whole swarm.'

'No, they're cannonballs, Captain.'

'That's another way of looking at it.'

The waiting continued. Some were beginning to hope that the battle would pass them by. Margont surveyed the battlefield. On the tops of the hills and on the slopes, in the smallest valleys and gullies, on the plains and even in the streams, as far as he could see, there were masses of soldiers. He had never seen so many. There were lines going into the attack, retreating or remaining still, squares, columns closely packed or split up, scattered hordes, fluctuating groups, soldiers isolated, lost or dug in, troopers whirling around or charging *en masse* . . . Coils of white smoke showed where muskets or artillery guns were being fired. Whole areas disappeared from view beneath these fluffy clouds that then rose slowly into the air until they filled the sky. On the top of its hill the Great Redoubt was hidden by the smoke of its artillery fire. It looked like an erupting volcano.

Saber approached Margont. 'Prince Eugène has taken the village of Borodino. But it's probably a diversionary attack. The

Emperor's going to try to break through the Russian left so it's imperative that we take the Great Redoubt, otherwise our troops will be crushed by its guns and will lay themselves open to attack.'

Margont had realised that they had occupied Borodino. For the rest, he knew his friend only too well. Saber was smiling. He had some good news to announce.

'The Great Redoubt will be ours.'

The French artillery was pounding the Great Redoubt and the Three Flèches. To the left Eugène had indeed seized the village of Borodino but his progress had been halted. To the right the Three Flèches had already fallen – they had in fact been taken, lost and retaken. Ney's troops and those of Davout, Murat and Nansouty were trying to link up with Poniatowski's Poles, who were coming from the far right. But, from the village of Semenovskaya, which was set on a hilltop, the Russians overlooked the victorious French and were showering them with round shot, shells, grapeshot and bullets. Although Murat and La Tour Maubourg were attacking them with heavy cavalry – the Saxony Cuirassiers and Life Guards, and the Westphalian and Polish Cuirassiers – they were being counter-attacked by a wave of Russian cuirassiers. The Friant Division took advantage of the impetus of the allied charge to storm the houses. The confusion and slaughter were at their height.

All this time the 13th Light were chewing on blades of grass and kicking their heels. Aides-de-camp and orderlies kept galloping up, wheeling their horses round once or twice to calm them, handing over a missive and immediately setting off again. More and more of them kept arriving and they were in more and more of a hurry.

'The Redoubt! The Redoubt! The Redoubt!' Saber began to chant.

His company took up the cry. A superstitious corporal, terror-stricken at the thought and appalled that no one was listening to his pleas, brandished the butt of his musket ready to smash Saber's skull. The lieutenant had not noticed him because now all he could think of was 'his' Redoubt.

Margont grabbed the man by the sleeve. 'That's not a Russian. Control yourself.'

General Morand and his general staff galloped past the 13th Light. A few moments later, at about ten in the morning, the order was given to carry the Great Redoubt. The Morand Division began to march. Only the 30th of the Line and a battalion of the 13th Light were going to attack the Great Redoubt itself. The role of the other regiments was to take on the Russian troops deployed round about.

The infantry went forward perfectly aligned, coming under direct fire from the Great Redoubt. There was a buzzing that became a whistling sound, which got louder and louder, and then a breach appeared in the line. Another whistling sound and another gory void.

'Close ranks! Close ranks!' shouted the officers.

The soldiers moved closer together to fill the gaps but more shells exploded, more cannonballs struck them full in the chest or tore off their limbs, and there were more shouts of 'Close ranks! Close ranks!'

Lefine had followed Margont. He had told a sergeant who was unhappy at seeing him leave the 84th for the day: 'If you're going to die, it might as well be with your friends.'

'At this rate there soon won't be any ranks left,' he muttered.

'Who cares? We'll shout: "Close!"' replied Margont.

'Why are there so few of us to attack this redoubt? Who's the fool who gave this order?'

'Close ranks, Sergeant.'

'Yes, well, the other regiments in the division could also close ranks with us! I hate the army, which is only reasonable since the army obviously hates me!'

Margont was looking straight ahead and thinking only of keeping the ranks close together.

Galouche was reciting a passage from the Bible: 'And there was war in heaven: Michael and his angels fought against the dragon; and the dragon fought and his angels, and prevailed not; neither was their place found any more in heaven. And the great dragon was cast out, that old serpent, called the Devil, and Satan, which deceiveth the whole world: he was cast out into the earth, and his angels were cast out with him.' The Apocalypse. It was an appropriate choice.

The cannonballs were raining down more and more heavily, dropping, killing, bouncing off the grass, dropping back down again, killing once more . . . At last, the enemy was close enough and the line charged forward, yelling as it went. Grapeshot swept away whole ranks in a deafening din. The infantrymen following leapt nimbly over the dead and wounded and took their places. The attackers were in a frenzied state. Fear, vengeance, hatred, a desire for glory, and an obsession with fighting to avoid thinking about those dying around them – all these feelings mingled to produce an excited, exhilarated, enraged sort of euphoria. The Russians positioned on the edges of the redoubt had been pushed back or wiped out.

Disorientated by the smoke surrounding the entrenchment – a warm fog that smelt of burnt gunpowder – Margont fell into a ditch. He tried to get up but other soldiers tumbled on top of him, screaming with fear. He struggled and quickly got back on his feet to avoid choking to death under a human shroud. He was suffocating and could hardly see. There were flashes of light: men were shooting one another inside the ditch itself. Terror-stricken Russians had hidden there and were firing at anything that moved, killing as many of their own men as of the enemy. They were swiftly slaughtered. The French gave one another a leg up to get out of what a grenadier from the 30th quite rightly called a 'trap for prats' and went back on the attack.

The French were entering the Great Redoubt through the gaps made for the cannon or those caused by French artillery fire. Other infantrymen were clinging to the earthworks, digging their feet in and climbing up as best they could before shooting at the Russians from the top or throwing themselves at them. Some of the gunners were no longer even defending themselves but reloading their gun and firing so as to blow dozens of Frenchmen to smithereens. The cannon fell silent, the shooting gradually died away.

When Margont entered the stronghold, he saw Saber stroking a cannon as if it were the muzzle of a horse.

'You see, it was easy. I told you so!'

At that precise moment the Great Redoubt and the Three Flèches had been taken. The enemy line was seriously weakened. Ney and Murat asked for reinforcements so they could try to penetrate the Russian army. Napoleon sent them very few. He wanted to preserve his Guard. Sending it into the attack at this moment would probably ensure victory but not without sustaining very heavy losses. The situation was not yet clear and he feared a second battle the next day or the day after. Napoleon therefore wanted to win without deploying his Guard . . . if possible.

Seeing that all would be lost if he did not react, Kutuzov ordered a general counterattack, throwing considerable reserves into the fray. In the centre, the infantrymen of Lithuania, Ismailov and the Prince of Württemberg as well as the cuirassiers of Astrakhan and those of the Empress attacked the village of Semenovskaya while Barclay de Tolly and Bagration set about recapturing the entrenchments. On the Russian right, Hetman Platov's Cossacks and Uvarov's troopers went into action and, on the left, Olsuviev's soldiers came to support Tuchkov's in order to halt Poniatowski.

From the Great Redoubt a host of Russians could be seen, pressed shoulder to shoulder. Their courage bolstered by vodka, they formed a compact wall and were shouting 'Huzza! Huzza!' to thank the French for being kind enough to take them on. In the entrenchment, mainly occupied by the 30th of the Line because the other regiments were placed on either side of the position, the French were astounded. What was going on? Hadn't they won? Wasn't it all over? The French were firing from all sides but the Russians did not even slacken their pace. The seething green and white mass glinting with bayonets immediately swarmed over those who fell, giving the impression that the volley of fire had had no effect.

'For God's sake, are we firing at ghosts or what?' someone swore.

Margont saw Saber and a few men knocking down the double stockade that closed off the gorge of the redoubt. They were pushing with both hands against the tree trunks spared by the cannonballs or leaning against the wood. It was difficult to work out quite why they were doing this. Didn't they realise that the Russians were going to come back this way?

'Stop these idiots or I'll have them shot on the spot against their posts!' yelled a colonel, pointing at Saber and his men with the tip of his sabre.

Margont pushed his way through the throng of fusiliers to get to his friend.

'You're mad. What are you doing?'

Saber had seized hold of a tree trunk, which he was gradually bending. He was so stubborn that even if three men had got hold of him to remove him forcibly, he would have taken his bit of the stockade with him.

'The redoubt's lost! We're going to be swept up like dead leaves and the green coats will cling to this battery like limpets. The only way of getting back here will be a combined pincer attack, with the infantry head on and the cavalry to the rear. So we need to clear a path for our troopers!'

'A combined attack?' yelled Margont uncomprehendingly.

The previous night Saber had not taken account of the human factor in drawing his battle plans on the ground. That was one thing. But even now, when a human wave was about to engulf them, he was continuing to reason in a cold, mathematical way, a disembodied way, even. Saber collapsed, along with his post.

A trooper suddenly appeared in front of them. His horse was pawing the ground and tossing its head to shake the foam from its lips. The man and his mount were silhouetted against the light and their dark, proud, magnificent outlines were terrifying. He looked like one of the four horsemen of the Apocalypse. When the soldiers' eyes had adjusted to the light, they recognised Colonel Delarse. He had his back to the enemy. The Russians, who were getting closer and closer, were all attempting to cut down this officer, who some of them thought was Napoleon himself. Delarse pointed at the heart of the redoubt.

'Gentlemen, this is the gate to Moscow. Do not let them shut it again!'

A cheer went up at these words and shouts of 'Long live the Emperor!' rang out. Delarse set off again at a gallop, followed by a riderless black horse. Darval, his adjutant, had just rolled down dead at the foot of the earthworks.

The Russian horde swooped down on the entrenchment. Dark shadows appeared on all sides in the suffocating smoke caused by the firing. Flashes of light burst out constantly amidst a deafening roar. The Russians were trying to get in through the gorge but the French were blocking their way. Bodies were piling up on both sides. The Russians coming up behind flung themselves with all their might against their comrades to break this bottleneck. The soldiers of the 30th and the 13th Light were massing to counterbalance the Russian push. Those who were in the middle of this fray were caught in the vice. Squashed one against the other, some who had been killed could not even fall to the ground, giving the illusion that the dead had risen again to take part in the fighting.

Margont looked up. The Russians were firing from the top of the earthworks. Their bodies stood out so clearly that they were immediately cut down. Others took their places, only to suffer the same fate. The defenders of the gorge were eventually overwhelmed. Men were trampled to death whilst the Russians, whooping with joy, flooded in, running their bayonets through anything that moved. A petrified Margont thought of the amphitheatre in Nîmes. He had the impression of being in the middle of that ancient building, a wretched gladiator lost amidst a host of other gladiators. But there was no public, no Caesar poised to raise his thumb to bring the slaughter to an end. He saw green musketeers rushing towards him. A French fusilier next to him began howling with laughter. He was standing motionless, his weapon at his side, and laughing, just laughing.

Someone bent double in front of Margont. A piece of blood-soaked metal was sticking out of his back. Margont fired his pistol at the chest of an attacker. An indistinct figure charged at him, shouting at the top of his voice and wielding a bayonet. Margont dashed towards him, avoided the blade and thrust his sword into his stomach. To his right, someone fired a shot in someone's face. A hand caught him by the ankle. He leapt back without attempting to ascertain whether it was a Russian who had been knocked down or a wounded soldier asking for help. He was struck from behind on the left shoulder by a musket butt and lost his balance. He turned round sharply to discover an infantryman raising his bayonet to nail him to the ground. Margont had let go of his sword. He sprang forward, grabbed the Russian by the waist and both fell to the ground.

Margont got back up. The French were pulling back. He

noticed General Bonnamy, who was commanding the 30th of the Line and the 2nd Baden of the Line. Bonnamy was bleeding. A mass of Russians surrounding him were about to jab him to death with their bayonets. The fusilier was still laughing. He hadn't moved an inch. A Russian thrust his bayonet into his stomach. The Frenchman made no effort to defend himself. He collapsed. He had stopped laughing, recovering his senses only to die.

Margont retrieved his sword. The soldier who had attempted to run him through had picked up his musket. Margont trained his empty pistol at him. The Russian hesitated. Was he going to fight or give up? A stray bullet made the decision for him and went straight through his chest. Everywhere muskets were being thrown to the ground and hands were being raised in the air. The Russians had won. Margont caught up with those who were withdrawing but, since they had been surrounded, they would have to fight their way through the enemy.

Two-thirds of the 30th had perished in the redoubt and the area around it. But the survivors, added to those of the 13th Light and the other regiments, still made up a powerful force. They had begun to withdraw in good order when they suddenly turned into a surging mass. It was as if their minds had undergone a strange chemical reaction, producing a state of volatility. Paradoxically, their fear increased when the danger was receding since they were going back to their lines. A drummer had speeded up to overtake a grenadier and it was this trivial incident that had sparked off the stampede. The grenadier speeded up to overtake the drummer and soon everyone was running. Fear turned to panic and panic is the most contagious of all diseases. Margont looked back. The Russians were pursuing them.

'Fall in again or they'll slaughter us!' he yelled.

Saber, who was close at hand, shouted: 'You're a disgrace to our army! Fight for the honour of France!'

One was appealing to their reason, the other to their pride, but all the soldiers had turned deaf. The French ranks broke up in complete disarray and they began running faster and faster, hurtling down the slope of the hill in total confusion. Colonel Delarse positioned his magnificent brown horse across their path to bar the way.

'About turn! Stand up to the enemy!' he shouted. 'I recognise you! You're Lucien Malouin! Stop or you're for the firing squad! And you there, Captain André Dosse!'

His mount found itself surrounded by men on the run and was swept away by this human tide. Delarse was the only one standing up to the enemy but was going backwards despite himself. He was like a man astride a log being carried along by a raging current. Panic reached the point of madness. Soldiers began changing direction for no reason, accidentally bumping into their comrades. The stampede had turned into a sort of mysterious creature behaving irrationally, ignoring what was important and reacting excessively to the quite insignificant. So, if a foot chasseur ran to the left, the crowd immediately veered off in the same direction.

On the other side of the Semenovskaya Ravine, a dark blue mass was moving forward, perfectly in line. Its pointed bayonets were glinting in the sun, a brilliant and deadly streak of light. They were General Gérard's troops coming to the rescue of the routed Morand Division. The crowd could have continued to flee but it stopped and made an about-turn. Saber, who had just shouted, 'Stop fleeing like cowards!' had the delightful but false impression that he was the one who had effected this turnaround of events. Some of the soldiers who had kept on running broke their bones in the ravine or vanished behind clumps of bushes. Others did not rally until they reached the reinforcements. The wave of Russians smashed head-on into those daring to stand up to it but it was hit hard in return by the dark blue floodtide of Gérard's troops. The cannonballs made holes in the mêlée, which were immediately filled in. The shells sent smoke, earth and human remains flying into the air.

A carabineer next to Margont was reloading his weapon at top speed.

'You know what we are when all's said and done, comrade? Nothing but bloodstains.'

On the Russian left, Bagration declared that he would retake the Flèches or die. He launched a large-scale counterattack but the French smashed this action. Then a shell splinter broke Bagration's shinbone. The general tried desperately to conceal his wound but he eventually had to be evacuated. He had received a mortal blow. The news spread through the Russian army like wildfire. Bagration enjoyed such popularity that by about one in the afternoon the morale of the Russian left wing had fallen considerably. Also on the Russian far left, Kutuzov was beaten, this time by Poniatowski's Poles. Once more, Ney and Murat estimated that the Russian army could be destroyed if Napoleon sent in the Guard. Belliard, Ney's chief of staff, galloped off to find the Emperor.

Napoleon decided to send just the Young Guard into combat. But then he immediately ordered a halt to this manoeuvre. The reason was that on the Russian far right Uvarov's light cavalry and Platov's Cossacks had launched a counterattack. They were slaughtering the baggage escort of the Grande Armée, forcing one part of Eugène's troops and d'Ornano's cavalry to intervene against them. Napoleon could not afford to part with some of his Guard without first being sure of the stability of his left flank and knowing that they could not be skirted. Kutuzov used this unexpected respite to reinforce his centre by sending in Ostermann's corps, which was supporting his right and which was under relatively little threat, as well as the Russian Guard. So the Russian centre now had so many troops that it was futile to hope to sweep it aside. Napoleon responded by having a large battery of three hundred guns set up to crush the Russian army with its firepower.

At two in the afternoon the Russians were still in control of the Great Redoubt. The soldiers of the 13th Light were awaiting orders. The roar of artillery fire was frightening and soldiers had to shout in their neighbours' ears for any hope of being heard.

Margont was observing the battlefield through his field glasses. He could see troopers stirring up clouds of dust, coils of white and black smoke, dark patches moving across the hills and running into other dark patches coming up towards them before disappearing into the smoke.

'Are we winning or losing?' yelled Lefine.

'There's a lot of moving around. That's all I can tell you.'

Lefine took the field glasses and surveyed the scene. His face dropped when he saw the hordes of Russians that had appeared in the middle of the enemy position.

'Good God! Hell has got a bout of Russian indigestion and it's puking up all the ones we've already killed!'

He'd made a joke of it to save face but it was he who, at the prospect of more butchery to come, wanted to vomit.

'I can't believe there are so many Russians in the world!' he exclaimed. 'We've already wiped them all out! It's just their dead bodies rising up again. They pick up the pieces, gather around the rivers and have a big washday to make themselves more presentable. They bury the ones who are really too messed up: the ones chopped in half or squashed or with a head missing or in too many bits . . . Then they get back in line and there they are, starting all over again. With the Russians you've got to kill them and then kill their corpses, otherwise they come back to life.'

'I'm going to end up believing your theory of the Russian army's big washday. They're bound to send us in again to storm the Great Redoubt,' prophesied Margont.

'Here we are! More bad news! And this time it's enough to make you jump off the Pont du Gard.'

Saber was pacing up and down, his hands behind his back. Why didn't the Emperor send in his Guard to break through the Russian centre? he asked himself. He had noted the attack by the Russian cavalry on Kutuzov's far right but he was convinced that the French would hold out on that side and that this manoeuvre was just incidental.

Delarse galloped past, followed by two aides-de-camp, a captain and his former second-in-command's black horse.

'That one really gets on my nerves,' muttered Lefine. He turned towards Margont. 'He's earned himself a new nickname since his show of courage at the Great Redoubt: "Death-dealer". They really meant "Death-dodger" because he defies it so much but "Death-dealer" sounds better.'

'And what was his old nickname?' yelled Margont at the top of his voice.

' "Breathless." '

'What's mine, then?'

Lefine burst out laughing.

' "Bookworm", "the bookseller", and "Captain Freedom".'

'It's better than "Lefine the wheeler-dealer", "Lefine the nosy parker" and "hoodwinker".'

Lefine was outraged. 'That's an insult, sir. Who said that? It was that bastard Irénée, wasn't it?'

Piquebois was weaving in and out of the bodies lying on the ground. He grabbed Saber by the sleeve, rousing him from his daydreams just as the Imperial Guard was smashing the Russian centre to pieces and encircling the enemy wings . . . in his imagination. Margont and Lefine joined them beside Galouche, who was sitting down leaning against the trunk of a half-shattered birch tree. His hands were joined both for prayer and to try to stanch the flow of blood from his stomach. Saber sped off to look for a surgeon. Galouche motioned to Margont to come close to his ear.

'God's heard too many prayers at once today. He can't look after everyone . . .' He added with a smile: 'That's a very down-to-earth way of putting things. I lived life as a mystic and now I'm dying as an atheist. It's usually the opposite.'

'You're going to pull through!' Margont declared.

It was a platitude and he was annoyed with himself at not finding anything more convincing to say. Galouche was going to pat him on the arm but stopped. He didn't want to leave bloodstains on his friend's sleeve.

'Ask Lefine to give you lessons in how to tell lies.'

Delarse galloped past again, flourishing his sabre. 'Everyone to the redoubt! Everyone to the redoubt!' he shouted.

'Go there yourself, you git!' someone yelled.

The insult was lost in the cloud of dust thrown up by the colonel's horse.

'We might as well lie down where we are!' someone else chipped in.

A surgeon came running up. His clothes were dripping with blood, as were his medical bag and his shoes. He was sticky with death. Piquebois, Margont and Lefine shook their friend's hand for the last time. Saber waved at him from a distance as if expecting to see him again. Then he addressed all those who were willing to listen. The 13th Light had again lost a large number of officers, so they listened to this fired-up lieutenant as they would a general.

'Soldiers! These are the same Russians as those you crushed at Austerlitz, Eylau and Friedland. Let's charge at them, my friends, and walk over their bodies! They're used to it. They still bear the marks of our boots on their stomachs!'

Saber was cheered. A moment later the Morand, Gérard and Broussier Divisions, led by Prince Eugène himself, were moving up to attack the Great Redoubt. It was three in the afternoon.

The drummers were playing to urge them on, adding further to the commotion. The Great Redoubt was still swathed in the smoke from gunfire and only the flashes of firing pierced the thick white cloud. The shots once more caused havoc in the French line, churning it up and cutting through it.

'Close ranks!' Margont shouted automatically.

He forced himself to think of other things. He tried to recall Natalia's face. She was asking him to bring his book back and her clear voice eased the noise of gunfire and his headache. The ground began to tremble beneath his feet, as if Dante's Hell, which Brother Medrelli had so often told him about, were slowly opening its jaws to swallow up the world.

There were shouts of joy. A mass of cuirassiers and carabineers pounded past at the gallop. The cavalrymen were riding thigh to thigh, tight against one another like bricks in a wall. The sun glinted on their breastplates, helmets and sabres. The floodtide engulfed the Russian infantry and cavalry, sweeping them aside, and carrying on past the Great Redoubt. Eugène's troops started to charge. Suddenly, the Raevsky cannon stopped firing, as if by magic. The smoke cleared and inside the entrenchment metal gleamed in the sunlight. It was the cuirassiers of the 5th and 8th Regiments, led by General Auguste de Caulaincourt, who had just entered the Great Redoubt from the rear via the gorge. The French infantrymen, wild with joy, immediately climbed up the breastworks. The cuirassiers had decimated the defenders but were now being pushed back under fire from the last remaining Russians.

However, Eugène's soldiers were springing up to take over. 'Long live the cuirassiers!' the soldiers shouted, while shooting at Russians.

Margont noticed Colonel Pirgnon at the top of a breastwork. He was urging his men on, and they, uplifted by his courage, were passing him on either side and pouring into the redoubt. His presence, in such an exposed position, was considered an insult by the Russians. They took aim at him, cursing him as they did so. But for the devotion of his soldiers who pounced on them, and the smoke and general confusion, Pirgnon would probably have been hit. It was as if Delarse and he were in competition to see who was the more reckless. He remained there in full view whilst his soldiers stoutly defended what they had just named the 'Pirgnon breastwork'. At that precise moment, this man who so admired Achilles did indeed resemble the mythical warrior.

Margont entered the redoubt. The Russians were fighting every inch of the way. Some were sheltering behind heaped-up corpses of men and horses. Even some of the wounded had been thrown on to the piles. He had never seen anything like it. Shouting was coming from all sides. A Pavlov grenadier, recognisable by his mitre-shaped headgear, which this regiment had been allowed to keep because of its bravery at Friedland, charged at him with his bayonet. An infantryman from the 9th fired on the Pavlov. As this was not enough to stop him in his tracks, the fusilier jabbed him with his bayonet. The Pavlov fell to his knees but picked himself up again. It took another blow from the musket butt to knock him unconscious. The Frenchman was preparing to finish him off. Margont stopped him. He stared at the Pavlov. His arm and forehead were bandaged. He also had a deep gash to the shoulder.

'What next? Even the wounded are having a go!' Margont yelled.

The fusiliers continued to pour into the redoubt. Some infantrymen made a detour to avoid Margont. This poor captain seemed to be speaking to a dead person and they were more afraid of madness than of death. Next to him a boy of ten was crying. He was a Russian drummer. He had 'bird's nest' decorations on his shoulders and his sleeves were scattered with white braiding in the shape of an inverted 'v'. Squatting on the ground with his elbows on his knees, he was sobbing over his broken drum.

At last, the Great Redoubt was taken. Pirgnon, arms folded, was still on his breastwork. Margont set off in search of his friends. Lefine sprang up from behind a heap of corpses, his face smeared with gunpowder.

'So, you're still alive, Captain?' His blackened face was beaming with pleasure. 'He doesn't reply but he's still alive! Look at that swine Irénée!'

Margont turned his head. Saber was surrounded by two colonels and an infantry general. There were also numerous officers from the cuirassiers.

'I'm told that you were the one who cleared away the remains of the stockade blocking the gorge through which we entered the redoubt,' declared a colonel from the cuirassiers.

'That is correct, Colonel,' replied Saber, standing firmly to attention.

'What is your name?'

'Lieutenant Irénée Saber, Colonel.'

'Well, from now on you will be called Captain Saber. I shall see to it personally.'

The infantrymen again cheered the cuirassiers, who returned the compliment. But no one was happier than Saber.

Russian troops were still massed behind the Great Redoubt. Margont noticed Piquebois. He was standing on a pile of Russian bodies because there was nowhere else to put your feet. The bodies were a horrible sight, slashed and spiked all over. They were the bloody trail left by the cuirassiers of the 5th and 8th, the heroes of the Great Redoubt.

'Are you all right? You're not wounded, are you?' enquired Margont.

Piquebois made no answer. Motionless, he was staring at the Russian line.

'They're there. It's them . . .' he declared.

'Who?'

Margont looked in the same direction as Piquebois. He could see the Russian ranks further away, on the heights; he could make out the green lines of the infantrymen and black and white troopers in serried ranks.

'It's them, the Imperial Horse Guard,' Piquebois said, speaking the words with difficulty. He started to charge, shouting: 'To the death! Up and at the brats! Let's kill the lot of them!'

He was dashing towards them as cannonballs bounced around him. The hussar in him was awakening and he was furious. Piquebois became frenzied, as in the past at the height of the charge. He wanted to fling himself into the midst of the

Imperial Horse Guard and perish in the heat of battle, in a climax of blood, broken bones and severed limbs. Margont went running after him but would never have caught up with him had a shell not exploded near his friend. Margont picked Piquebois up, slung him over his shoulder and brought him back to the redoubt. Piquebois, half-conscious, was delirious. He could see the famous Imperial Horse Guard galloping along, roaring with laughter and pointing at him.

While the taking of the Great Redoubt was in its final phase, Kutuzov ordered his Imperial Horse Guard to charge the French cuirassiers. But French cavalry reinforcements were sent in. At the end of this massive clash between mounted troops the Russian cavalry was driven back and several enemy infantry regiments also received a mauling. By four o'clock the Russian left flank had fallen back. The centre, although seriously weakened by the loss of the Great Redoubt and the village of Semenovskaya, was still holding out.

Once more Napoleon wondered whether he should send in his Guard against the Russian Foot Guard, who had formed square, and the survivors of the other units. He had never encountered an enemy so ferocious and tenacious. He did not sense that the Russians were about to give in yet.

After much hesitation, he declared: 'Eight hundred leagues away from Paris you do not risk your last reserve.' He had his last reserve guns brought into position and gave this order to General Sorbier, who was commanding the Imperial Guard: 'Since they want more, let them have it.'

The Russians now had four hundred cannon firing at them. But Kutuzov stood his ground and answered back with his ordnance. This unprecedented artillery duel ended only when night fell.

The Grande Armée had lost thirty thousand men, killed or wounded, including forty-eight generals. Russian losses stood at fifty thousand. Fewer than a thousand of those had been taken prisoner. But the Russian army had not been destroyed, so the war was not over.

After holding a tense council of war with the heads of the general staff in an ordinary *isba*, Kutuzov decided to pull back his army. He preferred losing Moscow to losing both his army and Moscow. However, he had a victory message sent to the Tsar announcing that he had ripped the French army to pieces, destroyed the Imperial Guard, captured one hundred guns and taken sixteen thousand prisoners, including Prince Eugène, Davout, Ney and Murat. Only the claim involving Murat was true because General Bonnamy, after surviving the twenty bayonet thrusts he had received in the Great Redoubt, had proclaimed that he was the King of Naples in order to be spared. As fortune often favours pragmatists, Rostopchin, the governor-general of Moscow, ordered a Te Deum to be celebrated in the Upenski cathedral in the Kremlin and the Tsar promoted Kutuzov to General Field Marshal and paid him a handsome reward.

With the Russian army in retreat, the road to Moscow was now well and truly clear.

CHAPTER 25

HE was wandering amongst a vast expanse of corpses. To him, these bodies suggested dead leaves mistakenly carpeting a summer landscape. One scene had particularly struck him. Before his very eyes a cannonball had wrought havoc in a column of infantrymen. In a flash the projectile had blown off the left legs of seven soldiers who were advancing in single file. The man walked along in its wake, among the mangled victims, scattered limbs and pools of blood. Almost immediately he felt empty once more. A little further on, he noted the entangled bodies of combatants and imagined their struggle. However, the tumult of this slaughter soon faded from his mind, like a patch of fog dispersed by the wind. He crouched down to stroke the cheek of a Russian drummer boy barely twelve years old, hunched up, his stomach smashed to pieces by shell splinters. His gesture would have melted the hardest of hearts. It was not the child he wanted to caress, but death itself, and even that did not entertain him for long. He stood up, in a state of turmoil. He had witnessed an appalling butchery and yet he was already beginning to miss the suffering. He was afraid of no longer being able to escape detection. He felt the veneer wearing thin. He wondered how much bloodshed he would need to witness in order finally to feel assuaged.

*

The soldiers were marching stooped, their shoulders hunched. They looked like ghosts wandering in the night. Although he was as exhausted as the rest, Margont's impatient pace was at odds with this spectacle and either surprised people or annoyed them. Under the pretext of asking for news about someone or other, Margont visited the 9th of the Line. He made sure that Colonel Barguelot noticed him and the colonel hailed him jovially. His uniform was gleaming and he looked triumphant.

'Captain Margont! I'm glad you've survived. What a business! I was at the Great Redoubt during the afternoon assault, the successful one. I climbed up that wretched earth-work, sabre in hand, and there, with my fusiliers from the 9th, we caused a frightful slaughter. Frightful! It was indescribable! Indescribable! Everyone agrees that it was the fiercest part of the whole battle. You can't imagine what it was like!'

'I don't need to, Colonel, because I was there.'

Barguelot's jaw dropped. 'You were there? No, the 84th couldn't have been there because the Delzons Division . . . You're mistaken.'

'The fact is that for the day I was assigned to the 13th Light of the Morand Division.'

Barguelot was disconcerted. 'The 13th Light . . . Well, yes, I did see them, of course. But there was so much smoke that you couldn't make out a thing.'

'Perhaps you noticed Colonel Pirgnon, from the 35th? He was also at the Great Redoubt.'

'No. Not with all that smoke; it was worse than fog . . .'

It would have been difficult, though, not to have noticed Pirgnon perched on his breastwork. And, climbing up an earthwork without dirtying his uniform . . . Margont himself was so covered in soil that he looked as if he had just risen from the grave.

'I must leave you because I have to check up on the state of my regiment. I look forward to seeing you again, Captain.'

The two men parted. Margont caught up with the 35th of the Line. He was unable to meet Colonel Pirgnon, who was being treated for a superficial wound to the arm, so he ended up going back to the 84th.

Soldiers surrounding Saber were singing:

> Long live Saber! Long live Saber!
>   Our hero captured the Redoubt
> Of that there ain't the slightest doubt
>   Got himself a nice promotion
>   By his show of sheer devotion
> Long live Saber! Long live Saber!
>   In the army no one's braver!
> Long live Saber! Long live Saber!

Saber motioned to him to join them but Margont kept on walking and caught up with Lefine, who had done the rounds of his spies. He was going to have to take on more. Those allotted to Pirgnon had all been killed or wounded, and only one of those keeping a watch on Colonel Fidassio had survived. The same was true for Barguelot and Delarse. Neither Margont nor Lefine could believe such a death toll.

'Let's start with Delarse,' Margont declared.

'Our surviving spy lost sight of him for three-quarters of the time. What he was able to tell me was that Delarse took insane risks. He was at the head of all possible attacks. I don't know why the hell the general staff don't get a move on and put him up a rank or two. At this moment he's alone in his tent and won't see anyone. His new adjutant took him a meal on a tray and came out soon after with soup all over his uniform.'

Margont sat down and leant against a tree. He couldn't take any more. He thought he could still hear the sound of gunfire, distant and unreal. Lefine sat down cross-legged. His face, black with gunpowder, couldn't be seen in the darkness, and Margont had the impression he was listening to a report by a soldier who had been decapitated by a cannonball. Death pervaded all his thoughts.

'It's because General Huard has been killed,' Lefine continued. 'Delarse already saw himself promoted to general and put in charge of the brigade but he found out that he was going to remain a colonel and that he would be assisting Huard's replacement. Everyone found that disgraceful.'

Margont closed his eyes. 'Don't worry, I'm listening carefully. What about our Italians?'

'Even if most of General Pino's Italian Division couldn't get there in time to take part in the battle, Colonel Fidassio was there right enough. He showed immense courage.'

Margont reopened his eyes. 'What?'

'All the time he stayed at the head of his regiment and personally ran his sword through a Russian captain who had just shot his horse and was trying to skewer him. He took the dead man's gorget and put it around his neck.'

Margont instinctively touched his own gorget, the small

horizontal metal crescent worn by infantry officers, that last vestige of medieval armour.

'His soldiers nicknamed him "the lion",' Lefine added.

'Not very imaginative! Anyway, I must recant. I judged Fidassio too hastily. Because he wasn't coping with the responsibility of leadership and was panicking at the thought of it, I considered him incompetent and a coward. In fact he's only incompetent.'

'I personally don't understand the mysteries of this transformation.'

'He must have drunk some of that potion of yours.'

Lefine took his Austrian gourd – a trophy he had picked up on the battlefield at Austerlitz, so a sacred object and a lucky charm – and took a large swig.

'What's the second explanation?'

'I'm still convinced that the responsibility of being a colonel is beyond Fidassio. He can't make quick decisions and, when faced with a problem, hesitates like weighing scales that never manage to balance. But in a battle everything becomes clear. He's ordered to attack in column a given point in the enemy line, so he attacks in column a given point in the enemy line. There's no more self-questioning, no more decisions to make. Paradoxically, fear is the price he has to pay for his peace of mind. He makes up for his lack of judgement and competence with his courage. He's even happy because for once he knows what to do.'

'Close ranks.'

'That's more or less it. Obviously, if he has to take the initiative because everything's not going as planned, then . . .'

'Nedroni, help!'

Margont set about removing the soil from his uniform. 'Exactly. And how did Nedroni conduct himself?'

'As courageously as his master. The two of them are two sides of the same coin.'

'Yes, except that one side is worth more than the other. We don't know much about them, when it comes down to it. They're difficult to make out because they're always together. I'm sure that if we managed to separate them for a few hours we'd find out a lot more, just by observing them. Perhaps, then, it's precisely so that we don't find out too much about them that they are inseparable. It's as if each were hiding the dark side of the other; as if they were permanently back to back, covering for each other. But if Nedroni is concealing Fidassio's incompetence, what is Fidassio concealing about Nedroni?'

'A skeleton in the cupboard?'

'According to von Stils, our Saxon Life Guard, it's his homosexuality. Or else Nedroni has no secret and supports Fidassio in order to further his career. In any case, it's pointless hoping to find a way of separating them. The only solution would be to kill one of them . . .'

Lefine chuckled. It was so good to laugh.

'If we went for that option, Captain, I'd prefer it if we got rid of Nedroni. I fear him more than Fidassio,' he chipped in.

'Are you sure? When someone hits his master, even the most placid dog can go wild. The conclusion is that whatever the precise connection between them, Nedroni is bound to be in the know and will protect him no matter what. Your spies responsible for Pirgnon were killed but you were in the Great Redoubt with me.'

'He was incredible! I give him second prize for foolhardiness, a pass with merit. Delarse receives third prize.'

Margont folded his arms, looking amused. 'Really? I'm dying to know who won first prize.'

'General Miloradovich. I have a friend who's an interpreter in the general staff of our corps. A prisoner told him that Miloradovich wanted to prove that he was the bravest man in the whole Russian army so he sat on the ground where our guns were causing the maximum carnage and announced that he was going to have his lunch. That man is insane and gets a special commendation, "fit for the madhouse".'

Margont was full of admiration. 'How do you always manage to know everything about everything?'

'Because that's all I have to sell.'

'Pirgnon loves Greek and Roman mythology and is astonishingly knowledgeable about it. When he talks about it it's as if he was alive at the time. It's as if he thinks he is the reincarnation of a famous classical figure. He must imagine being the hero of an odyssey.'

'But if this campaign is an odyssey, it's obvious that Pirgnon is not its Ulysses.'

'What about Barguelot?'

Lefine became even more joyful. 'I've kept the best until the end! Poor Colonel Barguelot really is unlucky: when the Broussier Division attacked the Great Redoubt . . . he sprained his ankle again.'

'Oh! When you've sprained them once, these joints do tend to become unsteady . . . Why didn't he go into the attack on horseback, then? Had his horse sprained its hoof?'

'He'd left his horse in the rear.'

'It's true that it's dangerous to go into the attack too quickly.'

'You sometimes dismount before the assault yourself, Captain.'

'Yes, but that's in order to show solidarity with the men of my company. Besides, given how much marching we do in Russia, I wanted to be sure of keeping my mount. And, lastly, I did go to the Great Redoubt. Twice. It almost did for me, as well.'

Lefine wiped his face with a handkerchief in a vain attempt to clean it.

'Colonel Barguelot also ended up in the redoubt. He just arrived a tiny bit late, when it was all over.'

'His uniform was sparkling.'

'He skirted the redoubt and entered via the gorge. It was less dirty that way. He still almost got killed.'

'Really? Did he catch a bad cold?'

'He was limping along well behind his regiment, surrounded by a dozen soldiers – including our spy – when a Russian soldier who'd been pretending to be dead got up and attacked him with his sabre. Barguelot parried the attack so badly with his sword that, but for the speed of one of his men who stopped the Russian in his tracks by running him through, Barguelot's heart would have had a taste of metal.'

'So his title of "fencing master" is just one more piece of deception, is it? Excellent work, Fernand.'

The two men were in no hurry to catch up with their regiment. They knew it was the moment for counting the dead.

Men from each regiment were thinking of those they had lost or those hovering between life and death. The 84th had stayed in the second line so had not suffered much, but other regiments had sustained incredible losses.

Of Margont's acquaintances, Gunner Vanisseau had died. He had imitated birds and known how to attract ducks. Parouen had had both legs broken by a cannonball. He had been nicknamed 'the Pike' because he would swim in any stretch of water he could find and because he'd give you anything in exchange for a grilled fish. Partiteau had finished up not far from the redoubt, covered in bayonet wounds, like a pincushion. Oh, Partiteau! 'As stupid as Partiteau', 'as daft as a Partiteau', 'bird-brain Partiteau'. No one could be more simple-minded than he, so the army, with its habitual sense of humour, had put him in intelligence. Yet if you quoted a date, even one ten years back, he would immediately tell you if it was a Monday or a Thursday and would quote you the newspaper headlines – though, of course, he wouldn't understand a word of them. Agelle was dying in hospital with more lead in his stomach than you'd find in a cartridge pouch. He used to spend his evenings writing letters to his Suzanne, letters that were so riddled with mistakes as to be unreadable. In any case, his fiancée couldn't read. Zaqueron had been crushed to death under the dead body of a Russian hussar's horse. He had been such a good cook that one day the Emperor had made a six-league detour to treat himself at his inn. Noyet had been shot to pieces by a shell. He had never stopped talking, even when people had hit him to make him shut up and sometimes even during his sleep. They were already beginning to miss his never-ending chatter. Rabut was also missing. Oh, Rabut! The longest-serving man in the 9th. He had been nicknamed 'That's Poppycock'. The old sergeant seemed to have fought in all the Napoleonic wars, all those of the Republic and also two or three in the old days of the King. Whenever he had read the Grande Armée bulletins he had never failed to exclaim, 'Poppycock! Poppycock! I know it is, I was there, damn it!' Now here he was, finally dead. It was said that it had taken no fewer than three Pavlovs to get the better of him. Droustic, who was called 'the Bavarian', had been sabred to death. No one knew where his nickname came from and he got angry when asked. Sapois was waiting for a surgeon to carry out an amputation. He'd seen a cannonball rolling along and had wanted to stop it for fun. The result was a broken foot, the sort of foolish accident that happens to an inexperienced soldier. Mardet, from the 8th Light, had just given up the ghost after bleeding to death from a bullet in the arm that had hit him in 'the wrong place'. He had so many children that in a few years' time they'd be able to repopulate the whole company entirely thanks to him. The two Taleur brothers, who constantly looked out for each other, had been found within a few paces of each other. 'Cock-eye' had been run through by an Imperial Horse Guard's sabre.

This process lasted all night because they were still receiving reports of so-and-so's body being found, that so-and-so hadn't survived his operation or was lying in a cart for the wounded . . . There had never been so many dead and wounded, and the count was still not over. Even worse, it seemed as if it would never be over. And with each death, everyone had the feeling that a small part of humanity had just been lost for ever.

CHAPTER 26

O N 15 September the Grande Armée reached Moscow. Napoleon had admired it the day before, in the company of the vanguard, from Poklonnaya Hill, the Hill of Salvation. He had declared: 'Here it is, then, this famous city', before adding, 'It is high time.'

Reaching Moscow caused an indescribable outpouring of joy. The regiments could see the columns ahead of them gesticulating on a hilltop and shouting: 'Moscow! Moscow!' The soldiers simply could not believe it. They speeded up, muddling their ranks, which the NCOs, with much swearing, then had to attempt to disentangle. The Hill of Salvation was blocking the view; Moscow was still only a dream, a city they had heard so much about but which perhaps did not exist, a sort of Russian Eldorado. But once they had reached the summit, suddenly Moscow stretched out in all its immensity. Everywhere were church cupolas and gilded onion domes, splendid palaces, whole districts built of stone, vast avenues . . . Moscow, with its Baroque and Byzantine architecture, belonged to a different world from that of Paris, Vienna, Berlin and Rome. This was already Asia.

Margont felt as if he were discovering a city from the tales of the Arabian nights. He bowed down and made the sign of the cross out of respect for this wonderful city and because that was the custom for Russians when they gazed at this holy city from the Hill of Salvation. However, he crossed himself in the Catholic, not the Orthodox, way. Then, like everyone else, he began to shout: 'Moscow! Moscow!' because this word was so great, so magnificent, that it alone filled his whole mind. He repeated it, yelling for joy until he was hoarse.

Saber, arms outstretched to the heavens and sabre drawn, was exclaiming: 'Victory! Total victory!' Lefine, who was too much the pragmatist to believe in dreams, muttered, 'It's not possible, it's not credible . . .' Piquebois, wanting to greet the city in his own fashion, was stuffing his pipe with the last pinch of tobacco that he had kept for the occasion. His face seemed composed but his fingers were trembling. The fighting, the hunger, the extreme tiredness, the lost comrades: all were forgotten.

Feasting their eyes on palaces and the red ramparts of the Kremlin, the 84th went down towards the city in perfect order because they had to be impeccable to show themselves worthy of Moscow. 'I'm in Moscow': the phrase rang in their ears like the pealing of the bells of a whole city. Everything was over, no one doubted that for a second. The Tsar was on his knees and the Russian army in pieces. Alexander would sign the armistice and they would spend the winter here, with spoonfuls of caviar in their mouths, being treated like princes.

Disillusion set in as soon as they entered the former capital. The city was absolutely silent. The regiments and squadrons followed one another in columns but there were no crowds as they went by. For a moment they thought that the people had locked themselves away in their homes. But there were no faces to be seen at the windows. They realised that Moscow had been deserted. Panic and the evacuation orders given by Count Rostopchin, the governor-general of Moscow, had emptied the city. Of the three hundred and twenty thousand inhabitants, the only ones left were those of French, German or Italian extraction, the destitute, the wounded who could not be transported, and the deserters.

Margont looked about him on all sides. He marvelled at every sight. The wide, straight streets, some lined entirely with mansions and palaces surrounded by gardens the size of parks, offered superb vistas. The famous fortress of the Kremlin was the jewel of Moscow. Its surrounding wall of red brick was topped with white, swallow-tail battlements and it was protected by numerous towers. The walls allowed glimpses of gilded cupolas crowded together, turrets decorated with faïence and small bell towers. They envied those who would be privileged enough to have quarters there while they watched over the Emperor, because he deserved nothing less than the Kremlin.

Prince Eugène set up his headquarters in Prince Momonoff's palace, whose luxury bordered on the incredible. The 84th was allotted a sector. Margont, Lefine, Saber and Piquebois chose a pretty little house and went inside laughing, convinced that the worst was behind them.

Margont was in a deep sleep. His dreams were not in keeping with the day's brilliant spectacle. He saw an actor on stage, wearing a toga like a classical tragedian and holding a smiling mask over his face. The stranger changed his mask with such speed that Margont did not even have time to glimpse his face. This second, sad-looking character aroused pity. Another change made him resemble a child seeking protection. Then it was the face of an honest-looking man before becoming that of an adolescent enraptured by his own youth. The stranger was also a magician and he conjured up the masks at will. Margont was staring at the figure. He wanted to know if it had its own face or if it was only a hollow shell. But at the same time he wondered if it would be possible to tell the difference between this genuine face and yet another flesh-coloured mask.

He was roused from his sleep by someone shaking him violently. He had difficulty opening his eyes. Piquebois's face was leaning over his own.

'Quentin, for heaven's sake! The house is on fire! Wake up!'

A cloud of thick black smoke was already pouring in through the bedroom door while white smoke was filtering through the gaps in the floorboards.

'We've taken your belongings. The others are already outside. Come on!'

Margont got dressed in a flash. However, the two men were unable to get through the doorway. The corridor was nothing but a blazing shell. The constant sound of crackling flames could be heard, frequently drowned out by a great crash as part of the ceiling collapsed. They retreated back inside the room. Margont made a dash for the window and opened it. For a second he was taken by surprise. How could that be? Was it daylight already? Why hadn't he been woken up early in the morning? Then he realised that it was still the middle of the night. But in many parts of the city fires were devastating whole neighbourhoods and the brightness rivalled that of a summer afternoon. Down below in the street, Lefine and Saber were waving their arms about.

'What the hell are you doing, Quentin? Get out of there!'

Margont disappeared before returning with sheets and clothes in his arms. He knotted them together as fast as he could. Saber was holding a horse's bridle in each hand. The panic-stricken animals were neighing heart-rendingly. Lefine was having great difficulty controlling his terrified konia, which was edging backwards, not noticing that everything behind it was also on fire. Margont slid quickly down his makeshift rope, gritting his teeth as the material peeled the skin off the palms of his hands. Piquebois did likewise and the four men hurried away without having the slightest idea where to go to escape from the flames.

'Over there,' decreed Saber, rushing off in one direction.

They found themselves face to face with a group of hussars from the 8th Regiment who thought safety lay in the opposite direction. Most of them had not even had time to put on their pelisses or their shakos. Dressed only in dirty shirts and red trousers, they considered themselves lucky to have retrieved just three of their mounts.

'Don't go that way, the streets are on fire!' exclaimed Saber.

'It can't be worse than where we're staying!' retorted a barefoot trooper, who had flung himself on the neck of his beast to calm it down.

Another hussar was ranting and raving, sabre in hand.

'It's the Russians who are setting fire to their own city.'

'That's impossible!' said Margont angrily. 'It's some

irresponsible fools who've knocked over candles while ransacking houses or have lit fires and haven't kept an eye on them. It's drunkards who are the cause of this damn mess!'

But the hussar was categorical. 'I agree with you that drunks are responsible for some of the fires, but several fire-raisers have already been arrested. Russians. Some have confessed in front of the firing squad that Count Rostopchin gave the order to set fire to the city. He got policemen to disguise themselves as beggars and emptied the prisons. They've caught convicts who were completely drunk going along the streets throwing torches through windows.'

'I can't believe such a thing. They're liars,' Margont stubbornly maintained.

'Well, how do you explain the fact that there's not a single fire pump left in the city? Rostopchin had them all taken away!'

While Margont was trying to overcome his consternation, the two groups were arguing. Unable to agree, each of them decided to stick to their original conviction. Two hussars and the single mount they were sharing did, however, join Margont and his friends.

The heat was becoming extremely hard to bear. Sweat was pouring from their faces, running into their eyes, soaking their bodies and making their clothes stick to their skin. They passed between two rows of rustling, crackling flames. Explosions rang out at regular intervals, nearby or further away, sometimes isolated and sometimes in succession like a firework display. The sky looked amazing. It was a shifting kaleidoscope of colours: the black of the smoke merging into the black of the night, a thousand varying hues of glowing orange, the yellows sometimes paling into incandescence . . . It looked like a vast canvas smeared with thick layers of gouache. A mansion collapsed on itself with a terrifying crash. The horse belonging to the two hussars whinnied as it reared up. It brought its forelegs down heavily, almost crushing the foot of the one holding it by the bridle, and kicked out with its hind legs. The second hussar received the full force of one of its hoofs in his stomach. He was flung against a wall and fell, hunched up, to the ground. The mount reared once more and finally freed itself. It wanted to flee but, realising that it was surrounded by flames, it began to go round in circles. The buildings were threatening to collapse.

Margont shouted to the hussar to abandon his animal and to help his companion but the hussar stubbornly refused. Margont wanted to go to their aid but had to give up because the horse kept kicking out and whirling round on itself.

Lefine led his companions down a side street and they found themselves in a square. On two sides the buildings were on fire and the wind was blowing great quantities of white-hot ash about. It was like watching a gigantic swarm of fireflies landing all around. A volley of shots rang out and Margont realised that it was a firing squad shooting for all it was worth. The infantrymen were reloading as fast as they could. Some of them were walking among the bodies and finishing off the wounded by shooting them in the head. There were so many prisoners that they didn't even bother to clear the dead bodies.

'Who are you shooting?' Margont enquired of an adjutant, who was trying to speed up the executions while keeping an anxious eye on the spread of the fire.

'Fire-raisers. They're convicts and fanatics . . . Look at them. They're as drunk as lords!'

Faced with the muskets, some punched their chests to urge the French to open fire. The flurry of shots made Margont jump. A ragged individual, toothless and shaven-headed, approached him with a smile. Margont didn't recognise him. Was he a soldier he had fought? Someone he had met in Smolensk? The man spoke to him in Russian.

A corporal put a friendly hand on his shoulder and, responding to his smile, said to him: 'Come on, leave the captain alone and go back to your comrades. We're going to shoot you. You'll like that, won't you, getting pumped full of lead?'

The condemned man nodded his head several times. The corporal burst out laughing, proud to have made his point.

'The Russians have even emptied their asylums, Captain. They've put torches in the hands of lunatics and let them loose on the streets.'

Margont wanted to plead the man's case.

An adjutant, anticipating his protests, decreed: 'We are shooting all fire-raisers and I'll have anyone who tries to interfere arrested.'

Margont and his companions moved away while the simpleton leapt about with joy: it was his turn at last to stand in front of the wall where the men were giving a fireworks display with their muskets.

The men of the 84th decided to stay in this square until the blaze died down. But a shower of ash came and buried their hopes. The light-coloured confetti soon changed into thick flakes, which became so numerous as to make it difficult to see.

It was like being in the middle of a burning blizzard. Each intake of breath was agony because the heat made the lungs hurt and the debris caused endless coughing. Even drinking did not help. Worse still, the ash contained burning remnants.

A prisoner screamed as his mop of hair caught fire. The firing squad was not fast enough and had to complete its dirty task by rushing at the last captives with their bayonets. They didn't want to finish them off because they thought the fire would do it for them. The adjutant bawled out his orders. They would put the wounded out of their misery, then they would form a column and finally they would evacuate the square. But his men had already disbanded. Undeterred, the adjutant grabbed two saddle pistols and began shooting at those writhing in pain on the ground.

To their great regret Margont and his friends had to abandon their horses for fear of ending up disembowelled or having a hand severed if they kicked out. They dived into a narrow street but they could hardly see a thing because the ash was so thick. They covered their mouths and noses with bits of their shirts to filter the air. So as not to lose anyone on the way, they advanced in single file, holding on to one another by the belt. At the sight of so many riches going up in smoke, soldiers were rushing into houses in an attempt to rescue food and treasures from the flames. As he passed, Margont heard dozens of them screaming as a blazing roof fell in or sections of a wall collapsed on top of them.

At last they reached a neighbourhood that had been spared by the fires. The houses, built of stone, and the gardens, had acted as fire breaks. The considerable number of soldiers gathered here had formed a human chain right down to the Moskva. All sorts of containers were being passed from hand to hand to douse new pockets of fire. But more and more were starting up as blazing debris flew through the air in all directions.

'I told you it was this way,' Saber reminded them.

He was woken by an explosion nearby. As he dressed hurriedly he thought that the Russian army was attacking Moscow to dislodge the French, though he knew this supposition was absurd. Distraught soldiers came to inform him that the city was in flames and, at first, as he rushed out into the inferno with a few men, he feared for his life. Then, gradually, he became mesmerised. He took advantage of the confusion caused by the collapse of several buildings to disappear into the maze of streets.

While other people were running for their lives amidst this labyrinth of stone, wood and fire, he just strolled about. He gazed in delight at the houses devastated by flames. Near a crossroads he heard calls for help coming from a dwelling with a burning roof. He rushed up to the door. He could hear voices nearby. He seized his scabbard and placed it so as to block the handle. A moment later it turned several times but as its movement was impeded it could not loosen the bolt. There was frantic banging on the door while the handle continued to be jiggled to no effect. The bars on the windows prevented any other way of escape. People were shouting and pleading in Italian. There was a dreadful noise as the roofing collapsed, followed immediately by screaming, terrible screaming that was like music to his ears. The man imagined their bodies. He could see the flames licking their skin, turning it red and covering it with blisters. He pictured their hair and their clothes catching fire in one burst and their mouths and throats filling with fire at their last intakes of breath. He could hear the screams of pain of those transformed into human torches and, finally, the dull thud of the bodies falling. He breathed in the smell of burnt flesh. It intoxicated him like strong alcohol. He thought of the charred bodies, shrivelled by the burning of the tissues and the evaporation of their fluids. He would have liked to open the door to gaze upon these hunched-up corpses as black as lumps of coal, but he was afraid of being struck full in the face by a wave of flame set off by the draught. He put on one of his gloves to retrieve his burning scabbard and continued on his way.

His footsteps were guided by screams of agony. He noticed a man leaving a house that was reduced to a whirlwind of flames. He was one of the few inhabitants to have stayed behind. He was frantically beating his shirtsleeves to extinguish the white-hot debris scattered all over it. He smiled, thinking that the man was coming to his aid. A look of amazement spread across his face when he saw the pistol and the barrel of the weapon pointing in the direction of the house. He was being told to . . . go back inside. He put his hands up as a sign of surrender and moved slowly to the side to show that he would slip away without causing any trouble. The bullet struck him full in the chest. Two sentries, who had been present at the scene, ran up, muskets in hand.

'He was a fire-raiser. He was the one who set fire to the house,' the officer told them immediately.

The soldiers saluted and went off again. The man continued on his way, looking out for every opportunity to revel in the slaughter. After a time, even the fire of Moscow was not enough to slake his thirst for blood. Then he wanted to believe in God again in order to believe in the devil.

He imagined himself in Hell. The rustling and the crackling were caused by gigantic creatures devouring the damned. He conjured up the most loathsome monsters imaginable that would do justice to the sermons of the sternest of preachers: Cyclopean ring-shaped worms intertwined, their jaws swarming with tentacles that seized those trying to escape; flies' eyes whose myriad facets reflected screaming faces; mouths filled with rows of fangs that tore their victims to pieces . . . He could see immense shadows sprawling amongst the fiercest fires, crushing whole areas beneath their weight. More worms, covered in protuberances, laboriously hauling themselves out of a gigantic pit that went deep down into the infernal abyss, where everything was immeasurably worse than here. What existed within the secret of this chasm was beyond mere human understanding. The man took a few steps towards the abyss. He wanted to throw himself in, but the heat became too intense and forced him to retreat. He set off in search of streets that were enveloped in flames but where he would be able to move about. The night was still young. He would have more opportunities to see death and to kill.

CHAPTER 27

For four days Moscow burned. More than four-fifths of the city was destroyed. Twenty thousand people perished in the flames.

Margont and his companions had set themselves up in a suburb that was relatively unscathed. Margont decided to go back to his original quarters in the hope of retrieving some belongings. Several times he got lost in this apocalyptic landscape. While some streets were blocked with fallen debris, elsewhere the flames had opened up the thoroughfare by wiping out entire blocks of houses. The residences and bell towers that had previously acted as landmarks had disappeared. Margont was surprised by the capriciousness of the flames: sometimes for no apparent reason a house had survived in the midst of a wasteland of destruction. Soldiers from every regiment were beavering away amidst the foul-smelling wreckage. They unearthed valuables, opened up trapdoors leading into cellars . . . Many were drunk – drunk on vodka, rum, beer, wine, kvass, punch or a mixture of them all. Margont came across infantrymen dressed up as marquises, strutting about in fur coats and sable hats, cashmere or fox fur jackets . . . The women they were with, canteen-keepers and sutlers or Muscovites, were laughing as they gazed at their silk dresses woven with gold and silver thread, and their fingers dripping with rings and precious stones. The streets were littered with an assortment of objects: mirrors with elaborate frames, paintings, ivory combs, crockery, statuettes, candelabra, rings and necklaces set with malachite or semi-precious stones, ceremonial pistols, clothes, books, samovars, carvings, pipes . . . The looters were picking up any item they could find, only to throw it away again twenty paces further on when they laid hands on something more valuable. Margont caught sight of Piquebois, who was also trying to find their former quarters.

'Hey, comrade, what a sad sight!' Piquebois exclaimed. 'Looters and ashes. They've gone mad watching the city go up in smoke. It's impossible to control anyone.'

A smell of rose-tinted tobacco was coming from his silver Russian pipe.

'The most ridiculous thing,' he went on, 'is that they haven't understood a thing. What's valuable today is not gold but food. They'll make a fine sight when they try going back to France with their knapsacks overloaded and their stomachs empty . . .'

What Margont had just heard seemed obvious to him, yet at the same time he refused to believe it.

'Going back to France?'

Piquebois's face, usually so composed, looked worried. 'If the Russians have deliberately burnt down their capital, there's little chance that they're intending to make peace.'

Margont remained silent. Piquebois meanwhile was watching the few remaining inhabitants wandering amidst the wreckage. Most were desperate and in rags, alarmingly thin and starving. Some were tearing strips of flesh off the carcasses of animals to feed themselves. Others were diving into the Moskva to retrieve the wheat that the Russian soldiers had thrown in before evacuating the town. But the fermented grains made them ill.

'We'll soon look like them if we don't get a move on before the winter,' he prophesied.

The two men carried on walking.

'Lefine and Saber have managed to collect a considerable amount of food: cucumber, onions, beer, sugar, hams . . .'

'Hams?'

'Yes, hams. As much salted fish as you could wish for, fat and flour. But no bread. Potatoes as well.'

'All the same, we'd be well advised to start rationing ourselves now.'

Piquebois pointed at Margont with the end of his pipe to show his approval.

'Fernand is trying to get some horses for us. We'll need to be on our guard because, if the army really does have to withdraw, soon people will be killing one another for a mount.'

'And they'll end up slitting one another's throats for a potato.'

They stopped in front of a church that had been spared by the blaze. People were congregating there to pray and to find shelter. Margont gazed at the walls, which were painted red and a delicate green.

'It's incredible,' said Piquebois in surprise. 'There's no soot on the walls. I'm going to start believing in God.'

Margont pointed at the crowd dressed in rags.

'They're the ones who've cleaned it.'

They eventually found their former quarters. There was nothing left. However, someone had propped up a charred beam. A message written in French was pinned to the wood:

Frenchmen,

My name is Yuri Lasdov and this house was mine. I was only a shopkeeper, and this building and my two grocery shops constituted all my worldly goods. Just before fleeing the city with my family, I personally threw all my stock into the depths of the Moskva. I left one of my employees behind in Moscow to set fire to my beloved home in case any French dogs should take up quarters in it. I asked him to burn it down during the night in the hope that some of your kind would be roasted alive.

May Russia be the grave of France.

Margont went back to his new quarters. A lieutenant was pacing to and fro at the front entrance, waiting for him. As soon as he caught sight of Margont he looked up to the heavens in gratitude and hurriedly took him inside. Colonel Delarse was dying and wanted to speak to him.

'Has he been injured?' Margont enquired.

'No. An asthma attack. One of the worst he's ever had. It's because of the fire: he's inhaled ash.'

A Baden soldier dressed up as an Orthodox priest was drunkenly babbling away in made-up Latin, blessing the passers-by. The lieutenant angrily pushed him away with all his might as he passed, sending him flying on to the cobbles. The would-be priest called down on him all the curses of Heaven and Hell combined.

'He's spoken to the colonels in the division. Then he asked for you as well as several other officers.'

'I feel flattered to have been sent for. What's his reason for wanting to see me?'

'I've no idea.'

Colonel Delarse's quarters were in a mansion whose architecture was modelled on Versailles. Margont reflected yet again on the number of ties there were between Russia and France. This war seemed crueller than ever. Delarse was lying in a four-poster bed draped with veils to filter the air. Before even catching sight of him at the far end of his dark bedroom, you could hear him wheezing. The exhausted colonel was holding a pencil between his fingers.

'Good day, Captain Margont,' he scribbled on one of the sheets of paper lying on his blanket.

'Good day, Colonel.'

'I think it's the end. Spare me those "of course nots" and other such nonsense.'

Margont nodded. The air entered Delarse's lungs easily but then became trapped inside. Breathing out was slow and painful.

'I'm not afraid. I have two mothers, my own mother and death. Both nurtured me as a child, both cradled me in their arms, both think of me constantly and both occupy my thoughts too much. I write this because my mother was so possessive that sometimes she was more stifling than my asthma. I tried everything to fight death: to deny its existence, to despise it, to plead with it, to taunt it . . . In combat I ran every possible risk as if to say to it: "Come on, come and get me! Do what you should have done long ago!" Sometimes I would even think that the fact of my still being alive was one of the many small things that were wrong with the world and that I should put it right. Sometimes, contrarily, I would expose myself to enemy fire to prove I was immortal.'

The pencil moved across the sheets of paper with surprising speed and no sooner had Delarse covered one with writing than he let it drop to the floor and started on the next. It was true that time was short . . .

'One day I understood that by behaving like this I was merely re-enacting my childhood. Because even when I was well I needed to dice with death by playing silly games: jumping from tall trees, swimming as far as I possibly could . . . Anyway, the fact is that after every battle, once the danger was over and my concentration wandered, I was always surprised that I was still alive. One step forwards, two steps backwards. What cruel game was death playing with me?'

Delarse had become so emotional in writing these lines that his breathing quickened and became even wheezier, and his writing more untidy.

'While thousands of soldiers were covering themselves in eternal glory at Austerlitz, I was choking at an inn. That says it all, doesn't it? As an adolescent I read the biographies of Alexander the Great and Julius Caesar. Both suffered from epilepsy and I thought that my asthma would not count against me any more than their fits did against them. It looks as if I was wrong. But you must be wondering why I'm telling you all this. Well, your colonel told me that you were keeping a journal about this campaign. Is that correct?'

'Absolutely, Colonel. But I didn't realise that Colonel Pégot knew about it.'

Delarse's face lit up. 'So you're writing your memoirs, are you?'

'For the time being my plan is to launch a newspaper.

Amongst other things, I shall recount the Russian campaign.'

'Censorship will turn it into a walk in the country!'

'In that case, instead of cutting out the censored passages, I'll cover them in ink and people will go and protest beneath the windows of the prefect, brandishing the black pages.'

Delarse smiled. He did not have enough breath to laugh.

'On a more serious note, Colonel, I shall point out to my readers that it's an "official" version of the campaign. Then, as soon as I can, I'll publish the real version, in the form of articles, memoirs and first-hand accounts.'

'That's why I sent for you. I hope you will tell people who Colonel Delarse was. I have struggled to ensure that my life amounted to more than just my asthma. I do not want to be remembered as "the asthmatic colonel the Russians didn't even have to kill themselves". And then there's the general staff! They look at me in the pitying and frustrated manner of those watching a man die whilst implicitly criticising him for not cutting short this moment which is "painful to all concerned". Change that! Say what I did for the brigade. Talk about the Great Redoubt! Tell people that I lived life to the full, that I did great things, even though I was haunted by death.'

'I shall do so. Is there anything else they should know about you, Colonel?'

Delarse looked at him wearily. It was difficult to read his expression. Margont wanted to repeat his question but the colonel's new adjutant was already ushering in the next visitor. The fellow had taken it upon himself, given the circumstances, to speed things up.

*

That same evening Margont had to move once more because his quarters had been requisitioned by the Pino Division. He refused to set himself up in the house allocated to him.

'Too inflammable for my liking,' he declared, patting the wooden walls with the flat of his hand.

He discovered that Saber, almost as soon as he had been promoted, had pulled rank to take possession of a Moscow palace, driving out some Neapolitans who had angrily sworn to come back with King Murat in person.

The building was vast. It was big enough to accommodate what was left of the 2nd Battalion of the 84th. It had only one storey but it boasted twenty French windows, with windows just as big above. The entrance was so high and so wide that a trooper could have passed through it without having to dismount. Above it was a triangular pediment. Two elegant covered walkways branched out from the central part. Unfortunately, this semicircular construction led only to piles of ashes, so that the palace resembled a bull whose horns had been amputated. The building had been white but was now covered with black soot, in mourning for Moscow.

Margont climbed the steps leading to the entrance and turned round to survey the view of the garden. The rows of trees, the trimmed hedges, the pond, the colonnade surrounding a statue of Diana, the classical pavilion, the orchard: all that would have looked splendid were it not for the bodies that hung, swaying in the wind, from the branches of the fir trees and lampposts in the avenue.

'They're fire-raisers, Captain,' explained a fusilier, sitting astride the banister while polishing his weapon.

Margont did not rebuke him for failing to salute. This one was not disguised as an Orthodox priest, had not blessed him, was not drunk and was busy with his musket. That was already quite something. In the entrance hall a *voltigeur* let out a yell on seeing him. He had been assured that a Russian hussar had sliced Margont's head off at the Moskva. He fell down on his backside with shock, and immediately helped himself to another ladleful of punch from a large bowl. Margont, who strongly disliked seeing drunken men with muskets in their hands, grabbed hold of the bowl and angrily overturned it. The punch spread out in a sweet-smelling pool of vanilla, lemon and cinnamon. The *voltigeur* raised his arms in protest.

'Steady on there, Captain!'

He took out a worn handkerchief and started to soak up the alcohol with it before wringing it out over the container. There would be no problem finding scores of men wanting to drink it.

On the first floor, Margont came across a note pinned with a dagger to a rosewood door: 'Strictly reserved for Captain Saber, Captain Margont and Lieutenant Piquebois.' The room was long and narrow. Its walls, hung with red velvet, and its brown, carved ceiling added to its solemnity. A double row of candelabra provided the lighting but, for fear of fire, only a few candles had been lit. At the end of this corridor of darkness, in a pool of light, Lefine was sitting on a throne acting like the Tsar of all the Russias.

A corporal, bowing respectfully, was listening to him as he declared majestically: 'I dub you Knight of the Order of St Andrew, General of the Hussars of the Guard, Count of Smolensk and Prince of Siberia.'

'Oh, yes? Prince of Siberia, is it?' exclaimed Margont as he rushed forward to launch a palace revolution.

Lefine, who had celebrated Moscow by drinking punch, pointed at Margont and exclaimed: 'General, arrest this impudent fellow and send him to the salt mines!'

The newly promoted Prince of Siberia preferred to slip away discreetly while Margont grabbed Lefine by the collar.

'Well, what a sorry situation! You bestow all these honours on someone but as soon as the tide turns he just drops you.'

'Fate is so fickle . . . "Tsar for starters, muzhik for afters." Still, I unconditionally accept the armistice.'

Having pushed Lefine from the throne, Margont interrupted his admonishment to admire the fine piece of carving, the back edges of which consisted of two perfectly straight tusks engraved with the family coat of arms.

'According to a servant, these are the tusks of a narwhal,' Lefine commented.

'The tusks of a what?'

'Of a narwhal, those nasty underwater creatures which have a long tusk on their head, like swordfish. They spear shipwrecked sailors.'

'Oh, these aquatic animals don't catch as many victims as you do. I know what a narwhal is . . . but a throne of narwhal tusks? Whose house are we in?'

'A prince's. Another one.'

Margont went to sit down in a more modest armchair.

'I've got a plan for unmasking our man: we're going to set a trap for him.'

Lefine instinctively threw his head back. 'Ah.'

'I'm going to send him a letter blackmailing him.'

'But we don't know who did it.'

'Exactly. The idea is to send this note to the four suspects. I'll sign it simply "C. M.". Since the murderer knows my name he'll decipher it as "Captain Margont", whereas the others won't understand a thing and will think that a note not intended for them accidentally ended up in their hands.'

Lefine gave no sign of enthusiasm. 'Even if he's not the murderer, one of the suspects might still turn up at the rendezvous, out of curiosity . . .'

'No, because I'll choose as the meeting place "the Moscow home of the lady of Smolensk". I've made enquiries: Countess Sperzof did have a residence here.'

'Perhaps he killed her without even knowing her name.'

'It's possible but unlikely because, according to the servants, the countess didn't hide her identity from her casual lovers. In any case, the murderer stole her signet ring. I'm sure he kept it as a souvenir and a trophy. With a blazon it's easy to find out a name and with a name you can obtain an address. Especially when your life's at stake.'

'If I were him I wouldn't turn up.'

'I'm going to claim that my spy never lost track of him in Smolensk, that he saw him in the company of "the lady of Smolensk" and that he followed him to her house. Our man won't dare run the risk of not turning up in response to my "invitation".'

'He's going to wonder why you've waited so long before taking action.'

'Don't worry, I've already thought of an answer to that objection. It'll be explained in the note.'

Lefine stretched out his legs. They were still aching from all those forced marches.

'In that case, if I were him, I'd turn up and I'd kill you.'

'That's one of the two problems. But we won't be on our own. We need some trustworthy people who'll be able to keep this business secret. I've thought of Saber, Piquebois, Captain Dalero and our friend the Red Lancer. Five men lying in wait, plus me. If there were more than that we might be discovered.'

'What's the plan?'

'Our man turns up to pay me or to shoot me. That way I finally find out who he is. I try to get him to talk about his crimes, for example by asking him why he acted in this way. If he replies, then it's in the bag! You are witnesses to his confession and we arrest him. Prince Eugène will have to believe me when he hears my version corroborated by a captain from his own Royal Guard and a lancer from the Imperial Guard. And even if our killer doesn't answer me, we'll have evidence against him. He'll have paid a handsome sum in order to—'

'Or he'll have killed Captain Margont before our very eyes,' Lefine interrupted.

Margont did not react to this snippet of black humour, which in any case was no such thing. Lefine was rubbing his thighs to relieve his cramp but without success.

'What's the second problem?'

'If our man doesn't turn up. Then he'll find out that we've been leading him up the garden path. But what effect will that have on our investigation? None whatsoever.'

Margont jumped up from his chair. 'We're going to wait a day or so before going into action. If Delarse doesn't die of his asthma attack, as soon as he has recovered, he'll receive an anonymous letter . . .'

Lefine walked off, deep in thought. If he were the murderer he wouldn't pay up but he would definitely go to the rendezvous. Margont immediately set about writing his letter:

Sir,

I am aware of what you have done and am in a position to prove it. The reason is that the man I assigned to keep a watch on you in Smolensk has never let you out of his sight. He saw you meet up with the person I shall call 'the lady of Smolensk', escort her to her residence and then go inside.

I have reflected at length on what I should do. But after witnessing so many horrors in Smolensk, at the Moskva and in Moscow, I said to myself: why risk my career by attacking yours? The world clearly is not bothered about one more act of butchery. I have decided, therefore, to sell my silence: it will cost you six thousand francs, a substantial sum, but you will manage to amass it by taxing your soldiers for their booty (other officers are doing so). No precious objects. Pay me in money and jewels; they're easier to carry. I shall meet you on the 23rd at three in the morning, in front of the house belonging to 'the lady of Smolensk' in Moscow. Come on your own. Your absence will prove far more costly than your presence because I shall present my report to whom it may concern.

I look forward to an outcome favourable to us both.

C. M.

Margont folded the document and thrust it into his pocket. He got up, hesitated, and finally went to sit on that throne that fascinated him so much. He adopted a nonchalant pose, one leg crossed over the other and his arms spread out on the armrests. He imagined a court of generals, counts and countesses milling around to pay homage to him. There were Cossacks from the Guard and people were moving back to let them through, fearful of their unpredictability. The Red Hussars in their gold brocade uniforms were conversing with Uhlans and Imperial Horse Guards or with Mongol-featured emissaries from far-flung provinces. The most beautiful women from Moscow and St Petersburg were gliding about discreetly, hoping to attract his attention, but he had eyes only for the young Countess Valiuska.

Margont had the impression of being invincible, triumphant even. It seemed as if his sight was sharper and his hearing more acute. But he wasn't taken in. He knew that wine always seemed to taste better in gold goblets.

Colonel Delarse did survive his asthma attack and the two that followed. Margont contacted everyone he needed.

Fanselin was delighted to have been asked. 'A secret assignment? That's for me!' he exclaimed before adding in the confidential tones of someone who knows how to keep a secret: 'Is there a woman at the bottom of this?' Dalero also accepted, only too happy to be involved in an event that might further his career because, in his opinion, the Russian campaign was over. He estimated, however, that there wouldn't be enough of them so he brought along two of his grenadiers, Sergeants Fimiento and Andogio. They had broad, square shoulders and such enormous hands that one would have been enough to strangle someone with. Despite their immaculate uniforms and white gloves you could tell that if necessary they would be prepared to do a dirty job.

'I want him alive,' Margont ordered curtly.

He had to look up to speak to them and, with their headgear further emphasising the difference in height, it was like a David speaking to two Goliaths. But he had addressed them in such an aggressive tone that one of these giants turned to Dalero for support.

Dalero was gazing at his watch. With its white, gold-rimmed dial it looked very attractive in the white palm of his glove. Refinement seemed to suit Dalero.

'It's four in the afternoon. How are we going to proceed?'

The eight men had installed themselves in the ruins of Countess Sperzof's house.

'The letters will be delivered by messengers,' Margont explained. 'They're people I came across in the street. I've paid them in dried fish. The day after tomorrow they'll be given more food if they've done their job properly.'

'When is the rendezvous for?'

'Tomorrow night at three in the morning. We're going to position ourselves in our hiding-places straight away and stay there just in case our man does some reconnaissance well before the rendezvous or sends someone on his behalf.'

Margont showed them a plan of the area. The street the house was in had been severely damaged by fire. The handsome townhouses on either side of it were now no more than blackened façades, collapsed walls and decapitated columns. A series of gardens backed on to these ruins. Countess Sperzof's had survived. Others had been reduced to ashes. Opposite the meeting place was a street with piles of rubble and sections of wall on either side. There was also a crossroads nearby, several paces to the left. Only one block of houses had survived the flames. It was a building that had partially collapsed at its far end. A battalion of the 48th Regiment was quartered there.

Margont drew a cross on it. 'I'll be here, under the porch. This is the plan: our man turns up, I try to talk to him and, if he confesses his crime, you all emerge from your hiding places and converge on him, weapons at the ready.'

All eyes turned towards the dozen or so pistols that Margont had requisitioned. The weapons reassured them, despite their lack of precision and range, and the fact that they more often wounded than killed.

'I want to do all I can to make him talk, so no untimely intervention!' he emphasised.

'Only the man we're after can find this address. And he'll turn up with some gold. That's enough,' reckoned Dalero.

'We're dealing with a colonel: in a military tribunal his word will be given three times as much weight as all of ours put together. He'll say he just happened to be passing by, that he just had a discreet rendezvous with someone to buy something . . . We need irrefutable evidence, not suppositions or unlikely coincidences.'

Saber, Fanselin and Piquebois exchanged glances that betrayed their dismay.

'A colonel? We're not going to arrest a colonel, are we?' Saber eventually asked, convinced that he was about to clear up some misunderstanding.

Margont explained to them that they were indeed looking for a colonel. He told them there were very good reasons for this but he was not allowed to go into them.

'If some of you want to back out, I'll understand,' he added.

'You can rely on me,' Piquebois immediately replied.

Fanselin nodded. Saber agreed reluctantly. He didn't want to get the reputation of being a quitter, as there was no surer way of killing off all prospects of promotion.

'Therefore we need a confession,' Margont went on. 'If you see me raise my arm, come to my aid. It will mean that I'm in danger or that he's said enough to be arrested.'

'And what if he doesn't talk?' asked Dalero.

'I'll let him go. Then we'll discuss what to do next.'

That last point would depend above all on Prince Eugène's judgement.

'I want you to position yourselves in a circle around me. Then, in order to meet up with me, our man will enter the circle without realising it. There'll be no possible retreat. Piquebois will take up position in the next-door house to my right, Sergeant Fimiento in the one to my left. Lefine will hide in the garden to protect the rear. Fanselin and Saber will be in the street opposite the house. Captain Dalero and Sergeant Andogio will place themselves at the far left of our street, where it's intersected by the crossroads. Captain Dalero will be on the same side as me and Sergeant Andogio opposite, hiding in the ruins adjacent to the building where the battalion of the 48th has its quarters.'

'There are more men on the left,' Dalero pointed out.

'Correct. Because it's easier to hide there: the buildings are in a better state. But you told me that Sergeants Fimiento and Andogio were excellent marksmen.'

Fimiento smiled but it wasn't clear whether it was in response to the compliment or because he was remembering a few particularly well-aimed shots.

'I've positioned them at key points. Sergeant Fimiento can have the whole of our street in his line of sight as well as the one opposite this house. Sergeant Andogio is covering both our street and the crossroads. Any questions?'

'We're going to spend more than twenty-four hours hiding beneath the remains of walls in danger of collapsing and without making a fire – so having to freeze all night and eat cold food – is that it?' asked Lefine.

'Absolutely. Any more questions? So, let's wish ourselves good luck.'

CHAPTER 28

I T had been a long wait. At last the time fixed for the rendezvous had arrived and Margont was pacing up and down at the front entrance, surveying the area, his breath turning to steam. He thrust his hands deep into the pockets of his grey greatcoat. His fingers stroked the butt of his pistols. He had also brought his sword and a knife. He smiled at the thought that he hadn't been as well armed as this when he launched into the attack on the Great Redoubt. He was trying to guess which of the four faces he would find himself up against. He was also wondering whether the man would answer his questions. And if so, whether it would just be to allay his suspicions before trying to eliminate him.

After what seemed both a short and a particularly long period of time, he glimpsed a silhouette. His heart began to race. The passer-by was alone. He was coming from the right, Piquebois and Fanselin's side. He was walking slowly. He too was wearing a greatcoat and had his hands deep in his pockets.

Gradually, the distance lessened. The stranger had his collar turned up and was wearing a cap, so that it was still not possible to make out his face. When he was about a hundred paces away, he stopped. He was looking at Margont. Suddenly a shot rang out. Margont was hit full in the chest and fell. The stranger did an about-turn and started to run. The shot had been fired from the corner of the crossroads, where Sergeant Andogio had taken up position. Piquebois was the first to jump out of his hiding-place.

'There are two of them!' he yelled. 'Fanselin, come with me!'

He set off in hot pursuit of the figure, who was by now far away from the circle that was supposed to trap him. Fanselin suddenly emerged holding a pistol and ran to join Piquebois. Dalero and Saber rushed towards the marksman whom Fimiento was already aiming at. The man was lurking in the darkness. He had thrown aside his discharged musket and was taking aim at Fimiento with Sergeant Andogio's weapon. The sergeant was lying at his feet. Two shots rang out almost simultaneously. Fimiento's bullet lodged in the section of wall behind which his opponent had positioned himself and Fimiento fell to the ground immediately afterwards. The marksman dropped his second musket and then it was his turn to flee. He sped across the street and into an area littered with rubble.

When the fugitive failed to respond to his warnings, Saber opened fire with his pistol. Dalero did likewise. The two bullets were way off target. Lefine skirted the house and ran towards Margont, who was sitting up. His greatcoat had been holed near his right lung.

'It's all right. I'm not hurt, look.'

He opened his garment. He was wearing a cuirassier's breastplate. The piece of metal was thick enough to stop bullets and was pigeon-breasted to deflect projectiles.

'I borrowed it from a friend. I'm not wounded. It was the shock that made me fall. And the fear as well. Why did no one spot the marksman?'

'We were too busy watching the other one,' Lefine replied. 'He created an effective diversion.'

Margont picked himself up. He looked at the hole in the material.

'A hell of a shot . . .'

By now Dalero and Saber had also ventured into the rubble. Behind them lights and faces were appearing at windows and a sentry had sprung out from a porch.

'Who goes there?' he yelled.

'Friends! France!' Saber answered, to avoid getting a bullet between his shoulder blades.

There were piles of rubble that were liable to collapse underfoot, sections of wall from behind which someone could pounce on you, areas of shadow capable of hiding a marksman . . . Dalero and Saber, sabres in hand, were progressing speedily but cautiously. Saber noticed the man on the run disappear behind a heap of fallen masonry.

'Over there!' he exclaimed, pointing with the tip of his sword.

He wanted to press forward but the charred floorboards gave way beneath him and he went sprawling amongst the ashes. Dalero got slightly ahead of him. When Saber caught up with him, it was only to be told that the man had disappeared.

In the opposite direction Fanselin was still in pursuit of the other man, while Piquebois had stopped to lean against a wall. He still hadn't fully recovered from the concussion he had suffered at the Moskva. The figure turned round, pointing a pistol. Fanselin instinctively hunched his shoulders and bent over. But the marksman did not slow down and his bullet missed the lancer by a long way. Fanselin had noticed that the fugitive was in excellent physical shape. He ran very fast and had been doing so for some time. Sensing that if it came to endurance he would be the loser, Fanselin decided to use guile instead. When the man turned into a street, he himself went into a parallel one. He lost sight of him but could still hear his footsteps. Fanselin was trying to make as little noise as possible, even if it meant slowing down. The man almost gave him the slip but Fanselin made up for lost time by taking a short cut through the rubble. The fugitive turned round several times and, with no one in sight, thought he was safe. He changed direction and disappeared down an alley. Fanselin thought he was going to lose him for good but he glimpsed him again, separated from him by a row of crumbling houses. The man had started to walk to get his breath back. He wandered through the streets for a moment, frequently looking over his shoulder. Fanselin contented himself with following him in parallel, guided only by his hearing. Reassured at last, the man eventually reached a splendid-looking palace with several windows lit, even at this late hour. The two sentries guarding the railings surrounding the garden presented arms. He did not bother to look at them and went into the drive.

Fanselin edged closer and put his face to the icy bars. He recognised Colonel Barguelot.

Margont was examining Sergeant Andogio's dead body. The murderer had slit his throat. Dalero was gazing at the discarded musket.

'Line infantry musket first produced in 1777 and modified in 1801. How many of these are there in the army? Two or three hundred thousand? In any case, he certainly knows how to use it.'

Further away, infantrymen were hoisting Fimiento's groaning body on to a cart pulled by a scrawny horse. When Fanselin eventually returned, he took Margont and Dalero to one side to tell them what he knew. Then he left them on their own. Dalero was absently toying with the tassel of his sword-knot.

'Colonel Barguelot is popular with the general staff of IV Corps. He's invited the prince to dinner several times and His Highness has always come back from those evenings in a very good mood.'

'It's certainly true that Colonel Barguelot knows how to enter-tain. I can still remember the delicious meal he invited me to.'

'We can't arrest him when we have no evidence. Any tribunal would dismiss the case.'

'That's my opinion too. We'll have to continue spying on him. We know and he knows that we know. We'll have to see how he's going to react.'

Dalero glanced at the area of rubble in which his chase had come to a sudden end.

'If only we'd been able to lay hands on his henchman and force him to testify . . .'

'The day we finally have evidence of Colonel Barguelot's guilt, we'll force him to denounce his accomplice. I'm very sorry about your sergeants. If Fimiento had been wearing a breastplate like me . . .'

'If we'd all had breastplates, your friend the Red Lancer would never have caught up with Colonel Barguelot. So we need to wait. I hate waiting. What if we don't find any evidence against him?'

'Then we'll have to review the situation again.'

Dalero went to the cart in which Fimiento was lying, to try to get him more speedily transported to the nearest hospital. He grabbed the pommel of his sabre in his left hand and drew the blade about an inch out of the sheath before putting it back in. He repeated this gesture a dozen or so times without thinking.

CHAPTER 29

NAPOLEON had organised life in Moscow. He had been forced to authorise looting during the fire to enable his army to obtain food and clothing. Then he had strictly forbidden it. He had succeeded in restoring law and order and had set up a Russian local administration. The theatres had reopened. There were performances of *The False Infidelities*, *The Game of Love and Chance*, *The Lover as Author and Servant*, *The Three Sultanas* and *The Absent-Minded Lover* . . . There was even a ballet. People could also go to restaurants, admire the Emperor as he reviewed his troops, or watch the Guard on parade . . . But their hearts weren't in it because the expected victory was lacking.

Napoleon was waiting for negotiations to commence. He had sent Baron de Lauriston to meet Kutuzov to offer him peace. The crafty generalissimo was playing for time. He had dispatched an aide-de-camp to St Petersburg to pass on this message to the Tsar.

But despite the loss of Moscow, Alexander did not want to give in. He kept repeating that he would fight to the bitter end, and if he lost the last of his soldiers he would continue the struggle at the head of his 'beloved nobility and loyal peasants'. He was careful, however, to conceal his intentions from the French. The result was that while Napoleon was waiting for the peace, the Tsar and Kutuzov were waiting for the winter.

So, life in Moscow was tinged with anxiety for some, but enjoyable for others – those who had a blind faith in the Emperor and who had never heard about Russian winters. Colonel Pirgnon informed Margont that his plan for a Moscow Club would have to be 'temporarily postponed'. He too was worried about the future and didn't feel inclined to engage in witty conversation.

Margont explored every corner of Moscow. He walked along the red ramparts and gazed in awe at the cathedrals and churches. He visited the palaces and was always welcomed warmly by those quartered there when he brandished bottles of wine or gin. He also spent hours drawing. He cursed his lack of skill, but his sketches of a façade or a view were sometimes quite competent.

In the evenings he prepared dinner for his friends, partly because he enjoyed cooking, greedy as he was, and partly to keep busy. Lefine was involved in various shady dealings and regularly brought back new ingredients so that they could vary the way in which they cooked the inevitable salted fish.

Once they had eaten their fill, everyone settled down in the palace's most beautiful drawing room to engage in inexhaustible conversation over vodka, rum, coffee and tea accompanied by chocolates and caramels. Saber never tired of recounting how he had been promoted at the Great Redoubt itself. Piquebois talked of home; Margont about Russian culture; Jean-Quenin about medicine and ethics; and Lefine filled them in on the gossip: a general was having an affair with a Russian princess; some completely inebriated Bavarian gunners had attacked the Kremlin with their cannon, then been doused with water so that they would be presentable in front of the firing squad; the Emperor had ridden around in between reviewing the troops, and one night, instead of sleeping, he had drawn up a decree proposing to unite the actors of the Comédie Française into a company . . .

Fanselin often joined them. His sharp wit made him very agreeable company. He recalled his travels: places he had already been to and those still to visit, including Louisiana and Quebec, which he had even planned to liberate from the English with the help of a few friends, Red Lancers and grenadiers of the Guard. He was so enthusiastic that he made the impossible appear almost reasonable. They talked about the North American Indians who scalped people – though everyone was in agreement that they couldn't be any worse than the Russians – the Iroquois, who burnt their prisoners alive whilst apologising to them for making them suffer; the mysterious stepped pyramids of Mexico; the vastness of the New World . . .

They launched into endless arguments. Why had the Emperor still not issued a decree to free the muzhiks, the Russian nobility's serfs? What was His Majesty's plan now? Were the Russians at last going to give in? Well, of course they were! Not on your life, you must be joking! Your arguments are false because you're not taking the Russian mentality into account . . . Here we go, the librarian's going to read us another chapter! If you like the Russian mentality so much, go and marry your Countess Valiuska! They quarrelled, they made up and in the end were overcome by tiredness. Everyone then went off to bed, except Piquebois, who stood at the window and studied the stars.

Nevertheless, Margont was well aware that imperceptibly victory was turning into defeat. It was happening in small stages that were impossible to pinpoint, as when day changes to night, but the transformation was just as obvious. So he was preparing himself for every eventuality. Lefine had managed to buy two horses. Two horses between four didn't seem a lot but so many mounts had perished that in Moscow with two beasts you could form a squadron. Piquebois was stocking up with large amounts of food, exchanging bottles of vodka for wheat – a sort of reversal of the natural process – flour, eggs, a little meat and salted fish. There were also some kilos of sweetmeats that had been discovered in the remains of a shop. Margont had had two pairs of bearskin boots made for everyone. He had also had the jackets, cloaks and greatcoats lined with fur. He had bought ermine hats – at a knockdown price, only a bottle of vodka for a pair – muffs, gloves, hoods, bulky pelisses and trousers. Everything was available in Moscow. The soldiers had in fact dubbed the sale of booty 'the Moscow fair'. Margont disapproved of looting but not to the point of refusing to acquire clothes that would considerably improve his chances of survival.

On 13 October, a thin layer of snow covered Moscow. It quickly disappeared but it was only a foretaste. However, the month of October remained exceptionally mild and led Napoleon to underestimate the Russian climate. The Emperor continued to linger in Moscow. He wanted the enemy to believe that all was well and that he was intending to spend the winter in the capital. He thought that, between the Tsar and himself, the last to give in would be the winner. He was also aware of having reached the pinnacle of his glory. He was feared by the whole of Europe and everyone had to reckon with his policies. Ordering a retreat would be his first personal defeat. In addition, a retreat without an armistice would be a very perilous undertaking. Napoleon wanted to delay the moment when his star would begin to fade. He even tried to convince himself that the Tsar would negotiate in the end and that Russian winters were no worse than Parisian ones . . .

On 17 October, the tacit truce agreed between the two armies – a partial truce because the Cossacks and partisans were constantly harrying the French rear – was broken. At Vinkovo the Russians, who significantly outnumbered the French, took two thousand five hundred prisoners and seized thirty-three cannon. Murat, in typical fashion, counterattacked with a cavalry charge. The net result was two thousand dead on each side.

Napoleon ordered the departure for 19 October. He knew that the weather would be against him and that Kutuzov would do everything in his power to cut off the retreat so that the winter and resulting privations would destroy his army.

CHAPTER 30

WHEN the Grande Armée began its retreat, the crush was indescribable. The remaining hundred thousand soldiers and those accompanying them — wives, officers' servants, canteen-keepers and sutler women — had been joined by thousands of Muscovites of foreign extraction who feared reprisals on the part of the Russians. The streets were therefore jammed with barouches, carriages, carts, wagons, caissons, charabancs and every imaginable contraption. Several of these vehicles, weighed down with booty and passengers, had broken wheels and were blocking the way.

Napoleon still possessed a powerful army. Morale was high: they had faith in the Emperor. However, disorder was already undermining the effectiveness of the troops. In a clever manoeuvre, Kutuzov had stopped pulling back towards the east and had positioned his troops to the south of Moscow. Thus he was blocking the way to the rich provinces of the south and was threatening the French retreat towards Smolensk. While Napoleon had been reorganising his army and enjoying his conquest pending the opening of negotiations, Kutuzov had restructured his forces. He had recruited countless peasants who were convinced that the French had set fire to Moscow, were desecrating their churches (it was true that some cavalry squadrons, with a total disregard for religion, had turned churches into stables) and exterminating the people. He was also receiving a steady stream of reinforcements from all the provinces. He now had at his disposal one hundred and twenty thousand soldiers backed up by two hundred thousand militiamen.

Kutuzov, however, feared Napoleon and wanted to avoid direct confrontation. He hoped to use delaying tactics for as long as possible, allowing the winter and hunger to wreak havoc in the enemy ranks in order eventually to intercept the French army and destroy it.

As for Napoleon, he had planned to withdraw as far as Smolensk. He was intending to regroup his forces in the city and give them fresh supplies from the stocks of food he had built up there. He began by taking the Kaluga road, to the south of the road to Smolensk. Part of the Russian army, commanded by Lieutenant-General Doktorov, blocked his way. Fighting took place in Maloyaroslavets and the town was lost and retaken several times by Prince Eugène's troops. Seventeen thousand French and Italians fought against more than fifty thousand Russians. IV Corps lost four thousand men and the Russians twice that number. But Kutuzov had had time to link up with Doktorov. Now it was the whole of the Russian army that was obstructing the road to Kaluga.

Napoleon was faced with a dilemma. Either he continued with his plan to withdraw via the road to Kaluga, to which end he would have to defeat the Russian army despite its numerical superiority. Or he took the road to Smolensk again, which was shorter but, because it had been looted on the outward journey, would offer the army only very scant resources. On the advice of almost his entire entourage, Napoleon chose the road to

Smolensk. Several factors led him to prefer this option. In current conditions a battle against the Russians was particularly risky. He also believed that Kutuzov had pulled his army back a few leagues to take up a higher position than that at Maloyaroslavets. In fact, the Russian generalissimo, over-cautious as ever, thinking that the French were going to take the road to Smolensk again, wanted to avoid a confrontation.

Another incident also played a part in this decision: Napoleon had almost fallen into Russian hands. While he was on reconnaissance, six hundred Cossacks had sprung out of a wood. The duty squadrons had repelled them but for a few moments the Emperor had been threatened. The enemy would certainly not have withdrawn so swiftly if they had realised that they were dealing with Napoleon himself.

No one knows what would have happened if Napoleon had tried to force his way through to take the road to Kaluga. But what is certain is that the return journey via the devastated road to Smolensk was one of the main factors in turning the retreat into a disaster.

Kutuzov's army began a long march along the flank, keeping parallel to the French and forcing them to stick to the road to Smolensk. The Cossacks and other light cavalry troops as well as the partisans constantly harried the Grande Armée.

Margont, Lefine, Saber and Piquebois were in the process of preparing their lunchtime soup, rather a grand term for the vile liquid made from coffee and flour. They ate better in the mornings because Margont had advised Colonel Pégot to make the regiment march behind the mounted chasseurs. Thus, as soon as they got up, the soldiers of the 84th rushed to the encampment abandoned by the chasseurs and hurriedly devoured the horses that had died in the night, horses that had already been partly devoured by their riders. It was important not to wait until the carcasses froze because then it became impossible to cut them up, even with an axe.

On 27 October there had been a very heavy snowfall. This, added to the hunger and the anxious realisation that they were taking the road to Smolensk again, had begun to transform the army. The spirit of camaraderie was wearing thin. If you possessed horses or supplies of food, you had to guard them overnight to prevent them from being stolen. As for sharing, it was a concept that was rapidly disappearing. Margont was deep in thought about such matters while gazing at the snow-laden branches of the fir trees, when he heard Lefine laughing.

'Why do you put your hood on only at night, Captain? You look such a sight! Only your eyes are visible!'

'That's right. Have a good laugh. In a few days' time you won't be able to hear the nonsense you talk because your ears will have frozen and dropped off.'

'What? Is it going to get even colder?'

Margont was clutching his bowl of hot soup to warm his gloves.

'This is only the start,' he answered.

Every word he spoke produced coils of steam. He was dreaming of fig jam. As a child, he had got through whole jars of it as his mother looked on in horror, like any parent watching the excesses of its offspring. Although he gorged himself on this

373

jam, by one of those contradictions that make human beings such strange creatures, he sobbed his heart out if anyone tried to make him eat figs in the form of fruit. By adulthood he had become more sensible: he now loved both the jam and the fruit.

'What is there to eat this evening?' asked Piquebois.

'A raw egg and some sweets,' Lefine announced.

'Do you call that a meal?'

'In the 8th Light they only have sweets and caviar; in the 1st Croat they have beef that they wouldn't exchange for all the money in the world but they might exchange some for flour because, like us, they haven't got much of it. I'd need to exchange coffee and fish with Demay's gunners for some fodder, which I'd exchange with the 9th Chasseurs for the flour to—'

'All right, we trust you. Organise it as best you can,' Margont interrupted.

Morale was declining and yet the four men were among the more fortunate. Piquebois was watching over their bony, worn-out horses. He stroked them to apologise for the misfortunes they were suffering and to be forgiven for finally having taken to eating horsemeat. He swapped part of his meals for fodder and, at night, he tied the two bridles around his wrist. 'If anyone wants to steal them, they'll have to deal with Piquebois first!' he'd announced. And as everyone knew that he could still wield his sabre like a true hussar . . . One day, one of the mounts had slipped on a patch of ice and had accidentally thrown Lefine into the snow. The sergeant had cursed loudly as he got back on his feet and the two horses had immediately sought refuge with Piquebois.

Saber was munching a snowball to quench his thirst.

'It's unbelievable all the same! The army's in a bad state, I can tell you. It's been impossible for me to get my captain's epaulettes! I'm a captain on paper but not in uniform because of the poor organisation. What sort of impression are we going to give if, when the Russians attack, the captains look like lieutenants? This sort of laxity will be our downfall!'

'You're really getting up my nose!' thundered Piquebois. 'Go and take them from a dead body if it matters so much to you!'

'Are you mad?' stuttered Saber in horror.

'Well, well,' Margont said gleefully, 'you tell all and sundry you're an atheist, you make fun of me when I say a prayer, but it turns out you're superstitious. You've replaced God with black cats, rabbits' paws and tarot cards.'

Saber walked off in annoyance, trying to retain his dignity. 'At least I went up a rank.'

'And don't we know it,' retorted Piquebois.

Margont looked longingly at his bowl. Was it empty? Already?

'Cheer up!' he exclaimed. 'In two weeks we'll be in Smolensk. Talking of which, I suggest we drink a toast to the paradise awaiting us.' Then, raising a snowball, he said: 'To Smolensk!'

'To Smolensk!' Lefine and Piquebois repeated.

They toasted one another before gulping down the snow. The march resumed. What remained of the 84th, that is, fewer than eight hundred men, was making painful progress. Lefine looked up at regular intervals. A flock of black birds was following the never-ending column of the retreating army.

'Filthy crows!' he spat.

'It looks as if a Napoleonic crow has formed an avian Grande Armée and ordered the birds to mimic us.'

'I bet each of these pests has already chosen the soldier it plans to devour,' Lefine grumbled.

Margont pointed with his finger. 'Look, there's yours!'

'Don't say that! Must never say that, Captain.'

Margont's legs felt heavy. 'Let's keep quiet. We'd be better off saving our breath.'

'Yes, and in any case the words seem to freeze in our mouths.'

The road was littered with corpses. Soldiers were dropping from exhaustion, never to get up again. Some were almost naked: they had been stripped of their possessions.

'It's good, though, to say something from time to time,' Lefine added further on. 'That way you know you're not completely dead yet.'

'To take your mind off things, think about what you'll do when this war's over.'

'Go on to the next one, of course. There's nothing to think about!'

Margont spotted an infantryman cutting across the fields, struggling almost knee-deep in snow and waving at him frantically. Margont went to meet him. Lefine could tell how animated the conversation was by the amount of steam coming from their mouths. Margont came back looking worried and took his friend to one side.

'I made some calculations but I was mistaken. So I'm changing my strategy.'

'What does all this gibberish mean?'

'That we're going to have a talk with Colonel Barguelot. Now.'

Margont and Lefine caught up with the 9th of the Line. This regiment now made up only a small fragment of the never-ending black column winding its way through the snow, leaving a trail of corpses in its wake. It had almost ceased to exist at the battle of Maloyaroslavets. Margont had discovered from his spy that Colonel Barguelot was still alive. He had in fact been 'concussed by an explosion' that had left him unconscious at the rear for the whole duration of the fighting. He had only regained consciousness when it was time to withdraw. Margont approached the colonel who, on recognising him, stared at him in disbelief.

'How dare you come to see me? I'm going to have you shot on the spot!'

Margont handed him the letter signed by Prince Eugène himself.

'At least you've stopped sending me anonymous letters. Now you bring your notes yourself,' sneered Barguelot, snatching the missive from his hands.

He was astounded by what he read. His adjutant had unsheathed his sabre. Discreetly reading over his colonel's shoulder, he lowered his weapon.

'What does this mean?' Barguelot asked in a barely audible voice.

Margont put his document away carefully. He said nothing

and stared the colonel straight in the eye. Eventually he declared: 'You are blind in one eye, are you not, Colonel?'

Barguelot opened his mouth but was unable to speak.

Margont nodded assent. 'It's noticeable from close up: your two irises aren't quite the same colour.'

'Captain, you're mad! Your conduct is intolerable, unspeakable! It's . . . insolence! Disrespect! Mutiny!'

'Colonel, it so happens that we have both been victims of a plot. You are not the man I had arranged to meet in Moscow. You are not the man I am after.'

At the mention of the word Moscow, Barguelot reacted sharply. 'You're referring to your little ambush that came to an abrupt end!'

Margont indicated a copse of fir trees at the side of the road. The colonel, only too happy for a little discretion, did not need to be asked twice. His adjutant and Lefine followed the two men while the troops continued their laborious onward march.

'I could have had you shot! Attacking a colonel!' Barguelot said threateningly.

'You received a letter referring to a certain "lady of Smolensk", but I don't think you understood the message at all.'

'The letter was clearly not intended for me. What connection does it have with our business? And how do you know about it?'

'And yet you went to Countess Sperzof's Moscow residence, hence our encounter. Who gave you that address?'

'Why, you, of course! You're trying to make a fool of me!'

'I swear on my honour that I am serious. I repeat my question: who gave you that address?'

Barguelot looked taken aback. He stared in disbelief while instinctively tossing his head back. Then he became defensive.

'You're raving, Captain. I don't understand a word you're saying.'

'To begin with, you dropped hints to me, as if we understood each other perfectly, but now you are denying everything outright, as if to keep me at arm's length from this business. I'm very surprised at your sudden turnaround. I can only conclude, Colonel, that you are afraid of something. All this suggests a case of blackmail. What did someone know about you that scared you to the point of making you go to that meeting?'

Barguelot turned his back. 'I'm not listening to any more of this nonsense. Please excuse me but, unlike you, I have a regiment to command, Captain.'

Margont decided to pretend that he was well informed even though he was as lost as Barguelot. So he came out with a sentence that seemed to be pregnant with meaning although he was simply referring to a mystery he had been unable to solve.

'Was it to do with the real reasons for your appointment as Officer of the Légion d'Honneur, the honour that you were awarded such a long time after Jena?'

Barguelot turned round slowly. 'What do you want? Or rather I should say: how much do you want?'

Margont felt inwardly triumphant. He had always believed that despite the attractive and flamboyant way in which he wrapped things up, Barguelot's lies would never on their own have managed to earn him such an honour. Barguelot must then have cheated in some other way.

'Colonel, I wish simply to understand what happened. You

seem to think that I'm the one who invited you to this rendezvous in Moscow but it's not true. Who gave you this address? And how?'

'A Muscovite handed a letter to one of my officers. The anonymous message was for me and was asking me to go to Countess Sperzof's house for personal reasons. When I caught sight of you there I thought, quite logically, that you were the one who'd written it.'

'I must see the letter.'

'I burnt it.'

'You certainly did not! It's the proof that someone tried to blackmail you, and no one throws away a weapon that can be used against an enemy.'

Barguelot awkwardly unbuttoned his greatcoat and coat. His hand disappeared beneath layers of fur-lined material before reappearing with a letter.

'I would never have believed that people as cruel as you existed,' murmured Barguelot as he handed over the missive.

'You are wrong about me. As for the cruelty of the man I'm after, it is well beyond anything you can imagine.'

Margont unfolded the document.

Sir,
　　Some Légion d'Honneur you have here. Too good for you, anyway, because it is rather excessive merely for a sprained ankle at Jena. Instead of thanking the Prussians, would it not be better to thank a certain marshal who, annoyed at having been discovered in your bed with your young and beautiful wife, offered you a few compensations in the form of promotion and a decoration?

You certainly do not wish this business to become public knowledge. Neither do I, because what benefit would it bring to me? I fix the price of my silence at six thousand francs, payable in whatever form you choose. Try a little looting. In any case, I know you are wealthy, so you must have a money-box somewhere in your baggage. I will meet you on the 23rd at three in the morning in front of Countess Sperzof's residence. Its ruins are near the Kremlin, not far from the building in which the 2nd battalion of the 48th of the Line have their quarters.

Do not be late. It is so cold at night in Moscow . . .

'This is slander!' Colonel Barguelot added immediately.

'Who is aware of this "slander"?'

Barguelot was motionless. He was no longer even unconsciously moving about on the spot to combat the cold.

As he remained silent, Margont continued: 'Do you know Colonel Fidassio or Captain Nedroni?'

'No.'

'What about Colonel Pirgnon?'

'Vaguely.'

'That doesn't surprise me. But I think you know him more than "vaguely". On the one hand, you both serve in the same division. On the other hand, you have met each other at social gatherings in Paris. Or in Madrid. Undoubtedly in both Paris and Madrid, because neither of you would have missed a single reception for all the money in the world. Is Colonel Pirgnon aware of what this letter refers to?'

'It's true that Colonel Pirgnon got to hear of this vile piece of gossip because he was serving on the general staff of the marshal concerned.'

'He was the person you were expecting to see, wasn't he?'

Barguelot's face was a picture of distress.

'Yes.'

'Colonel, you'll never hear of me again. And this "piece of gossip" will not spread, I give you my word.'

Margont saluted and departed, leaving Colonel Barguelot completely at a loss. Lefine, puzzled by what was going on, hurried to catch up with his friend, who was trudging through the snow.

'I'd like some explanations!'

'I thought for a moment that Colonel Barguelot was our man. But there were two details, two grey areas, that didn't fit. Why had Colonel Barguelot refused the honour of a friendly crossing of swords with Marshal Davout and why would he never eat or drink in public? When he invited me to that officers' meal he didn't touch a thing. It's insulting when the person who's invited you doesn't even taste the dishes he's offering you. What could prevent a man from eating, drinking and having a sword fight? Then I thought back to an incident that Colonel Delarse had recounted to me. It involved a game of chess between that Russian chess player I met, Lieutenant Nakalin, and Kutuzov. In the course of the game Kutuzov knocked the chessboard over. I think he did so deliberately because he was losing. But his excuse was perfectly valid: he's blind in one eye and when you lose your sight in one eye it becomes very difficult after a time to gauge depth and distance. That's when everything fell into place: I thought that Colonel Barguelot must also have lost an eye. He hides it from everyone – except from his servants – because he's so concerned about his image that he can't abide this incapacity. The very idea of showing a weakness, of not being flattered and considered perfect, is unbearable to him. It's unthinkable for him to ask someone to cut his meat up for him during a meal, unacceptable to put out his hand towards a glass and knock it over . . . Besides, there was one detail that convinced me I was right. During that meal, when he wanted to propose a toast, his servant did not pass him his glass; he put it in his hand. A domestic would never behave so rudely without good reason. That's why Colonel Barguelot refused to cross swords with Marshal Davout and why he parried so badly the attack by that Russian officer at the foot of the Great Redoubt, whereas he actually had been a good swordsman in his youth. His wound even explains his repeated "sprained ankles".'

'How come?'

'Colonel Barguelot really was an officer of great courage. He proved it at the battle of Austerlitz but he never talks about this exploit, which is out of character. Do you remember the rumour you told me about concerning the wound he's said to have received that day? Well, I'm sure it's true. He must have lost an eye at Austerlitz. When he realised that this wound made him a partial invalid, that his image had been tarnished – because this is his strange way of seeing things – he was terrified. Colonel Barguelot is not afraid of death but of the image others have of him. It's his wound that has made him a coward. The conclusion I was able to draw from all this was that Colonel Barguelot was not our murderer. Because how the devil could he have escaped so acrobatically across the rooftops?

'We know that the man we're looking for probably knows

the identity of the other suspects. He himself had a note sent to Colonel Barguelot to get him to come to our rendezvous. It was an excellent idea. On the one hand Barguelot's arrival was a diversion that almost cost me my life. On the other hand we all suspected Colonel Barguelot. When I realised my mistake, I decided to make it look as if we were still convinced of Colonel Barguelot's guilt. I said nothing to you because the murderer needed to be convinced of this. But in secret I continued to keep our suspects under surveillance. Unfortunately, our man did not betray himself. I'd assumed that he would seek out another victim, in which case my spies had orders to intervene. Either out of suspicion, because he didn't want to, or because the opportunity did not arise, he did not strike. The murderer was the marksman in hiding. It couldn't have been Delarse: with his asthma he would never have dared to escape by wading through ashes. That left our Italians and Pirgnon. The murderer knew Colonel Barguelot well enough to find a way of forcing him to go to a remote district alone at three in the morning. But our Italians had never been outside Italy before. They hadn't taken part in any campaign and were mouldering away in their provincial garrison. They therefore had very few senior officers among their acquaintances. That's why I inclined towards Pirgnon.'

Margont waved the letter handed to him by Colonel Barguelot.

'Barguelot has just confirmed to us that Colonel Pirgnon was aware of the contents of this note! Although Pirgnon is capable of going into raptures over a poem or a painting, he seems to have no feeling for human life. His passion for classical heroes is morbid: he probably considers himself a sort of demigod, a superior being to whom other men's morals and laws do not apply.'

'What are we going to do? Inform Prince Eugène?'

Margont shook his head. 'Colonel Barguelot will never give evidence. That would mean admitting the truth of what was in that note. I think he'd be capable of blowing his brains out rather than face such dishonour. And Pirgnon is very well thought of in IV Corps. Are we really sure he'll be put on trial for his crimes?'

'Well . . . yes, surely.'

'Not surely enough for my taste. Especially amidst such chaos, where every senior officer who's survived is worth his weight in gold.'

Lefine blew on his gloves. 'I think I've guessed what Prince Eugène would think if we broke the news to him: "My God, how much simpler it would be if the Russians would just kill Colonel Pirgnon for us." '

CHAPTER 31

SMOLENSK was not the promised paradise. The damaged city had not been sufficiently restored. Many soldiers had to sleep outdoors in the snow. Food supplies had been badly managed and the reserves depleted by the troops passing through. An inefficient administration had been incapable of organising the distribution of resources properly and looting had resulted in considerable wastage. The Guard was the first to be served, something that Napoleon always saw to. The officers often received good rations but some regiments were given only a little flour, which some of the infantrymen swallowed immediately, just as it was.

Margont and his friends went to the Valiuski palace. Unfortunately, it was empty. One of the servants had stayed behind to wait for them. The Valiuski family had learnt of the French retreat and had decided to go to the Duchy of Warsaw to stay with relatives. They were afraid that the French would entrench themselves in Smolensk and that the Russians would attack them there. Margont thought that they probably also feared reprisals on the part of the Russians and preferred to let time heal the wounds. The servant went into a storeroom. He removed two planks from the wall to reveal a recess containing a package. Inside it was a ham, some rice, a jar of honey, a bottle of brandy, two sacks of flour and some potatoes: a treasure trove.

'That's all, because a lot of food was requisitioned,' explained the servant in an accent so heavy that they had to guess the meaning of most of what he was saying.

The man also handed Margont a letter. The captain went to his former bedroom, as if he was going to read its contents before going down to dinner with the Valiuskis, as if by returning in space to Smolensk he had also gone back in time and it was no longer mid-November but mid-August again.

Dear friend,

My father has decided that we should leave for Warsaw within the hour. It does indeed appear as if the campaign is not over and that more fighting lies ahead. Father had already greatly underestimated the violence of the attack on Smolensk when you came, so he prefers to take us away from the 'field of operations' (you know how fond he is of talking like a general). Contrary to what I had hoped, we shall not therefore be celebrating the peace with you in Smolensk.

My good Oleg has agreed to stay behind. He will hand you this letter as well as a little food. Unfortunately, your Emperor has requisitioned so much and the war has disrupted trade so badly that I cannot offer you more.

Keep my book or, if you have finished it, take some others. I hope we shall have the opportunity to see each other again in happier circumstances. It will be easy for you to find us: all the nobility in Warsaw knows the Valiuski family. But I realise that the combatants are unlikely to be liberated in the near future. Even if all French people are nothing but dreadful heathens, be assured that despite everything you are present in my prayers.

Countess Natalia Valiuska

Margont reread the letter several times, trying to hear the voice behind the words. This was only the first of a long series of disappointments. Napoleon had quickly realised that it was impossible for him to winter in Smolensk. The city was nothing but ruins and there was a shortage of food. Added to which, to the north-west Wittgenstein's fifty thousand Russians were increasing the pressure on Marshal Gouvion-Saint-Cyr, who had been defeated at Polotsk in mid-October. Similarly, to the south, the army of Moravia under the command of Admiral Chichagov, and reinforced by Tormasov's army, which had become available because of the peace with Turkey, had pushed back Schwarzenberg's Austrians and Reynier's French. The Grande Armée risked being surrounded by substantial forces. So the retreat resumed, with temperatures falling to twenty degrees below zero. There were only forty thousand men left in the army proper, with thousands of disarmed people as hangers-on.

Kutuzov was attempting to position his army between the different French corps in order to destroy them separately. At Krasny, on 16 November, IV Corps, which now consisted of only six thousand men, had to force its way through twenty thousand Russians, under the command of General Miloradovich, who were blocking its path. Two thousand French soldiers perished.

Colonel Fidassio was killed, his carotid artery severed by a hussar's sabre as he was personally launching a counterattack. His faithful shadow, Captain Nedroni, perished a few moments later, nailed to a birch tree by a Cossack lance. As for Colonel Barguelot, he was not at his post. He did not rejoin his regiment until the following day. He told how he had been captured by hussars but had managed to escape when a scuffle broke out between sentries guarding their prisoners and fanatical Russian peasants who had come to slaughter the captives. Colonel Pirgnon survived, despite the very heavy losses sustained by the Broussier Division.

Margont was in a sombre mood. His change of tactics, namely recovering the letter sent by Pirgnon to Barguelot, had led nowhere. Nothing in that document amounted to definite proof of Pirgnon's guilt. This lack of evidence annoyed him. He felt he was in the worst position imaginable: seeing a murderer free to come and go as he pleased just because there was one tiny piece of jigsaw missing to set the vast judicial process in motion. So he turned everything over again in his mind, thinking back to the scenes of the crimes, the discussions with witnesses, the clues . . . He imagined a thousand possibilities: setting another trap, telling Prince Eugène the whole story, talking to Pirgnon to try to . . . well, to try to do what exactly? All these thoughts swirled around in his head for hours before bringing him back inevitably to his starting point: he was completely stuck.

So he informed Captain Dalero of the progress of his investigation. He also handed a sealed letter to Saber, Piquebois and six other friends from different regiments. If Lefine and he were killed, these missives should be passed on to Prince Eugène.

The nights had become interminable. For sixteen hours the temperature fell to minus twenty-eight degrees. Margont, Lefine, Saber, Piquebois and thirteen soldiers were huddled together, a dark outline that gradually became covered in snow, like a blemish that needed to be blotted out of the landscape. They were all that was left of two companies that previously had consisted of two hundred and forty fusiliers.

Lefine, who was keeping guard, was constantly glancing at the watch Margont had lent him. He was waiting impatiently for the hour to end and wondered if there was any way of moving the hands forward by say, five, or seven, minutes . . . He kept the fire going with logs taken from the ruins of an *isba*. He was almost up to his knees in snow, which clung to him like a shroud as if inviting him to lie down and let himself be covered by it. His visibility was restricted by the snowflakes and the surrounding trees. He was vigilant, afraid that a Cossack might spring up behind him and slit his throat. Or perhaps a looter.

Suddenly, loud cries rang out: 'Huzza! Huzza! Paris! Paris!'

'To arms!' yelled Lefine, waving his musket in the direction of the din.

The snow began to move, and black and white shapes emerged, changing into men sitting up and searching for their muskets. There were a few shots, creating brief puffs of smoke in the wood, the sound of laughter and then nothing. It was the third fake attack of the night.

They tried to get back to sleep. The silence was disturbed by a soldier sobbing and the whispers of one of his comrades trying to comfort him.

Hunger was making Lefine want to scream, to kill. He was gnawing a root. It was not edible but in any case his teeth could not bite into it. It was just to have something in his mouth, to pretend to be eating something and to really believe it. The previous day he had heated up some water into which he had plunged two tallow candles and a leather belt. The candles had melted in this foul liquid and the belt had given it a vaguely meaty taste. He and his friends had then chewed interminably on the bits of boiled leather. Every other day they ate nothing unless they found a dead horse. Every other day they were all entitled to a potato or a piece of cake that Margont made from flour and snow. This 'miraculous meal' was soon only served every three days. Their two mounts had died and had immediately been devoured by all of them with the exception of Piquebois. Sometimes they also treated themselves to a small pot of horse blood. This sort of black pudding soup restored their strength. It was Lefine who prepared this dish, with a wooden spoon in one hand and a pistol in the other, the reason being that on one occasion some starving creatures had rushed at him and his pot. In the ensuing struggle, everything had been knocked over. Fortunately, chunks of frozen horse blood were appreciated just as much.

A silhouette wrapped in a blanket crossed the encampment.

'On your feet! It's time to march,' it shouted.

The soldiers got up with difficulty, numb and exhausted, and shook themselves. Many had thrown away their muskets, either to lighten their load or because they had no gloves, and contact between frozen metal and the skin was unbearable. The remnants of regiments had merged together and had been joined by stragglers. So there were dismounted cuirassiers, Bavarians, Westphalians, Württembergers, Saxons, a few velites, either on foot or 'on horseback but without horses' from the Neapolitan Guard, a handful of Poles . . . A good number of soldiers were rigged out in such a way as to make it impossible to tell which regiment they belonged to. They were wearing civilian cloaks, women's pelisses, gaudy tunics on top of their greatcoats, cashmere jackets, bearskins, bed sheets and curtains made into clothes, dresses, dressing gowns . . .

Margont straightened up, exhausted, famished beyond words and surprised not to be dead. He had grown up in an area where snow was a rare sight, and in the summer the scorching heat made it look as if the scrubland was on fire without ever burning up and that you were moving forward surrounded by invisible flames. That climate had enabled him to withstand heat but had also made him sensitive to the cold. Were it not for his natural foresight and what he had read about Russia, he would long ago have fallen victim to the first flakes of snow. He was wearing silk stockings, woollen stockings, leggings, corduroy trousers, a silk shirt, two waistcoats including one in cashmere, a padded jacket and a bulky fur-lined cloak with an ermine collar that half hid his face and whose skirts trailed along the ground. He also had on a woollen hood, a hat and a double pair of gloves thrust into a fox-fur muff. His feet were swathed in several layers of stockings and socks and protected by bearskin boots. Encumbered with all these layers, which made him into a sort of fossil, he looked like a thickset, clumsy giant. The sword at his waist was the only indication that he was a soldier, apart from the epaulettes that he had sewn on to his cloak. But all this did not stop his teeth from chattering and he felt as if he were a little child who had fallen naked into the snow. He took a few steps and already felt exhausted. They had slept too little, in appalling conditions, with the fear of never waking up.

He heard shouting and wailing. Some exhausted soldiers had fallen asleep on the ground and their faces were now stuck to the snow. Others had frostbitten cheeks and noses, and large patches of frozen skin were peeling away from their faces. Some people came to their aid but not many, it must be said. They had been through so much horror and were so afraid for themselves that they were now insensitive to everything. The bivouac was littered with the dead. People were looking for food around the corpses – a vain hope – and taking the clothes. As Margont passed close to a victim being stripped of his trousers by an infantryman, he heard a murmur of '*Mein Gott*'.

'He's still alive!' Margont exclaimed.

But the fusilier continued to tug at the trousers that the German was holding on to, a Württemberger to judge from the shape of his black-crested helmet.

'He's practically dead,' retorted the looter.

'So will you be if you continue,' Margont warned, putting the frozen barrel of his pistol to the man's temple.

The fusilier backed away, holding his bayonet because he'd thrown away his musket. The Württemberger was too weak to get up. Margont motioned to some Württemberg artillerymen, who were lamenting having had to abandon their guns in Smolensk because of the lack of horses to pull them. They referred to these pieces of ordnance as if they were human. When they recalled the moment they had spiked them – which involved driving a spike into the touch-hole to render them unusable by the enemy – they had tears in their eyes. The Württembergers moved forward suspiciously, then rushed to help their comrade as soon as they caught sight of him.

Lefine approached Margont.

'I don't even feel the cold any more!' he shouted gleefully.

Nevertheless, he had been shivering for almost a week.

'Don't lose heart. We'll pull through, Fernand!'

'Well, of course we will. Everyone's going to pull through! Talking of which, Pirgnon's going to pull through too.'

'No, not him.'

'So, with all that's happened you still believe in divine justice, do you? He's a colonel, so he eats much better than us. One of these days he'll step over our dead bodies laughing.'

Margont was trying to tread in the footprints in front of him so as not to exhaust himself unnecessarily by disturbing heaps of snow.

'My investigation's at a standstill for the moment but—'

'What a bad loser you are! Pirgnon's had us. He's had us. That's all there is to it.'

'The game's not over yet.'

Lefine pointed to a pile of corpses covered with snow. Men had huddled together to keep themselves warm but in the end the entire group had frozen.

'Even if you were frozen stiff like them, you'd still believe in victory. The Emperor should take you into his Guard! We're all going to kick the bucket! By the way, do you know what I think? That so many people are dying in this damned retreat that it could well happen to Pirgnon. A shot fired in a wood – by a Cossack, of course! – and that's it. No more Pirgnon. A Cossack who's as good a marksman as me, for example.'

Margont shuddered.

'No, Fernand.'

'Did you say something, Captain? With all this snow in my ears I can't hear a thing.'

'You heard perfectly well.'

'Why? Because it's wrong to kill a murderer?'

Margont stopped and turned towards his friend. 'Because it's meaningless. It would be absurd to become a murderer in order to eliminate a criminal.'

'What a noble sentiment and how well put. Another fine idea to form the basis for a book.'

'There's another reason. You'd be bound to miss him – especially as you can't stop shivering, like the rest of the army. But his escort wouldn't miss you. The snow would slow down your escape: his men would catch up with you or would only have to take aim as you floundered about in a snowdrift.'

Trails of steam poured out of Lefine's mouth.

'If Pirgnon had killed Natalia you'd agree with me. The two of us would have gone to pump him full of lead. Bang, bang! Yes, we would have been shot immediately afterwards but at least we'd have gone out on a high note instead of ending up as blocks of ice!'

'No!'

Margont had tried to shout but exhaustion took his breath away. Lefine was right and that unsettled him even more.

'I'll get him,' he concluded simply.

Lefine made a snowball, waved it in front of him, stood stiffly to attention and said: 'At your orders, Captain!'

The Grande Armée was now just one long caravan, a thick column of motley soldiers dressed up to fight the cold, and of carts and sledges interspersed with the occasional trooper. In some places people were crowded together and in others they were spread out, dangerously exposed and isolated, easy targets for the Cossacks. Only the Guard had kept up appearances. It advanced steadfastly in an orderly fashion, protecting the Emperor.

CHAPTER 32

O<small>N</small> 22 November, Margont was trudging through the middle of a wood of birch trees. It was foggy and it was snowing yet again. The soldiers' faces were gaunt, exhausted, dazed and sometimes blackened by the frost. Each one looked like a walking corpse. They advanced amidst the shadows, ghosts amongst ghosts. The fear of straying was ever present, because if you got lost there were Cossacks or partisans out there who would slaughter or capture you, according to their mood.

Fanselin had been walking with Margont and his companions since morning. His worn-out horse had slowed down so much that in the end he got left behind by his squadron. After his mount had died, Fanselin tried to cut across a forest but was caught in a snowstorm. When he at last got back to the army he found himself with IV Corps. He was wearing an enormous pelisse, a red one, needless to say. He felt it his duty to set an example and warded off his fears by laughter and bravado. As a result, he had a constant following of soldiers.

'I got completely lost in that forest and my only weapons were my two pistols and my lance,' he recounted.

He was so proud of his lance that every time he mentioned it, he flourished it and did battle with the branches of the birch trees.

'Of course, I was thinking about the filthy Cossacks! They appear from nowhere, shoot you in the back and by the time you've turned round, they're far away. And they can certainly gallop! It's hard work catching up with those scoundrels! They're devilish clever with their bark-coloured pelisses that make them invisible. You don't see them, you don't capture them and they vanish. In short, after a while, if you'll pardon this unsavoury detail, I started to relieve my bladder against a tree trunk when all of a sudden I said to myself: "Watch out, Edgar, make sure you're not pissing on a Cossack's boots . . ."'

His audience laughed, he stopped talking to save his breath and then, a few minutes later, he came out with another anecdote or philosophical observation. Fanselin had such confidence in himself and in the French, and the Guard enjoyed such prestige, that his presence lifted the soldiers' spirits a little.

The column was making slow progress. The road was littered with the frozen corpses of soldiers and half-eaten horses. There was also silver cutlery, vases and gold coins that people had dumped to lighten their load. Suddenly, there was a long whistling noise that became more and more piercing, followed by the roar of an explosion. A birch tree collapsed with a snapping sound and trapped some of the men in a tangle of branches. Cannonballs bounced this way and that. But the march continued. The troops were being bombarded at regular intervals by cannon that the Russians had had the detestable idea of mounting on sledges. The outline of a figure on horseback drew closer in the fog. Muskets were levelled in that direction because two times out of three a horse meant a Cossack. The figure suddenly emerged from the icy fog like an apparition. It probably was one. It was an adjutant, impeccably dressed, his trousers and gloves spotless. He was young and very angry.

'Soldiers, they're shelling us! Do something! Are you fighters or rabbits? Fix your bayonets and follow me!'

He galloped off in the direction of the enemy batteries, which were blasting away for all they were worth.

'Who was that?' asked a soldier wrapped in a series of shawls.

'The phantom of the Grande Armée,' replied a figure. 'The one that haunts us all.'

Fanselin began to talk again. Margont could hardly hear his voice any more. His lips, welded together by ice, and his legs were giving him terrible pain. His legs were so heavy to lift that he looked at them often, convinced that they had caught on something. They felt stuffed and swollen with pain. Sometimes the pain exploded into thousands of pinpricks all over his body. It was almost more than he could bear because it made him think of death and being eaten by worms. Worse than that: sometimes he lost all sensation in his lower limbs. It was as if he had lost both legs and they now belonged to someone else. So he extricated his hands from the depths of his muff and frantically rubbed his thighs to bring back the circulation. When the pain returned he felt as if his body was at last whole again. He looked enviously at those being transported on carts or gun carriages. But rest proved to be a trap. Death crept up in silence. The cold gradually numbed their minds and the passengers fell into a pleasant sleep from which they never awoke. The choice was simple: march or freeze.

Margont frequently thought about his childhood or certain moments in his life. He recalled in particular the birth of his friendship with Piquebois because that day he had almost died.

Piquebois, then at the height of his hussar period, had noticed him reading while he was slashing away at pumpkins on stakes topped with Austrian helmets. Piquebois, sabre in hand and probably running out of pumpkins, had called him a 'book-devouring little squirt'. He would have been only too happy to see the 'infantry librarian' unsheathe his sword. But Margont had replied that he only used his weapon for opening letters, not for slicing off the heads of French hussars. Piquebois had burst out laughing before dragging Margont off for a drinking session that it would have been unwise to refuse. However, these memories were rather a bad omen. When you reach the end of a long journey or a project that took a long time to complete, you often think back to its beginning. Margont had the impression that his mind was going back over his life one last time, before gently fading away . . .

A little further on, Lefine fell. Margont bent his knees to crouch down, which caused him intense pain, as if the bulging muscles in his thighs had ripped his frozen skin. He wanted to remove his friend's knapsack but was surprised by its weight. He opened it and discovered silver ingots, jewellery and gold plate. He started to empty it. Lefine groaned, stuck out his hand and with considerable difficulty picked up a gold snuffbox that he stuffed into one of his pockets. But Margont was throwing away far more than he could retrieve.

'I've left you your jewels. Otherwise you'd probably have stayed here,' Margont said in a whisper as he was out of breath.

Lefine was getting to his feet with the aid of Saber and Fanselin when loud cries of 'Huzza! Huzza!' rang out. In an instant, men on horseback swept down on the column from all sides at once. Most of the attackers were Cossack irregulars, Bashkirs and Kalmucks. Everything about them – their Mongol features, their strangely shaped red hats, the fact that some of them were armed with bows – caused fear and panic. Accompanying them were hussars, who yelled as they set upon the French with their sabres.

There was total confusion. Infantrymen were fleeing, putting their arms in the air or trying to defend themselves with anything that came to hand. Hands stiffened by the cold managed to wield muskets and fire at the horsemen or, more often, at the horses. The Russians, better fed, less tired, drunk with victory but also just plain drunk, were indulging in a massacre. The hussars galloped along the column laughing, leaving a bloody trail behind them. Fanselin wielded his lance. He had jammed the end of it against a large stone. A Bashkir charged at him, and the lancer, bending down at the last minute to avoid the point, impaled the Russian. He immediately clung on to the horse's mane but the animal did not interrupt its headlong charge, carrying the Frenchman away with it. Fanselin eventually rolled on to the ground. He picked himself up, pistol in hand, ready to grab hold of another mount. The Bashkirs who had witnessed the scene had no desire to take on such a madman.

Margont felt an uncontrollable frenzy come over him. He shot dead a Bashkir with his pistol and wounded another with his other weapon. This second assailant was bleeding from the shoulder. His weakened hand had let go of the reins and his horse was galloping round and round a cart. Margont wanted to finish the Russian off but his sword failed to pierce the thick cloak. So he seized the Russian and threw him to the ground. He sat astride him and brandished his knife. He wanted to gouge his opponent's eyes out to make him finally understand what suffering could be. He revelled in the Bashkir's fear. The man had a round face with prominent cheekbones. His head was shaven except at the back, where he had a long, dangling plait. He had a very thin moustache, the ends of which drooped down to his chin. His eyes were so narrow and slanting that his pupils were barely visible. Despite all these differences, Margont saw his own reflection in this face. The Bashkir had been hit; for him the war was over. Margont put away his knife, took the bag that the Cossack was wearing on his belt and moved away. At once he flung himself on his stomach because a Frenchman was taking aim at him, mistaking him for a partisan.

'French! 84th!' he yelled.

Realising his mistake, the marksman shot a Kalmuck for good measure.

The assailants left as suddenly as they had arrived. As they rode off, they thrust their lances into the backs of bodies, occasionally striking an infantryman who was pretending to be dead. A scream of pain told them when they had been 'lucky'.

Fanselin was engaged in a lance duel with a regular Cossack officer. The Russian was swiftly whirling his lance around to parry an attack. When he had deflected his opponent's weapon sufficiently, he stopped flourishing his own and thrust its point towards the Frenchman's chest. With surprising agility, Fanselin leapt to the side before counterattacking. Changing tactics, Fanselin pretended to attack with the point of his lance only to suddenly turn it in an arc and strike his opponent with the other end. The Cossack received a violent blow to the chin and fell from his horse. A chorus of explosions stopped the fleeing horse dead in its tracks. They were not going to let such a heap of meat get away. Fanselin kept the prisoner at bay with his lance.

'Long live our Red Cossack!' exclaimed Margont weakly.

More shouts greeted the 'Red Cossack' and Fanselin smiled at the compliment. The Cossack exclaimed 'Huzza!' and to general amazement hurled himself at the lance to impale himself. Fanselin immediately withdrew the point but it was too late.

Everyone rushed for the carcasses of the horses to eat their fill, gnawing on the bones like dogs, without even taking the time to cook them because the Cossacks were still prowling around.

Margont opened the Bashkir's bag. Inside it he found black bread mixed with bits of straw. The loaf had been baked any old how: it had been placed in an overheated oven and the outside was burnt and the middle still doughy. Margont bit right into it. He couldn't believe that he had almost tortured this Bashkir. Was suffering making him mad? He needed to build up some protection against insanity for himself. Instead of repeating that he was marching to the Duchy of Warsaw – which was still so far away – his thoughts turned to Colonel Pirgnon. Don't let him out of your sight. Keep your monster on a leash, he thought. He said to himself that he didn't have the right to let himself die or to lose his sanity, and that managed to put some life back into those aching blocks of wood that were his legs. The march resumed. Yet again.

*

Colonel Pirgnon was cursing the fog that was hiding the full scale of the disaster from him. In his opinion it was all up for the Emperor. The Russian armies were going to cut off the retreat and that would sound the death knell. The irony of the situation amused him, because while everything around him was dying, he himself felt reborn. His future at last seemed crystal clear. He went up to the soldiers in his escort who, blue with cold, were shivering near a fire. The frozen branches were bad for burning as they produced a sort of smoke but no fire or heat. However, the colonel felt a surge of contentment well up inside him.

On 25 November, the Grande Armée found itself opposite the Berezina. It was here that the Russians had planned to crush it. The Berezina, a huge tributary of the Dnieper, had not in fact frozen over. A hundred and fifty paces wide, almost ten feet deep and bordered by marshes and forest, it cut off the retreat. By now the Emperor only had at his disposal twelve thousand soldiers, half of whom made up the Guard. He could also count on reinforcements of twenty thousand men led by Victor, Oudinot and Dombrovski. In addition to these troops there were forty thousand civilians and stragglers, for the most part unarmed. The Russians, who numbered one hundred and twenty thousand men divided into three armies, had also been weakened by the fighting and the winter. Admiral Chichagov held the west bank of the Berezina and was supposed to prevent the French from getting through. To the north was Wittgenstein and to the east and south, Kutuzov. But the latter, still more than sixty miles away from the French, was not urging his army on. It was Napoleon's unprecedented prestige that had led the Russian generalissimo to commit this blunder, much to the consternation of his general staff. Napoleon had won so many victories that Kutuzov greatly underestimated the disorganised and weakened state of the Grande Armée. So, once more, he sought to avoid direct confrontation and to let the climate and the hardships do their work.

Napoleon managed a feat that saved a large part of what remained of his army. He sent a battalion followed by thousands of stragglers towards the little town of Borisov. Admiral Chichagov thought that this was where the French would try to cross and moved his troops opposite this position. However, the Emperor ordered General Éblé's pontoneers to build two bridges opposite the village of Studianka. When Chichagov was informed of this work he thought it was a manoeuvre intended to divert him from Borisov. When he eventually realised his mistake, the two bridges across the Berezina had been built in appalling conditions and the French had begun to consolidate themselves on the west bank. The first construction, which was fragile and with a deck that was sometimes at water level, was used by the infantry, and the second, more sturdy, by the artillery and vehicles. Napoleon had had thirty guns set up to protect them.

On 27 November, several corps, including that of Prince Eugène, now consisting of only one thousand eight hundred men, crossed the Berezina.

On 28 November, at seven in the morning, the Russians attacked both banks at the same time.

CHAPTER 33

O N all sides the sound of artillery fire, shooting and shouting could be heard. On both banks the French were attempting to contain the Russians, who were far superior in numbers. The remainder of Davout, Eugène and La Tour Maubourg's corps were continuing their retreat along the road to Vilna. On the east bank a considerable throng of civilians, deserters and stragglers had congregated. This dense mass was crowding together to try to get across the bridges. In the scramble people were trampled or crushed to death by carts; others were pushed into the water, black muddy water that was carrying huge blocks of ice and armies of corpses along with it. The Russian cannonballs smashed into the hordes from all directions. Part of the deck of the bridge collapsed at regular intervals, plunging clusters of people into the river. Then the pontoneers rapidly set about repairing it. Those who attempted to swim across the Berezina rarely reached the other side. On the east bank, General Fournier's eight hundred Baden and Hessian troopers launched charge after charge. They were supporting IX Corps, which was holding in check Wittgenstein's forty thousand Russians. On the other bank, Marshal Oudinot, wounded early on and replaced by Marshal Ney, was facing up to Chichagov's thirty thousand combatants with nine thousand men. Time was on the side of the Russians, who were gradually receiving reinforcements sent by Kutuzov.

The remnants of Colonel Pirgnon's regiment had slowed down and had not moved off from the west bank. As a result, Margont and Lefine had also slackened their pace. Saber had stayed with them. An aide-de-camp galloped up and halted his sweating horse in front of Colonel Pirgnon. The rider was exhausted. He was being sent with orders everywhere at once and had to force his way through the pushing and shoving crowds with the aid of his sabre.

'Colonel, you're marching too slowly. The retreat must speed up, the Emperor's orders!'

He immediately wheeled his horse round and set off again, yelling, 'Out of the way! Out of the way!'

Pirgnon went up to what remained of the 35th of the Line, who had been joined by some stragglers. Only he had heard the messenger's words.

'Soldiers, the Emperor is going to launch a counterattack of which we will form the spearhead. We're going to break through the enemy line. We shall be supported by several regiments and six battalions of the Guard as well as by all the troopers available. The Emperor is going to calm these muzhiks down and ensure the safety of our retreat!'

The majority of the soldiers obeyed and made up an attacking column. No one imagined for a single instant that Pirgnon could have been lying. All of them thought that the aide-de-camp in a hurry was galloping around passing on the order for this massive counterattack. They had faith in the genius of their Emperor, who once more was going to carry all before him. The Guard was going to be in at the kill, the Guard! The Emperor's favourite child, the élite corps that had never lost a single battle. Pirgnon managed to convince the remnants of other battalions and to rally some stragglers. Placing himself at the head of three hundred motley but fired-up soldiers, he launched his column straight at the thirty thousand Russians.

'What the hell is he playing at?' Saber exclaimed.

Pirgnon's small band of men went past the French line of defence. Those who were confronting the Russians, entrenched behind cut-down trees, snowdrifts or dead bodies, looked on in amazement. Groups of dark figures gesticulated as they went past, either encouraging them or trying desperately to make them change their minds. Margont saw Pirgnon turn round on his mount and wave his sabre above his head as he looked towards him.

'What reinforcements is he motioning to? Who's going to support him?' wondered Saber out loud.

'He's motioning to me,' replied Margont. 'He's a very intelligent man. He knows that I know. So he's bidding me farewell.'

'But what the hell is he playing at, damn it?'

'He's committing suicide. He's committing suicide with his regiment.'

The Russians reacted immediately. Two squadrons of hussars moved off and charged at the column from the side. In their headlong rush they took out rows of soldiers and broke up the formation into three sections. The troopers began whirling around the infantrymen, slashing away at will. Amidst the confusion the French tried to form square to defend themselves. Why had their cavalry not charged to halt the hussars? Why were the other regiments not coming to their aid?

'Let's go!' exclaimed Margont.

Saber was rendered speechless.

'Let's go, Irénée! We're not going to stand and watch. I'll see to Pirgnon and you get the survivors to pull back. Fernand, you go and find reinforcements.'

Lefine was no more talkative than Saber.

'Well, Irénée, do you want to end this campaign as a colonel or not?'

Margont set off towards the slaughter, with Saber following him. As he went past the French line he shouted: 'Cover us!'

Along the whole front the French were taking aim at the hussars and whoops of joy greeted each hit. To attempt a sally was unthinkable but at least they could support these reckless comrades with sustained fire. The hussars made easy targets but their commander did not want to let go of his prey until he was sure they were done for. He ordered the withdrawal only when the Russian infantry that was rushing forward made contact. A wave of Russians engulfed the attackers. They outnumbered them ten to one, and the hussars had left them enough time to encircle the French. Pirgnon had dismounted. He was delighting in this pointless butchery. For him these visions of combatants riddled with bayonet thrusts or shot at from all sides was a sublime spectacle, a gory feast. Here one of his lieutenants was being held down by two Russians while a third ran his bayonet through him. Over there a sergeant was being shot simultaneously by four infantrymen. Anxious faces turned towards him but he was smiling. The trapped French soldiers were fighting like lions to get back to their lines. Margont, Saber and fifteen or so volunteers fought their way through to them.

But as the seconds ticked by, the Russians were tightening the noose. The French had formed a circle with their backs to a wood, halfway between the Russian line and Marshal Ney's. A third of them had already been wiped out and bodies were dropping constantly. A shower of bullets rained on to them, mowing them down or hitting the tree trunks with the sound of hailstones.

Margont rushed towards Pirgnon, at the centre of his position. The colonel greeted him gleefully.

'I didn't expect you to come, Captain. You are not short of courage. That will make a few more corpses.'

Margont took off his heavy cloak and unsheathed his sword. Pirgnon had grasped his sabre. His smile was disturbing, loathsome.

'To begin with, I tried everything to fight against my bloodlust. I prayed to God, but in my imagination I tied women up and then tortured them. Then I began to work ceaselessly until I could no longer keep my eyes open. I thus reached a state of such exhaustion that I cleansed my mind of these images. But they resurfaced in my dreams, which mingled pleasure and pain, love and death. I was desperate. I exposed myself to danger in the Great Redoubt and waited there. The Russian bullets whistled around my ears and I came away with only a scratch. However, I have never stopped beseeching the Russians to do what I was unable to accomplish myself.'

Pirgnon seemed at ease amidst the chaos surrounding him. He spread his arms. 'Is it my fault if I am still alive?'

'In addition to Maria Dorlovna and Countess Sperzof, it was you who killed Élisa Lasquenet, the young actress, wasn't it?'

'Yes! Do you have any other crimes you wish to question me about? No? What a pity, your list will remain incomplete. Now my desires have won. No more remorse. I am a monster but that pleases me. And I dream of thrusting my sword into your body. Then, either I shall be killed in a final bloodbath or the Russians will spare me. Captivity will then be only an interlude before a whole series of "pleasant encounters".'

Pirgnon lunged at Margont but the captain swiftly pulled back. The colonel swung his sabre to behead him. Margont crouched down and thrust the point of his sword towards Pirgnon's stomach. The colonel, an excellent dueller, had anticipated this attack. The two blades met. There was a snapping sound as Margont's sword broke, struck on the flat by the thicker metal of the sabre. Margont immediately leapt at his opponent and stabbed him with the remains of his sword. Pirgnon fell to his knees, surprised at being defeated. He put his hand to his stomach and looked at the blood on his palm. He was amazed to discover that it was of the same colour and the same consistency as that of his victims. So, the blood of others also coursed through his veins . . . He collapsed.

Margont put his cloak back on. He felt neither triumph nor relief. He did not even have the bitter, cruel taste in his mouth of the 'justice' he himself had administered. His mind was blank. Fear quickly began to fill the vacuum until it occupied not only his mind but his whole body: he was surrounded by Russians, Russians eager to make the French pay for this campaign, Russians whose appetite for killing appeared insatiable.

His stomach churning with anguish and his reflexes sharpened by the instinct of self-preservation, he caught up with

Saber. His friend had gathered a group of about thirty élite soldiers, grenadiers, *voltigeurs* or men of resolve. These Frenchmen thought they were condemned to die and were preparing to charge in a frenzy. They wanted to kill. To kill out of hatred, out of desperation, to avoid thinking of their own deaths. To kill, kill, kill and in the end, alas, to die.

'This way! We're going to try to break out!' exclaimed Saber, pointing to the left with his sabre.

'But, sir, we need to try to get back to our lines,' a sergeant-major protested.

'That's obvious to anyone, so the Russians have positioned a company of grenadiers between our troops and us. But over there, look: you can see militiamen.'

To the left, behind the regular troops, there were indeed combatants with grey or brown cloaks. Some were wearing hats instead of their regimental helmets and, not having been issued with muskets even, were wielding pikes. Saber launched his attack. The Russians were not expecting it at this point and were caught unawares. Saber's group quickly dispatched the musketeers in the front line by battering or bayoneting them. Once up against the militiamen, who far outnumbered them, they took aim and fired the volley of shots they had held back until then. Given the situation, Saber gave the cruellest order he had ever issued: 'Aim at their faces.' When the militiamen, civilians with the sketchiest of training, poorly equipped and lacking experience, saw the faces of their comrades blown to pieces and turned into gaping, bleeding wounds, they threw their weapons to the ground and fled screaming. Then, the French launched themselves into the breach, shouting as they went. The circle emptied of its defenders like an abscess being drained. The survivors fled back to their lines under heavy fire, covered by Lefine, Fanselin and Piquebois, who had made a line of volunteers step forward a few paces. About a hundred soldiers survived this absurd assault.

Saber was carried along in triumph.

'That was a fine action by your friend. I'll refer it to the appropriate authorities,' Margont heard someone say behind him.

He turned round to see Colonel Barguelot.

'May I enquire what you are doing here, sir? Isn't your regiment on its way to Vilna?'

'That is correct. So it has no need of me for the moment. I shall easily catch up with it because one of my mounts has survived. This is where the action is, so that's why I'm here.'

With that, Colonel Barguelot went to give out his orders while the bullets struck the tree trunks around him, spitting splinters of wood on to his cloak. He rallied those running away and pointed out a position to be strengthened to the sappers. He had not been able to accept the idea of his cowardice being revealed. He could not bear his image to be tarnished. To salvage it he was prepared to do anything, even to die. Some of his soldiers, who had stayed to escort him, said to one another: 'There we were thinking our colonel was a coward, and now look at him in one of the most dangerous positions when he has no need to be there!' Barguelot was radiant. He was surprised, scared even, by his own courage. But he revelled in the admiration he could read on their faces. So he continued to force himself to make superhuman efforts to appear confident and genial. On seeing that Margont was not leaving, he had made up his mind to stay. He believed that the captain wanted to fight and he had not been able to accept the idea of this man acquiring a reputation superior to his own. And he also wanted to scotch the rumours about his conduct during the campaign. So he had seized the last possible opportunity to restore his family name and what he considered to be its incomparable aura.

He marched off to find Marshal Ney, one of the bravest men of all time, and when the marshal asked him in surprise the reason for his visit, the colonel replied: 'Marshal, if Colonel Barguelot has decided to go for a walk in a forest, not even fifty thousand Russians can make him change his mind.'

EPILOGUE

O F the four hundred thousand men of the Grande Armée who took part in this campaign, three hundred thousand perished or were taken prisoner. This disaster marked the beginning of the decline of Napoleon's reign. The Russians also lost more than three hundred thousand combatants (half of them because of the winter) but were able to recover from such a catastrophe.

Margont survived. He had great difficulty convincing Prince Eugène that Colonel Pirgnon was the man he had been looking for. The deranged Pole accused of Élisa Lasquenet's murder was freed. A few days later, Margont was promoted to lieutenant-colonel, cheerfully leap-frogging the rank of major, for 'his heroic action in the fighting at the Berezina'. He did not have time to go to Warsaw because the Emperor was already reorganising his forces in the knowledge that Prussia and a large part of Germany were going to take advantage of his weakened state to rise up against him.

Colonel Barguelot, who had proved himself a coward at the Moskva but a hero at the Berezina, was not relieved of his command and regained the confidence of his regiment.

Colonel Delarse also survived. Ironically, he attended a Mass held in memory of several deceased officers, some of whom had refused to put him in charge of a regiment because they thought his days were numbered. He was at last made a brigadier-general.

Saber was awarded the Légion d'Honneur for his action at the Berezina. The survivors of the 35th called him 'honorary colonel of the 35th of the Line'. This rank was no more than a mark of affection but it enabled Saber to proclaim to all and sundry that, as he had always said he would, he had ended the campaign as a colonel.

Lefine, Piquebois and Fanselin also escaped death on Russian soil.

No one had time to rest because in April 1813 the Saxony campaign began.

AUTHOR'S NOTE

The detective plot of this novel (characters and situations) is purely imaginary.

The 9th Infantry Regiment of the Line was in fact commanded by Colonel de Vautré; the 35th Infantry Regiment of the Line by Colonel Penant; and the 3rd Italian Infantry Regiment of the Line by Colonel Lévie. General Huard had only one aide-de-camp, Captain Cogniard.

Any similarity between the fictional characters of this novel and people who really existed is entirely accidental.

APPENDIX 1

Composition of the French Army at the beginning of the
Russian Campaign
Emperor Napoleon I
Prince Murat is Lieutenant-General

Emperor's Household
General Staff of the Grande Armée
General Administration of the Grande Armée
Imperial Guard (30,000 men)
I Corps (Marshal Davout) (70,000)
II Corps (Marshal Oudinot) (40,000)
III Corps (Marshal Ney) (35,000)
IV Corps (Prince Eugène) (45,000)
V Corps (General Poniatowski) (35,000)
VI Corps (General Gouvion-Saint-Cyr) (23,000)
VII Corps (General Reynier) (18,000)
VIII Corps (King Jérôme Bonaparte) (16,000)
X Corps (Marshal Macdonald) (30,000)
Prussian Corps (von Grawert) (17,000)
Austrian Corps (Prince Swartzenberg) (30,000)
I Reserve Cavalry Corps (General Nansouty) (12,000)
II Reserve Cavalry Corps (General Montbrun) (11,000)
III Reserve Cavalry Corps (General Grouchy) (7,000)

IV Reserve Cavalry Corps (General de La Tour Maubourg) (6,000)
Grand Artillery and Engineering Park

IX Corps (Marshal Victor) (25,000) and XI Corps (Marshal Augereau) (45,000) were held in reserve in Germany and would not become involved until the end of the campaign.

In total about 400,000 soldiers and 1,200 cannon directly took part in the campaign.

(The numbers given are intended for guidance only and vary considerably according to sources but the overall figure of 400,000 men is accepted almost unanimously by historians.)

APPENDIX 2

Detailed Composition of IV Corps
(or Prince Eugène's Army) (45,000 men)
Prince Eugène de Beauharnais

General Staff

13th Division (General Delzons)

1st Brigade (General Huard)
  8th Light Regiment
  84th Regiment of the Line
  1st Croat Regiment
2nd Brigade (General Roussel)
  92nd Regiment of the Line
  106th Regiment of the Line
Artillery
Engineers

14th Division (General Broussier)

1st Brigade (General de Sivray)
  9th Regiment of the Line
  18th Light Regiment
2nd Brigade (General Alméras)
  Joseph Napoleon Spanish Regiment

35th Regiment of the Line
3rd Brigade (General Pastol)
   53rd Regiment of the Line
Artillery
Engineers

15th Division (or Italian Division) (General Pino)

1st Brigade (General Fontana)
   1st Light Regiment
   2nd Regiment of the Line
2nd Brigade (General de Vaudoncourt)
   Dalmatian Regiment
   3rd Light Regiment
3rd Brigade (General Dembrowski)
   3rd Regiment of the Line
Artillery
Engineers

Light Cavalry Division (General d'Ornano)

12th Brigade (General Ferrière)
   9th Regiment of Mounted Chasseurs
   19th Regiment of Mounted Chasseurs
13th Brigade (General Villata)
   2nd Regiment of Italian Mounted Chasseurs
   3rd Regiment of Italian Mounted Chasseurs

Italian Royal Guard

Guards of Honour
Royal Velites
Regiment of Grenadiers
Regiment of Conscripts
Dragoons of the Guard
Queen's Dragoons
Foot Artillery

Artillery Reserve
Engineers

At the beginning of the campaign IV Corps was isolated and would meet up with the bulk of the army only after a few weeks.

APPENDIX 3

Composition of the Russian Armies at the beginning of the Russian Campaign

First Army (Army of the West)
General Prince Barclay de Tolly
(150,000)

Second Army (Army of the South)
General Prince Bagration
(65,000)

Reserve Army (Army of Galicia)
General Tormasov
(40,000)

Army of the Danube
Admiral Chichagov
(55,000)

Army of Finland
General Steingell
(15,000)

Garrison of the City of Riga
(10,000)

In total about 400,000 if the soldiers in the garrisons and depots, and Cossack irregulars are included.

Further books in the Quentin Margont series

WOLF HUNT

Armand Cabasson

In 1809, the forces of Napoleon's Grande Armée are in Austria. For young Lieutenant Lukas Relmyer, it is hard to return to the place where he and fellow orphan, Franz were kidnapped four years earlier. Franz was brutally murdered and Lukas has vowed to avenge his death.

When the body of another orphan is found on the battlefield, Captain Quentin Margont and Lukas join forces to track down the wolf who is prowling once more in the forests of Aspern...

Gallic Books

978-1-906040-83-3

MEMORY OF FLAMES

Armand Cabasson

March 1814. Napoleon's army is outnumbered and struggling to defend France against invasion by the European allies ranged against it. Paris itself is threatened.

When the colonel in charge of the security of Paris is found murdered at home, his face burnt and a fleur-de-lys pinned to his chest, it is clear that Napoleon's authority is being challenged by royalist plotters.

Who better to call in to uncover the plot than committed republican, Lieutenant Colonel Quentin Margont? Risking his own life, he must infiltrate the secret royalist society, the Swords of the King. But will he be able to, and why do Talleyrand's parting words as he sets off on the mission, 'Good luck, Lieutenant Colonel Margont,' have the ring of an epitaph?

Gallic Books

978-1-906040-84-0